Pacific Hope

Pacific Hope

A NOVEL BY
BETTE NORDBERG

BETHANY HOUSE PUBLISHERS

Minneapolis, Minnesota

Published by Bethany House Publishers
A Ministry of Bethany Fellowship International
11400 Hampshire Avenue South
Bloomington, Minnesota 55438
www.bethanyhouse.com

Printed in the United States of America by
Bethany Press International, Bloomington, Minnesota 55438

Library of Congress Cataloging-in-Publication Data

Nordberg, Bette.
    Pacific hope / by Bette Nordberg.
       p.   cm.
    ISBN 0-7642-2397-6 (pbk.)
    1. Married people—Fiction. 2. Pacific Ocean—Fiction. 3. Sailing—
Fiction. I. Title.
    PS3564.O553 P33 2001
    813'.6—dc21

                                  2001002325

To the Captain of my soul,
Who plots my course,
And trims my sails.
Who keeps an endless watch,
In fair wind or tempest.
Who guides me home,
Under the power of His own breath.
My hope lies in you alone.

BETTE NORDBERG graduated from the University of Washington as a physical therapist in 1977. In 1990 she turned from rehabilitation medicine to writing and is now the author of *Serenity Bay* and numerous dramas, articles, and devotions. She and her husband, Kim, recently helped plant Lighthouse Christian Center, a new church in the South Hill area of Puyallup, Washington, where Bette writes, directs drama, and plays keyboard. Married twenty-five years, Kim and Bette have four children, two in college and two at home.

The author may be contacted at her Web site: www.myfables.com.

Part
One

The Betrayal

Prologue

January 15, 1999

WHEN IT CAME to secret meetings, these two preferred their trysts on the San Francisco waterfront, believing that no secret remains better hidden than those left out in the open. This kind of camouflage worked best in the warm summer months, when tourism peaked and hordes of visitors jostled for space along the crowded sidewalks of Fisherman's Wharf. Then, the smells of seawater and hot dogs mingled in the light breeze and warm sunshine. Manic children climbed rails lining the sidewalks, calling to one another, skipping ahead of their parents, pointing and rushing from place to place along the waterfront. In the height of the tourist season, among crowds of people and children and activity, these two remained invisible, their presence inconsequential. Over the past five months, they'd counted on that.

In January, light crowds made it harder to remain inconspicuous; however, some emergencies demand flexibility.

On this day, dark clouds hung low over a granite harbor, and a cold wind sporting tiny speckles of rain cut through their clothes and burned their faces. They spoke quietly, their heads close together, as they leaned against a balcony railing, looking out over the bay. She wore boot-cut designer jeans, clunky heels, and a three-quarter length leather coat; he wore Levis, a jean jacket, and glasses with custom flip-up shades. From a distance, they gave the appearance of lovers, deep in ordinary loverly conversation.

"Are you certain?" he hissed. His tone held intensity unlike the happy antics of the tourists around them. A stout gray-headed woman moved quite near, propping her elbows on the rail to frame a picture of the bay. Suddenly, Cara Maria slipped one arm through his, kissed his cheek lightly, and began laughing as though at some hilarious joke. He turned, caught her in his arms, and held her close, listening at the same time for the click of the camera's shutter. They said nothing.

As the woman moved away, Cara whispered, "No one can be absolutely certain. But I trust my source."

"But you said no one would notice. Especially not the Feds."

"I can't predict everything. Who would have guessed?" She turned away from the banister, leaning back against it, bending one knee and raising her heel onto the lower rail. "My sources tell me that agents confronted him last week."

"Why?"

She noticed the pitch of his voice. Anxiety always gave it a tight, high edge. "Because they think that if anyone would have a tip, he would." She chuckled. "They said they came asking for his help. His expertise." She could not suppress the smile that rose to her lips. The irony of the agent's request had not been lost on her.

"What did he say?"

"My sources are good." She nodded and looked away. "But no one is that good. I didn't exactly tape the meeting."

"Does he know?" His face had lost its color; his eyes looked haunted.

"He couldn't possibly suspect." She moved away from the rail and glanced toward the crowd of tourists on the right. Hundreds of barking sea lions, lounging on floats near the dock, riveted the attention of nearby crowds. She started walking toward them, slipping her hands into her coat pockets.

"What now?" he asked, hurrying to catch her. His voice betrayed fear. He had much to lose; his face told her he believed they had begun sliding down the slippery slope toward losing it. Losing everything.

She stopped abruptly, tossed her hair away from her face, and turned to look at him. "Now we have to change our plans a bit."

"What do you mean?" He glanced up as two men frowned and stepped around them. Cara nodded in their direction and smiled suggestively. Then she turned back toward the bay and found an open spot on the rail.

He followed. Pinching the dark lenses from his eyeglasses, he dropped them into his chest pocket.

Still looking out over the bay, with Alcatraz in the distance, she continued. "We need to start our own surveillance."

His eyebrows rose. "Surveillance? How? How can we do that?"

"It won't be hard. I can handle it, easily." She stepped closer to him, slipping one arm around his waist. Giving a gentle hug she assured him, "I already have all the skills I'll ever need."

One

ON THE DAY the pictures arrived, Kate Langston jogged on Canyon Loop Road, down to Vista Del Mar, and then ran the last two miles along Richardson Bay at an easy lope. For years, ever since they'd bought the house in Tiburon, she had run this course from the other direction. But today a brisk westerly convinced her that running up the canyon with the wind at her back would make the climb to the top less taxing. This slight change in routine was Kate's only acquiescence to her forty-ninth birthday—now six months past. Still a compact size eight, Kate showed few signs of her age.

On this particular day, as Kate approached the house, palms resting on the back of her hips, dragging air into her lungs, it suddenly occurred to her that she had not yet picked up today's paper. She glanced longingly toward the house, paused, and with the back of one hand wiped away the cinnamon-blond hair stuck to her sweaty face. In the process, she tasted her own salty moisture and grimaced. Other women "glistened" when they exercised. Kate dripped. Honest perspiration ran off her face, down her back, and even into the recesses of her running shorts. She really wanted a shower and a drink of water.

Instead of cutting across the lawn to the front door, she stayed on the road, slowed to a comfortable walk, and headed for the mailbox. Reaching into the paper tube, she began scanning the headlines as she turned back toward the drive. Then Kate remembered the mail.

Normally, Mike brought in the mail. Not that her husband always arrived home first, but it was their routine, the comfortable pattern Kate and Mike had adopted somewhere over the course of their twenty-six-year marriage—a tradition left over from the days of babies and school schedules. Today, Kate had managed to escape from work early, the last photo shoot for the fall catalogue complete. She'd hurried along the thirty-minute drive from the office to their bay view home, eager to make her daily run while it was still light out. Now that she'd finished the run, perhaps she should bring in the mail. Sighing, she turned back to the box. Her shower and a bottle of cold water would have to wait.

The oversized mailbox held the usual collection of catalogues and bills. These she scanned with disinterest, glancing through to see if the latest Nordstrom sale catalogue had arrived. She needed a new jacket for work, and their spring preview collection featured a delightful tropical-weight wool jacket that Kate hoped would drop in price. It was featured in pumpkin, a rarity even in seasons of "warm colors." Kate was determined to have it, for she loved wearing the unusual, the bright—and nothing complemented her wiry frame and soft strawberry-blond hair like a warm gold, tomato red, or even pumpkin.

Disappointed, Kate found no catalogue, and she shook herself, determined to put away thoughts of the pumpkin jacket. "If I keep on like this," she chided herself aloud, "I'll buy the stupid thing at full price."

Letting out a little laugh, she turned her attention to the rest of the mail. As she sorted, an oversized first class envelope seized her curiosity. Addressed to her, with bold handwritten lines, the envelope bore no return address. She looked for a postmark and found it had been mailed in Los Angeles. Strange. Kate could think of no one who would send her a package from Los Angeles.

She tore it open, still standing on the side of the road, sweating. Her damp fingers found only pictures inside—eight-by-tens—and this surprised her. She was not expecting photos, though at work she handled them daily. She turned them over in her hands to discover a set of glossy color prints, blurred but still identifiable—each with the same unavoidable message. Kate's husband with another woman. And the woman was someone she knew.

The pleasant fatigue of exercise gave way to nausea and dizziness, and the rest of the mail fell from beneath Kate's elbow. Her heart raced, as it had when she climbed the canyon, and she stumbled slightly, her strong legs trembling at the knees. Kate glanced around for a place to sit. She found nothing and landed heavily on the grass and gravel below her. Dazed and shocked, she leaned back against the mailbox post, grasping desperately for a reasonable explanation. No run had ever left Kate Langston in this condition. The pictures had kicked her in the solar plexus of her soul, and her raging body retaliated. She rolled onto her side, letting the gravel dig into the bare skin of her upper arms. She didn't cry. She made no sound. Kate Langston lay motionless, in utter stupefaction.

———

At that same moment, in Sausalito, a half hour from their house, Kate's husband, Mike, was about to receive a kick of his own.

Designed personally by Mike Langston and named after their daughter, the Keegan Building housed the corporate offices of DataSoft. Resting squarely in the middle of the newest and most expensive downtown corporate area in Sausalito, the building appeared neither striking nor imposing. Rather, typical of the many office complexes surrounding it, the Keegan stood a modest four floors high, enclosed entirely in reflective glass.

Inside, however, the building was very different. There Mike wanted to create a respite from the work world of competition and drive. Just inside the front doors, a dark mahogany reception desk sat before a massive two-story fountain of teal patina. On either side, twin stairways of gray-green marble and black pipe ascended to the next level. From the second floor, glass offices overlooked the opulent lobby.

The fountain, illuminated by carefully hidden spotlights, featured a mermaid hand-feeding a porpoise family. Water, flowing in graceful arches, cascaded down over the mermaid and across the friendly faces of the waiting mammals. Mike Langston intended for DataSoft employees to enjoy moments of restful contemplation on black park benches surrounding the fountain. He believed that the sound of flowing water brought tranquility and peace. That was the way Mike wanted it. A building full of tranquility. Peaceful workers—working productively.

Mike also took great pride in the office he occupied on the southwest corner of the fourth floor. A business suite, yes, but it also reflected an elegant and masculine comfort. He had selected the leather couches in the waiting area himself, along with the lights recessed into ceiling soffits. Mike Langston loved details and prided himself on the selection of fixtures and cabinets. The details that some considered trivial, Mike believed separated DataSoft from the rest of the corporate world. Mike's attention to minutiae had single-handedly turned DataSoft into a model of corporate success.

On this day, as Kate lay collapsed by her mailbox, Mike met with his partner and longtime friend, Doug McCoy, cofounder of DataSoft. In the corner of the giant office the two men sat around one end of a black granite conference table. Through office windows behind them, bustling views of harbor activity and city sounds would have distracted most men. But not Doug McCoy. And definitely not Mike.

Doug was the techie, the "propeller-head" behind the DataSoft empire. He knew the inside of the personal computer as well as Mike knew the ins and outs of business and marketing. Together they made a powerful pair. They had had few disagreements in their fifteen years as partners, due in part to the willingness of each to trust the expertise of the other.

DataSoft had evolved to follow the development of the computer world. They had created and sold many different products. Most recently, DataSoft scored big in designing and selling commercial Web sites for retail sales. Doug's expertise enabled them to create software that safely encrypted and transmitted orders and payments for anything the Web had to offer. And lately the Web had come to offer everything. With more business than they could handle, DataSoft team members felt constant pressure to keep up, produce, and promote.

Mike and Doug owed their success, in part, to their division of labor, a division so complete that each partner had several teams that reported only to them. Mike handled wholesale shipping, accounting, customer service, marketing, and technical support systems. Doug handled research and development, product design, and production systems. Only in support did their authority overlap; Doug trained technicians about the product itself, and Mike designed the parameters and policies under which they worked.

This afternoon, the two found themselves at odds with each

other. "I've told you," Doug pled, "I can solve the problem. We just need more time."

"I've given you more time." Mike stabbed at the table with his index finger. "There isn't any more to give. We've already released a press report on the project. We said May first, and we have to make the deadline."

"Okay, if you can't give me more time, then at least give me more people. I can finish with a bigger staff. I know we can work out the bugs." Doug pushed his wire-frame glasses farther up onto his nose. "Let me hire some of it out to subs."

Mike took a deep breath and tried to slow the intensity of the conversation. Rubbing the dark shadow of his afternoon beard, he stood and walked to the window. He folded his arms across his stomach, staring but not seeing the city scene below his window.

"I'll think about it," he said at last. Turning away from the window, he moved to his massive desk and touched the telephone. "Brooke," he said into the speaker. "See if you can get Cara Maria up here."

"Yes, sir," came the polite response.

"What do we need Cara for?" Doug stood suddenly and came to the desk. "It's a simple matter of permission. You give me permission to get the staff I need, and I'll meet the deadline. We don't need Cara Maria in on this." Doug leaned forward as he spoke, a position that might have encroached on the space of others. Mike knew better than to take offense, for his partner was very near-sighted.

"Cara Maria is the Chief Financial Officer here. She runs the numbers." Mike heard the tight edge in his voice and stopped to take a calming breath. "We hired her to help us make decisions just like this one."

"Mr. Langston," a young female voice came over the speaker again. "Cara says she has an appointment in fifteen minutes. Will that be enough time, sir?"

"Yes, fine," Mike answered gruffly. "Just get her up here. And ask her to bring her numbers on the Patterson project."

"Right away, sir."

"Doug," Mike straightened and slid his enormous chair under the desk. "It's time you got a picture of my side of this company. I've let you have your way for the last fifteen years. I've never held you to a production schedule. Whatever you wanted, you got—even when it hurt the company to do it. But that has to change." Mike stood and walked back to his chair at the conference table. "You can't live in the world of 'throw money at it' forever." Leaning against his chair, he continued, "I suggest we look at the numbers together for once and see just exactly how much we already have invested in this project."

Exasperated, Doug sighed deeply. "Don't treat me like a child." He paced along the conference table, turning suddenly and running one hand through his curly blond hair. "I have as much invested in this company as you do."

Frowning, Mike sat and leaned down to adjust the thick athletic socks above his Wilson court shoes. For a moment he wished he were at the club instead of the office. Compared to conflict, slamming a tennis ball across the court would be sweet relief. Much easier than reining in his undisciplined partner. Doug seemed to grow more difficult every day. Why had he let things go this far?

"Invested, perhaps," Mike agreed. "But I don't like being the brakes on your irresponsible management. This project should be wrapped up by now."

They heard a knock on the door, and Mike stood to answer. Cara Maria Calloruso passed through the doorway with the grace of a runway model. Behind her, Mike caught the delicious scent of her expensive perfume. Today, she wore black in the shape of a St. John suit, fashioned of wool crepe. The long narrow skirt, enhanced by a deep off-center slit, and a long jacket fit the curves of her lean figure perfectly.

Mike glanced away as Cara walked across the room. For a moment he wondered if she planned the effect this kind of suit had on him. Her beauty always left him feeling like a preteen, gasping for air. She wore her glossy black hair twisted loosely behind her, held in place with a jeweled stake. Loose strands hung fashionably along the sides of her face. She moved confidently to the table and chose the chair beside Doug, who seemed suddenly to forget his irritation. He jumped up and held the chair for her. Mike took the seat across from Doug.

"The Patterson numbers," she said, opening a file. Sliding it across the table, she asked Mike, "Now, what is this about? Why the sudden need to see me?" She glanced back and forth between the two men.

"I just wanted to have you here to confirm our current status." Mike leaned back and put both palms on the arms of the mahogany chair. "Mr. McCoy here thinks a delay for product release is our only viable option."

"It would certainly make things easier for him," she said, turning her attention to Doug. "But we've published the release date. We already have orders for more systems like it." She glanced back at Mike. "We can't change the release date now."

"That's what I said," Mike confirmed. "But Doug doesn't agree."

"Not quite true," Doug interrupted. "I can make the date, I just need more engineering hours to do it."

"How many more hours do you need?" Cara asked.

"I think with four guys and another month, we could work out all the bugs."

"But we're already over budget." Cara Maria leaned back, using both hands to brush the hair away from her face.

"I told him that too." Mike held his hand lightly across his mouth trying to suppress a smile. "But he doesn't see that as a problem. I asked you to come in and help me convince him."

Cara reached for the file and shuffled through the papers inside. "Here," she said, handing a copy to both Mike and Doug. "This is last month's accounting for the project to date. As you can see, we're already twelve percent over our projected budget."

Mike reached into the front pocket of his cargo shorts and retrieved a hard-shelled glasses case. Placing the half lens carefully on his nose, he adjusted the position of the report and began to read. "What have you done to adjust?" he asked briskly.

"Nothing yet," she answered. "Of course there's the possibility of a price increase or perhaps a decrease in production costs. But it's too early to tell yet."

"So what? We charge a little more," Doug offered.

Cara Maria exchanged glances with Mike. "Doug, I can't do that," her voice held a calm, deliberate tone. "We have competition. We aren't the only ones trying to create this kind of product. We can't expect to make money by selling ours at the highest price on the market."

"We can't win by marketing an imperfect product either." Mike heard emotion and frustration in the tone of Doug's voice.

"I know that product development can be frustrating," Cara spoke gently. "But DataSoft has committed on this project. We have to finish on time."

Mike interrupted, touching the back of her hand. "Okay. Let's think about this. Doug needs more time, but we can't give him that. What about hours? Can we give him that?"

"I'll have to look into it," she said. "I think we should put a limit on it though. No blank checks." Her brown eyes smiled at Mike.

"All right. I agree. You work the numbers, and let me know exactly what we can reasonably spare. Get back to me, say Friday?"

Cara Maria reached for the file and straightened the papers. "I'll do that. Now you two try to keep our expenses under control. We aren't trying to launch the space shuttle, you know. We don't have a government budget." She closed the file and stood gracefully. "Now, unless you need anything else, I must be going. I have an appointment."

"Thank you, Cara," Mike stood and pushed in his chair. "I wonder, could you get a copy of that spreadsheet to me?"

"No problem," she said, stepping toward him. Tipping her chin, she looked directly into his eyes. A smile touched her lips. "I'll have Josh bring one up this afternoon."

Mike walked her across the office, his hand lightly touching the small of her back. Opening the door, he held it as she passed through.

"I'll get back to you," she said, and disappeared.

As Mike moved back to the corner window, he noticed that Doug had helped himself to another full cup of coffee. Doug seemed morose, and his emotional state would be a more urgent problem than the production schedule. Mike would have to nurse Doug back to enthusiasm if he ever hoped to have the product on time. Mike sighed deeply.

A voice came over the speaker. "Mr. Langston, there's a delivery for you."

"So take it, Brooke."

"I offered, sir, but the delivery person says he has to have your signature." She paused, and he heard muttering. Brooke continued. "He says that he has orders to put it in your hands only."

Reluctantly, Mike agreed. "All right, bring him in."

The door opened again, and his secretary entered followed by a delivery boy in jeans and Birkenstocks, his hair tied back in a long greasy ponytail. He walked straight to Mike and held out a manila envelope. Mike accepted it and began to open the double seal on the envelope.

The young man stepped forward, holding a clipboard in one hand and a pen in the other. "I'm sorry, sir, I need a signature."

"Oh, certainly," Mike agreed. Without comment, he placed his own bold initials on line thirty-four. "That will be all, Brooke," he said, dismissing them both.

When the door closed behind them, he turned the envelope over in his hand and discovered his own name scrawled across the front in bold dark strokes. No return address. No clue as to the envelope's origin.

While Doug sat drinking coffee on the leather couch, Mike went to his desk. From the top drawer he withdrew a gold letter opener and tore open the envelope. An angry oath escaped from his lips, drawing Doug's attention. Doug stood and crossed to the desk where Mike stared openmouthed at a stack of glossy eight-by-ten color photographs.

Mike was dimly aware of Doug moving around behind his chair and looking intently at the top photo and then back at Mike. But Mike continued to stare down at the image he held in his trembling hands. In it he saw the bare back of a woman wearing a deep crimson evening gown. She danced with a man in a tuxedo. He did not need to look further. He knew the woman. He knew the place. And he recognized the face of the man whispering in her ear as his own.

Two

March 24, 1999
Tacoma, Washington

WAYNE FRAZIER always drank his morning coffee at the same place—a dark, quiet café off of Sixth Avenue, near Highway 16. Since everyone in the Tacoma office of the Washington State Patrol knew where to find him, turning off his cell phone didn't protect him from official intrusion.

"Wayne," his waitress called from the front counter, "the office." She nodded at the phone.

"I need to find a new spot," he muttered as he hit the Power button on his phone and dialed. Waiting for his dispatcher's voice, he took a long sip of hot, dark liquid. At least he'd been smart enough to order his coffee to go. Wayne waved at the waitress as he walked past the counter.

"Sorry to bother you, Wayne," the voice apologized. "It's the bridge."

As a senior member of the Washington State Patrol Incident Response Team, Wayne often found himself assigned to work accidents on the Tacoma Narrows Bridge. This one, the dispatcher reported, involved at least one fatality. That meant a closed bridge. Closed bridges decimated traffic flow through both of the major freeway systems in the city. "There goes the morning," Wayne said to himself as he flipped on the emergency lights and pulled his patrol car into traffic.

The Narrows, connecting metropolitan Tacoma with the Kitsap Peninsula, served as a constant thorn in Wayne's professional life. The current bridge, built in 1950, replaced "Galloping Gertie," blown down in a nasty 1940 windstorm. On the day the replacement opened, she claimed the title of third longest suspension bridge in the world. Wayne believed she was also the biggest piece of trouble in the world.

Spanning six thousand feet and arching nearly two hundred feet above the water, the bridge offered breathtaking views of Mount Rainier, the city of Tacoma, and tidewaters boiling out of lower Puget Sound. Unfortunately, the Narrows Bridge sometimes took away more than breath; sometimes she took lives.

In the forty-nine years since she opened, populations on both sides of the bridge had mushroomed. Afternoon traffic often backed up more than five miles as commuters headed toward the relative quiet of rural communities west of the city. Accidents sometimes snarled traffic for five or six hours, leaving stranded drivers on both sides frustrated enough to abandon their vehicles in search of meals and bathroom facilities. The four lanes of the bridge could not keep up with the present demand.

And accidents happened with frightening regularity. None of her designers had anticipated the need for center barricades. Accidents that would have been simple fender benders on other highways often developed into head-on collisions on the bridge.

Wayne looked at his watch. Eleven o'clock. Today, at least, he hoped that commuters wouldn't be involved. With any luck he could finish his investigation and have the bridge open again by late afternoon.

In spite of his flashing lights, approaching the bridge proved difficult. Frustrated drivers in idling cars already crowded the freeway near the bridge deck. In a desperate attempt to avoid the wait, other cars jammed the exit ramps. Wayne pulled onto the shoulder and inched his way past irritated and impatient drivers. He rarely had to use his siren, but today the blaring wail seemed to be his only option for moving cars out of the way.

As he approached, he found himself startled by the scene. A fire truck, parked sideways, completely blocked the highway more than a quarter mile from the bridge deck itself. Firefighters in yellow slickers stood huddled behind hastily built barriers.

"What in the world?" Wayne parked his patrol car and climbed out. Approaching the officer nearest the barrier, he said, "Wayne

Frazier, Incident Response." He flashed his credentials. "What do you have?"

"Joseph Bordeaux, sir." The younger officer nodded. "I haven't heard much. But I do know it involves a propane tank, a logging truck, and a private vehicle."

Wayne noticed the intense high energy in his voice. Bordeaux's dark disheveled hair peeked out from the edge of his hard hat, and his face revealed thick black stubble. "Okay. Fill me in."

"Yes, sir." The two men walked quickly toward the bridge. "Happened about fifteen minutes ago, from what I've heard. A westbound logging truck lost a wheel. Dropped over just before the bridge crest."

"Lose his load?"

"No, sir. But he did cross the center line." At this Wayne shook his head. The man continued, "An eastbound tanker tried to avoid the truck and lost control. He swerved into oncoming traffic, and that's where the other car came in. Oh yeah, I hear we had a couple of rear-enders in the aftermath."

"A fatality in the other car?"

"Yes, sir."

"Any chance of fire?"

"I hope not. The place is full of officers. We've evacuated five city blocks on the west end, sir. We don't know what's left in the tanker." Suddenly Wayne stopped walking. Bordeaux took two full steps before he realized that he'd left Wayne behind.

Frazier made a long slow turn, a full circle, observing the streets and buildings near the freeway. So that explained the eerie calm around the accident scene. It was the quiet that bothered Wayne. No flares. No sirens. No vehicles. No people. The evacuation had been startlingly complete.

"All right, Bordeaux. Thanks. Now get back there and make certain nobody gets through that barrier." Wayne pointed back to the truck.

"Yes, sir." The man in the yellow slicker jogged back to his barricade.

At the bridge deck, smoking wreckage greeted Wayne. Though he'd investigated fatal accidents for more than seventeen years, he'd never gotten over the damage inflicted by the collision of a fast-moving vehicle and a stationary object. Glass and metal debris covered all four lanes of highway. A patrol car, parked sideways, blocked traffic on the far side of the bridge. Beyond that, for as far as Wayne could see, cars waited impatiently to cross the bridge. On the north railing, a propane tanker hung precariously by its left front wheels. In the center, near the crest of the span, a logging truck lay folded in half, the cab on its side. Miraculously, the logs held on. Somehow, the driver had been able to slow down. Or perhaps the traffic itself had been moving slowly. Almost exactly between the two trucks lay the crushed remains of a small blue sedan.

Even from this distance, the damage startled Wayne. The car seemed to have been completely flattened, looking more like a pop can than an automobile. The driver never had a chance.

Two full blocks from the wreckage, in a parking lot hidden behind a bridge post, officers and witnesses stood huddled together in small groups. "Wayne Frazier. Incident Response," he said, showing his identification to the first group of police officers.

They nodded, grim faced and stiff. Fifteen feet away, a tall man standing near the open door of a police cruiser broke away and moved toward him. "Wayne, glad they sent you." He held out his hand.

"Mel." The men shook hands, and Wayne gestured to the propane truck. "What do you know about the tanker?"

"The driver is okay, but he's pretty shaken up." He jerked his thumb toward the cruiser. "Over there. He says it's empty. But we're not moving till someone gets here to tell us it's safe. I think it's leaking."

"Have you called?"

"They're on the way."

"What about the car?"

"No hurry. He's gone."

"How many?"

"Just the driver. A white male."

"ID?"

"Working on it."

"Okay, Mel. Let's get started."

The coastal air grew colder, and a light breeze began to blow, but it was not until tiny drops of rain fell onto Kate's cheeks that she rose from the ground to a sitting position. Her fatigue had changed to exhaustion; the warmth of exercise now turned to chill. Kate struggled to understand the pictures. Who sent them? What did they mean? Some part of her refused to believe the story they told.

She struggled to her feet, still holding the photographs. Brushing dry grass and pebbles from her arms, she noticed the rest of her mail fluttering away in the rising wind, caught in the grass, and tumbling end-over-end across the street. She felt cold, very cold, and she wanted more than anything to hide in the sanctuary of the house. For a moment she fought the urge to tear the pictures into tiny pieces. Let the wind carry them away. Instead, she stooped to gather her lost mail. When she was finished, she turned back to the house.

By the time she entered the kitchen door, Kate was shivering violently. The cold she felt came not from the temperature but from something seeping into her soul. Though she did not understand the pictures, she could not doubt their message. Kate placed the photographs along her kitchen counter and looked carefully at each one. Kate knew something about photos. She worked with them nearly every day. Perhaps she could find something, some hint about their authenticity. Deliberately, methodically, she searched for signs of alterations that might deny their claims. Though she longed to find them, searched diligently for them, she found no signs of modification.

Her careful scrutiny, begun in hope, instead left her convinced. Mike was cheating. Her shock gave way to anger, and the violent shivering of her chill was augmented by the shock of betrayal. How dare he? After all these years. Her thoughts darted about on the horizon of her consciousness, alternating between continued disbelief and intense, almost primal, rage.

In spite of the obvious truth in the pictures, Kate's brain, or perhaps it was more her heart, did its best to reject the facts. It couldn't be. But it was. He wouldn't. But he had.

Suddenly, like the stranglehold of a surprise attack, Kate's heart felt yet another violent squeeze. What about the children? How could she face Drew and Keegan? What would she tell them? She knew that this truth would destroy the supreme admiration they had for their father. They loved him. Adored him. And she understood that. Whatever had gone wrong with the marriage, Mike had always been a good father. Both children led successful, faith-filled lives. There could be no better testimony to Mike's devotion and profound love for his children.

Kate shook herself from her memories. She should not blame herself for how this would affect the children. She had not done this. Mike had. If the children were hurt, it was Mike who hurt them. The more she thought, the angrier Kate felt, until finally the truth drove itself home. Whatever else she believed, she could not deny the facts. These pictures were facts. In anguish, Kate bent over the counter and dropped her face in her hands. Giving way to intense grief, she sobbed violent, angry tears, beating the counter with her fists, until the chill of her body and the betrayal of her soul coalesced into uncontrollable trembling.

No. Kate clenched her teeth. *I can't cry. I didn't do this. He did.* She stood, dragging open palms over her cheeks. *This isn't my fault.* The sobbing left her gasping for air—dry rasping sounds escaped her throat with every breath. *Why should I punish myself?*

She gathered the pictures and stuffed them back into the envelope. Then slowly and deliberately, she organized the mail into a neat stack, put the largest envelopes on the bottom, and left it by the telephone. She left the surprise envelope among the rest of the mail, and even as she did so, she wondered why. Kate, a woman of action, of decision, could no longer explain why she did or felt anything.

Her tears would not obey her own deliberate instructions, and she nearly slapped herself in the intensity with which she wiped her eyes. She opened the refrigerator and filled a clean glass with filtered water. Standing in front of the sink, she took a moment, willing herself to calm. Then she drank deeply, letting the cool liquid fill and distract her disturbed emotions.

I can't stay, she determined. *I don't want to ever see him again.* Leaning against the sink, with the glass still in her hand, she glanced around the kitchen and noticed a single light blinking on her answering machine. Somehow, something as ordinary as a telephone message now seemed completely irrelevant. In an instant everything had become irrelevant. In just twenty minutes, Kate's life had passed from the ordinary forever.

This must be how the Titanic*'s passengers felt on the night it collided* *with an iceberg,* she thought. In the midst of a pleasant evening, just one tiny collision—one little brush with ice—and the ship suddenly filled with water. And while the band played and people danced, while waiters served sumptuous meals, the hull drank the ice-cold water of the Atlantic Ocean.

Kate felt as though her life had suddenly collided with an iceberg. Nothing would ever be ordinary again. Her marriage, her family—all lost. All sinking below the icy water of infidelity.

Ignoring the answering machine, Kate went upstairs. *I need a shower,* she thought. *A shower will help me sort this out.*

———

In a state of complete shock, Mike did not try to hide the pictures from Doug. In fact, he continued to shuffle back and forth between the images, seeking desperately to identify when and where they were taken. He could not escape the resounding question. Who? Who had taken these pictures? How had he been caught? They had been so careful, so secretive. In his mind, he had never expected to be discovered. No one would ever know. He turned the envelope over again, looking for clues. It bore no mark other than his own name.

Doug cleared his throat noisily and walked to the window. He stood, quietly gazing out over the waterfront.

"Oh, God," Mike moaned, leaning back and throwing the pictures to his desk in one motion. "Oh, God, what have I done?" He turned his chair to the window and rubbed the palm of his right hand over the bald spot at the crown of his head.

"It looks to me like you've been having a good time," Doug responded, his tone cool and even. "I admit, you two had me fooled. I'd never have guessed."

"Shut up. Just shut up." Mike leaned his forehead on his right hand and groaned.

"Right." Doug chuckled. "And now you're telling me you're suddenly repentant?" He turned to face his partner. "Cara's great looking. Who'd have thought she'd go for you?"

"Get out." Mike wheeled his chair back to the desk, resting his forehead in his hands. "Get out now, before I do something I'll regret."

Still smiling, Doug exited, closing the office door quietly behind him. As he heard the door close, Mike picked up the pictures again. This time, he examined them more carefully. A tiny Post-it note attached to the lower right corner of the last picture rewarded his search. There he found the handwritten words *Kate should find these interesting.*

Mike stopped breathing. Whoever had mailed these pictures had more in mind than causing Mike Langston misery. The object of the deed seemed to be the complete destruction of his marriage. But even as he thought these things, he realized it wasn't the truth.

If anyone had destroyed his marriage, Mike had. No one else had betrayed Kate. And whatever damage had been done occurred long before these pictures were mailed.

A new wave of anguish rolled through Mike's stomach, and he suddenly envisioned himself facing Keegan with the news. Dear, beautiful Keegan. With hair as curly as her mother's and as dark as his own, she was the perfect embodiment of their physical union. Fiercely idealistic, Mike could clearly picture her horrified expression while he tried to explain his infidelity. Anguish would fill her lovely features, and then loathing. The loathing would be for him. What could possibly have convinced him that this present misery was worth the transient pleasure of sexual fulfillment? The realization of his own foolishness filled his body. Why had he not pictured this face, his daughter's face, in the moment of his own temptation?

This vision, combined with the unbearable pain Kate would feel, wrenched the place where Mike's soul and body met. Nausea squeezed his insides. Feeling completely and totally defeated, Mike cried out, "Oh God. I never meant for this to happen. I never meant . . ." Giving in to his sorrow, he buried his face in his arms and wept.

Three

STANDING IN THE SHOWER, Kate lifted her face to the hot water, letting it pour down over her head and mingle with her tears. At least in here, no one could accuse her of losing control. In all this water, no one could ever prove she was crying. She turned her back to the spray, deliberately relaxing, willing the water to ease the tension of her back and neck. Hot water might relax her muscles, but it could not resolve the persistent gnawing in her gut. Kate Langston knew she would never be the same.

She tried instead to soap away her pain. Filling a bath sponge with vanilla shower gel, Kate lavished her skin with suds. She scrubbed until the friction turned her skin pink. Still miserable, she gave up, resting her forearms against the tiles of her walk-in shower. As the water beat against her skin, she let her tears flow again. Kate felt utterly drained.

She dried off carefully and stepped from the shower onto the bath mat. At some point during her shower, Kate realized she had to leave. She needed time, space, and someplace to go to think things through. She could not face Mike yet. Not until she could do so without tears. She would never allow him to see how much he'd hurt her.

After towel-drying her hair, she dressed quickly in lightweight jeans and a hooded sweatshirt. She found her favorite sneakers and stuffed her feet in without pausing for socks. Tying her shoes quickly, she turned to face her image in the mirror. Already the skin around her eyes had swollen, and in the khaki green of her irises she thought she recognized pain. Projection, she objected. No one else can tell. She pulled out a hair pick and began to untangle her shoulder-length curls. She had no desire to fuss with them. She would drag out the knots and leave her hair to dry, a wavy, curly mess. It didn't matter what she looked like, not today.

At the bathroom cupboard she removed her cosmetic bag. Holding it below the counter with one hand, she dropped toiletries into it with the other. Pausing, she dug through a drawer for sunscreen and applied a palmful to her freckled cheeks. Kate's fair skin posed a constant hazard, and life in Northern California demanded that she pay close attention. Either she wore sunscreen constantly or she wore dense freckles forever. Even in the aftermath of deep shock, Kate remembered the daily post-shower regimen of sunscreen.

From the closet she pulled a small carry-on flight bag and took it into the bedroom. Without thinking, she opened drawer after drawer and threw items into the bag. She folded nothing, counted nothing. She simply wanted out. Tomorrow was Thursday. With only two workdays left this week, she needed only enough to last until Monday. She wanted to avoid seeing Mike through the weekend. She needed time. By then she would have a plan.

When she tired of packing, Kate leaned over their king-sized bed and tried to zip the zipper. She tugged and pulled, but the zipper resisted until Kate finally had to sit on the bed and restuff her clothes into the bag. Again she pulled, until her hands ached and the zipper left an angry indentation on her right index finger. Suddenly the zipper pull fractured, and as it gave way, Kate fell over backwards. It was too much. This whole thing was far too much for one afternoon. Again she gave in to tearful grief.

Much later, Kate became aware of a faint pink light filling her bedroom. The setting sun had turned the western sky coral and blue, bathing the room in reflected color. Normally Kate delighted in the colors of the sunset. But today, as she became aware of the color reflecting off the bedroom ceiling, she felt only intense, heavy grief.

"Oh, Jesus," she said aloud. "What is happening to me? What will I do now?" Only silence answered her question, a silence that was neither peaceful nor profound. She found it only empty and full of pain.

Sitting up, she pulled a pair of jeans from the bag and threw them against a bedroom chair. Then she used her bare fingers to drag the zipper on the flight bag closed. She blew her nose and carried the bag downstairs. Mike would be home soon. If she wanted to escape without seeing him, she needed to leave now. She went out through the kitchen door and noticed as she passed that the light on the message machine now blinked two quick blinks instead of one. Someone had called while she was in the shower.

She pressed the Message button and leaned against the counter. "Welcome. You have two new messages," the automated voice declared. "Wednesday, 3:52 P.M."

The machine clicked, and her daughter's voice rang cheerfully through the kitchen. "Hey, Mom. It's Keegan. I just finished my last midterm, and I was wondering if we could do lunch this week. What do ya think? Give me a call. You know the number." There was a pause, and then, "Oh yeah, I love you. Say hi to Daddy." The line went dead, and for an instant Kate heard the hum of a dial tone.

The mechanical voice interrupted, "Wednesday, 5:20 P.M." The next voice she recognized as Mike's—intense and serious. "Kate. Mike." She heard a pause, then a tiny catch in his voice. Pain? She couldn't be sure. "We need to talk. It's very important, honey. Call me. Please?" His voice pled the request.

"End of new messages," the machine continued. Kate pressed the Erase button. She would not return Keegan's call, nor would she talk to Mike. Not now, with her emotions as raw and odorous as week-old fish. She could not. Taking a sheet of paper from the drawer below the phone, she scrawled a note in black felt-tip letters.

I've taken a time out. Don't call! With that, she picked up her bag and walked out the kitchen door.

———

The legs, which swung gracefully from the driver's-side door of the classic silver Mercedes, were long and shapely, all the way to the short black knit skirt clinging to lean thighs. The valet, who opened the car door, made a valiant effort to appear uninterested. But as his eyes drifted back to perfect legs in shimmering hose ending in stylishly tall heels, he seemed to surrender to the woman's beauty. His mouth dropped open, and he remained for a moment, frozen.

The woman hesitated, still sitting in the car, as she surveyed the covered driveway carefully. Holding her hand aloft, she indicated her willingness to be helped from her car, and the valet immediately sprang to her aid. The rapid response indicated his commitment to duty. No doubt, he would surely have run into a burning house to escort this beauty from danger. Today, all he could offer was his hand.

Cara Maria Calloruso chuckled at the obvious fall of the overdecorated valet. Aware of her own striking appearance, she stepped in front of the doorman. As she approached the restaurant entrance, she enjoyed the awareness of eyes following her progress. People often wondered if Cara were a movie star. They whispered in awestruck tones as she passed by. She relished the stir she caused whenever she entered a room. In fact, she took great pleasure in causing a stir.

So, with a flourish equal to that of a famous star, she approached the maître d'. "Excuse me, I am to meet Mr. Mike Langston," she said, removing her sunglasses and tossing her glossy dark hair behind her shoulders. Her beautiful olive skin and dark brown eyes had the desired effect, and the host dropped his pencil to help her.

"Of course," he said with too much cheer. "Mr. Langston is expecting you. Come right this way." He led her into the main dining room, bright with natural light. She noticed only a few people in the room, which she attributed to the late afternoon hour. Cara Maria felt surprised and pleased to meet Mike in such an unsequestered location. Perhaps things were about to change between them. Though she never expected to fall for Mike, the idea of winning his public affection sent a thrill of victory through her heart. Deliberately, she took a calming breath, determined to fight the giddy excitement rising in her chest. She strode into the dining room with sultry steps.

The maître d' escorted her to a table directly in front of floor-length windows overlooking the street, where Mike sat drinking coffee. Cara Maria placed her purse on the chair, which her host held for her, and gracefully took the seat opposite Mike. She dismissed the host with a faint smile and slight nod, and he backed away appreciatively.

Cara smiled coyly and rested her elbows on the table. Setting her chin on well-manicured hands, she said, "Hello, love." She tossed her hair again. "What a surprise to meet you here, in front of all these people." She gestured to the room. "To what do I owe the pleasure?"

"Hello, Cara. Thank you for coming," he answered, fingering his coffee cup. Mike did not look up. It surprised her that he refused to meet her eyes. Frustrated, she reached out to touch his forearm. He pulled away and sat up in his chair. Still, he did not look directly at her.

"What is it? What's wrong?" she questioned, suddenly aware of a new distance between them that frightened her. No one ever dared step outside of Cara's magnetic control. She'd never experienced this kind of indifference—such a clear refusal to submit to her beauty.

"This," he answered simply, and leaned down to his briefcase. Bringing out an envelope, he slid it across the table to Cara Maria.

Wayne waited more than an hour to have the propane tanker officially pronounced empty. By the time he gave the go-ahead to begin the accident investigation, the Department of Transportation had already called twice to ask about reopening the bridge. During the last call, Wayne had nearly lost his temper. After seventeen years, they certainly should know that Wayne Frazier did not hurry—especially when something about an accident felt wrong, as this one did. This accident felt horribly wrong.

Before long, officers with clipboards and measuring tapes tramped across the highway, carefully measuring skid marks and taking notes. A team of photographers documented every possible angle of all the vehicles involved. Back at the parking lot, witnesses huddled in police cruisers waiting to be interviewed. Wayne made certain that the treads on the logging truck, smoother than a clean windowpane, had been photographed and measured. Those tires clearly violated state law. But he suspected something else, something more.

From long years of experience, Wayne knew trucking companies tried to keep expenses down in order to save on overhead. Sometimes they did so illegally. In this case the bald tires led him to wonder how many other aspects of maintenance had been overlooked in the interest of economics. He gave orders for the rear trailer hubs to be taken to the lab as evidence. Perhaps the wheel bearings and brakes were long overdue for attention as well.

When Wayne felt completely satisfied that all the relevant information had been gathered, he gave permission to begin towing the vehicles. The police crew ordered a crane to lift the tanker from the bridge rail. In the meantime, Wayne stood watching as firefighters struggled to remove the body from the flattened blue car. These men knew their stuff, and Wayne respected their expertise. They had already cut into the frame and top of the car. Still the remaining damage kept them from pulling out the victim. As he watched, the men began to cut away the base of the steering wheel.

"Wayne!" Mel Stanton jogged toward him from his patrol car.

"Yeah?" As his friend approached, Wayne found himself envying his shape. Wayne had let his old body go. Jogging didn't seem to be much of an option anymore.

"We have a little problem with the driver here. I thought you should know."

"What is it?"

"Well, the plates are registered to a black GMC Suburban."

"Oh yeah?" Wayne turned to look directly into Mel's eyes. "That was no Suburban."

"Yep, stolen about four months ago in Idaho."

"Great." They stood silently watching as two firefighters climbed onto the roof of the car. Carefully, the men leaned in. Squatting low over the opening, they began to lift the man from his seat. "Okay. Check and double-check his ID. And Mel?"

"Yeah?"

"Would you keep the press out of this? I have a bad feeling here." Wayne glanced back to the overpass behind him, where onlookers had gathered like bluebirds on a fence. Mel followed Wayne's glance. People loved watching police investigations.

Wayne felt like a goldfish. "Don't say anything at all about the car—or the plates. Just tell the press that we can't release the name of the victim until the relatives have been notified."

"Got it."

"When we get him out, I want prints. And get Forensics in here. Maybe we'll get lucky."

Kate spent the rest of the evening sitting in the breakfast nook of Sally Crandall's house in the woods. "Here, have some more coffee," Sally said, filling Kate's cup. She set the pot back on the burner.

"Thanks, Sally." Kate did not move, did not look at her friend.

Sally slid into the seat opposite Kate and dropped two teaspoons of sugar into her own cup. She stirred quietly, thoughtfully. Finally she said, "Wake up, Kate. You can talk to me. What are you thinking?"

"Nothing, really. I guess I just got lost somewhere."

"I understand. But tell me again. Was there anything else in the package? Anything besides the pictures?"

"Whoever sent those pictures didn't need to add anything. The photos said it all."

Kate shook her head in a vain attempt to drive the images from her mind. But the images remained, seared permanently into her memory. She looked up to find her friend searching her face, blue eyes intense and hurting. Still holding the mug between her hands, Kate noticed for the first time that Sally was aging, getting gray. *Is this how Mike sees me,* she wondered? Kate's eyes filled with tears, and she looked down at the table, blinking rapidly.

"It's hard to believe." Laying her spoon down next to the mug, Sally sighed. "I never would have guessed it—not of Mike."

"Obviously, I didn't guess either." Kate wiped the corner of her eye, where a tear threatened to escape without permission. "I always wished there was something more between us. You know, some little spark. But I guess I thought this was how love settles after so many years."

"Have you told the kids?"

"Oh, heavens no. Drew is just settling in at his new job. And I just can't tell Keegan. It would kill her. She called about doing lunch. But I can't talk to her. Not yet."

"What about Mike? Does he know that you know? Have you two talked?"

"What's to talk about?"

"Maybe it isn't how it looks."

"You didn't see the pictures. It can't be anything else."

A thoughtful silence settled between the two women, a silence born of heavy emotion and deep grief. Tears had been shed, hugs had been given and received. "Well," Sally began gently, "you're welcome to stay here as long as you need to. We have a guest room with a private bath. It's upstairs away from all of our noise and interference. It should give you plenty of space to think and pray."

Though Sally and Don Crandall owned the sportswear company where Kate worked, their relationship could more accurately be characterized as friends than employers and employee. For the past ten years, Sally and Kate had shared everything—work and church and family.

The Crandalls attended the same small community church as Mike and Kate. Though her own children were grown and gone, Sally continued as the Sunday school superintendent. Her husband, the founder of the business, had an insatiable love of carpentry. He spent most Saturdays down at the church helping with the latest addition—a multipurpose room. Sally and Don were old guard at the little church. No matter what their community of faith needed, they came through.

In this latest crisis, Sally had come through again. Kate squeezed her friend's hand. "Thanks. You guys are about the only thing I have left to depend on." She took another sip of coffee. "I'll be all right. I just need a little time to think."

"What you need right now is some rest. This is too much for anyone to handle—at least all in one day." Standing, Sally picked up her mug and carried it to the sink. "Come on upstairs, Kate. I'll have Don bring up your things." She put an arm around Kate's shoulder and guided her toward the entry hall. "Let's open up your bed." They walked upstairs together. "Some sleep, and some prayer, and some time, and who knows? Things might not be as bad as they seem right now."

Kate stopped suddenly and turned to face Sally. "Look, you have no idea." Her voice felt dark, the words falling heavily from her lips. "Nothing will ever make those pictures seem better. I don't ever want to see Mike again, not as long as I live. I'm through. Done. It's over."

Sally offered no argument, gave no objection. She simply folded her younger friend into a loving embrace and held her. "I know, dear," she murmured gently, patting her back. "I understand. Really, I do."

Four

IN THE HOTEL RESTAURANT, Cara Maria Calloruso wasted little energy inspecting the photographs Mike gave her. Her lovely mouth changed into a tight, dark line, and her skin blanched from its rich European olive to the color of unfired clay. She stuffed the pictures back into the envelope and spun them across the table to Mike. "Where did those come from?"

"They came this afternoon—by private courier," he answered, taking another drink from his mug. In a desperate attempt to distract himself from the woman seated across the table, Mike focused on the dark coffee aroma wafting up from his mug. He tried not to notice her lovely legs, crossed at the knees, or the single black shoe dangling from her shapely foot. He tried. Though he had committed his mind to a new course, his body seemed to have a will of its own. Mentally, he flogged himself. *Focus, Mike. Stay focused.*

Cara acknowledged his answer with a nod and flagged a waiter with a graceful sweep of perfectly manicured fingers. The waiter came immediately. "I'd like wine," she said simply.

"Of course, ma'am. Which do you prefer?"

"Something dry," she cooed. "Surprise me." The waiter bowed, beaming pleasure as he hurried away to select exactly the most appropriate afternoon wine for the lovely lady.

As the waiter turned to leave, Mike observed Cara Maria with a new detachment. This change in thinking had begun when he first saw the pictures. Her interaction with the male staff of the restaurant over the past few minutes only confirmed it. No longer did he find her enchanting. Instead, as he watched, he saw the bluer, blatant truth. He recognized the black and white of it. Cara was a seductress, a tease. And he had surrendered to her spell with the same predictability of this young waiter. He remembered her entrance into the office this afternoon before the pictures had been delivered. He remembered how the scent of her passing in front of him had left him dizzy. He thought of how many times her beauty had left him staggering, swaying foolishly, and he felt a sudden intense shame. Only a fool would fall for a shell. Cara Maria was nothing more than a Barbie Doll with skin.

Cara knew exactly what she was doing, he realized. And he had been stupid enough to fall for it. For a moment, self-loathing threatened to engulf Mike. But he shook himself free. For now, he had a more important task.

Cara smiled softly at Mike. "So now that we've been discovered, what next?"

"Next, nothing." He kept his voice flat, unemotional.

"What do you mean, nothing?" For an instant, she seemed to struggle to maintain charm and composure. "Darling, we've been exposed," she said. "It has to change the game plan." She reached across the table, caressing his hand with the tips of her fingers.

"You're right. It does," he answered, pulling his hand away. "And it's over, Cara." He sighed, sitting straighter in his chair.

Finally. He'd said it.

She drew back. "Over?" The smiling waiter reappeared with a full carafe and two tall chilled wineglasses. Cara forced a tantalizing smile. He bowed. "A glass for you, sir?"

"Nothing, thank you." Mike held up his hands.

With great care, he poured for Cara Maria. "It's on the house, madam," he said. Again the bow. The smile.

"Why, thank you, kind sir," she drawled. Her face came alive. Ever the tease, she tipped her chin toward him, her gaze locking his.

When the waiter left, she leaned forward again, speaking with fierce intensity. "We've been caught. So what? People would have discovered us sooner or later anyway. Maybe this is for the best. We can finally make our own life together, without all this sneaking around."

"There won't be any more sneaking, Cara. You aren't listening to me." Mike leaned forward in his chair, his voice intense. "I mean it. We're through. When I saw those pictures today, I realized what I've known all along. It's all wrong. We're wrong. It has to end."

"Wrong? What could be so wrong about what we share?" She must have heard her own rising volume, for she glanced suddenly around the room. Lowering her voice, she made another attempt. "It wasn't wrong; it was wonderful. You told me yourself. It was wonderful."

"I was wrong, Cara. I've wronged you, and I've betrayed Kate." His voice threatened to break. "And now it's over. Done."

"I don't mean to be stubborn here, but we do work together." She folded her arms across her chest. "Whether or not we continue, we will see one another."

"I know, I've thought of that."

Tears threatened to spill from her dark almond-shaped eyes. "It will hurt, you know, seeing you when I can't have you."

"I've thought of that too." Mike avoided her eyes, trying to stay separate, unfeeling. This meeting had turned out to be much harder than he'd expected. All along, he'd told himself that he could end this fling at any time. That Cara didn't really care for him. This was another lie he'd allowed himself to believe. Another lie in an unending cascade of lies, threatening to destroy his life.

Even though he'd seen things as they were and made up his mind, it seemed overwhelmingly difficult to undo the mess. But he had to. In the silence that followed, he drank a mouthful of coffee and closed his eyes. He summoned Keegan's face and imagined telling his daughter the truth. In that same moment, he breathed a prayer asking for strength. Whether from the prayer or the image, he found the courage to continue. "I want you to resign, Cara."

Shocked, her body straightened—every muscle suddenly seemed taut, attentive. "You can't ask me to do that. I've put my life into your company. I've kept you out of debt and in the public eye. You owe your success to me."

"Not true." Mike shook his head sadly. "We've all worked hard to get where we are. And now it's time to make some changes." He took another drink and then stared out at the people on the sidewalk. Happy people, with peaceful, unshattered lives, hurried by the window.

Mike suspected that Cara Maria had never begged for anything in her life. And most likely, she'd never lost a man in her life. He knew she'd never been fired before. His decision seemed to un-nerve her. He'd effectively demolished her pride. Her response came as no surprise. "All right. Fine," she said, throwing her cloth napkin on the table. "If that's the way you want things, great. So I resign. I'll expect a decent recommendation."

Mike nodded without looking at her face. "I've done more than that," he said. "It's my fault that this whole thing has happened. I've made some contacts." He removed another envelope from his briefcase and slid it across the table. "I've written personal letters to several companies. They're all there. You can have your pick of a number of positions."

She took the envelope without looking inside. Tense anger had frozen the features of her face. "I'm not about to thank you."

"I don't expect that." Mike felt complete misery. Not only had he destroyed his own family, but Cara's professional life as well. There could be no more painful place than this. "I'm so sorry," he whispered.

Suddenly, Cara Maria slid her chair back and rose to her feet. "I never wanted you anyway," she hissed. "You were nothing more than a toy to me." She trembled slightly. "So the toy is broken." She shrugged, "I'm finished anyway." Cara stalked out of the din-ing room still clutching the envelope in her right hand.

Even angry, Cara Maria Calloruso was very beautiful. Mike no-ticed that all the men in the room turned to watch her leave.

————

Somehow, Kate made it through Thursday, though she accom-plished very little. Through her secretary, Kate had refused more than ten calls from Mike. Late in the morning, he'd arrived at her office breathless and anxious to see her. Fortunately, Kate had al-ready left for lunch with Sally. Her secretary had assured Mike that she would call. She did not.

Friday morning proved to be easier. A meeting with the design team for the spring collection promised to keep her thoughts oc-cupied. Their primary objective was to decide on the spring color palette. But Kate realized immediately they would not reach their goal.

Everything on the catalogue pages had to match and blend, and getting the buyers, the designers, and the entire marketing department on the same page required more diplomacy than even Henry Kissinger possessed. She might as well try to redecorate the Museum of Natural History in an afternoon. Sally Crandall seemed frustrated as well, and Kate wanted to call in the firing squad. If she hoped the meeting would keep her mind off her troubles, Kate found herself sadly mistaken. Instead, while the team argued, Kate drew tiny cartoons of Mike's face, thin hair on top, smiling cheerfully over half-rimmed reading glasses.

At the end of the second hour of negotiations, Kate's assistant knocked at the door. "Mrs. Langston, Mr. Langston is on line three." Kate glanced around at her coworkers. From their expressions, she could not tell how much they knew. Certainly, Kate's assistant had her suspicions. "Joy, I can't take a call from Mike right now. Please tell him I'll call when it's convenient." Hiding things irritated Kate, but she refused to explain her personal life to her secretary.

Joy obeyed without question. She backed out of the room. "Yes, ma'am," she said, frowning.

The meeting continued, but they made no progress. In spite of intense discussion and heavy campaigning, Kate found the meeting far too passive to drag her thoughts from her own emotions. The door opened again, and Joy stuck her head through.

"Joy, really. I told you I couldn't be interrupted," Kate scolded.

"Mrs. Langston, I thought you might want to take this call." Joy glanced around the room. "It's your mother, long distance. She sounds very upset."

With an enormous sigh, Kate excused herself. How dare Mike call her mother into this? Wasn't it enough to destroy her life, without involving her parents? They were elderly, not well enough to take this kind of stress. Her fury increased with every step.

In her private office, Kate fell into the desk chair and picked up the phone. Very nearly barking, she answered, "This is Kate Langston."

She recognized her mother's voice, weak and tearful. "Kate, I'm so sorry to bother you at work." The voice broke, and Kate heard gentle weeping. Still believing the call was about Mike, her anger threatened to boil over.

"Yes, Mom. What do you want?"

"Kate, it's your father." Her mother took a deep breath. "He's had another heart attack."

Exhaling, Kate leaned back into the chair. Her heart sank, and she felt such fear that she nearly choked. "Oh, no. Mom, is he . . .?"

"No, Kate, he's going to be all right. For now." Her mother sniffed. "The doctor says it was a pretty rough one, though." She drew a long breath. "Honey, I wouldn't bother you, but he's asking to see you."

"To see me?"

"Yes, Kate, he wants you to come."

Kate grabbed a handful of hair from behind her neck, twisting it up onto her head. She leaned onto the desk, still clutching the phone. Her tears began anew. *Even in California,* she thought, *when it rains, it pours.*

———

"Ad out," Mike Langston called. His brows, etched in concentration, dripped sweat onto his cheekbones. Mike brought his racket down swiftly, carving a perfect arc through the air behind him. As the tennis ball rose gracefully into the air, Mike dropped his racket–elbow high, with his hand behind his shoulder. Then snapping his wrist, he slammed the ball toward the net.

David Holland sprang toward the ball. "Long," he called as the ball skipped across the court beyond the service line. His face broke into a large grin. Mike missed his second serve, as well, giving Dave the game. "I win again," he laughed. Dave wiped his forehead with the sweatband around his wrist. Unsatisfied, he leaned forward and mopped his dripping face with the front of his T-shirt. "Something must be bothering you. I never get to kill you this bad."

Ignoring him, Mike strode to the bench beside the court. Without a word he stuffed his tennis racket into his bag and picked up his sweatshirt.

"So what is it?" David asked, crossing the court to the bench.

Mike glanced around the tennis club and noticed that the center court had emptied. "Don't," he warned. He threw his sweatshirt over one shoulder and turned to leave.

"Come on, you can't fool me." Dave pulled the strap of his own bag over his shoulder and hurried to catch up with Mike. "That wasn't a game. That was a cream." He smiled as he gestured toward the tennis court. "So what is it?"

"Look," Mike stopped suddenly, turning to face him. "I lost. That's all. I'm off my game. That doesn't give you permission to become my therapist."

"Okay. I'm backing off." Dave raised his hands in a gesture of mock surrender.

Mike's face softened for a moment, but he shook his head and turned back to the locker room. Dave followed a few steps behind. "I'm right, though, aren't I?"

"You never give up, do you?" Mike said without looking back. He put out his right hand and slammed open the swinging door to the men's locker room. "No wonder you made the cut for dental school. You're so stubborn."

"But I'm right, aren't I?"

"So what if you are?"

"So, if I am—right, I mean—you look like you could use a friend." He followed his tennis partner through the door. "How about coffee?"

"All right. Coffee," Mike agreed, surrendering.

———

Six hours after the accident, Wayne sat staring at the computer in his Tacoma office. The cursor blinked accusingly. He'd missed lunch, and the donut he'd eaten with his morning coffee left him with low blood sugar and a nasty headache. Wayne had trouble concentrating on the report in front of him. At least he'd ordered the bridge open by early evening. But snarled traffic would last until nearly midnight.

Perhaps he should write another letter to the Department of Transportation advising them to place a concrete traffic barrier down the center of the bridge. A barrier might have saved the life of the driver in the blue car. Without a fatality, the bridge would have been reopened in two hours. At least plans for a new bridge had already been drawn. If Wayne could survive two more years of days like today, another bridge would open. No one would ever cross into oncoming traffic again. Wayne picked up his coffee cup and discovered it empty. He stood to get a refill.

The ringing phone jarred him. Setting the cup down, he

reached for the phone, glad for an interruption.

"Wayne. It's Mel." A male voice boomed from the earpiece.

"How'd you know I'd be here?"

"Didn't. Thought I'd leave a message. We did prints on the driver."

"What'd you find?"

"Nothing. He's clean. At least he doesn't have a record. But that's not all."

"Okay. Tell me."

"Had a fake driver's license. Gives an address on Elm about two blocks into Commencement Bay."

"So we got a dead guy living in a house that doesn't exist?"

"Yeah, killed in a car with stolen plates."

"All right. Want to meet me at the yard?"

"Just say when."

Five

"LISTEN, FRANK," Kate said early Friday afternoon, "I know what I'm doing here. You saw the pictures." She leaned back in her seat and took a deep breath. "I'm paying you by the minute for your time, and I don't want to spend my money arguing with you about this."

The man sitting across the desk sat quietly for a moment, his fingers laced across his broad belly. "Katherine, please. I'm only asking you to postpone your action, not change it. If, after you give this some real thought, you still want a divorce, I'll help you in any way I can. But, after all these years, what's the hurry?" Frank Bickman spread his hands away from the arms of his chair in a pleading gesture. "Maybe it was just a fling. A misunderstanding. Are you sure you want to throw away everything just because of some pictures?"

"Frank, listen to me. You're my lawyer—not my counselor. I haven't thrown anything away. Mike did. I thought I could trust him. I thought I knew him." Kate paused, battling tears. How could she convince Frank about the truth of the situation? "It isn't that he made a mistake or that he had an error in judgment. He took my trust and destroyed it." Kate's voice quivered as she spoke. "I'm only cleaning up the mess." She dropped her forehead into the fingers of her left hand, massaging the skin vigorously. *I won't cry,* she told herself firmly. *I've cried enough already.* "I won't live with someone I can't trust."

"I'm afraid these kinds of messes aren't like dirty laundry,"

Frank said gently. "You can't just throw them in the wash and hope it comes out clean. The stains stay forever." He paused, then continued more earnestly, "What about counseling? Have you spoken to your pastor?"

"There isn't anything to talk about. I can't—look, just start the proceedings. That's all I'm asking."

"One more question, Kate. What about the kids? Have you said anything to them?"

"Not yet. And I won't—for a while. They have lives of their own now. I'm not going to bring them into this for now. Please, Frank. Just do it."

"If you insist, I'll draw up the papers."

"Thank you." Kate stood, smoothing the lap of her trousers. Extending her hand, she said, "I'm going to Kansas to see my folks for a while. You can contact me there."

Ignoring the hand, Frank Bickman came around his desk to take Kate's shoulders. He pulled her into a gentle embrace. "I've known you all your married life," he said. "I never thought I'd see you here like this. I'm so sorry."

Kate let him hold her for only a moment before pushing him away. "Me too," she said, brushing tears from her eyes. "I'm sorry too. But here we are. I just have to get over it, that's all," she said, pulling a tissue from her pocket. "Just get on with my life." She pinched her nose with the tissue and took a deep breath.

"Well, then, Kate, I'll be in touch. We don't have to go through with it, you know. I'll do as you ask, but if you have a change of heart, just call me. You wouldn't be the first to change your mind."

————

At the Covington Hills Country Club, most everyone ate lunch in athletic wear of some kind—designer tennis dresses, running suits, golf clothes. Most had just finished a round of golf or several sets of tennis. Some attended the morning step aerobics classes, and others simply dressed the part and came for lunch.

Mike and Dave arrived before the lunch crowd and settled into a quiet corner table over the eighteenth green.

"I'll have white wine," Mike said to the waitress who seated them.

Dave pulled his chair into place and raised his eyebrows. "Just water, thanks," he said. The waitress, dressed in a black skirt and white tuxedo blouse, handed menus to each of them and turned to leave. Dave opened his and allowed the silence to linger. After a brief reading, he closed the menu and set it aside. "So what exactly is going on?" he asked.

"You don't give it much time, do you?"

"We both know why we're here. So let's cut to the chase." He took a sip of water. "Why do you look like you're about to be arrested for murder?"

Mike unfolded the white linen napkin and spread it carefully on his lap. Leaning his elbows onto the table and folding his hands, he stared off at the putting green outside the window. "I screwed up, Dave."

"Okay, so you screwed up. Everybody has at one time or another."

"Not like this."

"All right. Nobody has ever done it this bad. What did you do?"

The waitress arrived with a glass of wine and set it gently on a paper coaster in front of Mike. He lifted the glass and took a long swallow. Setting the glass down, he continued, "There's a woman at work," he began. "I, uh . . ."

"You had an affair."

"Yep. That's about it." Mike lifted the glass and swallowed another gulp. He felt the same enormous shame wash over him just like it had on the day the pictures arrived. "I don't have an excuse. It was stupid. I love Kate. I never meant to hurt her."

"So she knows?"

"Now she does."

"She caught you?"

"No, and that's the weirdest thing." Mike put his glass down. "I got pictures. Delivered to the office." Turning the wine stem slowly, he watched the liquid trace a pathway on the inside of the glass. "I don't know where they came from—who sent them. I just know Kate got them too."

"What pictures?"

Mike looked up at his friend.

"Okay, I know what pictures. Your face tells me everything. Where did the pictures come from?"

"I've no idea. I've tried to figure it out, but I keep coming up with a big zero." Mike shook his head and continued. "They were taken in public—but who did it and why? I can't figure it out. Anyway, I went home Wednesday and found a note from Kate. It said, 'Don't call.' She got the same exact photographs in the mail. I found them in an envelope on the kitchen counter." Mike shrugged. "She saw them, all right. I went to see her at her office the next day—her secretary told me she was out. But I'm not so sure. I can't get her to answer the phone. I leave messages, but she won't call." He tapped the table with the palms of his hands and leaned back in the leather chair. "I think it's over. She's done with me."

"What about you?"

"What do you mean?"

"I mean," Dave leaned forward in his chair, his elbows on the table, "what do you want?"

"I want my wife back." Mike paused, and his voice took on an angry edge. "I can't believe how stupid I've been. I want to roll back the clock. I want to erase this whole thing from my memory." He sighed. "I want to protect Kate."

The waitress returned to the table and took out her tablet. "Are you gentlemen ready to order?" She was young and pretty, and she smiled appealingly at the two men.

"We are," Dave answered. "I'll have the grilled chicken salad. How 'bout you, Mike?"

"I'm not hungry." He lifted his glass for another drink.

"He'll have the club," Dave answered. "And we'd both like coffee. Black."

She wrote down their order, took the menus, and left them alone.

"Seems to me, there isn't any way for you to get all of what you want."

"Thanks for the encouragement."

"Look, Mike," Dave took on an advisory tone, "you know you can't turn back the clock. But we've been in business long enough to know that you can get most anything you want—if you want it badly enough. Because when you set a goal, you go after it. It consumes you. You spend every waking minute trying to figure out how to get the thing you want. The rules are the same at home as they are in business."

Mike looked at Dave as though he had lost his mind. "What are you talking about?"

"What I mean is simple." Dave took out his fountain pen, lifted Mike's wineglass, and slid the coaster out from under Mike's drink. He started writing. "You can't hit a target you don't aim for. You know that as well as I do."

Mike looked across the table, trying to see what Dave had scribbled on the paper, but Dave's large hands covered the words. "I will tell you this. Ten years ago, I sat in the same place you are right now. I thought the world had ended. Valerie threw me out."

Mike stared up at his friend. "You never told me that."

"It isn't something I'm proud of. There isn't a day that goes by that I don't wish I could undo the pain I caused. But I can't."

Mike read sincerity in his friend's features. "But you and Val. You made it. You're together." The waitress returned, carrying a salad in one hand and the club sandwich in the other. The men leaned back, giving her room to work.

Holding a tall pepper grinder, she smiled at Dave, "Fresh ground pepper?"

"No, thanks."

"Can I get you gentlemen anything else?" Another charming smile.

They shook their heads. She nodded and retreated. Dave lowered his voice and continued, "Getting mixed up with another woman was the biggest mistake I've ever made. The details aren't important. Val and I decided not to make it a feature of our life together. But just because we don't talk about it doesn't mean it didn't happen." He poured hot mustard dressing onto his salad. "It did. And I'm to blame. And if I could make the whole memory disappear, I would." Somehow, without him saying it, Mike understood that Dave would offer no further details.

Mike made no move to eat. "You're preaching to the choir." Shaking his head, he continued, "But it's too late. Kate will never forgive me."

"Have you broken it off with the woman?" Dave asked as he swallowed the first bite of his salad.

"Yes."

"Really—off?"

"Yeah. I showed her the pictures. I said it was over."

"Okay, I'm going to trust you on that. But I'll remind you of this: You can't move forward if there is any chance of her being around. She has to be gone. Completely unavailable." Dave reached for a roll and pulled it open. Slathering a glob of butter across it, he continued, "Then, what I'm going to tell you will work. It's simple, but it isn't easy."

Dave slid the coaster across the table to Mike. "You can't pretend this whole thing didn't happen. You can't wish it away. You've taken a good first step, but it's only a beginning. With a ton of work, you can get your wife back. I've known Kate long enough to know." He stopped and took another bite. "She loves you, Mike."

"That's why she left me."

"Probably."

"What?"

"Listen, Mike. If she didn't love you, she wouldn't care if you had an affair. But she does. She's as mad as a mother bear." He took a swig from his water glass. "I'm telling you. That's love."

Mike looked at the words Dave had printed neatly on the coaster. *Priorities. Relationship. Goals.* Mike could see how these words affected a business—but marriage?

Dave spoke again, "How many times in your career have you made a business mistake?"

"More than I can count."

"Me too. And every time I make a mistake, I can count on these three words to tell me where I went wrong. Every time. I go back and find that something is out of balance. I've let my priorities get out of order. Or I've forgotten to maintain a relationship. I've misplaced the goal. One of these things is off. Every time."

Mike nodded. Things in his life had more than gone out of balance. They were completely upside-down. Where did it start? He couldn't think. Memories swirled around in his head, refusing to let him get a handle on the beginning. Why had he let it happen?

"So fix it," Dave concluded.

Mike couldn't believe his ears. While his own world threatened to close down around him, these were the only wise words his friend had to offer? "Fix it?" He stared back at Dave.

"Exactly. Just like in business. Figure out what the goal is. Don't let anything get in the way. Make it the priority. The first thing you concentrate on every morning. The last thing you think about every night. Pray about it. Dream about it. Study it. Work at it. And above all else, do whatever you have to do to earn her forgiveness. Prove her trust."

"I told you. I think it's too late."

"You wouldn't say that about a business relationship." Dave swished a piece of chicken around in the dressing. "You'd try to fix it. You'd do whatever it takes to make things right. You'd grovel. You'd give away stuff. You'd think of it as a post sale. Don't you think Kate is worth the same effort?"

Mike's face softened, and he almost smiled. "You think she'd even listen to me?"

"I can't speak for Kate," he answered. "But for me, I'd say this. If you don't try, you'll not only regret what happened between you and this woman—but you'll never forgive yourself for not trying. You'll wonder for the rest of your life." He lifted a bite of salad to his mouth. Staring out the window, he chewed thoughtfully for a moment. "One regret is enough for any man to live with."

Mike took a bite of his sandwich. In the lengthy silence that followed, they watched a foursome putt out on the last green. When the group came near the restaurant, Mike noticed that the men of the foursome were older than the women who played with them— much older. As he watched the women fawn—flirting and touching—Mike felt a wave of revulsion crash over him. Had he looked this foolish with Cara?

"Don't be afraid to ask for help." David's voice startled him. "You'd call in a consultant for your business if you needed it. Do the same for the family. Get help. Get serious."

For the first time, Mike felt a glimmer of hope. A challenge? Yes. But hope. Suddenly hungry, he dove into his sandwich, and for the first time since seeing the pictures, Mike actually tasted what he ate.

———

When Wayne pulled into the impound yard, Mel was waiting for him in a down parka. With his shoulders raised high, white wisps of breath blew from his mouth. Mel had abandoned his regulation clothes for warmer ones. Of his uniform, only his hat remained. March rarely got this cold in Tacoma, and Wayne knew that Mel hated the cold.

"I gave orders to search the car," he said, coming toward

Wayne, both hands hidden deep in his jacket pockets.

"Good to see you too."

"Something bothers me about this accident, Wayne," Mel answered. His tone remained low and serious. "I just have a gut feeling."

"Well, then, let's go see what your gut knows that we don't."

In the office, they presented identification to the clerk at the desk, a bored-looking young man glancing through a *Car Trader* magazine. He stood, tossed the magazine on his desk, and turned to escort them out to the bay where the little blue vehicle had been stored. "It's a Honda," Wayne said, talking over his shoulder at Mel. "That much we know from the VIN number. We also know the Honda was jacked in Bellevue two months ago."

"The owner should be happy to know we've recovered his car."

Wayne stopped well away from the wreckage. In its current shape, the Honda had virtually nothing left to identify its original make and model. Only the color remained.

The clerk nodded again and turned back to the office. "Nice guy," Mel smiled. "But he talks too much."

Wayne focused on the remains of the Honda. In addition to the cut made in the roof at the accident scene, the rest of the roof had now been completely removed. They watched as a technical officer, in heavy overalls and a protective helmet, worked with Jaws of Life, cutting into the trunk of the car. Seeing Mel and Wayne, he set down his equipment and walked toward them, removing his gloves. They shook hands.

"Find anything?" Mel asked.

"Nothing yet. The inside of the passenger compartment was clean. Nothing at all to identify him. He had lunch at McDonald's, probably on his way to the bridge." The technician scratched his nose with one of his gloved fingers. "The carpet and upholstery are still wet with Coke."

"How long till you get into the trunk?"

"Almost through now," he answered. "I've cut a lid. I just have to pry off the section. Should be a few minutes."

"We'll wait."

"No problem." The man smiled and flipped his helmet visor down. Returning to the trunk of the car, he lifted the tool and finished a small section of the hole he'd been cutting. Wayne and Mel watched quietly, anxiously. Moments later, the tech lifted a spreader from the pavement beside the car.

With a wicked screech, he tore the metal lid from the opening he'd created. Both officers moved closer, leaning in to inspect the inside of the trunk. Behind them, the technician said, "Here, try this." He brought a large flashlight to the hole and stepped closer, brushing the darkness with its bright beam.

"We're in luck," he said. "Lots of stuff in here." Holding the light in place, he moved out of the way, so the men could see inside.

"A briefcase," Mel said. Then he gave a long, low whistle. "Here, give me the light." Leaning over the back of the car, he held the flashlight at a peculiar angle and craned his head to one side. Curious, Wayne stepped closer.

"Can you see it?" Mel asked.

"No. What?" Wayne dropped his head almost onto his shoulder trying to catch the viewpoint that so excited Mel.

"There—spilling out of the case. See it?"

Wayne reached up and snatched the light from his friend. Bending forward and easing his head slightly to one side, suddenly he did see. He saw it all very clearly.

"What is it?" The technician was obviously curious as well.

"Credit cards," Wayne answered, straightening up. "By itself, the cards aren't enough. But with stolen plates and a stolen car, I think we may have stumbled onto organized crime. Maybe even racketeering."

Mel spoke up. "Maybe a hundred cards—spilling all over the trunk of the car. Either this guy has a big problem with debt, or we got some fake cards here. Add that to the fact the license plates are from a car stolen in Idaho . . ."

"Across state lines," the technician added, understanding dawning across his face.

"And we have racketeering. Maybe." Wayne handed the light back to Mel. "I want a report by tomorrow morning. Everything you can come up with. Don't miss a single item." After twenty years on the force, Wayne should learn to trust his instincts. He'd felt it the moment he'd gotten to the accident. The whole thing had been wrong. Very wrong.

Six

AFTER HER FRUSTRATING APPOINTMENT with Frank Bickman, Kate stepped off the elevator into the lobby of the Leschi Building and stopped. Rain, driven into full-length lobby windows by a strong southerly wind, pelted an angry percussion on the glass. Drops of water bounced up off the sidewalk. People outside dashed through the elements, covering their heads with newspapers and briefcases—whatever they had handy. Kate noticed a woman entering the lobby in a trench coat stained dark with rain.

When she'd parked her car barely an hour ago, the sun had warmed the city to a comfortable seventy degrees. Kate had chosen to leave her coat behind. Big mistake. Now she wore only a pale blue linen suit and suede shoes. Mud would ruin the suede, and wind would frizz her hair into a mass of knots more difficult to unravel than a hank of handspun yarn. She looked around the lobby for a newspaper machine. For fifty cents, the *San Francisco Chronicle* would at last be worth its cover price. At least it might keep her hair dry on the way to the car. Her shoes would be a total loss.

Kate dropped change into the machine and bought a paper. Draping it carefully over her head, she held it firmly with both hands. Then, stepping into the circular doorway, she started out of the building. The sound of wind penetrated the passageway with a horrible rattling. As the revolving door spilled Kate out onto the sidewalk, gusting winds nearly ripped off her jacket. She dropped her head and moved closer to the building in a vain attempt to avoid the worst of the weather. Holding her jacket closed with one hand, she clung to the paper with the other.

As though in unison, all the people on the sidewalk had chosen the same tactic. Bumping against one another and fighting for protected sidewalk space, the crowd surged forward. With another hour before she had to return to work this Friday afternoon, Kate let her thoughts wander back to her attorney's office. What had he advised? To wait? How could he suggest that she wait while her husband carried on with this woman? The request made her angry all over again. While she was in this half-conscious state, a man suddenly stepped from the doorway in front of her, startling her so much that she jumped.

Gripping her arm hard, he pulled her into the dark alcove.

She gasped and nearly screamed before she recognized his face. "Mike!" She tore his hand from her arm. The newspaper blew away, whipping down the sidewalk until rainwater eventually pasted it to the concrete in a wet heap. "Mike, what are you doing here? Following me?"

"Kate, we have to talk."

"I don't have to talk. I have nothing to say to you." The wind whipped at her hair, and she used one hand to brush it from her mouth. She felt tiny curls beating in the wind around her face. Setting her face into a deadpan expression, she refused to allow Mike to read her emotions.

"You're right," he said. "I didn't mean to frighten you. I was waiting for the rain to let up when I saw you walk by. I just want to talk."

Kate looked up into his brown eyes and recognized the intensity there. How handsome he was, even after all these years. Certainly he'd aged. Still his dark brown hair showed just the slightest frosting of gray over his ears and near his face. Only the deep lines around his eyes betrayed his age. His body had matured. His shoulders were broader, stronger, and his lean, youthful shape had thickened to that of a mature man. Actually, because Mike hated the idea of growing fat, he was more physically fit now than when they had married.

A group of teenagers running down the walk brushed against her shoulder, bringing Kate back to the present. She would not be distracted by memories of the man she remembered. She couldn't. She turned away and began walking toward the car.

"Can't we have dinner?" he called, hurrying to catch her. "Don't you owe our marriage that much?"

The words felt like scalding water. As anger rose in her stomach, horrible bitter words came to mind. But she would not give him that satisfaction. She would never let him see how much he'd hurt her. "How dare you insinuate that I owe you anything," she spoke quietly through clenched teeth. She wanted to scream, but she would not. "After what you've done, you have a lot of nerve even speaking to me." She started to walk away, but then she remembered.

Turning back, she saw Mike standing there in the rain, his expression frozen by something—grief or shock—she couldn't be certain. The wind blew his hair wildly around his head, exposing his bald spot. For a moment his helplessness threatened to soften her resolve. And then she remembered the pictures.

"Don't you dare speak to our children about this." She spit the words. "They're trying to live their own lives. Drew has a new job. Keegan is struggling through school. I don't want them drawn into this now." Her voice broke, and for a moment, it sounded to her as though she were pleading.

She took a breath. "We can tell them later—when things are settled between us. But it isn't fair for you to torture them too." She stopped and brushed her hair from her face. "I'm leaving for Kansas in the morning. You can reach me through my attorney."

On Saturday, Mike woke feeling heavy and defeated. With Kate gone, he had no reason to stay at home. He got up early, made himself a full carafe of French press coffee, filled his commuter mug, and got into the Mustang. Thick clouds hung low over the bay, cooling the air, threatening rain. He left the top up.

Four blocks from the house, a strange noise caught his attention. Tipping his head, he leaned forward in the seat listening intently. There it was again. He pulled to the side of the road and put up the hood. Leaning over, he tugged and pulled, tapped and twisted, looking for an explanation for what he had heard. Nothing. For a moment he remained there, resting on the radiator, wondering if Kate had been right all along. She hated that he'd restored the Mustang. Hated that he'd spent an entire winter rebuilding the thirty-two-year-old engine. He pictured her leaning against the garage door questioning him. "Why don't you just buy a new car?" she'd asked. "We can certainly afford it. More than the time you're wasting on this heap."

How many other times had he ignored her, refused to listen to her advice? He slammed the hood harder than necessary and returned to the driver's seat.

On the way to the office he stopped at Maggie's Donuts and chose the Lucky Thirteen Special. Under normal conditions, Mike avoided donuts. But suddenly his life had taken a wide swing from normal. With everything else falling apart, living a long and healthy life seemed an unreasonable goal. He'd managed to mess things up so badly—why make his life last any longer than necessary? What difference would a few donuts make? He parked the open box on the seat beside him and finished three before he reached the highway.

A light drizzle began just as he turned into the office lot. He parked in his reserved place and used his key card to open the electronic doors of the office building. Buzz, a haggard-faced overweight security man, sat at his console reading the Saturday sports section. In front of his desk, four television screens played images of empty office areas.

Spotting Mike, Buzz suddenly folded his newspaper. "Hey, Mr. Langston."

"Hey, Buzz," Mike returned, stopping at the counter. "How is that new Japanese pitcher doing?"

"It's no good, sir," Buzz said, shaking his head. "He pitched yesterday. His first outing, and he didn't last four full innings."

"Well," Mike smiled, "it's only spring training. Maybe he'll improve." He patted Buzz's desk and gave him a thumbs-up sign. Buzz picked up the paper to read, shaking his head doubtfully. "Has to, sir. He's got nowhere to go but up."

On the top floor, the elevator doors opened to a delightfully deserted office space. No lights. No humming computers. No ringing telephones. No pagers. Mike drank in the peace and quiet. On weekends, the silence of the office reminded him of the way things were before success caught up with him. He liked being here by himself. He liked the steady, unbroken pace of working alone. He'd actually been a little sorry when his thriving business took that small pleasure from him.

As he passed his reception area, he smiled at Brooke's immaculate desktop. He'd never understood how she could do that—wipe her desk clean of all evidence that she'd ever been there. He glanced at her telephone and found a neatly stacked pile of messages all addressed to "Brooke." The thought pleased him in an odd way. Even secretaries faced the unending demands of others.

Pulling out his keys, he reached for his own door and unlocked it. As he hit the switch, bright fluorescent light flooded his private office. He locked the door behind him and moved to his desk, where he brought his computer to life. At the credenza, Mike grabbed the coffeepot and took it to the bathroom for water. With fresh grounds in the machine he started the brew cycle.

Mike always had a clear plan of action on these kinds of days. Today he needed to think through the problem of hiring a new Chief Financial Officer. More than that, he needed a plan for running things without Cara until she could be replaced. Finding someone would not be difficult, just time-consuming. At this point, Mike felt completely certain that he would look for either an ugly woman or a capable man. He would never make the same kind of mistake again. No. In fact, Mike felt fairly certain that he would gradually replace every beautiful woman in the company.

As the smell of coffee drifted up from the machine, Mike grew impatient. He pulled the pot out from under the spout with one hand while he held his mug under the stream of fresh coffee with the other. Rich dark liquid filled his cup. After putting the pot back, he sat down at his desk.

Tapping his keyboard, Mike mused over his problem. How long would it take to find the perfect replacement? And how would he keep the business running smoothly in the meantime?

With a click of his mouse, he opened his organizational plan and brought up the Finance Department. Perhaps a replacement for Cara could be found within the company. That would be the most efficient move, saving the time needed to bring an outsider up to speed. Curious, he brought up each of the profiles of the men working under Cara Maria. The chief of Accounts Receivable was a capable CPA from Boston. But as Mike scanned his resume, he remembered him as a recluse with no real management experience.

Then there was the new Budget officer. Mike typed in the name. "File unknown." Funny. Why no file? Was he new to the system?

Mike picked up his telephone and buzzed Brooke's desk. He let the phone ring several times, but it was not until her voice mail picked up that he remembered: Brooke didn't work on Saturdays.

He looked at his watch. Well, he could walk down to Finance himself. Cara kept a wall chart of her department personnel in the conference room. Perhaps Mike had misspelled the man's name. That might explain the absence of a file.

He found the Budget and Finance Department as deserted as his own. The light coming in from outside windows lit the area off the elevator adequately. But as Mike worked his way down the interior corridor, the light grew too dim for him to see. He remembered the conference room being on the right, just two, maybe three doors down from the reception area. Feeling his way down the darkened hallway, he let his right hand slide along the plaster, over one door, then two. As he reached the third door, Mike clearly heard voices.

What? Who would be working here in the conference room on a Saturday morning? And why were there no lights? He knocked twice on the door and turned the knob. Locked. The voices inside hushed. He knocked again, then heard steps moving slowly toward the door. He stepped back into the dark hallway.

As the door opened, Mike was surprised to find Cara Maria standing with one hand on her hip, the other on the knob. Though the lights were off, the outside windows clearly illuminated the inside of the conference room. Sitting at the desk behind Cara, Mike saw his partner, Doug McCoy.

———

Kate first heard the voice at thirty-thousand feet, just after the cabin attendants finished picking up breakfast trays. Sitting in an aisle seat over the wing, Kate leaned her seat back in an attempt to enjoy a cup of after-breakfast coffee. Her neighbor, a mother traveling with a preschooler, suddenly needed to get out of her seat. "Excuse me," she said, rolling her eyes at the child. *The bathroom,* Kate assumed, and she stood up, sliding into the aisle to let them pass. The mother clamored out, followed by a reluctant blond boy, being dragged along by one hand. The boy stomped on the toe of Kate's shoe as he passed.

Kate frowned and reached down to brush off her shoe. Returning to her seat, she closed her eyes, resting for a moment. She knew they would be back soon. *Don't get too comfortable,* she told herself. Then she heard it. As clearly as a human voice.

"Trust me."

Trust me?

Kate opened her eyes and looked around the cabin. Neighboring passengers seemed absorbed in their own little worlds. The man across from her banged away at a laptop computer. The teenager directly behind him sat with his eyes closed, shaking his head in time to music from oversized headphones. She brought her seat up. Had she imagined it? She leaned into the aisle, looking around for any possible explanation.

Kate had never heard anything quite like that before. By the time the mother and child returned to the two seats beside her, Kate had decided that her own overactive imagination had created the voice. Even so, through the rest of the flight, Kate listened with one ear as though she expected to hear the words again. But she did not. And the silence unsettled her as much as the words themselves.

At the Kansas City Airport, Kate walked directly to the baggage claim area, expecting to find her olive green suitcase. The carrousel circled as expected, but her bag did not appear. Her fellow passengers eventually wandered away, leaving Kate to search among the misplaced luggage waiting in piles near the baggage office.

She did not find her bag there either. She breathed a deep sigh and looked around to find the Customer Service area. After a week like hers, losing her suitcase seemed—almost expected somehow.

Inside, a young woman, wearing lines drawn carefully with eyeliner around both eyes and nearly black lipstick, welcomed Kate with a sultry southern accent. "May I help you?" Her voice held disinterest.

Kate read the name on her employee name tag. Sylvia. "Yes, Sylvia, I just came in from San Francisco, and my baggage hasn't arrived." Kate pulled her baggage claim check from her purse.

"Are you sure?" Sylvia said, without looking up. Kate noticed that she continued to work at a clipboard on the counter below her. Multitasking.

Kate rolled her eyes. "I've stood at the carrousel for the past thirty minutes while everyone else on my flight claimed their bags. I've looked through every piece of luggage in the area. I think it would be safe to say that I'm quite certain. You've managed to lose my suitcase."

The brown eyes looked up and widened slightly at the intensity in Kate's voice. "Well," she drawled, "then I'll just have you fill out this form for lost bags." She slid the form across the counter and laid a pen on top of the paper. "Be sure to fill in all of these blanks, and we'll see what we can do."

Kate felt her own temper rise. She took a deep breath, swallowed hard, and very gently put her hand over the form. With exaggerated care, she took the paper and stepped back from the counter.

Just as Kate turned, Sylvia said, "Don't worry about your bag. We'll find it. Trust me."

Trust me. Those words again.

They didn't find her bag.

Kate picked up her rental car, a small white Toyota, and headed west on I–70. Having grown up in Lawrence, Kansas, Kate knew her way around this land like her own bedroom. She glanced up at the first mileage sign. Fifty miles to Lawrence. Good. She needed every one of those fifty miles to prepare herself. Even at this point, she hadn't decided whether or not to tell her parents the truth about Mike.

Seven

FROM THE THRESHOLD, Mike watched as Doug's expression moved quickly, transparently, from intense concentration to surprise and from surprise to unmistakable irritation. Mike wondered why.

"What can we do for you, Mike?" Cara Maria asked.

Mike stepped into the room and noticed again that they had not switched on the lights. "I came down to check the spelling . . . uh," he gestured with his thumb toward the white board at the end of the conference room. Giving up on his own explanation, he put both hands on his hips. "What are you guys doing here? I mean, after all, it's Saturday."

"We do occasionally work on Saturday," Doug answered.

"I mean together. Here."

"We've been discussing my replacement." Mike heard defensiveness in Cara's voice. With the grace of a dancer, she moved away from the door and leaned against the conference table, crossing her arms at her waist.

Mike noticed that she wore tight-fitting jeans and a light cashmere sweater with a hint of furriness about it. The color was electric, some shade of pink that set off her hair and the deep brown of her eyes. He winced and glanced away.

A small smile played at the corner of Cara Maria's mouth. She'd noticed his reaction. "Doug had some suggestions as to who should be my replacement."

"Great, I'll be glad to hear them." Mike glanced around the

room and shifted his weight from foot to foot. "As a matter of fact that's what I'm working on today." They offered no further comment as Mike walked over to check the spelling on the board.

"Well, now that I have the name off the wall chart . . ." he let the sentence trail off. Somehow it seemed clear to him that he had already been dismissed. Closing the door gently behind him, he left them together in the unlit room.

Mike fought with irritation all the way back to his own office. One part of him fumed. What were they doing there together in the gloom like that? Another part of him dismissed his questions as foolish jealousy. After all, Cara Maria could spend her time with any man she chose. He no longer had an interest in her. But Doug?

For the rest of the morning, Mike worked out an elaborate plan for hiring a new Chief Financial Officer. He would suggest to the board of directors that DataSoft hire an interim CFO. In the meantime, he established a timeline for the permanent replacement. Mike put together a summary of all the people holding top positions under Cara Maria. If he were lucky, one of them just might be the right person to tide the company over after she left. He had only two weeks to put his plan in place.

Just as the last page of work came off the printer, a terrible hunger pang twisted his stomach. He looked at his watch. Nearly two in the afternoon. No wonder he felt so hungry. He stood and poured himself another cup of dark coffee, adding milk from the fridge below the counter. The addition might stave off starvation. He took a gulp and grimaced. The coffee had been brewing all morning, condensing itself into a thick sludge that reminded him of motor oil.

After five solid hours of uninterrupted work, Mike's legs felt tight and sore. To move around a bit, he walked to the window. The morning fog had lifted, leaving behind a beautiful, though cool, afternoon; although out over the bay, fog still clung to the water.

The slam of a car door brought his attention to the parking lot below him. He looked down and tried to guess where the sound had come from. As he watched, he saw Doug walk across the lot and open the passenger-side door of a silver Mercedes parked in Doug's private space. Mike recognized the car.

While he stared, the engine started and the car pulled away.

Kate found the Kansas interstate congested—especially for late Saturday afternoon. Because of slow traffic, she decided to tuck her rental car into the slow lane and let others set the pace for her. She used the time to think and soak in the beauty of the Kansas plains. She'd forgotten how flat things were here, how far you could see. She enjoyed the pastoral view of passing fields, now fallow, of old barns and fences and cattle. When the filtered clouds above her began to reflect the pink of the sunset, Kate realized she had not yet decided how much to tell her parents.

She drove through downtown Lawrence, enjoying the ambiance of tree-lined streets and Victorian houses. In the years since she'd grown up here, her hometown had more than doubled its population. But now, on this March afternoon, the town looked like nothing more than the small, lazy college town she remembered as a kid.

She approached the hospital, watching carefully for a parking place. Just as she turned into the lot, a van pulled out of a spot near the side entrance. She zipped the rental into place and turned off the engine. At last, something had gone right.

"Well, thanks for something, God," she muttered, slamming the car door.

Kate entered the hospital through automatic sliding doors and headed down the long hall to the lobby. At the volunteer desk, she found a candy striper slumped in a rolling secretarial chair, completely absorbed in a romance novel. To Kate, the girl appeared to be approaching a boredom meltdown. She glanced up from her book. "Can I help you?" she asked in a weary monotone.

"Yes," Kate answered, "I'm looking for a patient room number. Thomas Patrick Killian, please."

The girl slapped her novel over and scooted the chair toward a metal book that opened to alphabetically filed three-by-five cards. She flipped through the entries. Stopping at the "C"s, she slid her finger down the names. "Cassidy, Cavanaugh, Christian, Cornell . . ." she muttered. With a stifled yawn, she dragged her finger down the cards in front of her. "Curtis . . ."

"Killian," Kate interrupted. "That's K-I-L-L-I-A-N."

"Oh," she said, nodding her head. "K." Then she giggled to

herself. "Okay. Get it? Oh. K." She laughed, delighted with her own humor, and flipped through the alphabet to the "K" section. "I've got it. Killian, Thomas P. He's in room 232. That's down this hall and up the first elevator to the right." Picking up her novel, she turned it over again, dismissing Kate.

Kate found the second-floor cardiac unit without any problem. But no one sat at the desk of the nurses' station. Kate wandered through the hallway trying to appear inconspicuous while looking for her father's room. At least she wasn't a patient looking for a nurse. Just then, from the hall, Kate heard her mother's calm voice. Rosemarie Killian spoke quietly and soothingly, though Kate had no idea to whom she spoke.

Her eyes filled with tears she could not explain.

"Mom," she said, entering the room and dropping her purse onto an empty chair.

"Katherine," her mother answered. Turning from the bedside table, she stepped toward her. "Oh, Katherine, you're here," she whispered, her voice trembling. She stepped into Kate's arms, and they stood for a long moment, holding one another at the foot of the hospital bed. "I wasn't sure you'd really come." She squeezed her daughter hard, and Kate felt her mother cling to her.

"How's Daddy?"

"He's slept all morning. He's been so tired since this last attack." Rosemarie stepped back and wiped her eyes with her fingertips. "He'll be so glad you've come."

Kate moved to the bedside, where she put both hands on the rail and leaned over her father's sleeping face. "Daddy," she whispered. He stirred. "Daddy, I've come to see you. Just like you asked." She reached down and touched his forehead. "Daddy?"

Thomas's eyes fluttered open, and he turned his head to focus his eyes on her face. "Oh, Katie-Doll." He smiled, though it was not the broad grin Kate remembered from her childhood, but a rather feeble, trembling little smile. As she gazed at her father, she marveled at the change she saw in him. This was the face she remembered—the same soft full face, with the same immaculately trimmed white mustache, the same gentle eyes. But she recognized that her father had changed. And the change frightened her.

He put his fists down near his hips and lifted himself higher in the bed. "Oh, Katie, my love, I'm so glad you came." He reached to her face and touched her face gently, rubbing her cheek with his thumb. Kate, all grown up and nearly fifty years old, loved the caress. She laid her hand over her father's, holding it to her face. Something inside of her had longed for her father's touch. Then leaning down, she scooped him into her embrace.

———

Even after watching the car leave the parking lot, Mike could not shake the peculiar feeling of seeing Doug and Cara Maria together. He stood staring out over the empty lot for a long time, drinking coffee and thinking.

Mike finally put away his work, gathered his briefcase, and went down to the car. In the cool spring air, his hunger came back, and he decided to walk down the street for a hamburger. He wouldn't have to cook for himself later if he ate a late lunch. Throwing his sweatshirt over his shoulder, he started down the street.

Mike had known Doug McCoy for more than twenty-five years. They'd become friends when they both worked for another Bay Area firm. Though not at all alike, their differences made for a strong friendship. Mike loved people. Doug loved anything technical. Mike loved making money, and as it turned out, he was very good at it. He specialized in the business side of the computer industry. Doug loved the computer itself and turned out to be as good with a computer as Mike was with a balance sheet. Their mutual respect for each other's abilities led them to the decision to start their own company. For nearly three years, they had spent every spare moment planning and scheming. Eventually, after borrowing twenty thousand dollars, they had begun the fledgling company in Mike's garage.

During their scheming days, Mike had started attending church. Doug didn't mind this as long as Mike's new infatuation didn't interfere with the business. When Mike's church attendance turned into a real commitment of faith, Doug had laughed so hard that Mike felt embarrassed and hurt. After that, Mike kept his newfound faith to himself. Still, Doug ridiculed Mike relentlessly, and even as he thought about it, Mike felt self-consciousness warm his face.

Mike rounded the corner onto Bridgeway and walked up to the order window at the Dairy Bar. He chose a double cheeseburger with bacon and a large marionberry shake. Today, with both donuts and bacon, Mike had begun to live dangerously. As he sat outside waiting for his order, he watched traffic and wondered about Kate. How was she? Had she made it to her parents' home safely? Normally, she would've called to report her arrival. But he knew better than to expect that now. If he couldn't save his marriage, he realized he would be spending the rest of his life wondering about Kate.

For a moment, Mike gave in to the intense loneliness he felt, sitting there at a picnic table all by himself. Doug had been through this—this death of a marriage. But when it happened to Doug, Mike had made no real effort to support his friend. By then the two men had grown apart, both struggling to manage their own areas of responsibility in the flourishing business. Whenever they were together, they worked to solve problems. As the business grew, their private time became nonexistent. As a result their friendship had suffered a slow death. Today, Mike felt guilty for that as well. He had not been there when Doug needed him. What else had he missed? What other things did he not know about his partner?

Mike ate his lunch slowly. Ordinarily, a double cheeseburger would be a luxurious treat for a disciplined man. Today, it tasted flat and unsatisfying.

———

Kate chose a chair near her father's bedside. Her mother sat across from her, in front of the windows on the opposite wall. From her seat in the corner, Kate watched her parents intently.

Rosemarie Killian, once a redhead, now possessed a full head of white hair with a few remaining strands of the original color. She had the same fair, freckled skin that Kate inherited. But because she faithfully followed a daily skin care regimen, never allowing direct sunlight to touch her skin and always wearing a hat, Kate's mother, at seventy-two, had soft translucent skin the color of fresh cream.

Raised in Louisiana, Rosemarie still spoke with the softest of drawls, though she denied her accent whenever anyone questioned her about it. Kate noticed it this evening in the lazy vowels her mother caressed as she spoke. "Patrick, are you comfortable?" she asked, using his middle name, as everyone did. Kate's dozing father did not reply.

Rosemarie pulled a small stitchery project from a tote bag beside the chair. A lap hoop held her latest wall hanging, a quilt of mustard and warm greens with the tiniest bit of purple. From her chair, Kate did not recognize the pattern as she leaned forward to look.

Kate noticed that her mother wore a silk blouse with a paisley scarf draped artfully over one shoulder. Below this, she wore an ankle length wool skirt in a soft taupe. Her feet sported fashionably squatty shoes. She didn't look like someone visiting a hospital. She certainly didn't resemble anyone's mother. Actually, Rosemarie Killian looked more like a model for *American Maturity* magazine.

Like Kate, her mother loved color and texture. Though Rosemarie had never been a professional woman, her sense of style and proportion convinced Kate that her mother might have made a very successful interior designer. As it turned out, Rosemarie expressed her artistry in her hobbies, quilting and sewing, and in her meticulous choice of clothing. But more than anything, Rosemarie loved decorating, rigorously following the adage "Your home is your calling card."

As Kate watched, her mother stopped her work in midstitch. As though struck by some sudden urge, Rosemarie put her handwork aside, stood by the bed, and spoke in low soothing tones to Kate's father. "How are you feeling, Patrick?" she asked. "Would you like us to leave you for a bit so you can take a little nap?" She lifted his hand from the sheets and gave it a little squeeze. He didn't answer.

She selected a tube of hand cream from the bedside table and squeezed a little onto the palm of her hand. "Your skin is getting so dry here." She rubbed the cream onto his hands, making tiny soft circles on his fingers. "This should help." She continued her gentle massage, rubbing her thumbs in circles over each cuticle. "I should cut your nails for you though." She brushed her fingers across his nails. "Maybe I'll bring a manicure set tomorrow."

Reaching across his waist, she took his other hand and started her little ritual again. "There, isn't that better?" He opened his eyes and smiled up at her as she leaned down to give him a kiss. While Kate watched, she noticed that the kiss lasted a moment longer than most. It seemed urgent, frightened somehow. Her father's lips stayed behind for an instant too long, expectantly, hungrily, even after Rosemarie pulled away. Watching the love that flowed between her mother and father made Kate's eyes fill with tears.

"Can I get you anything, dear?" her mother asked Patrick.

"No thanks, Rosie." He smiled.

"Mom," Kate said, "why don't you go down to the cafeteria and get some coffee? The break will do you good."

"Oh." She hesitated, glancing from Kate to her husband. "Oh, I hate to leave him." She seemed too uncertain to make a decision.

"I'll sit here. He won't be alone."

After assuring them that she'd be right back, her mother left the room, and her dad closed his eyes again.

Kate let her tears flow unchecked. This was how marriage should be. How hers was meant to be. No wonder having it end hurt so much.

————

"Excuse me," a man's voice said. "Is this seat taken?"

Mike Langston looked up to find his tennis partner standing in the center aisle. "Oh no, sit down," Mike answered, scooting over. The woman sitting on the other side of Mike glanced up suspiciously. He ignored her.

"Thanks." David Holland dropped into the padded chair beside Mike. David's tall, heavily built frame caused a little shudder in the floor as he sat. He leaned over to Mike and whispered, "Haven't seen much of you here lately." His eyes rolled up gesturing to the sanctuary around them.

"Where's Valerie?"

"Fours and fives," David answered. "You avoiding my question?"

"Yep." The volume on the electronic piano rose, and the pastor moved to the podium. Grateful for the interruption, Mike stood. Dave shrugged and followed. The worship service began as always, with bright victorious music. The people around him joined in clapping and singing. Mike didn't feel very joyful. In fact, the music and the mood of this place actually seemed to make his pain more pronounced. He would have left, but David Holland, a former UCLA defensive tackle, now blocked his access to the aisle. Mike had no choice but to stay. Somehow, he made it through the worship service.

By the time the sermon began, spring sunshine seeped through the stained-glass windows above the sanctuary. Golden colors spilled over the people as they listened attentively. Mike grew more miserable with every moment. Coming to church alone had been a mistake. Here, in the middle of all these people, he felt the full weight of his own guilt and loneliness. And to make matters worse, the sermon subject came entirely too close to home.

Sunset Community Church, located in Tiburon, had recently begun a study of the Book of John. To be truthful, Mike hadn't heard the whole series. David's accusation had been completely correct. Mike frequently excused himself from church, saying he was too busy. In the years after his grown children had left home, Mike had often let Kate drive off alone while he cloistered himself in his downstairs office. Sunday mornings proved to be quiet and productive, and he enjoyed the leisure of working at home. Sometimes, instead of staying in his office, he worked around the house, fixing chairs, painting, working on yard chores. None of it essential at the time, yet Mike had convinced himself that it was.

Why had he let that continue? It wasn't as though Mike didn't believe in the importance of church. After all, when the children were little, he'd never missed a Sunday. Kids needed to be in church. They needed the fellowship, the involvement, the moral guidance. . . .

The thought stabbed him. Moral guidance. Adults need moral guidance too.

"And this woman was caught in adultery." Adultery? The word seized Mike's attention. He squirmed in his seat. Why today, of all days, would Pastor Rick choose to talk about adultery? Mike didn't want to listen. He felt heat rise in his own cheeks. He glanced to the aisle, hoping that somehow David had mysteriously disappeared so he could slide out unnoticed.

But David gazed thoughtfully toward the front of the auditorium.

"Caught in the act," Mike heard the pastor say. "In the very act."

Mike forced himself to hold very still. He had been caught in exactly the same way. His shame threatened to swallow him whole, and he made a vow to never come back to church again. The pastor's voice faded as Mike saw again the grainy color photos he'd pulled from the envelope. How he hated himself. For the hundredth time he wondered how he could possibly have gotten involved in something so completely despicable.

And then the thought came to him: Had someone told Pastor Rick about what had happened? Had he staged this entire service simply to destroy the few remaining fragments of Mike's self-esteem? This thought made Mike angry. Very angry.

In this frame of mind his decision to stop attending church seemed completely justified. After all, his pastor and his best friend had conspired against him.

Eight

ON SUNDAY MORNING, Kate's mom insisted they eat a healthy breakfast before going to the hospital. Expounding on the importance of the first meal of the day, Rosemarie prepared Cream of Wheat, toast, and fresh Texas grapefruit. But in spite of her mother's enthusiasm, neither of them felt like eating. They fiddled with their food, taking a few meager bites, and gave up. They dressed quickly and set out for the hospital.

They had not been in the room five minutes before a nurse entered, noisily pushing a blood pressure cart. "Time to check your vitals, Mr. Killian," she announced cheerfully.

Her father glanced at Kate and rolled his eyes. Kate could not suppress a smile.

She watched as the nurse placed the cuff above her father's elbow and pumped it full of air. Then Kate heard the whoosh and saw the silver fluid in the pressure gauge drop. "Good," the nurse said. "I like those kinds of readings." She stuck a thermometer into his mouth and continued without taking a breath. "How are you feeling this morning, Mr. Killian?"

Keeping his lips closed, he muttered an indistinguishable answer.

" . . . For a man who's had a heart attack, huh?" She laughed at her own joke. "How about a little walk? Say out to the nurses' station and back?"

Patrick shrugged and lifted the covers to move them away. The nurse lowered the bed rail by hand and used the electric controls to bring him to a sitting position.

Rosemarie seemed frightened to have Patrick walk. "Walking won't hurt him, will it?"

"Oh no. He needs to get up. It's time."

"Well, then," Kate's mother responded with wide eyes, "I think maybe I'll go down and get some coffee while you're up."

"We won't be long," the nurse reassured her. "Just a little walk."

"I'll stay and help," Kate volunteered.

Leaning over the rail, Rosemarie kissed Patrick and squeezed his hand.

When Rosemarie had gone, the nurse asked, "Now, where's your bathrobe?" Without waiting for an answer, she moved briskly to the wardrobe and looked inside. "Hmm, not here." Her father slid his feet over the edge of the bed and waited patiently, his hands in his lap.

"I think that's it—over Mother's chair," Kate said.

"You must be the daughter this fella was bragging about all morning yesterday."

"I don't know about bragging," Kate smiled. "But yes, I'm his only daughter."

Turning away, the nurse draped the robe over her father's back, holding it so he could tuck his arms inside. The IV tube slid into the sleeve as well, leaving Patrick precariously tied by a short hose to the pole beside the bed. The nurse allowed him to tie the belt himself.

"Okay, whenever you're ready, Mr. Killian."

Kate's father used both fists to push himself up. He stood swaying slightly while the nurse held him under one elbow. "Be sure and get your sea legs before you start off here." She reminded Kate of an aerobics instructor at a health club—the kind who kept telling you to breathe. As if you might forget.

"I'm fine. Just been down too long, that's all." Kate's father straightened slowly to his full height. He took a step, one small wobbly step, and paused, swaying. Then, picking up momentum, he shuffled step by step toward the door. The distance, though no more than twelve feet, seemed like a football field to Kate. And the man heading for the goal line did not resemble the healthy basketball player and gardener whom she called Daddy. No, the ancient resident of some dilapidated nursing home had mysteriously replaced Thomas Patrick Killian. This man—this tottering old man—was her father.

Watching, she felt a stab of pain. Though she realized her parents would not live forever, this stark reminder of her father's age seemed too abrupt, too painful. She did not want to face their mortality—especially not now.

Kate suddenly decided to follow behind them, hoping that activity would drive the fear of losing her father out of her consciousness.

Patrick made it to the threshold of the room and paused. Exhausted, his shoulders stooped, and his head protruded forward in the peculiar fashion of the very old. The nurse encouraged, "Just a little farther? You wouldn't let the Jayhawks quit here, would you?"

He turned to look directly at the nurse, and Kate noticed the slightest hint of a smile under his mustache. Then, it seemed that Patrick measured the distance to the nurses' station with his eyes. Shrugging, he took a timid step forward. One, then two, and again he made slow progress down the hallway. From behind, Kate tried to coach. "You're doing great, Dad. Really impressive."

"That's enough," he said suddenly, out of breath. "I can't go any farther." He took a deep breath and began a wide turn back to his room, shuffling again, each step taking longer to complete. By the time he reached his bedside, his face had grown pale, and his hands trembled with exhaustion. He rotated abruptly and dropped onto the bed, which rolled away slightly as he landed.

"Now, Mr. Killian, that wasn't safe," the nurse chided. She bustled around his knees to help him remove the bathrobe. "You need to sit—not fall—on the bed. Otherwise the thing will roll away, and you'll be on the floor. Then we'll be treating you for a hip fracture as well as a heart attack." She laughed again.

Kate's father said nothing. Instead, unable to sit any longer, he tried to lie down. Falling onto his back, he threw his legs upward in a vain effort to conserve whatever energy he had left. One foot managed to land safely on the bed, while the other slipped off. He lay there panting, one leg on, one leg dangling over the side.

The nurse bent to retrieve the delinquent foot and slipped one arm under Patrick's elbow. Kate hurried around to the other side. "Here, Dad, let me help you slide up the bed."

"Wait a minute." The gray-haired nurse pushed a button, and Kate heard the sound of the bed motor. "It'll be easier if I bring his head down a bit." Her father seemed for a moment to slide farther down the bed. "All right now, we'll lift and you push, Mr. Killian." She shouted as though Kate's father had suddenly grown completely deaf. "One, two, three . . ." With a heave the two women lugged Patrick's body into place. "Now, Mr. Killian, you'll have to do better than that, or I'll end up in the hospital myself." The nurse patted him lightly on the shoulder and paused to replace his sheets and blankets.

She lifted one wrist and checked her patient's pulse. Satisfied, she continued, "Now, why don't you take a nice long rest. I think I've managed to wear you out." Carefully, she lifted the bed rail and wrapped the call button cord around the upper bar. "I'll be right out at the nurses' station if you need me." She patted Patrick's hand lightly and left the room.

When the door closed, Kate stood beside the bed holding her father's hand. She watched as he closed his eyes and sank into what seemed to be a deep and immediate sleep. Gently, she lowered his hand onto the sheets, caressing it lightly.

Kate let her thoughts wander. When she was little, Kate loved to hold her father's hand while they walked through the streets of downtown Lawrence. As part of the Jayhawks' coaching staff, people viewed Kate's father as a local hero. Everyone knew him. Folks regularly stopped to comment on the season's progress or a recent injury. Kate knew that most fans second-guessed every coaching staff decision. But in all those walks with her dad, she'd never heard an unkind word directed toward her father. In those days, when they walked hand in hand, Kate always felt herself to be kind of a fairy-tale princess. The daughter of the King of Basketball.

Now it seemed that Kate had become the princess of a dying man. How she wished he were well. She could tell her father the truth about Michael. He would understand. And she would ask his advice. He would know what she should do. He would calm the storm of fear and anger threatening to take her under.

But Thomas Patrick Killian was not well. In fact, he seemed to be hovering frighteningly close to death. Now, when she needed him most, Patrick fought his own battle and could not spare any energy to help his daughter with hers. Kate's tears splashed on the sheets near his hand, and she took a moment to pray for him.

There, in the silence of the empty room, she heard something new. Or perhaps it wasn't really new. Perhaps this was only the first time she had noticed it.

The sound reminded her of a runner who had just finished a long uphill climb. A labored breathing, deep and almost gasping—as if the air in the room were suddenly insufficient—like someone desperate for air.

Only her father wasn't running up a hill. Lying flat on the hospital bed, he slept peacefully. And the sound of his breathing frightened Kate more than anything she had ever heard before.

————

Mike slaved his way through Sunday afternoon, feverish in his anger toward his pastor. He mowed the lawn and used the blower to clean the driveway and sidewalks. He used the string trimmer along the edges of the grass and then attacked a weedy patch out by the street. The trimmer quit twice, and in his fury, Mike managed to force it back into service. At one point, he managed to so tangle the string that he threw the bobbin into the bushes and stomped back to the garage. With a new string in place, he let fly at the dandelions as if he were personally responsible for national weed security.

Still fuming, he turned Kate's small vegetable garden by hand, stomping his shovel into the solidly packed weeds that had invaded the space over the winter. With each piercing, he kicked the back of his shovel. Each kick brought pain resonating into his foot and ankle. Mike wanted to have the garden ready for Kate's spring planting. But some part of him argued that she would never plant this garden again. Lifting angry shovelful after angry shovelful, he enacted his refusal to give in. She would come back. She had to come back. His personal debate continued until at last he had turned half the garden.

Still he drove himself. Eventually, his T-shirt, pasted by sweat, clung to his skin. His soft executive hands bloomed fresh blisters. This pain he could not ignore, and he pulled off his leather gloves to find pale bubbles oozing pink fluid onto his skin.

Furious at the new wounds, he threw his gloves onto the ground and sank to his knees. "Jesus," he cried out. "Jesus, it hurts too much. Please help me."

Mike slid over into a sitting position, hugging his knees with his elbows, his hands hanging loose from his wrists. Dropping his head between his forearms, he let tears drip unchecked onto freshly turned soil. Mike Langston sat like this, echoing his silent pain to the heavens, begging for help—though speaking no words—until the late afternoon breeze and his own perspiration combined to leave him chilled and exhausted. The sky over the bay turned pink, and Mike, now stiff and tired, rose to pick up his leather gloves and walk toward the house, leaving all his tools outside.

Inside, Mike faced haunting reminders of Kate. Her artwork hung on the walls. Her fabric trimmed the kitchen windows. At the desk in the kitchen, he found an unfinished grocery list, a recipe card, and a reminder to pick up a gift for a friend's birthday. Every part of this day seemed to cause new anguish. Resigning himself to suffer, he climbed the stairs to the bedroom, determined to shower and waste the evening in front of the television.

Though he felt clean, the shower did not ease his torture. He came downstairs to a silent, dark house where an intense loneliness overcame him. The hours in the yard had left him hungry and exhausted. Going to the refrigerator for a sandwich, he passed by the kitchen telephone. The light on the message machine blinked, indicating messages not yet erased. Mike counted the blinks and noted with disappointment that no new calls had come in. He had hoped to hear from Kate by now.

He opened the refrigerator and stood dully in front of the door, mulling over the items inside. Making a sandwich suddenly sounded like a supreme effort, much more than he could handle. Mike pulled out a half gallon of whole milk and drank from the carton.

Draining the milk, he threw the container into the garbage can under the sink, wiped his lips with his hand, and leaned thoughtfully against the kitchen counter. Staring at the water beyond the window, Mike noticed that feathered clouds had surrendered to high, thick cloud cover. A change in weather. Perhaps rain? He searched for the sun and found it low on the horizon. While he watched, the brilliant globe sank so quickly that it seemed to drop as he watched.

The setting sun brought a strong memory of Kate. These kinds of sunsets were her favorite, with high blue-gray clouds reflecting a brilliant pink. She should be expressing her pleasure over the sunset to him from this very sink. She would have her hair tied back in some fabric thing, with tiny wisps of curls hanging loosely about her face. She would smell of hard work and raspberry shower gel, and he would come to the sink and take her in his arms. . . .

The progress of his thoughts made his heart want to explode. She should be here. Standing next to him, watching the sky. But she was not. And he had no one to blame but himself.

He shook himself. *If she's gone and it's my fault, then I'll fix it,* he said to himself. And then aloud he said, "God help me, I'll make up for this. I will win her back."

He pictured her again on the street outside their attorney's office, telling him she was going to Kansas. *Why not? Why not go home to your parents when your husband turns out to be a jerk?*

He reached across the counter for the telephone. He would call her there. He would persuade her to come back. She had to. He would make her. He ran his finger down the auto dial list and recognized Kate's handwriting with fresh pain. He punched Auto 6 and waited for the phone to ring, hoping that Kate would answer and that he would think of something to say.

────

Rosemarie Killian returned to the hospital room soon after her husband had been tucked safely back into bed. Kate watched her lean over the bed rail and scan her husband's face anxiously. She pulled at his sheets, making a fuss over the wrinkles in the bedclothes. Then she caressed Patrick's hand lightly. Satisfied, she smiled at Kate and turned to sit. "How did it go?"

"He walked all the way into the hall. Almost to the nurses' station."

"Yesterday, they only had him sit in the recliner," she said. She still seemed to disapprove.

"Mom," Kate hesitated, not wanting to worry her mother. "He seemed so out of breath when he got back in bed. Is that . . .? Uh, what does the doctor say about that?"

"Do you want his words exactly?"

Kate nodded and smiled, hoping that she looked more coura-geous than she felt.

Her mother cleared her throat, and said, "The doctor says this heart attack was a 'doozy.' That was his exact word."

"What does that mean?"

"It means that we're lucky he lived through it." Rosemarie's voice clouded with a tremor. "And I think it means that we may not get to keep him for long." She brushed a single tear from her cheek.

Kate had no words. The two women sat in the glow of the light over Patrick's hospital bed, gazing at him. His desperate struggle for air seemed to have passed, and he slept peacefully, heavily, without moving. At last Kate spoke, "Well, we've been here all morning. Do you think we should say good-bye? You look like you could use a rest yourself."

Her mother nodded. Then, glancing around the room, she looked almost as though she were lost. "I hate to leave him here."

"I know, Mom. But he'll be fine. He needs his rest."

Rosemarie gathered her purse and the wicker basket that housed her quilting. She placed them on the chair while she put on her raincoat. Then, leaning over the bed again she whispered, "Patrick." He opened his eyes. "Patrick, Kate and I are going home now. Do you want me to bring you anything?"

"No, Rosie," he whispered. "I'm fine, really. Just tired." He gave a weak smile.

She caressed his hair with her right hand, tucking stray pieces into place. Gently, she smoothed his forehead and patted his cheek. "We'll see you later, my love." She kissed him. He nodded, and the edges of his mouth formed a weak smile.

Kate moved to the bed rail. "Good night, Daddy," she said. "We'll be back." She leaned over him and scooped his head into her hand, pressing against his cheek with her own. "Love you, Daddy."

"Take care of your mom for me, Kate."

"Of course, Daddy. That's what I came for."

The two women walked to the elevator in silence, each absorbed in her own thoughts. Kate marveled at how she could feel so many things at once. Here she was, in her father's presence, very much a little girl, though she had already celebrated her forty-ninth birthday. Thomas Patrick Killian, now old and frail, would always be Kate's daddy. And at the same time, Kate stood waiting for an elevator with a woman who needed her—not just as a daughter, but as a friend.

Kate did not generally allow herself fits of introspection, but at this moment she felt overwhelmed by the changing roles she'd experienced in the past two days. And for a moment, she wished that she could talk to Mike about it. But she couldn't. She wouldn't talk to Mike about anything ever again.

Arriving at home, Kate found her suitcase dropped carelessly in the middle of the front porch. "Nice of them to tell me they were delivering my stuff," she said as she bent to confirm the name on the baggage tag.

"At least they delivered it." Her mother had just turned the key in the lock when they heard the kitchen phone ring. "Oh, dear," she sighed, "that always happens." Her full hands struggled with the doorknob. "It never fails. I'll get inside and whoever is calling will have hung up."

"You could get voice mail, Mom."

"Not me. I hate having to talk into that machine of yours." Rosemarie managed to open the door and squeeze into the entry hall. Dropping her things as she walked, she hurried through the hallway to the phone. Kate followed her inside, lugging her purse and suitcase. She dropped her car keys on the hall table beside an enormous bouquet of white lilies.

"Just as I said," Rosemarie's shoes clicked across the wood floor, "they hung up."

"They'll call back." Kate started up the stairs. "I'll put my things upstairs, and then I'll come down and fix us a little snack."

"Oh no," her mother objected. "I'll fix the food. That way, you'll have time to call Mike. You haven't had a minute to call him all day."

———

Mike put the telephone back in the cradle and sighed a long, anguished sigh. No answer. His anger, seeping out, left him completely empty. The sun had set; the kitchen took on the glow of twilight. Still, he didn't move. Instead, he poured himself a glass of cold water, sat on a barstool, and let his mind wander over his years with Kate.

Up until now, before this terrible betrayal had taken their love away, had he ever longed for her as he did at this minute? Why not? When had he begun to take her for granted? Why had his work so consumed him? When had their relationship grown comfortable instead of warm? Companionable instead of passionate? Was this the path of all marriages?

He let his mind wander back over the years the children were home, when all family activities revolved around the children's sports and school events. He remembered family vacations to Hawaii, watching soccer games in pouring rain, and long drives across the state to basketball tournaments. He remembered being dragged to spring music recitals and holding hands with Kate through endless programs of musical torture while they waited impatiently to hear the kids. He and Kate had been closer then. But where had it gone?

The ringing phone snatched his wandering thoughts. *Kate!* He grabbed at the phone, knocking over his glass and spilling water across the counter.

"Hello," he said, catching the glass as it began to roll. Water ran off the counter onto his pants. He grimaced.

"Hello, Mr. Langston," a female voice replied. "Sorry to bother you." His secretary rarely called him at home. What did Brooke need tonight?

"Oh, no problem," he lied. Disappointment flooded him, and he sat heavily on the stool. "What is it?"

"I was just thinking. Would you like me to arrange for a limousine for tomorrow?"

"Tomorrow?" Mike asked, scanning his brain for some memory of an appointment. He found none.

"Yes, sir," she hesitated. "I, uh . . ." she hesitated, clearly uncomfortable. "Well, normally your wife takes you to the airport."

"The trade show," he remembered. Mike had been slated to attend a technical show in Las Vegas starting on Monday evening and continuing through Thursday. "I hadn't thought about it, Brooke. Is Doug going?"

"Yes, sir," Brooke said.

"Are we at the same hotel?"

"Yes, sir. But Mr. McCoy flew in last night, sir. I confirmed his flight Friday afternoon."

"All right. In that case, I'll just take the Mustang," Mike said. "I can leave it in an airport lot. It won't be a problem."

"So is there anything I can do before you go? You put all of the flight information in your briefcase on Friday. You should find everything you need in the travel packet."

"No, Brooke." Mike smiled to himself and slipped one hand into his pocket. Brooke usually managed to give him the information he needed before he asked.

"Well, then, I'll let you–"

"Wait. When did the PR team fly out?"

"They left Wednesday, sir. They had to set up the demo booth and get it tested before the show opened."

"Thanks, Brooke," Mike said. "You always take care of everything."

Hanging up, Mike sighed deeply. It wasn't easy to save a marriage and keep a business running at the same time. He wiped the counter and turned out the kitchen light. His presentation needed work, and he had packing to do.

Nine

By Monday morning, the Washington State Patrol had tied the stolen credit cards to the Internet. Having no resources to pursue that kind of investigation, Wayne was more than happy to dump the dead driver on the FBI—figuratively speaking, of course.

The FBI, however, proved less than enthusiastic.

At their Seattle office, the Bureau assigned the case to Norm Walker.

Lately, Norm hated his desk—especially on Mondays—which he regularly scheduled as the day to force himself to catch up on his paper work. Whenever Norm felt trapped with his computer, he eased his discomfort with a little snack. Any comfort food would do—so long as it contained large amounts of sugar. So on this Monday morning, Norm leaned over, pulled open the lower desk drawer, and lifted out a jumbo-sized box of Vanilla Wafers. Shaking it, he heard the few remaining cookies rattle against the sides of the empty box; Norm made a mental note to restock his supply. After a morning like this, he deserved a new box. No, he deserved a new case. He'd stop at Costco this weekend.

Norm Walker despised reports. He hated typing. After all, when he'd joined the Bureau, all reports were done the old-fashioned way—with an ink pen. Secretaries typed anything really important. Things had changed over the years.

He grabbed a handful and sat thinking for a moment. With only ten months until retirement, how many more reports might he have left to type? At three per week, twelve per month, Norm figured he only faced 120 more. The calculation did not cheer him. The FBI had been a demanding boss, but for the most part, Norm Walker had no real regrets. He liked his work—at least the parts that didn't tie him to his desk. He leaned back, trying to concentrate on the report staring back from the computer screen. The prosecutor waited. He stuffed the last cookie into his mouth and brushed his palms together, dropping crumbs onto his lap. At last, he began to type, hitting one key at a time with his two index fingers.

"Hey, Norm." Gwen Saunders leaned impatiently against his cubicle wall. As always, she wore an impeccably tailored pantsuit and minimal makeup. In her forties, Gwen had a kind of commanding presence that didn't require artificial help. In one hand she held a manila file, and she waved it toward him. Her mouth wore a tight smirk.

He sighed. More work. "Morning, Gwen."

"Got one for you." She smiled. The tiny hint of dimples deepened into crevasses.

"I figured. There's no rest . . ."

"And you're as wicked as they get." She tossed the file on his desk. "It's a John Doe. Remember the accident on the Narrows?"

"With the tanker?"

"That's the one. Turns out the car was stolen." She reached up to tuck dark hair behind one ear. She'd been growing it out, and now that it reached chin length, it regularly fell into her eyes. This made her crazy, Norm knew, and she'd developed a regular habit of yanking it behind one ear. Norm controlled an urge to smile. "The driver's ID was false, and the plates were fake too," she added.

Norm raised one eyebrow and leaned back again in his chair. "Not federal offenses yet." He reached for the box on his desk and fished at the bottom for another cookie. "So why us?"

She smiled. "True. But they found quite a treasure in the guy's trunk." Her chin tipped to one side, nodding at the file on his desk. Her expression dared him to guess what might have been hidden there.

He didn't bite. "Oh yeah?"

"Credit cards. All kinds."

He sighed. "A conspiracy?"

"Maybe. Right now, that's what the State suspects." Her mahogany eyes narrowed. "Anyway, it's ours now."

Norm set one elbow on the arm of his chair and fingered his lip. "Don't the locals do anything anymore?"

"Nobody has the funds or the skills to handle this kind of stuff. At least they gave us everything they had. All legal. Very neat." She nodded again at the file.

"All right. I'll read it. Do you have a list of the card numbers?"

"I made a copy."

"Okay. Then pull the bank records and get back to me. If we're lucky, it's just someone with a credit problem, and we can go back to chasing the really bad guys."

"Done," she agreed. "Later."

———

On the fifth day after Patrick's heart attack, Kate and her mother rose early and hurried to the hospital. "I hope we arrive before the doctor does this morning," Kate's mother fretted from her seat in Kate's small rental car.

"Mom, it's only seven o'clock," Kate soothed. "I've never known a doctor to make his rounds this early. We won't miss him." As the stoplight in front of her turned yellow, Kate bit her bottom lip, fighting the frustration of hitting a red light.

"Well, I didn't see him yesterday," her mother answered.

Kate knew she meant the doctor. "What happened?"

"I went to the ladies' room." Rosemarie Killian's hands tumbled in her lap, a gesture of anxiety Kate remembered from childhood. "I don't understand why they haven't done something about your dad. A surgery, or something."

The day before, Kate had gone out for coffee—not that lame black stuff, but a latte, which she found at a coffee shop several blocks from the hospital. Unfortunately, the doctor had appeared when both women were away from Patrick's side. "What did Daddy say?"

"He said that everything is going just as the doctor expected." Kate's mother turned suddenly to face the window at her side and covered her trembling lips with one hand. "I know that Patrick knows something. But he won't tell me." She took a deep breath. "I'll just have to ask the doctor myself."

"We'll find out this morning, Mom." The light turned green, and Kate accelerated gently. "Almost there." She reached over to pat her mother's knee. "It'll be okay, Mom," she reassured her.

Kate and her mother rode the last few blocks in silence, each woman occupied with her own thoughts and anxieties. Kate turned into the visitor lot closest to the hospital entrance. Prowling the rows, she looked for an empty parking space. Her mother continued to stare without speaking, hands fretting. While Kate searched, she worried about her mother.

Her parents had been childhood sweethearts, together most of their lives. What they shared was more than love. It went beyond passion. Her parents had grown so close that they seemed to have developed a sort of telepathy—a single-mindedness. Her parents' relationship had been strong even when Kate was a child. But it had continued to grow, especially after her father's retirement. The bond between them had thickened and shortened, until the two now seemed to resemble a joint performance given by a pair of street mimes—exact mirrors of one another, moving together perfectly. Though still clearly separate individuals, they had somehow grown into a single living organism.

Still fretting, Kate pulled the car around yet another row of parked vehicles. What would Rosemarie do if her other half suddenly ceased to exist? Without her mirror image, would despair drive Rosemarie to death as well?

While Kate examined her fear, it surprised her that she did not worry about losing her father. Though Kate loved her father fiercely, she had prepared herself for his death many times as his heart had deteriorated. Patrick had had his first bypass surgery the same year Drew, her oldest, had started the third grade.

Kate remembered how one night, after an evening of playing bridge with friends, her father had surprised everyone by passing out on the front sidewalk of his home. The doctor had found seriously clogged cardiac arteries and suggested a bypass. Her father's surgery had nearly frightened Kate to death, and Patrick Killian knew it. He had been more concerned about Kate than his heart.

On the evening before surgery, Patrick had asked for time alone with Kate. When the hospital room had emptied, he'd simply said, "Kate, I'm all right about this. I want you to be all right too."

"Daddy, I'm just so afraid for you." Her tears flowed freely over her cheeks.

"I know, Katie-Doll." He had taken her hands in his own, patting them gently. "But you need to understand that I am completely at peace. If anything should go wrong during surgery, I don't want you to grieve. I know where I'm going, Kate. If I die, I won't really be gone. You need to believe that I've gone on ahead of you." He nodded and smiled a soft, gentle smile. "And if I go ahead, then you can bet I'll be waiting for you when you get there." Kate had bent over her father and wept into his hospital gown.

"Daddy," she'd said through sobs, "I still need you. Please don't go anywhere."

Patting her shoulder, he had whispered, "I'm not planning on it, Kate."

Though nearly fifteen years had passed since that first surgery, the memory felt as fresh as their morning breakfast. Patrick's heart had given them many scares. Always, his first concern had been for his family's fears. He worried most for Rosemarie and Kate. Today, while she searched for a parking space, Kate worried for her mother.

———

Mike Langston had never really liked Las Vegas. He couldn't understand why the computer industry insisted on having their conventions in this bustling, overcrowded, brightly lit hustler's haven. As he stood in the registration line of the hotel lobby, Mike tried to ignore the unending noise and the garish decor surrounding him. A throbbing headache seemed to grow with every breath he drew. He made slow progress in the line as they processed one registration at a time. Eventually, he found himself near the front, waiting impatiently for his turn at the desk. The oversized woman in front of him seemed to have difficulty with English, but Mike couldn't make out the origin of her accent. He tapped his foot on the red floral carpet and tried to control his frustration. Finally, he faced a beautiful Asian clerk at the registration desk.

"May I help you, sir?" she asked politely.

"I need to check in."

"And the reservation name, sir?"

"Michael Langston."

She typed furiously into her computer. "Ah yes," she crooned. "DataSoft." She slipped a form into a clipboard and placed it on the counter in front of him. "I just need you to sign here." She smiled and turned back to her screen.

"Great." He put down his bag and briefcase and picked up the pen. "I'm wondering if you can tell me," he said, signing with an unreadable flourish, "has Doug McCoy checked in yet?"

"Let me check, Mr. Langston," she answered politely. "Could you spell that for me?" Her hands posed gracefully above the keyboard.

Mike spelled the name slowly, though with little patience. After all, how many ways could you spell McCoy?

"Yes, he has, sir."

"What room is he staying in?"

"I'm sorry, sir. I'm not allowed to disclose that information. However, if you'll proceed to the lobby telephone right over there, I can connect you to his room." She pointed across the corner of the lobby to a red telephone attached to the wall. Mike sighed in growing frustration. "No thanks, I'll just go upstairs." Out of obligation, he smiled at her and picked up the envelope that held his door card.

As he bent to retrieve his suitcase, she called over him, "May I help the next guest, please?"

Mike found the elevators and pushed the button, grateful to find a bank of six elevators with only a few patrons waiting. Aspirin. That would be the first order of business. Then he would stash his suitcase and find the DataSoft demonstration booth. The elevator announced its presence with a sophisticated *bong*.

No, he thought suddenly. He would try to call Kate again. Certainly he would catch her at home eventually—that is, if she'd told him the truth about going to Kansas. He moved into the elevator and stood near the back wall. It didn't matter where she had gone. He would find her and make her listen.

———

Kate followed her mother into the hospital room. There, sitting fully dressed in a bedside chair, her father sat waiting, his eyes twinkling. His breathing sounded less frightening this morning; his cheeks had more color. That brought Kate some relief. He definitely looked better.

While her mother bent to kiss and greet her husband, Kate exclaimed, "Daddy, what are you doing up and dressed?"

"I'm waiting for the doctor."

"Wonderful, we aren't too late," Rosemarie said. Standing beside his chair, she held his hand in hers. He seemed perfectly content to let her stand up, holding his hand up tightly against her chest.

"Here, Mom, let me get you a chair." On the window side of the room, an empty chair flanked an unoccupied hospital bed. Kate went around the bed and began to push an enormous vinyl recliner across the floor. The legs scratching across the linoleum made a horrible racket as she fought with the chair. Kate shoved and pushed, eventually running the chair into the wall as she came around the end of the bed. Pulling the chair back in order to try again, the reclining mechanism engaged—throwing Kate back into the windowsill. "Shoot," she sputtered, the nearest Kate ever came to an oath. She put the chair back into a sitting position and tried again. This time, she rammed it into the bed frame.

"Good thing that bed is empty."

Surprised, Kate looked up. Her father's cardiologist leaned leisurely against the doorframe. Today he wore scrubs and booties, and a blue face mask dangled from paper strips around his neck. He had tucked the end of his stethoscope into his chest pocket.

Humiliated, Kate determined to ignore him. If he cared about the furniture, he could at least come over and help. She tried to pull the chair away from the bed and toward the window, but the bed frame held the chair firmly locked in its clutches.

The doctor set a medical chart down on the nearest counter and strolled toward Kate. "Here, let me help you. Whoever designed these rooms must not have meant for anything to move in here."

"I've got it." Kate blew stray cinnamon-blond hairs from her eyes and shoved the chair again. This time, the chair jumped free and rammed itself into the wall at the end of the bed, leaving a small but obvious scar in the plaster.

Apparently unwilling to let this stubborn woman destroy the hospital, the doctor bent to lift the chair from the floor. "Excuse me," he said, hoisting it up and over his head. He cleared the offending bed and brought the chair around to drop beside Kate's father.

"Thank you, kind sir," Rosemarie said, smoothing her skirt and sitting with a feminine air. "Dr. Stewart, you've met our daughter, Katherine?"

"Yes, once, I believe." He extended his hand, "Nice to see you again." His eyes smiled as though laughing at her.

"Thank you, Dr. Stewart." She slid her hand out of his firm handshake and made an awkward move for the banquette chair she'd occupied the evening before. Kate felt some irritation. She knew her mother considered her dismissal of the doctor to be rude. But Kate could not stand the patronizing sparkle in his deep blue eyes. She would have gotten the chair herself—eventually.

He went over to the counter and picked up the aluminum chart. "Tell me, Patrick. How are you feeling?"

"Much better," her father answered.

"I see you went for quite a walk yesterday." Dr. Stewart flipped through the pages of nurses' notes.

"Seemed farther than it was," her father agreed, smiling.

Dr. Stewart put the chart down and pulled his stethoscope from his pocket, rubbing it against the palm of his hand. "Well, then, how about we have a listen?" He stepped over beside his patient and bent down. "Lean forward," he said. He pulled Patrick's shirt away from his waistband and rolled it gently to his shoulders. Putting the piece onto her father's back, he listened intently. As he checked several locations, his face remained carefully impassive, revealing no clue as to what he heard. He slid the shirt into place, and said, "Now the front." Patrick pulled his shirt up, and Kate watched as the doctor repeated the procedure in front. At last satisfied, Dr. Stewart straightened up and smiled at Patrick. "Well, how do you feel about going home today?"

Patrick Killian smiled and slapped the arms of his chair. "That'd be great."

"All right then, I'll write out the prescriptions for discharge, and as soon as we can get the pharmacy to send things up, we'll send you home." Dr. Stewart returned to the chart and concentrated intently on the notes he wrote there. Something about the peculiar look of his arm hooked up around the chart made Kate realize that he was left-handed.

Her mother's voice startled her. "But, Dr. Stewart, I don't understand," she said. "You haven't done anything about this heart attack. Why haven't we considered a procedure—like a bypass or something?" While she talked, one hand gestured vigorously and the other held Patrick's tight.

"We did talk about that, right after we admitted him." Dr. Stewart closed the chart and slipped his pen into his chest pocket. Kate noticed that his face darkened slightly and that the tone of his voice deepened. She felt a sense of dread and leaned forward to listen. Her mother had not mentioned this conversation.

"Not really," her mother objected. "We said that treatment depended on how bad this attack turned out to be."

"That's right." He leaned against the counter and crossed one ankle over the other. "We said that if the damage were severe enough, we wouldn't be able to do any of the treatments we've considered in the past."

"I can't bring him home without fixing it. We have to do something."

Kate heard desperation in her mother's voice and watched as tension etched deep lines in her mother's forehead. Somehow, without knowing, Kate sensed what was coming.

"Mrs. Killian," Dr. Stewart spoke low and soft, "I thought you understood. This last attack has damaged the entire anterior wall of your husband's heart. We aren't able to do anything more at this point. The damage is so severe that his heart couldn't stand any more corrective treatment."

Tears slid from her mother's eyes, past her cheeks, and dripped onto her silk blouse. Patrick tightened his hold on her hand, using his other to softly rub Rosemarie's forearm. "I . . . Why, there must be something," she objected.

"Rosie," Patrick began, "I don't want to do anything more. I'm going to go home and take good care of myself and do all the things the doc here tells me to do. It isn't like I'm going to die tomorrow."

Her tears began to flow in earnest. "But we have to do something, Patrick."

He reached over and enveloped her in a loving hug, smoothing her hair and whispering into her ear. Kate found the moment so tender, so personal, that she had to look away. Suddenly embarrassed, her mother wiped her eyes and leaned against her husband's shoulder.

"Mrs. Killian," the doctor tried again, "truthfully, we don't know what will happen at this point. Some people live for years with a badly damaged heart. I have many patients who learn not to stress their hearts, who exercise gently and regularly. They eat well and even outlive some of my more healthy patients. I don't think this is quite the death knell you imagine."

Kate's mother did not answer.

"So then," her father began, "let's get this discharge on the road."

Ten

CLOSE TO NOON ON TUESDAY, Norm still hadn't read the file Gwen had delivered to his desk. Of course, if the crime had involved a kidnapping or murder, he would have considered it bedtime reading. But Norm knew better. This was just some smart kid's attempt to milk the world for spending money. And the kid had died in the effort. Norm would get to it, but he felt no hurry.

His busy investigative schedule left him with little patience for reading lengthy reports. Who had time to read in the midst of a calendar full of meetings with investigators, appointments with witnesses, and suspect interviews? Still, after nearly thirty years with the FBI, Norm had developed a system. He managed to find time to read and also to reward his effort for doing so.

Frequently Norm had to testify in federal court. Sitting in a holding area off a courtroom—sometimes for an entire afternoon, sometimes for days—Norm waited while the federal prosecutor choreographed his courtroom witnesses.

These moments Norm saved for reading. And today he had chosen to reward himself for completing the odious task with a dozen glazed donuts from the bakery on Third and Pacific, located right across from the courthouse. He patronized the shop so much that all the counter help knew him by name.

He'd just settled in with his stack of files when the door opened, and Gwen stuck her head inside. "I heard I might find you here," she said.

"Yeah, maybe for the next two or three days," Norm nodded.

"Come on in and get a load of my new office."

"Nice," she said, looking around the holding area. "Spacious for a guy about to retire."

"Yeah, have a seat. What do you need?"

She pulled a chair away from the conference table and put a pile of computerized readouts in front of Norm. "The results of our search. They're fake credit cards."

"We knew that."

"We suspected that," she corrected him. "But these are good, very good. Turns out that over the past four months, none of them have been used criminally."

"Okay, so we got to 'em first." He slid his donut box toward her.

"No thanks," Gwen smiled. "Actually, it isn't even really clear where the numbers were lifted."

"No overlap?" he asked, biting into an old-fashioned.

"Not only that, the cards are from about twenty-five different states."

"They had to come from somewhere." He brushed the table free of crumbs and pulled the pages toward him.

"Well, the Internet seems to be the big common denominator. That's why the Patrol gave us the file. We just confirmed it. All of these folks are Internet users."

"Same store?"

"Nothing that simple."

"What do you think?"

She hesitated, tapping the papers with her index finger. "I think we need the computer club."

"Who?"

"The boys who know the computer world inside out. I think these numbers got lifted off the Net—somewhere. I don't know where exactly. Either by an insider or by a hacker. I have this feeling . . ."

"Oh yeah?"

"I can't explain it. I just think this is bigger than it looks."

He nodded, "I've known you too long to ignore your feelings." He closed the file. "But we still have another avenue."

She raised her eyebrows.

"We have a John Doe. If we could figure out who he is . . ."

"Was."

"Right. I meant was. Then we could see if our driver left any clues of his own. Maybe in his apartment or in a bank account. Maybe a safe-deposit box." He pulled a pen from his shirt pocket. At last this case seemed to be developing into something interesting. "We do have a picture?"

"Yeah, the license is phony. But the picture seems to be the guy in the car."

"All right. Let's circulate the picture. Didn't he have lunch somewhere?"

"The report says there was wet pop on the floor of the car and McDonald's trash all over."

"All right, let's start with that. Let's find out where he bought the food. It had to be somewhere close to the bridge. Maybe he's a regular."

"Sure." She made a note to herself. "What about the computer angle?"

"All right. Give the boys in the club a call. And check with the Federal Computer Incident Response. See if they have anything that matches our situation."

She smiled and stood up. "Well, seems I have my work cut out for me."

"I wouldn't want you to get bored."

She walked to the door, shaking her head. "Working with you? Boredom is never an option."

———

Mike had difficulty making the electronic door card open his hotel room door. In frustration, he dropped all his bags to the floor and wrestled with the handle as though it were simply being stubborn. When at last the door light turned green, he let himself into the executive suite Brooke had reserved.

But Mike didn't notice the plush Oriental carpet or the tufted white upholstery on the nine-foot couch. He didn't see the solid cherry cabinets or appreciate the crystal chandelier over the conference table.

Instead, Mike walked directly to the adjoining bedroom and threw his things on the king-sized bed. Picking up the bedside phone, he dialed Kate's parents' number. By now, he knew all ten digits by heart—memorized from the many times he had tried to reach her during the past twenty-four hours.

Mike let the phone ring seventeen times, counting every ring. He looked at his watch twice during the wait and calculated the time difference between Las Vegas and Lawrence, Kansas. Where could they be? And why hadn't Kate's parents joined the twentieth century? If only they would buy an answering machine. He imagined Kate's dad puttering among his flowers in the backyard and tried to imagine what tasks the garden would demand this time of the year. None came to mind.

Since Mike and Kate had more money than they could spend, Mike had hired a lawn-care crew to weekly maintain the grounds at their Tiburon home. Mike worked outside only when he wanted to—like Sunday when he'd taken his anger out on the yard. Unlike his father-in-law, Mike never felt any real appreciation for horticulture.

Kate's father, on the other hand, loved his garden. Every year since his retirement, Patrick had transformed yet another area of lawn into a reckless display of color and scent. Whenever Mike, Kate, and the kids visited Kansas during the summer months, Patrick's hobby kept fresh-cut flowers on every tabletop in the house. He spent hour after hour, day after day nourishing, weeding, trimming, and encouraging his flowers to grow. The spectacular result had once been featured in a regional edition of *Sunset Magazine.*

The second time Mike checked his watch, he remembered suddenly that he had promised to check DataSoft's display area. They had scheduled a press conference at the demonstration area for later this morning, and Mike was expected to be on hand for the announcement of their latest online shopping cart technology. Later that evening Mike would be the keynote speaker for the convention itself. Reluctantly, he hung up the phone and dialed the front desk.

"I'm expecting a very important message," he barked at the operator. "I want you to make certain it's delivered directly to me. I'll be in the Great Plains Ballroom."

"Yes, Mr. Langston," she answered with deference.

Mike hung up, wondering where the bark had come from. Truthfully, he didn't expect Kate to call. He didn't expect to hear from Kate ever again. He would never hear the little giggle that punctuated her sentences or the breathy sigh that betrayed serious thought. He would never hear her call him "Mick." The anguish that washed over him bent his knees and collapsed him onto the bed beside the phone. He leaned forward and covered his face with his hands.

Moments passed, but his anguish did not abate. The ringing phone jarred him, and he jumped up to answer it. "Yes?"

"Mr. Langston, this is Denise down in the ballroom."

"Oh yes, Denise." He vaguely remembered her as an assistant executive in Sales.

"Sir, I asked for you at the desk, and they told me you had just checked in."

"Right. What can I do for you?"

"Well, sir, I was wondering if you knew where Doug McCoy is?"

"Isn't he with you?"

"No, sir." A pause. "Actually," she said, hesitating. She seemed to choose her words carefully. "He came in the first day, but we haven't seen him in the booth since. I mean, I'm sure he has a lot of work of his own." Mike recognized her feeble attempt to backtrack. "I just have some questions," she continued, "and I've had to make things up as we go along. If you could come down and check on things, sir, I'd feel a lot better."

"I'll be right down." Mike hung up the phone, rubbing his forehead with the fingers of one hand. What in the world was McCoy up to? At the most important trade show of the year, Doug's team needed him. He should be there to supervise the testing of the demonstration area. Where was he?

Mike went to the bathroom to brush his teeth and wash his face. One thing was certain, if he caught up with McCoy in the ballroom, Mike would certainly give him a piece of his mind.

———

On the afternoon of his second day back at home, Patrick slept peacefully in a reclining chair out on the screen porch. Rosemarie had tucked him carefully under a blue-and-white wedding-ring quilt, determined that he should not become chilled. His metal-framed glasses were perched precariously on the end of his nose, and his white mustache fluttered with every breath. A tall glass of decaffeinated iced tea sat untouched beside him. The day had grown unusually warm for spring in Lawrence, and the thermometer beside the potting bench registered seventy-four degrees.

Kate's mother sat rocking in a wicker chair, close enough to her husband to touch him. In the afternoon sunlight, Rosemarie Killian carefully hand-stitched a small pink crib quilt, destined for the grandchild of a close friend. With flagging interest Kate read the latest novel from John Grisham. She'd bought it at a San Francisco Airport newsstand, hoping a page-turner would keep her from focusing on her own problems. It did not. Giving up, she turned down the corner of the page and put the book on the table beside her. Over the past week, Kate had lost her ability to focus on anything.

Kate watched with amusement as her mother's gaze flitted from her tiny quilting stitches to her husband and back again. It seemed to Kate that Rosemarie noted every rise and fall of her father's chest. Her eyes constantly checked his position, his comfort, his color, and his breathing. She could not have been more attentive as a paid employee from the hospital. Though Kate understood her mother's concern, she wondered how long Rosemarie could keep it up. How long could she go without sleep while she listened to him breathe, waking every time he turned over in his sleep?

Her mother looked thinner, her face more deeply lined, even in the four days since Kate had arrived in Kansas. The area below her eyes had grown darker, puffier. Was this the price of love?

Kate gazed out over her father's garden. Even in early spring, the grounds showed the constant care her father lavished on the yard. The winter lawn had already begun to grow green with the help of fertilizer. Her father had banished weeds from the flower beds and trimmed and staked the perennials in preparation for heavy blooms. Could her father resist working in his Eden long enough to allow his heart to heal? Even now in this lush space, she knew he would long to complete some bit of unfinished gardening business. When he felt well enough to complain, he would point out every flaw and elaborate on every bit of work being neglected during his recovery.

The telephone interrupted Kate's thoughts, and she stood to get it. "No, Kate," her mother objected, "let me answer." She moved her quilt into the basket beside her and stood. "I'm expecting Dr. Stewart to check on us this afternoon." She smoothed her skirt and brushed a wisp of hair into place as she started for the kitchen. Even at home on the porch, Kate's mother wore a skirt and sweater. Slowly, Kate sat down, resuming her mother's vigil. Surprisingly, neither the ringing phone nor their conversation disturbed Patrick's sleep.

Rosemarie came back to the porch carrying the cordless phone. "For you," she said, smiling broadly. "It's Keegan." Rosemarie handed the phone to Kate, tucked the quilt more securely over her husband's shoulders, and went back to her chair.

Kate took the phone. "Keegan, what a surprise!" She tried to make her voice sound buoyant, but the effect wasn't quite what she hoped for.

"Mom, what is going on?"

"Grandpa has had some heart trouble. I came home to help out for a few days."

"Mom, I know that. You told me that when you said we couldn't get together for lunch. I know all about Gramps. But why didn't you tell Daddy?" Kate heard anger and confusion in her daughter's voice.

"Try to calm down, dear."

"Daddy called here asking about you. I wasn't home but he left this weird message. He knew you were in Kansas, but he didn't know anything about Grandpa. What is going on between you two?" Keegan's voice had grown too loud, too anxious, and too close to tears. Kate glanced up to find her mother staring curiously at her.

"That's a good question. I don't know the answer," Kate answered calmly, deliberately. "The doctor says he needs lots of rest, and they're adjusting his medicine. We'll just have to see."

"Mom. I'm not talking about Grandpa!" Keegan nearly screamed. "Answer me."

"All right." Kate took a deep breath and glanced up at her mother. "Things are a little—well, strained between Daddy and me right now. I don't want you to worry about it. I can't explain it all. But I will. Give me some time. I promise, I'll explain later."

"Mom. You're frightening me."

"There isn't anything to be frightened about. Really. Besides, Keegan, just because you are an adult doesn't mean that you are suddenly my confidante. I need some time to figure things out. Really, I have to go now." With some effort, Kate managed to get Keegan to hang up. Gently, she set the cordless phone down.

"Kate, what is going on?" her mother asked, nodding toward the telephone.

"It's nothing to worry about, Mom. Just some stress in the family. Keegan has to get to a class now," Kate lied. "Just wanted an update about Daddy. I'll call her later when she has more time to talk."

Kate picked up the novel and opened it to her bookmark, feigning great interest. Just as she settled back into her chair, she looked up to find her mother's dark brown eyes regarding her curiously.

Rosemarie sat quietly without picking up her project. Her chin rested lightly on her hand, and her white hair appeared blond in the sunlight. She continued to rock, but the look on her face clearly revealed her thoughts. Kate had not fooled her mother.

Kate's mother would not press her. Rosemarie would bide her time. Eventually she would dig out the truth. But not now. At least not yet.

———

Exiting the elevator to the lobby, Mike fought his way through the crowds of company representatives, sales teams, and "techies" who had turned out for the computer show. No matter which way he turned, it seemed that Mike fought a great river of humanity flowing in the opposite direction. He shouldered and sidestepped his way through the exhibition area, eventually arriving at the space set aside for DataSoft. Mike noted with some satisfaction that a large group of observers had gathered around the roped-off demonstration area.

DataSoft had hired a lovely blond actress—at Actors Guild prices—dressed her in a skintight sequined gown, and staged a mock game show in the area just outside their booth. Beside the woman, a tuxedoed man spoke into a microphone, coaxing the milling spectators to participate in a word game. Anyone guessing the secret computer phrase won a prize—the value of which depended on the spin of an enormous notched wheel. The blonde smiled charmingly and played her "Vanna White" role with relish, hips swiveling and long fingers gracefully pointing to the game board. As the group of onlookers grew, Mike's sales team eagerly handed out promotional coffee mugs.

Mike shouldered his way through the crowd to a folding table at the rear of the booth. "Where's Doug?" he asked the team manager.

"Haven't seen him," Dennis answered without looking up from his laptop. "Should show up pretty soon, though, the presentation for the press release is in thirty minutes."

"Did he say where he was going?"

Dennis looked up with a puzzled expression, as though Mike had suddenly gone deaf. "I said I haven't seen him."

"You mean not at all?"

"Not since Saturday, actually."

"Hasn't anyone been looking for him?"

"I've heard Lisa has given herself an ulcer trying to find him. You might check with her." He gestured to a petite woman in a dove gray business suit.

Mike knew Lisa well; he'd managed to steal her away from a Los Angeles competitor. Sidestepping another group of prospective clients, he sighed and waited while she handed out brochures and business cards. She shook hands with one of the men and encouraged him to call her at the office. "I know we can take care of that problem for you." She waved and turned away, nearly running into Mike.

"Lisa."

"Mike! Am I glad to see you," she smiled with obvious relief. "I thought Doug was going to do the technical presentation. I've been wild with worry."

"He is."

"What? Then where is he?"

"I'm trying to figure that out," Mike answered, irritation in his voice. For as long as he'd known him, Doug had always worked on his own time clock. But usually he managed to be responsible enough to finish what he started and show up when expected. "Do you know his room number?"

"Sure, the team had dinner together our first night in town. I got off the elevator with him." She shrugged, looking toward the crowd surrounding the booth. "But you won't find him there. I've called his room dozens of times." She lowered her voice to an urgent whisper. "I've left messages. I've asked around at other demonstrations. I've even tried to see if I could spot him around the show. But he's vanished."

A team member excused himself and stepped between them, laying cable along the floor. "You guys talking about Doug?"

She looked at him, her eyebrows raised. "You've seen him?"

"Sure," he answered, rolling the cable in an attempt to force it to lie flat. "I saw him in the casino last night." He gave the cable a shake and moved on.

"Okay," Lisa nodded. "He hasn't vanished."

"No, he's just been misplaced," Mike agreed. "That is, until I find him." He glanced around the booth and lowered his voice. "Then he's going to vanish. Because I'm going to kill him with my bare hands."

"Idle threats," she said, grinning. But her smile was shortlived. Mike saw it disappear. "I wonder if you could hold off on killing him?" She brushed nervous perspiration from her forehead. "At least until after you give his presentation." She nodded toward a camera crew striding through the crowd. "It's time," she whispered.

Mike turned to follow her gaze and let a slow oath escape his lips. "Now what?"

"I'll stall them. You talk to Dennis and figure out what we have planned." She turned him by his coat sleeve back toward the table and plastered a sunny smile over her lovely face. *I have to admit,* he thought, *she's got guts.*

Dennis managed to walk him through the demonstration they'd planned for Doug to give. "These guys don't know technical from astrophysics. You'll be fine," he assured Mike. When the lights came up, Lisa made her way to a narrow glass podium perched at the side of a small stage a few steps off of the coliseum floor. Her white-blond hair and vibrant blue eyes made a lovely picture. "And today, ladies and gentlemen, we have a big surprise for you. May I introduce the president and CEO of DataSoft, Mike Langston."

Mike moved forward to the sound of polite applause. His heart thundered, and his anger grew with every step. Where was Doug? Why had he left Mike to cover for him? Mike felt a column of cold sweat dribble slowly down the small of his back. In the business world, giving an unprepared presentation constituted suicide. At that moment, Mike felt very much like a Kamikaze heading for a crash dive. The only ship to sink today would be his own. If he managed to live through this, Doug McCoy would never take another breath!

Mike managed to bluff his way through the speech, certain that his flaming cheeks gave away his secret. He kept his introductory remarks as nonspecific as possible, emphasizing the history of the company and its rapid growth over the past three years. The team cued a PowerPoint presentation at the first hint of his floundering. Gratefully, Mike gave up the podium and took his seat.

Near the end of the presentation a voice beside him said, "Not bad for a paper pusher."

Mike turned to stare at Doug McCoy. "Where on earth have you been?" he demanded, vicious anger coating every word.

"Relax, I heard it all. You did pretty well, considering you can't turn on the computer without help."

"Forget how I did. Why didn't you show up?"

"Quiet, big man. Members of the press are still in the room. We wouldn't want them to speculate about division in the ranks, now, would we? Might affect the stock value." Doug joined the applause as the program ended. "Pretty good, actually."

Mike fumed. At least his partner could apologize.

Without explanation, Doug stood, stepped in front of him, and hurried to catch an acquaintance. What could possibly have gotten into Doug McCoy?

At last the crowd dwindled. Hotel employees began to remove folding chairs, noisily hanging them by their legs on a cart. Mike eyed the room and found Doug. He made his way toward him and grabbed him. "Tell me the truth," he demanded, turning Doug to face him. "Where have you been?"

"We're in Las Vegas, pal." Doug patted him on his arm, then removed Mike's hands from his jacket lapels. "To tell the truth, I've been winning. Big time." Still smiling, he turned away and disappeared into the mass of conventioners. Mike stared after Doug, his mouth hanging open in disbelief.

Eleven

EARLY THURSDAY MORNING, Kate found her mother in the kitchen, sitting at the round pine table she kept in the breakfast nook. Holding a pen in her left hand, she glanced up from the small piece of paper she had been concentrating on. "Morning, sweetie. Coffee's just finished." Sunlight poured in paned windows, and steam rose from her mother's china cup. Freshly cut flowers rose from a vase at the center of the table. Even with her husband's illness, Kate's mother still behaved like Martha Stewart.

"Thanks, Mom. Coffee sounds good," Kate said, bending to kiss her mother's cheek. "What are you up to this morning?" She plucked a mug from the rack beside the kitchen sink and filled it to the brim with fresh coffee.

"Just working up a grocery list." Rosemarie Killian gave a long sigh.

"I hate shopping for groceries too," Kate agreed. "But it isn't that big of a deal, is it? Why the big sigh?"

"Oh, nothing really. I just have so many things that I should do. All over town." She set her cup down. "Shirley Adams said she'd do the shopping for me. But I can't ask her to do everything."

"Couldn't I do it?"

"No, sweetie. There's too much. I have dry cleaning and an order in at Calico Corner and groceries. I should go to the bank."

"So what if you go and I stay here with Dad? It'd be good for you to get out."

Her mother gave Kate an anxious look. "I hate to leave him.

He's only been home a couple of days."

"I'm a grown-up, Mom. He's as safe here with me as he is with you." Kate pulled out a chair and sat down opposite her mother. "I promise to keep a close eye on him."

"The doctor said he should go for a walk today."

"It's warm enough. We could take a meander through the backyard."

"I wouldn't be gone for long," Rosemarie said, as much to herself as to Kate.

"I know."

"Well, it would be a big help." She hesitated, putting a finger to her lips.

Kate smiled and reached out to pat her mother's hand. "Trust me, Mom. I won't allow anything to go wrong until you get back."

"Thanks a lot," her mother frowned. "All right. I guess I'll go clean up."

Two hours later, Kate waved to her mother and closed the front door. Rosemarie's anxiety had manifested itself in a carefully printed list of things for Kate to do in her absence. She'd attached it to the front of the refrigerator with a basketball magnet. *Move the clothes from the washer to the dryer. Give Dad his morning medication. Make Dad drink a full glass of water with his medicine. Add a half teaspoon of fiber to his morning juice. Fix only decaffeinated coffee!* Kate smiled. In all of her childhood, Kate had never doubted her mother's devotion, but Patrick's most recent heart trouble brought out a level of paranoia she had never witnessed before. Maybe this happened to every married couple after fifty years. Mild paranoia seemed more reasonable when she thought of it that way.

Turning from the front door, Kate walked past the entry hall table where her own wedding picture had been proudly displayed for twenty-six years. Kate told herself not to look at it, but her eyes refused to obey. She paused, reaching out to touch the gilded frame. Who were those two foolish children standing there? Why had she believed that their love could last?

With a pang Kate realized she would never know fifty years with the same man. Mike's choice made sure of that. Kate would never know the kind of devotion and love that her mother knew. Tears came to her eyes, and this time they were as much out of grief as they were of anger. Kate would never experience the horrible love-fear her mother felt for her father. And suddenly she felt robbed.

Mike's relationship with Cara robbed Kate of her future—of the years and experiences she'd dreamed of and planned for. They would never share retirement. Never sit together for Keegan's wedding. Never share the grief of lost parents or the delight of a new grandchild.

But Mike's adultery had managed to steal her past as well. For the rest of her life, the memory of their years together would be tainted. His betrayal had divided her life into two distinct categories—each intricately tied to his affair. Kate would forever mark time with two words: "before" and "after." And the pain, the sudden realization of it, sucked the air from her lungs and left her standing in the hallway, bleeding to death from an invisible wound.

———

Normally, Ray Taylor pruned his fruit trees in January. Pacific Northwest winters nearly always included at least one long spell of high pressure. The resultant clear skies and dry weather made the task of pruning safer and less miserable. Ray preferred to prune when the weather turned dry and cold.

But this year, unrelenting rain and a mild attack of arthritis in his left knee forced Ray to wait until much later for warm, dry weather. On this sunny last day of March, Ray left the house early, armed with his trusty tool bucket and pole trimmer.

Forty years ago, he and his wife, Jeannie, had planted two rows of dwarf fruit trees near the property line behind their home. A long expanse of grass separated the orchard from their tiny two-bedroom house. On this particular Thursday, wearing rubber boots and canvas overalls, Ray started with the trees farthest from the house. He hoped to have his five apple trees finished by noon. After lunch he would attack the cherry tree by the fence. Or perhaps he would chop the tree down.

When Ray bought the tree, the salesman had assured him it was a dwarf. But this particular cherry seemed to ignore all instructions regarding size; every year it threatened to explode into a giant tangle of unwanted shoots. He hated that tree. He would have enjoyed chopping the thing down—if it hadn't been for Jeannie's cherry pies. Those pies had managed to save that tree for a long and healthy life.

Ray worked steadily, diligently, and had just begun the last of the apple trees when Jeannie, his wife of fifty-two years, called him for lunch.

"Almost finished with this tree," he called to her.

"Hurry, it's getting cold."

He took his time, pruning with care and dropping the limbs onto a pile away from the tree. When the shape of the branches satisfied him, he picked up his loppers, his pole trimmer, and the bucket and crossed the back of his property to the offending cherry. Taking a rag from his back pocket, Ray opened a small container of rubbing alcohol. He poured it onto the rag and began slowly cleaning the cutting surface of his loppers. Ray refused to transmit disease from tree to tree. As he worked, his stomach growled. And then he noticed the dogs.

Though Ray had never actually met his newest neighbor, he hated the dogs that lived next door. The two German shepherds barked incessantly, snarling and threatening whenever anyone approached the fence line. Ray tried his best to ignore them, but because of their relentless barking, he had taken to sleeping with his bedroom window closed. This irritated him. He liked sleeping in cold fresh air.

Jeannie felt more frightened than annoyed by the dogs and worried constantly about their younger grandchildren. "What if those dogs get out? I've heard of children being attacked by loose dogs."

Ray tried to reassure her. "They're behind a chain link fence, Jeannie. They won't get out. The kids are fine." Truthfully, he felt the same uneasy fear. But he would not admit it.

Today, though, as he cleaned his tools he noticed something missing. The morning stillness had not been broken by the obnoxious barking of the shepherds. Why not? Perhaps they weren't out today. Just as he tucked his rag into his pocket, he heard a soft, pitiful whine. Curious, he stepped closer and peered through the wooden slats of his own fence. He saw both dogs lying down inside their kennel. From his viewpoint, he could see their doghouse at one end, the dogs outside, and the concrete ground covered with excrement.

The dogs lifted their heads to peer at him, whining mildly. Still they didn't bark. Ray walked over to a nearby stump and held on to the fence as he stepped up. The rattling fence aroused the dogs.

With obvious effort they stood and barked—sickly, weak barks.

Ray saw more clearly from his position on the stump. Beside the doghouse, large blue feeding dishes stood completely empty. The dogs had no water, no food. Since he'd last seen them, both dogs appeared to have lost weight. The skin over their rib cages distinctly revealed bones. The pelvises of both dogs showed clearly below their fur. These dogs hadn't been cared for in days. Ray's heart softened, and he wondered where their owner had gone. Why had he left the dogs to fend for themselves?

Ray stepped down, crossed the lawn, and brought back the garden hose. He couldn't feed the animals, but he could make sure they had water. Stuffing his finger into the hose end, he sprayed water over the fence into the kennel. The dogs backed away from the stream. When at last he dropped the hose, both dogs crowded the bowls, eagerly slurping up water.

By the time Ray turned the water off, he'd decided to call the Humane Society. No matter how much he resented those dogs, Ray would see to it that the authorities removed them from the neighbor. The young man who lived next door didn't deserve to keep animals.

————

After breakfast, Patrick Killian insisted that he did not need or desire Kate's supervision. And, because she wanted to appease her father's pride, Kate agreed. From the kitchen, she listened as he walked slowly upstairs to the master bedroom.

It frightened her to leave him alone. But she refused to discourage his independence. He insisted on doing everything for himself, resting between each phase of activity. Stealthily, she climbed the stairs and stood in the hallway outside her parents' bedroom door, listening to every creak and groan coming from the room where her father dressed. She heard him pant while he stood to pull up his trousers. She heard the bed groan while he sat down to put on his socks. She heard slow, shuffling steps while he walked to the dresser for something he'd forgotten. She felt foolish spying like this on her own father. Her heart pounded in her ears while she leaned into the door, straining to hear every sound.

What if something happened to him? A noise from the room caught her attention. He'd dropped something. A shoe? She forced her feet to stay outside. A long pause. He rested. Before she realized it, tears filled her eyes. When she felt certain her father was safe, she tiptoed back down the stairs to the kitchen to finish the breakfast dishes. He would never know that she had eavesdropped.

The dressing ordeal left Patrick exhausted, and he slept in his favorite chair until noon. While Kate worked on her mother's household chores, she kept one ear tuned for her father. A soft coughing noise told her he had wakened. She went in to check on him. "Feeling better?"

"Oh, much." He smiled and rubbed the stubble of new beard growing on his face.

"Mother tells me you need to take a little walk today." Kate sat on the ottoman beside his feet. "You want to walk through the backyard with me?" Her fingers gently massaged his shin.

"Oh, I suppose I could manage the yard," he agreed.

She brought him a light cardigan from the hall closet and stood ready to help while he got up and put it on. He shuffled through the kitchen out to the screen porch with Kate standing very close behind. She opened the door for him, and he reached out to hold the doorframe as he lowered himself down the two steps to the yard.

A gentle breeze rustled the tiny new leaves in the trees over their heads. The air smelled fresh, full of new blossoms and scents of spring. Kate took a deep breath, "Isn't it wonderful, Daddy? I love spring."

He stopped a moment, shifting back and forth on his legs. "I love every season, Katie-Doll." He moved forward again, and she worried that he might have trouble on the gravel walkway. Feeling embarrassed by their changing roles, she asked, "Do you want to hold my hand, Daddy?"

He smiled, a loving, knowing smile and slipped one arm through her elbow. Slowly, they meandered down a winding pathway toward a small pond her father had built before Kate graduated from college. She missed the sound of water trickling over rocks from one level of the pond to another. His heart attack had interrupted his spring gardening ritual, and he had not yet started the circulating pump. She wondered if he would ever feel well enough to keep the garden again.

Her father paused a moment, resting.

She stood waiting beside him. "Do you want to go back inside now, Dad?" she asked.

"No," he answered. "I want to go out to the barbecue bench and sit a few minutes." Kate looked up, gauging the distance to the property line. When she was a child, her father had built a swing set at the farthest end of their property. She and her friends had played for hours there. Later, when she was in elementary school, Patrick had constructed a tiny playhouse beside it. When they'd outgrown the swings, her father had put in an enormous frame for a home-made ice rink that became a neighborhood attraction.

When winter temperatures plummeted, all the local children came to Kate's backyard to skate. The boys played hockey there, while Kate and her friends pretended to win Olympic skating medals. When Kate was in high school, her father had converted the rink into an outdoor picnic area. He built a brick barbecue, added a fire pit, and placed teak benches around the perimeter of the circle he'd paved with brick.

Today, it seemed as though those benches were miles away.

After several stops to catch his breath, they reached a seat under a spreading Chinese elm. Little spots of sunlight filtered through the branches above them onto the bench. Warm scented air brushed her face. It seemed to Kate that her father collapsed onto the bench. He sat without speaking for several minutes. Again, she heard the panting and fought her own fear.

"Do you remember what we used to do out here, Kate?" he asked, looking up into the tree.

"We used to talk."

"I remember how you used to tell me everything out here, under this old tree."

"I remember, too, Dad." She thought about their conversations. They'd talked of high school dates and disappointments. Of college plans and course work. She'd first told her father about Mike under this very tree.

"So tell me, Kate." He leaned back on the bench, folding his hands in his lap.

"What, Dad?" A little chill ran along her back and up her neck. She shivered.

"Tell me. What is really happening between you and Mike?"

Twelve

MIKE DROVE INTO Sausalito early on Friday morning, determined to catch up on his own work, which included preparation for an upcoming board of directors meeting. The show in Las Vegas left him cranky and tired. He'd tried to telephone Kate numerous times over the three days he'd been out of town, all without success. Eventually, in desperation he'd called Keegan. Mike believed he could find out about Kate without telling his daughter about their marital difficulty.

"Dad, they've probably been at the hospital."

"Hospital?"

"Of course. Grandpa's been in coronary care for almost a week now. And you know Grandma," Keegan continued with a chuckle. "Mom's probably had to pry her away from Grandpa's bed every single night before the nurses kicked them out."

"Right. Of course."

"Dad, you did know about the heart attack, right?"

"Sure, I just didn't think about the hospital," he lied.

His lie did not fool Keegan. In fact, he felt certain he'd stirred up a hornet's nest of anxiety. Keegan did not understand why her father seemed so confused about Patrick's illness. Now, thanks to Mike's call, she believed something had gone horribly wrong between her parents. He hadn't meant to frighten Keegan. But he had, and like the damage in his marriage, eventually he'd have to try to undo this as well.

Turning the corner onto Stanton, he bought a latte at a drive-through two blocks from the office. The woman who frothed his milk looked like she was new at her job; she struggled with the grinder and splashed milk all over her apron before finally presenting Mike with his drink. When he carried it across his lap, Mike spilled most of the drink on his khaki shorts. The girl hadn't secured the lid to the cup. Scalding liquid splashed across the cotton of his pants and his right thigh, leaving a nasty red splotch on bare skin. Mike chose to forgo his usual tip. He leaned down and poured what was left of his drink into his broad-based aluminum commuter mug. Then he swabbed at his lap with the napkins she offered through the car window. He cursed his Mustang for not having a cup holder. *Of course, no one had a cup holder in 1968,* he thought. Back then, people worked and lived on the same street. Having a cup holder would not have saved his leg; only an employee who knew what she was doing might have prevented such a nasty spill. Nothing irritated Mike more than incompetence. He shifted into first and pulled into traffic with a screech of his tires. He'd have to try and wash out the stain at work.

At Brooke's desk, he picked up a five-inch stack of mail. On top of the pile, she'd secured a pile of yellow phone messages with a giant paper clip. Mike's mood sagged further. His work would have to wait until he sorted through the messages. Then, of course, there would be another sixty e-mails waiting on his computer. In an effort to stay calm, he told himself he'd have time to do the preparation after lunch.

"By the way, Brooke," he began, balancing his coffee cup and the stack of papers with one hand, and his briefcase in the other, "any messages from Kate?"

"Not this morning, sir," she answered quickly, lightly. "But Cammie from Technical is waiting in your office."

Mike tucked his emotions away, refusing to let his disappointment show. After a short delay, Brooke's words broke through his internal preoccupation. "Does she have an appointment?"

"I don't have a record of one. I thought maybe she'd talked to you."

"What does she want?"

"I don't know. She said it would only take a second."

"Brooke, I've told you not to do this to me."

"I know," she sighed. "But Cammie said it was urgent. And you didn't have anything on your calendar." Brooke's phone rang. "When I got here, Cammie was panting around out here like a rabid animal." She held her index finger in the air and answered the phone in a singsong, "Mr. Langston's office."

"All right, all right." Mike shrugged and turned toward his office door. Reaching for the knob with one hand, he dropped part of his mail on the floor. Behind him, Brooke promised to transfer the call, pushed a button, and hung up.

"I'll get it, Mike," she hurried around her desk, opening his door for him. While she scooped envelopes off the floor, he brushed past her.

Mike dropped his briefcase beside his desk and set down his coffee. This day did not promise to be very productive. As he dumped the mail on his desk, Cammie jumped up from her seat on his couch, throwing aside a magazine she had been reading. "Mr. Langston," she said.

"Good morning, Cammie," Mike said quietly. "Have a seat, and I'll be right with you." He took a moment to settle his things onto his desk, opening a drawer for a pen and a small writing pad. These he carried along with his mug to the chair before her. He sat quietly. "Now, what can I do for you?"

Cammie, who looked to Mike to be in her mid-twenties, wore stretch denim capris. Her boy-cut hair glowed in a peculiar black-burgundy color. With one hand, she fiddled incessantly with one of the ten or more earrings that lined the lobes of both ears. *Kids,* he thought as he waited for her to speak.

"I'm sorry, Mr. Langston," she said, breaking the silence. "I know you're just getting back to the office," she continued. "And I would have made an appointment. But, well, I think this is urgent, and I don't know where to go with it." She crossed one ankle over her other knee and began fiddling with the buckle of her sandal.

"What is it, Cammie?" He tried to keep his tone casual, though he resented having her come to him with her troubles. Officially, Cammie reported directly to Doug, as did all of the Technical team. He made a note to himself. At some point, he needed to speak with Doug about the supervision of his team.

"Well, sir, I'm working on the new system for Tebett Marine Industries. And I'm having this strange problem." She shook her head in a vacant, pensive way and stared off into space.

"And the problem is?" Mike prodded.

"Well, sir, the system has bugs. Weird things. Things that shouldn't be happening."

"Aren't bugs normal? Isn't that what you always get at the start of every system design?"

"Some are, Mr. Langston," she agreed. "And I do expect them. In fact, we schedule time for debugging every system we design for our clients. But this is different stuff. Stuff I haven't seen before."

"I think I understand. But why don't you talk to Doug about this? Isn't he the one you normally talk to about these things?"

"Normally I would. But in this case I thought you should know."

"Cammie, I don't supervise the technical side of our work. Why would you bring this problem to me?"

"Because it's Doug's project. He's the primary designer."

"And have you talked to him about it?"

"I've tried. But it isn't easy. He brushes me off. Like he doesn't want to talk about it. I've even tried to get the team to meet with him on it."

"What happens?"

"Well, sir, I feel like I'm talking behind his back." She stirred uncomfortably and then shrugged. "I've never gone over Doug's head before."

"Listen, I'm having trouble following this. You're going to have to be more specific."

"Okay." She scooted away from the back of the couch. Carefully, she placed her hands together in her lap, fingertips touching, and took a deep breath. "Well, he isn't in the office much, Mr. Langston. He comes in late and leaves early. His secretary tells me he's working from home."

"Well, that's possible, isn't it, considering the kind of work he does?"

"I suppose," she agreed, shaking her head. "He can get into our system from home. But he isn't getting anything done anymore. The programmers and designers—we're all frustrated. We're working for a guy who never shows up. He doesn't know what's going on, and he doesn't help us fix the problems we do have."

"I see." Truthfully, Mike didn't see. He had no idea why Doug had suddenly become extra weight in his own department. He thought about his friend, about the conversations they'd had in the past couple of months. What had happened to Doug? Why did he act so strangely? Had Mike missed something? Had he become so involved with Cara that he had managed to ignore the health of his own partner? "I see," he repeated. "All right, Cammie. How about you give me some time to work on this?"

Suddenly appearing very relieved, Cammie stood, wiping perspiration from her palms onto her denim pants. "Well, I just felt you should know. Thanks for letting me see you without an appointment." She stuck out her hand, which Mike shook. It was cold and moist.

"I'll get back to you," Mike said, escorting her to the door. "And you keep in touch, okay? Let me know if you have any ideas about what might be going on." When the door shut behind her, Mike stood for a minute lost in his thoughts, his hands pressed on his hips. He shook his head. *Now what?*

How quickly things could go from bad to worse. Kate had deserted him. He had frightened Keegan to tears. His father-in-law had suffered a heart attack. Now his partner had begun acting so strangely that worried coworkers had gone over his head. What had turned Mike's world so completely upside-down?

————

When the doorbell finally rang, Ray Taylor answered it. A plumpish young woman, in tight green denim and a dark khaki uniform shirt, stood on their small doorstep holding a clipboard. "Hello," Ray greeted her, pushing open the screen door with one hand and extending the other. "I'm Ray Taylor. I called about the dogs."

"My name is Shannon," she said, shaking his hand firmly. "Thanks for calling. I'm from the Humane Society."

Ray nodded. "I found the shepherds this morning. I don't think they've been cared for in days. No food, no water. I called as soon as I discovered them."

"Can you come outside and show me?" The woman stepped back. Her thick brown hair, held loosely in a big funny clip, bounced with every move.

"Certainly," Ray answered. "Be right back, Jeannie," he called over his shoulder as he stepped out the front door. "Actually, you can see them best from the fence in my backyard. That's how I found them." He led the way around the Taylor garage into the side yard, where huge lilac bushes blocked the view of the neighbors. When they reached the stump, Ray held out one gnarled hand. "If you stand here, you can see."

She took his hand and stepped onto the stump. Balancing high on the toes of one foot, she held the other leg out stiffly at her side. "Oh, hey, babies," she cooed at the dogs. "Are you all right over there?" They let out a pitiful whine but did not bark. She jumped onto the grass, shaking her head. "I see it all the time, but it still gets to me."

"So can you go in and get the dogs?"

"Nope," she answered firmly. "I have a very strict set of rules to follow. We have to post the place first." She lifted the first sheet of paper on her clipboard and began writing. "It's a forty-eight-hour protocol. I can't take anything until I've posted a notice on the door. Then, after forty-eight hours, I can come and get the dogs."

Ray nodded. "I guess I understand. The whole place is locked up tight."

"Actually, it'd be easier for neighbors to help the animals than for me. We have to be so careful about going onto private property." She paused, her pen still on the paper. "Do you know who lives here?"

"No. The owners moved away about ten years ago. It's been a rental ever since."

"What about the address?"

Ray shook his head. "We can get it off the front of the house." He pointed at the fence. "Will they live for forty-eight hours?"

She continued filling in the form on her board. "Starvation, believe it or not, isn't considered life threatening. I can only break in if they are obviously in immediate danger of death. Like if they were hanging by a collar or something."

The feelings Ray experienced surprised him. After so many sleepless nights, why did he care about what happened to those stupid dogs? But he did care. "I used the hose to get water to them. But I can't get food to them—unless I throw it through the fence one piece at a time."

"If you'll do what you can, Mr. Taylor, I promise to come back as soon as possible to get the animals. It's a shame for people to have pets when they don't take care of them." Together they walked back to the front yard, where the woman headed straight to her truck. She pulled a package of tacks from a plastic case in front of the passenger seat. "Let's go post the front door."

Ray led the way as they crossed to the neighbor's driveway and walked up the broken sidewalk to the front door. Ray hadn't been near the house in the ten years since the owners had moved. He found himself noticing the cracked, uneven sidewalk, the faded siding, and the peeling wooden doorframe. He saw dirty drapes, torn and hanging unevenly from the rod over the living room window. He had a funny feeling; he should have been paying more attention. He'd lived here nearly all his married life. Why didn't he know more about his neighbor?

Shannon managed to tack the bright yellow notice onto the front door and turned back to Ray. "I'll come back tomorrow and check on the dogs. If things are looking a lot worse, maybe I can convince a judge to let me bypass the second twenty-four hours." She patted Ray on the forearm. He followed her back to her truck. "In the meantime, Mr. Taylor, I'd appreciate it if you'd do what you can from your property line." Her face seemed tight with emotion.

This woman really did care about those two noisy animals. Shannon slid into the driver's seat. "Be sure to call if anything changes." She pulled the door shut.

As her little truck pulled away, Ray felt relieved. He'd done the right thing.

————

Kate leaned back on the bench and turned toward the house. "I don't want to talk about it, Daddy."

"Katie-Doll," her father began gently, placing his hand over hers, "certainly you didn't think we'd miss it."

"No, I would have told you as soon as you felt stronger."

"You've been here almost a week. Your mother heard you crying in your room. The thing with Keegan didn't fool us. And last night while you were out on your run, Mike finally caught your mom at home." He lowered his chin and leaned toward her gently, asking with infinite kindness, "What happened, honey?"

In spite of her determination to avoid them, tears filled Kate's eyes and ran down her face. "I don't know," she whispered, brushing her cheeks. "Oh, Daddy, I don't know."

He put an arm around her shoulders and pulled her into his chest, letting her cry. "There," he said, patting her shoulder. "I'm so sorry, Katie-Doll. So very sorry."

She let the tears roll. Until this moment, Kate had focused every ounce of her energy on fighting the reality of it all. Wanting to keep these horrible feelings of loss and anger and utter hopelessness deeply buried, she'd refused to confront the truth. But now, even as a grown woman—nearly fifty years old—being here under the tree again and talking to her father brought all of her emotions to the surface. Bubbling up, spilling over, they flooded the air around them. Kate felt as though she would drown in grief. For long moments they sat there, she crying, he comforting, until with a deep shuddering, she seemed to come to the end of it. She rubbed her dripping nose with the back of her hand. He reached into his pants pocket and removed a cotton handkerchief.

"What happened, Kate?" he asked, offering it to her.

"He, I . . . oh, Dad." She blew her nose and then sighed. "A woman."

"Mike? It can't be." He seemed incredulous. "How do you know?"

Kate sniffed and wiped her nose again. "I saw pictures, Dad. It was Mike—no question. I even know the woman."

"I'm so sorry, Kate." He patted her upper arm with the palm of his hand. More comforting. More tears. "What will you do, Katie-Doll?"

"I've already done it, Dad." Kate took a deep breath. "I went to see a lawyer . . . before I came." She let out a long, shuddering sigh. "I filed for divorce."

"Oh, Kate."

"You don't have to feel sorry for me, Dad. I'll be all right."

"But what about Mike?"

"What do you mean, 'What about Mike?' " Her voice rose defensively. "Why should you care about Mike? He's the one who made the decision. Not me. I didn't choose this."

"Kate, he's been in our family for almost thirty years. We love him as much as we love our own children."

"After what he's done? You care about him after this?"

"Kate, I'm not excusing it. I'm not approving it. Surely you know better than that." Her father took her chin in his hand and turned her face toward him. "But I know that this decision will destroy him. It will devastate him as much or more than he has hurt you. What about him? Have you talked to him? What does he want?"

Kate turned her face away. "I don't care what he wants. If he cared about me, he would never have done it. Why should I care about him now?"

"I understand how you feel," her father agreed. A breeze stirred the leaves in the tree above them, and the air seemed to have grown colder. "What about the kids? I'm assuming you haven't told them?"

His questions brought fresh tears, and for a moment Kate wondered if the reservoir would ever run dry. "No. I told Mike not to tell the kids. And I can't explain it to Mom yet either. At least not until we decide what to do. The kids have their own lives now, and I don't want to worry them. Not yet."

He nodded. "I'm so sorry, Kate," he said again. "There isn't anything I can do to fix this. But I can do one thing. I'm going to pray. I think we need a miracle."

Kate sat up straight. "Dad, I don't want a *miracle*." Kate mocked the word. "I just want to stop hurting. I want to get on with my life."

"Sounds like you're running, Kate."

"Remember me, Dad? I love to run."

"I know, Katie-Doll. But *this* running won't get you anywhere."

"Dad, I don't want to get anywhere. I just want to get over Mike. I want to stop hurting." She brushed her tears away, and as her father reached around her shoulders she sank against his warm chest. "I just want to stop hurting," she said again, her voice breaking. While her father held her, Kate gave in to her tears once again.

Thirteen

ON FRIDAY EVENING, Mike arrived home too exhausted and keyed up to relax. He tried to mop the kitchen floor but couldn't find the bucket. He dragged a basket of dirty laundry downstairs and began sorting whites from colors. In his eagerness to accomplish his task, he bumped his head on the corner of Kate's folding table. Intense pain folded his knees, and he sat on the floor rubbing a nasty bump. Forget the laundry; he had plenty of underwear. He heard the phone start to ring and ran upstairs, hoping it might be Kate.

Instead he heard Dave Holland, calling to ask if Mike would like to join him for a day sail. Mike needed the break, and he agreed enthusiastically.

———

Mike arrived at the marina just before eight on Saturday morning, carrying a nylon day bag packed with snacks, his camera, his favorite fleece pullover, and an old Helly-Hanson jacket. A low tide had dropped the floating dock so much that the ramp going down hung at a steep angle. Mike stepped carefully, holding on to the rail with one hand, his bag in the other.

From out of his bag, the moldy smell of his old sailing jacket seeped into the morning air. Last night, the stench had nearly knocked him over. He'd dug the jacket out of a basement storage closet and soaked it in the laundry tub with a bit of bleach. Hours later he'd hung it in the shower to dry. The effort had been largely wasted. Now the jacket smelled like mold *and* bleach.

In spite of his stinky jacket, Mike looked forward to the day. He'd had a rough couple of weeks. So much pressure. So much to figure out. So many decisions to make. Perhaps the wind would blow the confusion from his mind and give him a new sense of direction in the tumult that had suddenly overcome his normally predictable life.

Mike walked along the dock looking for individual slip numbers. He had not yet seen Dave's new sailboat and could only identify it by the number of the berth.

Smells of diesel fuel, saltwater, and creosote-soaked timbers floated in the air. He heard the slap of water on the dock and the squeak of dock sections rubbing against one another with the motion of his steps. Cold air cut into his lungs, and he felt invigorated. The dock rolled gently, and gulls cried out to one another in the air above him. When had he last gone sailing? Not since the children had entered high school. All at once, the feeling of wind in his face, the sound of slapping sails, and the joy of rising and falling with the motion of the waves all came back to him. It suddenly dawned upon Mike how much he missed it—missed everything about being out on the water.

In the old days, he and Kate had owned a twenty-eight-foot cutter—nothing fancy, really. With just a small cabin, the *Day Tripper* had been a maneuverable, seaworthy little vessel. Mike and Kate had never taken her offshore, never more than five nautical miles beyond the Golden Gate. Instead, they'd enjoyed many weekends in and around the San Francisco Bay Area.

Often when the kids were young, the four of them would spend part of a weekend cruising and picnicking, eventually stopping at a public dock not far away from their home slip and camping for the night. Those were happy days, he remembered, back when he still had Kate's love and trust.

While Mike enjoyed simple family sailing, his tennis partner and friend, Dave Holland, had gotten deeply involved with racing. Occasionally Mike crewed for Dave in local races, learning much about sailing and boat handling from Dave. Once, when a crewman suddenly became ill, Mike had taken his place in a Trans-Pacific race. They'd had a wonderful, though exhausting, trip to Hawaii, and

Mike had always wished he could retrace the passage at a more leisurely pace.

When the children entered high school, Kate and Mike decided to stay closer to home. Though Dave continued to sail, Mike sold the family boat. The Langstons never again sailed as a family. This morning, walking along the dock, Mike wondered why not. A gull dove low over the water, crying as she fell, and Mike glanced up just as she scooped some treasure from the surface of the dark, sparkling water.

"Mornin'," a voice called. "You look lost."

A man in a worn flannel shirt sat with his back to the sun, sanding teak trim. He stood up as he spoke to Mike.

Mike stopped. "Good morning," he answered, smiling. Mike might miss sailing, but he would never miss boat maintenance. Mike hadn't yet found any slip numbers, and he had to admit that he needed help. He shifted his bag to his other hand. "You're more right than you know." He laughed. "Could you tell me how to find slip 131?"

"Sure," the man answered, scratching the top of his gray head. "Just go down to the end of this dock," he began, waving a sheet of folded sandpaper. "Then take a right around the corner. Should be the third or fourth dock off the left side."

Walking away, Mike gave a little wave. "Thanks."

Following the man's directions, Mike discovered that the boats farther from the parking lot were bigger and more expensive than those tied closer in. What kind of vessel had David purchased? Along this dock, owners proudly labeled each slip with engraved plaques. Without further help, Mike found the row he sought. Slip 131 had a beautiful bronze plaque set into concrete. *Slip 131*, it read, *Dave and Valerie Holland.*

Mike glanced up from the sign to the boat and felt a wave of surprise. There, floating majestically beside the dock, sat a startlingly beautiful white cutter. Mike guessed her to be nearly forty-five feet long, with a spacious cabin and a roomy midship cockpit. Mike gave a low, appreciative whistle, and in response Dave's head popped out from below the dodger. His sandy brown hair stood on end, and he had grease smudged across one cheek.

He grinned. "Like it?"

"She's beautiful," Mike said with genuine enthusiasm. "If I'd known you made this much money doing dentistry, I'd have gone back to dental school years ago."

"Yeah, and that coming from a real poverty-stricken beggar." Dave chuckled. His head disappeared below, and when he came up the companionway he wiped his hands on a blue mechanic's rag. "So stop your gawking and come aboard the *Second Chance*," he said, waving Mike on deck with the rag.

Mike reached for a lifeline and climbed on. The boat barely swayed in response. Shaking his friend's hand, he said, "She's beautiful, Dave. When can I start the tour?"

"How about now?" Dave smiled broadly. "She's forty-five feet, six inches long. A Liberty Cutter, built by Shin Fa. Handles like butter on hot toast."

"When did you buy it?"

"Val and I bought her in Texas. Brought it home last spring. Took two vacations to get it all the way home."

"Must have set you back a chunk."

"Too many root canals to count." He smiled again and put his hands on his hips. Mike nearly laughed out loud. His giant friend stood in the cockpit bursting with pride. Wearing blue plaid shorts gathered below his bulging tummy with a black leather belt, knobby knees peeked out below the hem of his long shorts. His hairy legs, particularly thin for a man of his bulk, were punctuated with dark socks and the most enormous Top-Siders Mike had ever seen. Above all this he wore an unbuttoned yellow Hawaiian print shirt, exposing a badly stained T-shirt. For a moment Mike imagined what smug remark Kate might make about Dave's appearance. *Something like "I hope Valerie dresses him for work,"* he thought.

Dave began the tour, gesturing to the sunken space containing the large aluminum wheel. "Well, you've seen the cockpit," he said, waving his hand wildly. "But did you see the autopilot? I had that installed last summer. Brand new."

Mike noted comfortable mats on the cockpit benches and bent to lift one. "Storage," Dave said. "You know, emergency kit. Abandon ship accessories. Flotation markers. Flares. Stuff like that."

"What kind of engine?" Mike looked out over the stern.

"Not so fast." Dave wagged an index finger. "Everyone knows you save the best for last. The engine room has to be last. Come on down to the cabin." Dave turned sideways and led the way down steep companionway stairs. Belowdecks, Mike admired the blond wood lining the main salon. He'd never seen a large boat with more storage than this. Cabinets lined every wall.

Clearly Dave intended this to be a man's tour. He had no intention of admiring the woodwork. They moved first to the forward cabin, where Dave opened the door to the forward head. Behind the marine toilet, he demonstrated the sail storage compartment accessible from both the deck and the cabin. After this, he proudly showed off the galley and its large refrigeration unit and three-burner stove. Mike admired the double sink and the storage lockers located under the floorboards. The cabin featured a roomy couch and a broad wooden table.

At the navigation station, Dave stopped to demonstrate the radio, his seaboard laptop, and other technical amenities. He culminated his tour of the domestic area by showing Mike the aft cabin and the master head.

"See?" he said, stepping inside the fiberglass enclosure. "Enough room to stand up—even for me. And no weenie little toilet to sit on while you shower. No, sir. In here, there's a whole bench. You can sit and soap to your heart's content."

Dave clearly valued a roomy bathroom. Mike smiled. "Now *that* makes the whole boat worth buying."

"Absolutely. If you're gonna spend a few weeks on board, you gotta have room to spread out. Be comfortable."

"Weeks? You guys planning to spend weeks on this thing?"

"Val and I are taking three months to do part of the South Pacific. That's all we'll be able to do this year. It's been our dream for as long as I can remember. So I just hired a kid out of UCLA to cover the office for me, and as soon as he passes the state boards, I'm outta here."

"Why not go after you retire?"

"I could wait till then," he agreed, nodding, "but who knows if I'll live that long? Sailing is really a sport. I don't want to wait until I'm too old to be safe. Besides, I think it'll be kind of romantic, you know? Cruising the palm-lined beaches of the Pacific Islands."

"I've always wished I could do that," Mike said. "But our business wouldn't allow it. I just can't be gone that long."

"This could be our last opportunity to fulfill our dream," Dave slapped his back. "I'm going for it."

"So that's why you named her *Second Chance?*"

Dave laughed. "Actually, that was her name when we found her."

"No kidding?"

"Yeah, apparently the owner had always wanted to circumnavigate the world. But his first boat was lost in a dock fire. He bought this one with his insurance money and named her *Second Chance.*"

"So the boat has been around the world?"

Dave chuckled again. "He never made it. Turned out his wife couldn't handle the cruising life. He had to sell, and we got to buy."

Mike couldn't help but notice the parallel in his own life. He'd lost everything too; but no one insured relationships. His only chance was to salvage what he'd lost. He shook himself from his own morose thoughts. "So what will you do with the boat after this trip?"

"Not sure. May dry-dock it for the hurricane season and go back next year. Or I could have it shipped home. Depends on how things go." He stepped out of his roomy bathroom and closed the door. "Maybe I'll just sell the practice and never come back." He had a dreamy, faraway look that surprised Mike.

Dave had never shared anything like this before, and it took Mike by surprise. To Mike, work was what you did—full steam ahead—until you finally dropped dead in the saddle. But he also felt something more than surprise. With a pang of guilt, Mike admitted to himself: He felt envy.

The hours and years he'd devoted to his business had paid off handsomely. Yet in this moment, it hit him how the business had given back nothing of lasting value. Sacrificing everything to grow a business had cost Mike exactly that. Everything. The now-familiar feeling of heaviness filled his stomach and his heart.

"Ahoy, maties!" a voice called from dockside. Dave smiled, excused himself, and slid sideways past Mike to head up the companionway stairs. Clearly, Dave was expecting someone. It hadn't occurred to Mike that they might have company.

"Rick, good to see you," Dave called cheerfully. "Get on board, and we can shove off."

Mike followed Dave upstairs and pulled himself onto the deck. Still under cover of the dodger, Mike peeked out through a plastic window and recognized the man standing on the dock, grinning foolishly, speaking with Dave. Rick Hansen, pastor of Sunset Community Church.

Suddenly, the thought of going on a day sail seemed like a very bad idea.

———

"Honey, that woman is back." Ray Taylor's wife knelt on the couch in her living room, peering through a tiny viewing space she'd created by pinching the center of the drapes with her fingers. She tipped her head to one side to adjust her viewpoint. "And the sheriff is with her."

From the kitchen, Ray poured coffee into a large mug. "Good," he said. "I can't be bothered trying to throw food over the fence to those stupid dogs anymore." He stepped into the living room and paused directly behind his wife where he could supervise the situation.

From over her shoulders, he saw a police cruiser parked on the street directly behind the Humane Society truck. Parked together, the two vehicles blocked the neighbor's driveway. Shannon, again wearing jeans and her hair in a clip, sauntered over to the cruiser. A tall dark-haired officer got out of the cruiser and followed her up the driveway toward the backyard of the rental house. "I think I'll go over and see if they need my help."

"Don't be silly. They don't need an old man's help." Dropping the drape in place, she turned to face her husband. "You've done everything that you can. Now just let them do their jobs."

Ray looked into his wife's pale blue eyes and saw a glimmer of stubborn determination. "Those dogs aren't any threat to anyone now," he said. "They're barely alive."

"Ray, just stay here."

"I'll only be a minute." He pulled his hooded sweatshirt from the hook in the hallway and opened the front door. "If they really don't need me, I'll be right back." The door closed solidly behind him. Before he'd stepped onto his driveway, the drapes at the living room window parted again, and his wife's nose and mouth were clearly visible from the yard. Ray felt a shiver of irritation. *Seventy-two years old and she still wants to mother me,* he thought, zipping the sweatshirt up to his neck.

Next door, the sheriff's officer stood bent over the gate into the neighbor's backyard. He held long-handled bolt cutters just above a heavy padlock. Ray nodded at the woman standing behind him. "Morning, Shannon."

"Good morning, Mr. Taylor." She smiled. "This is Officer Gordon."

The man struggling with the padlock stopped working long enough to look up and nod. As he fought with the lock, his forearms bulged.

"You could just cut a hole in the fence," Ray offered.

Shannon smiled. "No, we'd like to be able to shut the place up after we're done." She tipped her head at the officer. "We're responsible after we break in."

With an audible snap, the cutters broke through the padlock. "There we go," the officer said. He stood and pulled the lock from the fence. "After you, Shannon." He leaned over the gate and slid the latch open. The gate swung into an unkempt yard. Grass, unmowed through the latter part of the fall, stuck up in thick clumps. Though most of the grass had yellowed over the winter, large fuzzy sections of healthy moss made patches of brilliant green.

"One more lock to go," Shannon said, lifting his toolbox for him. "Hurry, Marcus. Those poor dogs are in really bad shape." They proceeded through the gate in front of Ray.

Moments later, while the whining shepherds watched, they broke the padlock on the kennel. As soon as the door opened, the dogs' demeanor changed. Their passivity suddenly became fierce anger, violent territorialism. Barking and threatening, the dogs rushed the gate.

"What happened?" Marcus asked as Shannon backed away immediately and slammed the door closed.

"Starving animals don't change. Their personality only gets magnified by the illness."

"Well, then," Ray volunteered, "you guys are in for a real struggle. Those dogs are demons."

"We're going to need the rabies pole," Shannon said. "I'll go get it." She hurried to her truck. "Be right back."

From just outside the dog run, Ray and the sheriff's officer exchanged pained glances. The smell from the kennel threatened to seize Ray's stomach and turn it inside out. He backed several steps upwind and turned his nose to the breeze. The kennel smelled much worse than he'd anticipated. He hoped Shannon would hurry.

She returned carrying a long aluminum pole with a wire noose hanging from one end. "I'll need you to manage the door, Mr. Taylor," she said. "And, Marcus, once I get this dog all the way to the truck, I'll need your help to coax him in."

Ray suspected that the sheriff would have to do more than coax.

While Ray opened the kennel door, she slid the pole inside. The dogs, barking and growling, charged the pole, their paws stiff in front of them. One dog managed to grab the wire noose with his teeth and pull. It seemed to Ray as if he might drag Shannon into the kennel for dinner. In spite of his own good intentions, Ray wanted to slam the door shut and let the dogs starve.

Shannon spoke a litany of soothing words, her voice high and feminine. "Oh, baby, come on," she urged. "Let me take you out for some dinner, huh, sweetie?" With a perfectly timed lunge, she managed to get the surprised dog to let go, and in one movement she had his neck held tightly in the wire loop. She backed away from the kennel, step by slow step, dragging the growling, complaining dog toward the door.

At the same time, Ray backed up, holding the door with one arm as she dragged the dog outside. The sheriff, standing on the other side of the door, dropped the latch into place. "I'd rather manage criminals," he mumbled, following her to the truck.

When they arrived at the truck, Shannon had already opened the door of a crate. Deftly she used the pole to lift the dog's head and neck up. At the same moment, Marcus lifted the dog's rump and gave a shove. The dog had no choice but to follow. With the dog inside, Shannon managed to pull the noose free and slam the door behind the shepherd. "One down," she said, locking the cage. "Good job, Marcus. You can start breathing again now." She slapped him on the shoulder and headed back for the second shepherd.

Thankfully, the second dog seemed less inclined to fight. Whether more weak from starvation or having learned a lesson from his kennelmate, the shepherd even jumped into the van without any help from Officer Gordon.

Shannon locked the second container and turned to meet the two men as they exited the backyard. "Well, that's that. I'll have the vet take a look at them as soon as we get back." She stuck out her hand, "Thanks for helping, Marcus. I know you'd rather be cruising for speeders." He shook it, smiling.

They all walked toward the police car. "Now I still have to find out who the owners are," Shannon said, crossing her arms over her chest. "Mr. Taylor, are you certain you have no idea who lives here?"

"Never met him, officially," Ray answered. "The house has been a rental for about ten years. People come and go all the time." He stopped walking to stroke the stubble of his beard. "I only spoke to the fellow once, when he parked his Honda in front of my driveway. I couldn't get my Winnebago out."

At that moment Marcus Gordon suddenly stopped. Something Ray said seemed to trouble him. The rental, maybe?

"A Honda?" Marcus asked. "Did you say a Honda?" He put one hand on his hip, and with the other, he rubbed the back of his neck. "What did I just read about a Honda?"

"You got me," Shannon quipped. "I didn't know you guys could read."

His look gave her an unspoken rebuke. "No, really. A rental. And starving animals." He dropped his hand. "Mr. Taylor, do you remember what color the Honda was?"

"Of course. It only happened about two weeks ago. The car was blue. The guy had a blue Honda."

Fourteen

ON SATURDAY MORNING, Kate's father had his first appointment at the University Fitness Center Cardiac Rehab Program. The intake process began with an appointment with a registered nurse. Normally the recovery group had a lengthy waiting list, but her father's many years of teaching and coaching gained him an early entry. Most people in their community considered Kate's father a basketball legend. For once, being a legend paid off.

By ten-thirty, Patrick sat in the passenger seat of her rented car, kissing her mother through the car window. Kate tapped one finger impatiently on the steering wheel and looked with feigned interest at a bush planted near the driveway.

"Now, Patrick, please be careful, dear," Rosemarie said, stepping back from the car. She put her hands deep into her apron pockets. From the driver's seat, Kate saw her mother's hands clenched in tight fists through the apron fabric.

"Rosie, I'm not going down there to play full-court basketball," her father answered patiently. "I'm just going to meet the nurse and learn about the program."

Rosemarie smiled, a patient, cooperative smile. But the smile did not reach her eyes, where tears threatened to spill over.

"We'll be back in time for his afternoon nap," Kate added. *That is, if we ever leave the driveway.*

"Be careful driving, dear."

"Right, Mom. Been driving for thirty years now." Kate leaned forward to grin at her mother through the window.

Patrick patted the hand Kate rested on the gearshift. "Better head out." He smiled and tipped his head slightly to indicate his overanxious wife. This morning's outing had become far more traumatic than it ought to have been. The disagreement started, though gently, over breakfast. Rosemarie did not want to let Patrick leave for his appointment without her. Patrick wanted Kate to take him. Through the entire episode, Kate remained neutral. This fierce protectiveness in her otherwise quiet and gentle mother surprised and amused Kate. She enjoyed watching. In the end, of course, Patrick won.

Kate drove through town without speaking, always aware of her fragile and ever-weary father. She drove carefully, avoiding potholes, changing lanes slowly, and turning wide, soft corners. Pretending to concentrate on the traffic, Kate kept one eye secretly focused on her father. She watched his hand—his fingers, actually. Kate could tell by the position of his fingers how he felt. If they lay completely relaxed, she felt safe. She took her time driving to the rehab clinic.

When she arrived, Kate parked and walked her father inside. A nurse, who appeared to be half Kate's age, met them in the waiting area, wearing Hawaiian print scrubs and high-tech running shoes. Patrick told Kate to go waste an hour. "There's a new outlet mall in town, down on the river," he said. "I'll be fine here."

"We have a comfortable lounge," the nurse added. "He can wait for you there after we're finished." The perky box-blonde smiled and took Patrick's arm, as though there could be no further discussion. Suddenly Kate realized what her mother must feel whenever she surrendered Patrick to the medical profession. She watched him walk slowly down a long empty hall beside the nurse. When the two disappeared into a doorway on the left, Kate felt a sudden, strong urge to sit in a chair and hover until he returned.

———

Rick threw his gear bag onto the deck and climbed aboard. "You can stow that below," Dave called from the wheel. He flipped switches and turned the key. Obediently the boat engine turned over with a throaty rumble below the deck. A cloud of blue exhaust puffed up behind the boat. "Mike," Dave called again, "how 'bout you take care of the lines?"

Mike dropped over the side and landed with a thud on the dock. He released the bowline first and threw it aboard. Then he unleashed the stern line, dropping the tail below his feet. Dave threw the spring lines to the dock, and Mike coiled them cleanly. As Dave pushed the throttle forward, Mike held the stern line, walking the sleek sailboat out of the slip. Just as her midsection cleared the end of the slip, Mike jumped on board.

"Thanks, Mike." Dave's head bobbed like a sandpiper, glancing around the harbor. He kept one hand on the wheel and the other on the throttle, turning the long hull tightly, efficiently, between the docks.

Mike walked forward, pulling fenders out of the water and dropping them into frames waiting on deck. The motor chugged, and they progressed slowly out of the marina toward the breakwater. In the eastern sky, a low-hanging sun cast a fierce reflection off the sea. Mike tucked his Oakland A's hat low on his forehead and pushed his sunglasses up higher on his nose.

Though still early, heavy boat traffic headed out of the marina, and Mike kept his position forward, watching the water for Dave. When they had safely cleared the jetty, Dave prepared to raise the sails by swinging the boat into the wind and cutting the engine to Neutral. Mike glanced to the top of the mast, high above the deck. There, floating freely above them, a tiny arrow pointed into the wind.

"All right, let's bring up the mainsail," Dave called. Rick, holding on to the edge of the dodger, seemed unsure of what action to take. Dave noticed. "Rick, why don't you step back here and start to take the cover off the main?" Rick stepped onto the rear bench of the cockpit and began untying the canvas loops holding the sail cover down. As he untied, he tucked the loops into the back pocket of his jeans. Mike moved to where the boom attached to the mast and began removing the cover. While his crew worked, Dave steadied the loose end of the boom. Removing the cover, Mike began folding it, working from the mast toward the back of the boat. Rick, who was folding from the other direction, met him at the middle, and for one awkward moment the two men faced one another, each holding a length of dark green canvas. Mike glared. Rick smiled.

"Good," Dave called approvingly. "Why don't you stow that, Rick? You can put it in the cabin. Mike, could you hoist the main for me?" Mike, grateful for the interruption, shoved his end of the canvas into Rick's chest and worked his way forward along the narrow walkway. He attached a clip to the top of the mainsail and fed the sail into the groove on the main mast. Mike hadn't hoisted a sail in years and never one as big as this. Certain the lines were clear, he moved back to the cockpit and wrapped the halyard around the winch. Then he began the vigorous pulling required to raise the sail. It felt wonderful—the wind, the motion, the work. *Today could have been healing*, Mike thought. *If Rick had stayed home.*

As it was, today would not even be pleasant, let alone healing. Clearly, Dave had planned an ambush. Like all big-game hunters, Dave planned to trap and corner some unsuspecting animal. *And I'll bet I know who the quarry is*, Mike thought with resentment.

Pulling the last four feet of line felt like dragging a truck up Telegraph Hill by hand. His arms and back ached with effort. Mike had managed to raise the sail nearly to the top of the mast before he decided to use the winch handle.

"Great," Dave said, grinning. "Mike, would you adjust the main? She seems a little sloppy at the mast. And Rick, how about you let out the jib?"

"The jib?"

"That's the sail in front." Dave pointed at the roller fuller. Mike and Rick busied themselves with their appointed tasks, while Dave smiled liberally from the cockpit. *He missed his calling*, Mike thought. *Dave should have been a whaling captain. He'd have given Ahab a run for his money.*

With both sails fully up, Dave approved their work. "Take the jib, Mike," he instructed. "And Rick, you manage the main for me. Let the line out gently as the bow turns. When the wind catches, we'll be off and flying. All you have to do is tie her down and relax." Dave throttled up and put the engine in gear.

Mike smiled. Most captains would have cut the engine and used the sails to turn into the wind. But Dave seemed eager to be underway. When the boat turned to port, both sails filled, pushing them off to the right. The boat began to slide forward through calm water. Dave cut the engine, and the sudden silence seemed to be a physical relief. Only the clanking of rigging and the lapping of seawater could be heard from the deck of David Holland's *Second Chance*.

Dave settled into the cockpit seat. "All right, Mike, why don't you take the helm and set a course for Ayala Cove?"

"Aye, aye, Captain," Mike saluted jauntily.

"And, Mr. Hansen, you man the mainsail. I'll watch the jib."

"Aye, aye," Rick agreed, gazing up at the sail above him. Rick clearly had never been aboard a sailboat before. His face seemed forever frozen in a delighted, almost childlike grin. Looking all around, he could not seem to absorb enough. Soon he and Dave sat forward, heads close, shouting questions and answers about the boat.

That suited Mike just fine. He loved the feel of Dave's new boat, maneuverable but not overly so. He liked the sleek, comfortable design. If Dave and Rick decided to spend the whole day talking back and forth and ignoring him, Mike would be very happy. He liked feeling the boat respond to his hand, feeling the light cold wind blow over the water. He decided to enjoy the day, no matter who had been invited to come along.

———

"For heaven's sake," Kate chided herself out loud, "my father is certainly old enough to go to an appointment alone." The receptionist paused in her typing and glanced up at Kate. Kate waved and said, "Be back in an hour."

For a moment, Kate stood in the parking lot wondering what to do. How could she kill an entire hour? She scolded herself for not bringing along a book, or at least stationery. She might have written to Keegan. At some point she would have to fully explain their mysterious phone conversation. But the thought of having to untangle the mess her life had become only made Kate overwhelmed with sadness. She would explain eventually. But certainly it would be easier when she understood it all herself. And for now, she did not.

She had started the car and pulled into the street before she remembered the huge bookstore that had recently moved into Lawrence, not far from the clinic. She could always get lost in a bookstore. And if nothing else, she could enjoy a cup of real coffee in the little café inside. No more of that disgusting decaffeinated stuff her mother brewed. Kate longed for leaded coffee, the kind that gave you a real boost. She turned onto Iowa Street, smiling to herself. *If I didn't know better, I'd think I was addicted.*

Only a few customers occupied the store so early in the morning. Kate bought coffee and began to browse. She ignored the Contemporary Fiction section and went straight to History and Travel. Browsing through titles, she wandered along the perimeter of the store, lost among the books. Occasionally, she pulled one from the shelf and leafed through the pages. Always, she replaced it and moved on. Eventually, she worked her way back to the center of the store where shoppers crowded the bargain book area. Kate looked through these titles quickly, hoping to find a gardening book her father might enjoy. As she came around a corner, she nearly ran into a tall woman with almost black hair. Coffee splattered the front of Kate's linen jumper.

"Oh, I am so sorry," the woman crooned.

"No problem." Kate brushed at the spots with her napkin.

"But it is. I've got it all over your—Kate? Kate, is that you?"

Kate looked up. The woman did not look familiar, yet there was something in her voice. Her eyebrows rose, communicating her uncertainty.

"Wendy. Wendy Stoltenberg." The woman held out one hand. "We went to school together."

Suddenly, something about the squint of the brown eyes, the freckles on the nose, and the tilt of the chin brought memories flooding back. Kate and Wendy had been lab partners in home economics. Together, they had "dip, level, and poured" their way through baking powder biscuits, yeast bread, pie dough, and every other requirement of high school girls thirty years ago. Neither of them had enjoyed cooking. But they'd managed to giggle their way through their entire senior year without being expelled from class.

"Wendy, I can't believe it. Running into you like this." Kate smiled. She took Wendy's hand and pulled her into a gentle embrace.

"I work here now," Wendy said, gesturing to the store. "What are you doing in town? Visiting the folks?"

"Yeah, Dad's been sick. I came to help Mom."

"Oh, I'm sorry. Do you have time to talk?"

"But you're working."

"Just let me tell someone. I'll take my break now—with you." She hurried away toward the checkout area.

Moments later, they sat in comfortable overstuffed chairs in the coffee shop. "So, Kate, what have you been up to? I haven't seen you since our last reunion."

"Well, I've been doing some work for a small sportswear company in the Bay Area."

"What kind of work? And what about your family, the kids?"

"I do their catalogues for them," Kate smiled. "The kids are great. Keegan is enrolled in law school, and Drew just started a job as a civil engineer in Salem, Oregon."

"Oh man, life changes when the kids leave for good, doesn't it?" She sipped at her coffee, which must have been hot. She grimaced and blotted at her lips with her napkin.

"I guess it does," Kate agreed. "What about you? When did you move back to Lawrence?"

"Three years ago. I left Daniel." She said it matter-of-factly, with cold precision, as she might mention selling a car.

"I'm sorry, Wendy."

"Don't be. Best thing I ever did." She toyed with her napkin, gazing dreamily at the table.

"Why did you leave? You guys were childhood sweethearts."

"I think that's it. I just got bored. He settled into this horrible rut, as though I didn't exist anymore. The kids left, and I felt like I couldn't be any more alone than I already was with him. So I left."

"You divorced him?"

"Yep. I'm not really sure he even noticed. Anyway, I work here, which might be better if I didn't spend half of every paycheck on books." She laughed. "Our kids are all out of state, so it didn't matter where I decided to live. I've always loved Lawrence, so I came home."

Kate couldn't help wondering if Wendy had told her the whole truth. But she didn't feel comfortable asking for more information. Tactfully, she changed the subject. "What is Dan up to now?"

"I don't know, really. He hasn't remarried, but that's not too surprising."

"What do you mean?"

"Well, dating in your late forties isn't quite the thrill it was as a teenager. The closer I get to fifty, the more I think maybe I'll live alone the rest of my life."

"That isn't so terrible. You're happy, aren't you?"

"Oh sure. I'm happy by myself." Wendy's answer sounded

cheerful enough. But her eyes told a different story, a much sadder, much lonelier story. And though the two women parted with a hug and a promise to keep in touch, Kate drove back to the cardiac rehab clinic with a new and painful feeling in her own heart.

Would her eyes someday betray the same haunting loneliness? Did they already?

Fifteen

DAVE PROMISED HIS CREW a mouth-watering lunch of broiled steak, as soon as they properly tied up. But the way things were going, Mike had just about given up all hope of food. In spite of this, his hunger had become an unrelenting elephant inside him, and he could almost smell barbecued beef. He heard his stomach growl.

Though Mike had been instructed to aim the big sailboat for the docking buoy, Dave's thunderous backside, hanging from the bow in front of him, blocked all view of the water. How could Mike aim for a buoy he could not see? Silently, he coaxed his friend. *Catch the buoy, Dave; I'll starve to death if I have to come around again.*

He turned the boat directly into the wind, hoping to slow her down. But the massive sailboat slid forward fast—too fast. Dave raised an index finger and pointed to his left, shouting, "Port, helmsman. Hard to port."

Rick smiled conspiratorially at Mike, who eagerly turned the wheel. If there was any way to catch that stupid float, Mike was determined they would.

"I got it," Dave yelled in triumph. "We're on."

Mike glanced at the horizon, gauging the direction and speed of the wind. Winds remained light, perhaps five knots. Glancing at the depth sounder, he concluded they had plenty of leeway for a leisurely and safe lunch. "Drop the sails, Captain?"

"Drop the sails." Dave came around the side of the deck, balancing like a black bear on a tightrope. "And now, gentlemen, I will dazzle you with my culinary expertise."

Shortly, Dave stood over sizzling steaks, with a meat fork in one hand and an ice-cold Coca-Cola in the other. He wore a white barbecue apron tied around his middle, the straps barely reaching around his girth. Mike and Rick relaxed in the cockpit nearby, each holding a can of pop and sharing a deep bowl of sour-cream-and-onion chips.

The sun rose high, and in spite of soft fluffs of white clouds, the morning had warmed to a comfortable seventy-two degrees—unusual for early spring. The wind on the water kept things chilly, and all three men wore windbreakers. But there was more than just cool air between them.

Mike and Rick exchanged few words. Instead, Mike leaned against the wall of the cockpit, trying to appear relaxed, yet wondering when it would happen.

Perhaps now. Over lunch. Yes, that would be the ideal time for Rick and Dave to bring up Mike's "moral failure." They would do it together, seeming innocent enough, trapping him in his infidelity and then going in for the spiritual kill.

They ate steaks, potato salad from a grocery deli, and fruit that Dave brought out in a Tupperware container. They followed it all with thick wedges of boxed cheesecake. "Oh man, cheesecake," Rick said longingly. "This is absolutely my biggest weakness."

Rick didn't appear to have any weaknesses. His long frame was both lean and fit. Mike tried hard not to envy his young good looks. Rick, barely older than Mike's own son, had taken the senior pastor position at their church five years after graduating from seminary.

Mike watched while Rick made an event out of his first bite. He seemed to roll the cake around on his tongue, leaning back and immersing himself in the rich, sweet taste. The sunshine, reflecting off the water, had turned his broad forehead pink. He looked relaxed and happy in spite of the burn.

Smiling broadly, Rick sighed. "Thank goodness I don't get this every day." His smile seemed almost disarming. Moaning, he continued, "I'd weigh four hundred pounds by next Tuesday."

After they stowed their trash and put away their leftovers, dishes, glasses, and the grill, Dave patted his palms on his thighs. "Well, fellas, what do you think, time to head back?"

"Yeah, I should," Rick agreed. "Tamara will be going nuts by herself with the babies." He drank the last bit of his pop. "What about Valerie, does she mind you taking an afternoon with the guys?"

"Not at all. She has months of this to look forward to." Dave stood and took Mike's empty pop can.

"Hey, Mike," Rick looked directly at him, his eyes looking innocent. "Where's Kate been lately? I missed her this last Sunday."

Here it comes. Mike felt his shoulders tense and the muscles in his jaw tighten. Despite the fact that he'd anticipated this and believed it to be the purpose for the whole trip, he didn't know how to answer. No words surfaced.

"She's in Kansas," Dave intervened for him. "Visiting her folks."

"Oh, well, when you talk to her, tell her I missed her." Rick's eyes reminded Mike of the color of a Caribbean lagoon. His smile seemed genuine enough. "I haven't been here long, but I've always appreciated Kate. Such a sunny lady. So much to give."

Dave just stood there, unmoving.

"So, all right, guys," Mike said, "say it. I know you brought me out here to nail me. So do it. Get it over with. I know that's what you've had in mind all along. I knew you were after me last Sunday in church. So here I am. Let me have it."

Rick looked stunned, as though he'd been slapped. "What are you talking about?" He glanced at Dave. "What is he saying?"

Dave shrugged, looking uncomfortable. He sat down beside Mike.

"You know exactly what I'm talking about," Mike answered. Though he'd promised himself to stay calm, he'd already lost it. He felt all the anger from last Sunday rise from his gut. The pent-up tension made him wish he could go running, sweat it out somehow.

"Actually, Mike, I don't think he does," Dave said calmly, quietly, from the cockpit bench. Looking back and forth between the two men, he continued, "And I'm not really sure what makes you think that."

Mike fought to keep his voice calm. "I sat through that whole sermon last week. I knew it was about me." He stood confronting the two of them. "A woman in adultery. You told him, didn't you, Dave?"

"No, Mike. I didn't."

Only the wind, gently rocking the lines against the mast, broke the silence of the three men. Rick stared at Mike with an expression of utter confusion. Then suddenly, understanding dawned. His eyes widened and his lips tightened. Rick let a long, slow sigh escape from between tight lips.

Mike crossed his arms over his chest and stared at the shoreline just over Rick's head, trying to look tough, unfazed. In truth, he felt deeply embarrassed. From his own bottomless shame, Mike had assumed the guilt of both his friend and his pastor. How wrong he had been. A deep burning sensation rose in his neck and covered his cheeks.

Rick finally found his voice. "Mike, I'm sorry. I didn't know."

"I can't believe you think I'd go straight to the pastor to report everything you told me." Dave sounded hurt and angry.

"I'm sorry, Dave. It just looked like too big a coincidence." Mike spread his hands and sat with a thud on the bench. "First the sermon, then this morning the pastor just happens to come sailing with us. I thought you guys planned this. A group confrontation. I thought you brought me along to try to get me to clean up my act or something." He glanced away again. "I misunderstood."

"It sounds like you've already come to the end of your 'act.' " Rick's voice took a gentle sympathetic tone that brought Mike close to tears.

His relationship with Cara Maria had been such a mistake, such a huge mistake. One that he couldn't undo. And though he'd tried so hard, Kate still refused to speak to him. "I don't know what to do. Kate won't speak to me. But what should I expect? It's like you said in church. Adultery. She can't ever forgive me." He leaned forward and covered his face with his hands, pressing hard on his eyelids. The weight of his enormous loss seemed to come crashing over him again. "I don't know what to do," Mike whispered.

"Well, for one thing, I think you'd better start taking notes on the sermon."

"What?" Mike looked up to find Rick's blue eyes twinkling over a hesitant smile.

"The sermon last Sunday happened to be about adultery. But you missed the point. The heart of the message was forgiveness. Not condemnation. Not judgment. Not rejection." Rick leaned forward and patted Mike's shoulder. "I can see you weren't listening. Not that I blame you, actually."

Mike looked at Dave, who was stretched out against the cockpit, soaking up the sun. The soft smile on his face told Mike that he enjoyed his friend's intense discomfort. "What are you smiling about?" Mike snapped.

"Oh, nothing. I just remember feeling exactly like you do right now."

"Mike, listen, God doesn't ignore adultery," Rick said. "But He doesn't use it as an excuse to throw us away either. I mean, think about it. He's a perfect, holy God. Of course sexual sin offends Him. It's very serious. The guys who caught the adulterous woman were counting on that. They figured Jesus would 'off her.' What they didn't understand was the power of forgiveness."

His young pastor's vocabulary amused Mike. But he shook his head, refusing to accept such a simple explanation. He'd thrown his marriage away. "How can I ever hope to be forgiven?"

"God is in the forgiveness business. If He can forgive you, Kate can too." The silence between the men lengthened while Mike considered his pastor's words. The wind whistled, and the sun peeked out from behind a small cloud, brightening and warming the boat deck. At last Rick said, "But you can't give up, Mike. You must pursue her, just as God pursues men."

"How? She won't even answer my calls."

"Why can't you go see her?"

"In Kansas?"

"Mike, last I heard, airplanes fly to Kansas all the time. All you need is a ticket."

A strong current pushed against the side of the boat. The three men sat together silently while the boat bobbed in the tiny waves of a changing tide. They had moved passed the angry silence of suspicion into thoughtful consideration.

"Well," Dave said, slapping his thighs, "since we've settled that issue, what do you say we get this raft moving?" Rick offered his hand to Mike. They shook hands, and Mike stood.

"It won't be easy, you know. And you can come talk to me anytime," Rick said. "There is hope, Mike."

"And I'm living proof of it," Dave agreed, grinning broadly. "Now, go cut us loose, will ya? Before this tide washes us out to sea."

Ray Taylor could not understand what he might have said to grab the sheriff's attention. But when Marcus Gordon held his index finger in the air and sidestepped quickly around Shannon, Ray knew something was up. As Marcus began running toward the cruiser, Ray followed as fast as he could.

Sliding into the driver's seat of the car, Gordon picked up the microphone on his radio. "Dispatch, this is Bravo 471," he said, his voice businesslike.

"This is Dispatch. Come in, Bravo 471," a female voice answered.

"Yeah, Marcus Gordon here. Yeah. Hey, I'm out on a call with the Humane Society, and I've run into a question. I'd like some details on an accident. Could you check with the State Patrol and find out if anyone has identified the driver killed on the Narrows a couple weeks ago?"

"Stand by, 471. I'll try to get that information."

For a moment, it felt to Ray as though he'd become a participant in a scene from one of his favorite cop shows. He couldn't help the excitement he felt as he watched Marcus tapping away on the keys of his laptop computer.

"Bravo 471, this is Dispatch."

"Go ahead."

"That is a negative. WSP tells me that the driver has not yet been identified."

"Can you tell me again what kind of car he was driving?"

"Yes, I'm looking at the report right now. A navy blue '96 Honda Accord."

"Bingo. Thanks, Dispatch. By the way, did the driver have a picture on his license?"

"Affirmative."

"Did the picture resemble the driver?"

"I'd have to check with the investigating officer."

"Is the picture in the accident report?"

"Affirmative. The report includes a photo."

"Can I have the report number?"

As the woman's voice called off the numbers, Ray watched Marcus bring up the blurry image of a man's face on his small computer screen. The sheriff suddenly turned the screen toward Ray. "Is this your neighbor?"

Ray squinted and tipped his head so that he could focus through the lower portion of his glasses. "Yep. That looks a lot like the guy who lived here. Can't say for sure. But seems an awful lot like him."

Shannon glanced from Ray to Marcus, obviously confused about what exactly the sheriff had discovered.

"I think that's all we need." Officer Gordon shut his computer and set it on the seat next to him.

"I don't understand," Ray said. "Why is my neighbor's picture in your computer?"

"Because, if I'm right, your neighbor is dead," came the quiet response. "Killed in that accident out on the bridge."

Ray felt the impact of the news go through his whole body. He glanced toward the truck, where the dogs inside had fallen silent. "Well, that explains the dogs."

Marcus spoke to Shannon. "I'll call for backup. They'll send a squad car with a better picture. We'll try to get confirmation from the neighbors and the utility company."

She nodded, her face serious.

Marcus turned to Ray. "This may also explain why he parked his car in front of your driveway," he said.

Ray looked up questioning. "What do you mean?"

"Stolen," Marcus said. "He parked in front of your house so that you'd be questioned if anyone spotted the car. You'd be interrogated, and he'd have time to run before anyone figured out the car was his."

"Oh boy. Better not tell Jeannie all this." Ray glanced back and forth between Shannon and Officer Gordon. "She spends all her time looking out the front window as it is. You tell her about this, and I'll never get her away from that hole in the curtain." He ran one gnarled hand through his thinning white hair. "Nope. This one, we'd better not tell Jeannie."

Sixteen

PATRICK'S APPOINTMENT left him exhausted. As a result, Kate and her parents spent a quiet Saturday afternoon at home. Patrick slept through most of it.

Sunday dawned cool, with heavy, low clouds. At breakfast, Patrick insisted on attending the early church service. "You can drive me directly to the front door and pick me up there after the service."

"But it's too much for you, Patrick. Too soon."

"Rosie," he pled, "nothing will do me more good than being with my family at church. I'll just sit in the back, and we'll sneak out when it's over."

Kate's mother eventually gave in. Patrick hugged her warmly, kissed her on the forehead, and sent her upstairs saying, "Now, you'd better start getting ready, or we'll miss the anthem."

Moments after the benediction, Kate and her parents struggled through a crowd of well-wishers, handshakes, and hugs, the three of them trying desperately to escape the foyer. Patrick's face tightened with fatigue, and he took slow, heavy steps through the throng.

Kate wished they'd brought a wheelchair. Even though her mother pulled the family Oldsmobile into the covered driveway beyond the front doors, the distance to the car seemed like miles to Kate. She could only guess how it felt to her father. She held his left arm, feeling him lean heavily against her as he walked. If only Kate could get him home so he could rest undisturbed in the comfort of his recliner. There he would be free to sleep for the rest of the afternoon.

"Wait, Patrick," Charles Wold hurried toward them, wearing a broad smile and extending one hand. "So good to see you!" He shook her father's hand warmly.

"Good to be here," Patrick answered. Kate could barely hear his reply.

"We've been praying all week for you."

"Thank you. That means a great deal to me."

Charles carried on with a complete report of all the happenings at their latest Men's Committee meeting. Kate wanted to strike Charles with her purse. Why didn't he notice the exhaustion that nearly bent her father in half? Patrick waited graciously for Charles to finish, nodding appropriately as he listened. Eventually, Charles ran out of breath, promising to call and check on Patrick during the week. "I'd like that," her father answered. The two shook hands again, and Kate whisked Patrick away before anyone else could come up to them bursting with news.

She tucked her father into the front seat and pulled the seat belt across his lap. Too tired to resist, his head slumped back against the headrest, and he closed his eyes. This outing had been too much for him.

When Kate settled into the backseat, Rosemarie put the car in gear and pulled away. Kate saw her mother's face glance at her in the rearview mirror, and she recognized deep concern filling her mother's brown eyes.

Kate leaned forward, her hand on her father's shoulder. "Daddy, should we stop for something to eat on the way home?"

"Not hungry," he answered without opening his eyes.

Again, mother and daughter exchanged glances. Kate noticed how tightly her mother held the steering wheel and the tense position of her shoulders. *Mother is afraid*, Kate thought. Reaching forward, Kate gave her mother's arm a gentle squeeze. "We're almost home, Mom."

Rosemarie Killian managed a feeble smile. "I wish we'd stayed home. Your father could have certainly missed church this week."

Kate nodded at the face in the mirror. All the way home, Kate thought about her mother's devotion. She recognized it in hundreds of tiny ways. Today in her fear over Patrick's fatigue. Saturday morning in her refusal to let him out of her sight. She saw it in the elaborate chart she made to keep track of his medicines. Every morning Rosemarie carefully laid out his medicine in tiny piles along the kitchen counter. Then, with all the dosages on her list accounted for, she scooped the pills into a plastic pill dispenser. She would not tolerate having Patrick miss or delay a dose. She even set the kitchen timer to keep track of the schedule.

Years ago, Kate might have thought of her mother as weak or overdependent. Today, her mother's obvious concern deeply touched Kate. No. She felt more than touched; Kate felt envious.

Even in her best years with Mike, Kate hadn't felt the kind of passionate devotion she observed in her mother. And now, she never would.

As the landscape blurred by, Kate blinked back tears. She could not stop the thoughts that rushed through her mind with the speed of passing scenery. She remembered her early years with Mike. How excited he had been to start his own business. She thought about how happy she and Mike had been when they became parents. She remembered the nights he'd stayed up late to plan and scheme and worry about how to make the business grow.

Kate thought about the trappings that went along with children. She remembered those early years when a weekend away with the kids looked like a cross-country move. She remembered Mike carrying high chairs and playpens out to the car and how they would collapse together in laughter as he tried to stuff everything into the trunk. Kate remembered Mike suggesting they rent a moving van for a weekend at the ocean. She remembered weeks at Mount Hermon. Camping trips with church friends. How could he throw away so many happy memories? What did Cara Maria have that could possibly make him want to throw it all away?

Stabbed again by his betrayal, Kate wondered for the thousandth time how long she would wander in the land of unrelenting pain. Once again she imagined the pictures. Blinking hard, she tried to drive the images from her mind.

Kate brushed tears from her face and sat up in her seat. She had not made this choice. He had. Mike had chosen to throw everything away. Now Kate needed to let go. No more memories. No more wondering. They were done, finished. She made a silent vow to stop such worthless trails of meandering thoughts. She had to. She needed every ounce of energy to begin again. To start her life over.

As Kate's mother turned the final corner onto their street, Kate pulled a tissue from her purse and ran it along her lower eyelids. She did not want globs of black mascara to call attention to her tears. Crumpling the tissue, she stuffed it into her coat pocket. Her mother pulled into the driveway.

Gathering her things, Kate looked up at the front porch and gasped.

Mike sat on the front steps waiting for them.

Rosemarie Killian looked directly at Michael and said, "Now I wonder . . ." She turned off the engine, looked at the porch again, and cried out, "Oh, it's Mike. Patrick! Mike has come." Before Kate could reply, she heard her mother's seat belt bang against the car window. Rosemarie opened her car door and slid out of her seat all in a singular motion as she hurried toward the front steps. Mike came forward to meet her, wrapping her in his arms. From her seat in the car, Kate watched the two, wishing she didn't care that her mother seemed so glad to see Mike. Rosemarie fawned over him, and Mike accepted the attention with the grace of a long-lost son-in-law.

Trust me. Kate heard the voice again, and the sound of it—the strength of it—seemed to force the irritation out of her chest like the compression of air from a cushion.

Sighing, she released her own seat belt and got out of the car. She reached for her father's door and opened it, offering a hand. "Now, this is a surprise," he said softly, smiling up at Kate.

"It is to me."

Patrick pulled hard on the door and managed to drag himself out of the seat. "You okay?" she asked.

"I'm fine." He stood hesitating a moment. "Just a little weak in the legs." Finding his balance, he sighed, straightened, and started up the front walk. Kate slammed the car door. With no choice but to follow, she pulled her purse over her shoulder, shoved her hands deep into her coat pockets, and fell in step behind her father.

"Dad, how are you feeling?" Mike asked, coming forward, ex-tending his hand.

"Better, Mike. Much better." Patrick pulled Mike into his arms, giving him a long, warm embrace. "Glad you could come," he said softly into Mike's ear. Something about her father's affection irritated Kate. She felt a moment of betrayal, as though her father had not heard—or worse, had not believed—the story she told him. How could he show so much kindness, so much warmth, toward the man who betrayed his own daughter?

"Kate," Mike said, stepping toward her. He took her right hand gently and bent to kiss her cheek. Nothing in his action gave any indication of the tension between them. For this, at least, Kate felt grateful. The smell of Grey Flannel drifted to her nose. The same cologne she had bought him every Christmas since Drew started high school.

"Mike." Time seemed to stand still for a moment, her parents waiting awkwardly behind them.

"I brought you flowers," he said, turning back to the porch where he'd been sitting. He reached down and lifted a large bouquet of coral roses. "I don't know how fresh they are. I bought them at the airport." He handed the gift to Kate.

"Thanks." She sounded lame and she knew it. But she could think of nothing else to say. They stood there staring at one another until Kate, unable to bear it, glanced away. She coughed.

Her father broke the awkward silence. "Well, then, let's not stand out here. How 'bout we go inside?" With one arm, he made a sweeping gesture toward the front door. "The key, Rosie?"

"Oh, yes. My manners." Rosemarie fumbled with her key ring, searching for the correct one. At last, she stepped onto the porch and unlocked the door. The raised-panel door swung open quickly, and she stepped inside. Slipping off her raincoat, she said, "I have grilled chicken for salad and fresh rolls." She moved gracefully to the hall closet and draped her coat on a padded hanger. Lightly, she pulled the silk scarf from around her neck and slid it down one coat sleeve. "Daddy is exhausted," she said, hanging up her coat, "so let's have lunch right away. Then he can take a long nap." She hurried through the hallway to the kitchen door.

Her father closed the front door. "I think I'll just sit down a minute," he said. "I am a little tired."

"Good idea, Dad," Mike agreed. "Can I get you anything? Water?"

"No, thanks."

"Then, I'll help Mom with lunch." He pointed to the kitchen with his thumb and turned away.

Kate, left standing alone in the entry hall, still held her coat in one hand and the wrapped roses in the other. She'd never heard Mike offer to make lunch before. When she went through the kitchen to the back porch, her mother had Mike tying the back of her apron.

Kate found a tall crystal vase below her father's potting bench and rinsed it out in the garden tub. She unwrapped the roses and broke the rubber band holding the stems together. She opened a drawer and began to look for trimming scissors. The stems should be trimmed before being put in fresh water. What was she thinking? She slammed the drawer and turned to the roses. Picking them up in a heap, she stuffed them into the vase. *That's what I think of his flowers,* she thought. As she turned to go back into the house, she heard the voice again, *Trust me.*

"Oh, shut up," she said, loud enough to startle herself.

In the kitchen, Kate found her mother bending over the open refrigerator door, her apron tied neatly behind her, a platter of chicken breasts waiting on the counter. The sound of the vase hitting the kitchen counter caught her attention. "Oh, Kate, if you'll slice this," she said, gesturing to the plate, "Mike and I can put the salad together." She pulled green peppers, spinach, romaine lettuce, and boiled eggs from the refrigerator. "Here, Mike, why don't you start on the lettuce and spinach?"

"Sure," Mike agreed, turning to the sink with a bag of lettuce.

Careful not to touch Mike, Kate pulled a large knife from the block and slid a cutting board out from behind the sink. On the outside, Kate continued to help with lunch, completely unaffected by her husband's arrival. Inside she fumed. He had nerve, that much she had to give him. How dare he just show up like this, acting for all the world like nothing was wrong? What a fake!

But what else should she expect of Mike lately? Deception. Lies. Without her permission, the pictures appeared in her mind again— neatly lined up on her kitchen counter. She blinked fiercely, her heart pounding, her chest struggling with shallow trembling breaths. She would not cry. Not here. Not in front of him. Instead, she allowed her anger room to grow. Still holding the knife, she brushed at her left eye with the back of one hand, as though trying to scratch some inconvenient itch.

It made her even angrier to be standing here in the kitchen preparing lunch with him. Like nothing had happened. It wasn't chicken that Kate wanted to slice into tiny little pieces. No, she'd like to use the knife on Mike.

———

Norm tried never to call Gwen at home. She worked hard to keep her work life separate from her family. Sometimes, though, it couldn't be helped. His good news had to be an exception. Late Sunday afternoon, he dialed her number. "You busy tomorrow morning?" he asked.

"What did you have in mind?"

"A search warrant."

"Sounds fun. Where?"

"We found the dead guy's house."

"Who did? Where?"

"Pierce County sheriff, out on a call with the Humane Society. On the Kitsap Peninsula. A neighbor identified our dead driver from his license photo."

"Great. I'm so sick of McDonald's I could scream."

"Well, it worked. You found the place where he bought his lunch. Too bad no one could tell us if he was a regular."

"I think half the McDonald's staff must be new every single week. How can the customer be a regular if the employees aren't?"

"True. Big turnover. Mostly kids. It was a long shot."

"So where do we meet?"

"At the Federal Way Park and Ride, on 320th—say around ten? I'll get a warrant and pick you up in a company car."

"Sounds good." She hung up.

Short and sweet. Why couldn't all women be more like his partner?

———

While her mother made small talk, Kate could barely swallow, let alone finish her meal. But she was not the only one. She noticed that her father, pale with exhaustion, leaned heavily on one arm while he picked at the salad before him. Kate suspected that more than fatigue lay behind his hesitation. In spite of a long history of heart disease, Patrick Killian still thought of himself as an athlete. His body, tall and lean, still craved thick dressing and heavy butter. Though his doctor had ordered a change in diet, her father resisted. For Patrick, Sunday wasn't Sunday without a big pot roast and mashed potatoes. Today, he seemed too tired to complain. Perhaps even too tired to eat.

Kate felt sad watching him move his salad around with his fork. Over the years, Patrick had grown to expect things the way he liked them. And now, if he wanted to survive, things had to change. She understood. She felt the same way. If she wanted to live through Mike's betrayal, she had to learn to let go of her dreams and expectations as well. Like the desire to grow old with Mike, to enjoy weddings and grandchildren together, and eventually retirement. All of her dreams and wishes had to change. He'd taken that from her.

"And how are things at the company?" her mother's voice startled her.

"About the same. Busy." Mike took a drink of milk and dabbed at his mouth with a napkin. "We had a show in Vegas last week," he said. "Otherwise I'd have come out with Kate." No mention of the pictures.

"Successful?" Her father asked, interested.

"Oh, I couldn't say yet," Mike answered. "Actually, it was a little strange. Doug seems to be acting—I don't know—weird lately. Not like himself."

"He and his wife ever get back together?" Rosemarie asked.

"I don't think that will ever happen," Kate answered firmly. "It's been years, Mom. Not every marriage has a happily-ever-after ending."

Her father shot her a reproving glance. "Have you talked to him about it?" he asked Mike. "I mean, his behavior."

"Not yet. I've had my own fires to fight."

"I understand." Her father nodded. "But there's nothing like straight talk. Getting things out in the open. Otherwise things fester."

Mike seemed to consider the advice. "You're probably right. It's just that lately, everything I say to Doug seems to make him angry."

"Why?" Kate's mother sounded surprised, as though nothing Mike could say would ever anger anyone.

"I don't know. It's like he thinks I'm being bossy. Too—I don't know—parental?"

"What kinds of problems?" Patrick set his napkin beside his plate and leaned forward.

"He's missed some product deadlines. And his staff has even complained to me about his performance."

"That seems out of line," Patrick observed.

Mike shrugged. "It is. But I've had to fire our financial officer." Mike looked pointedly at Kate, staring directly into her eyes. She noticed his brown eyes glisten. "And I've been busy trying to find the right replacement. So I haven't had any extra time to worry about Doug."

"Honey," Rosemarie said to Patrick, "aren't you hungry? You've barely touched your dinner."

"I guess I've lost my appetite," he said. Smiling, he reached out to pat her hand. "Good lunch though, Rosie. As good as you can do without real food." He chuckled and pushed back from the table. "Now, would you excuse me? I think I'll go lie down for a bit." He stood and slid his chair under the table.

"Good idea, Dad," Mike agreed. "I'll help Mom with the dishes."

"You'll do no such thing," Kate's mother stood. "There's hardly anything here. Why don't you and Kate go for a walk or something? You haven't even seen each other for a week." She picked up two dinner plates. "I'll have this clean in a jiffy. Then I can sit down with the Sunday paper."

Kate started to object.

"Now, I don't want any arguments. Go on, you two, before it rains."

"Sounds like a good idea, Kate. Like to take a little walk?"

They'd trapped her, and she knew it. She took a deep breath and gave a little smile. "I guess I'll go change my clothes."

Seventeen

WHEN KATE CAME BACK downstairs, Mike was waiting for her by the hall table. Behind him, artfully arranged coral roses framed a gilded mirror. Her mother had trimmed the stems and added greenery.

"All ready?" Mike asked.

"Sure." Kate reached for an umbrella from the pot beside the front door. Outside, a light mist threatened to grow into rain. Before they reached the sidewalk, Kate raised the umbrella and held it tilted protectively toward Mike. At the front gate, they turned and walked silently down the street.

"Are you surprised to see me?"

"Of course."

"Why didn't you tell me that your dad had another heart attack?"

"I didn't think you'd care."

He took the jab with only a flinch. "I do care, Kate. I love your parents. As much as my own."

"So it's just me you hate?"

He stopped suddenly and turned to face her, taking her elbow. "Don't, Kate. Please don't do that."

"Do what?" she asked, looking up at Mike, determined to remain calm, composed.

"Kate, I want to talk about things. I do. But not like this."

"Has it ever occurred to you that I don't want to talk? I don't want to hear anything you have to say. I've seen everything I want to know." She turned and began walking away, long quick steps carrying her toward the intersection.

Mike jogged a little to catch up, falling into step beside her. "We don't have to talk now. Not yet, if you don't want to." He slid his hands into his jacket pockets.

She did not answer. Instead, she reached the corner and turned away from him. He shook his head and followed. "Maybe you could just listen. I could talk and you could listen."

For a few steps, she didn't answer him. At last she said, "I can't stop you from talking. It's a free country." Glancing up, she added, "Just don't expect me to believe you. I'm not buying."

Kate stood in the mist, her golden hair getting wavier every moment, staring at him with open-eyed hurt. And he could think of nothing to say. Her last words had managed to open a hole in Mike's heart and drain every explanation from his brain. He could think of nothing that would ever change her mind. Nothing could ever win her trust.

He choked. "I'm so sorry, Kate."

It seemed to make her angry. Her lips tightened and her eyes flashed. She began walking again without saying a word.

"I don't know how it happened," he said. "It was wrong. I know it. I was wrong. I can't explain it. Don't you think I've tried to figure it out?" His voice trembled, a deep uncharacteristic tremble. "But Kate, I love you. I know you can't believe that right now, but I do love you." He brushed his nose with the sleeve of his sweater.

She didn't answer.

"I got the same pictures you did. I think they came the same day. Only mine came by courier. I was at work, the pictures came, and I knew."

She broke in, "You knew you'd been caught."

"No, that wasn't it at all."

Animosity filled the air around Kate. Her expression had grown tight, controlled. They continued walking. She pulled the umbrella down until it almost rested on the top of her head, and Mike could no longer see her face.

He spoke to the umbrella, imagining her face. "When I saw the pictures, I realized how much I hated it. Hated what I was doing." He could not read her eyes. Did she understand? Could she believe him? "I mean, I knew it all along. Really I did. I won't lie to you."

"Now, that's a novel idea."

"I mean it. The pictures—somehow the pictures gave me the courage to end it. I needed courage."

"It took a lot of courage to start it, Mike." Hatred permeated her voice.

"I know you believe that, Kate. But it isn't true. It happened, but I don't know how. It hadn't been going on all that long, really." He took a deep breath and spoke in a low anguished voice. "What you must believe now is that it's over."

"Oh, really. I must believe?" Her voice dripped sarcasm. "That's entertaining. Now I must believe." She chuckled. "No, Mike, you're wrong. I don't have to ever believe you again. If you came here trying to save your mighty estate, you can relax. I won't try to break the bank. I only want what's mine. I have a career and money of my own. You don't need to apologize to me in order to save your business. I don't want your business."

"Kate, you haven't heard a word I've said," he said, exasperated. "I want you, Kate. In this whole world you are all I want. I didn't know it. I got lazy. I got stupid. I admit that. But now I'm begging you to give me a chance. Give us a chance."

They walked on silently. She never even glanced up at him. Hours seemed to pass; still she said nothing. At last they reached a small city park where benches surrounded a playground. Kate chose a seat, still holding the umbrella low over her face. Mike sat beside her, feeling all hope seep from him. He'd come halfway across the country to make her understand. But no words seemed sufficient. She did not want to listen. His shoulders ached with the burden of utter hopelessness.

And then he realized she was crying.

By the time Kate and Mike walked back to her parents' home, light rain had given way to a full-strength downpour. Overhead, a black sky, impelled by a cold spring wind, formed a perfect background for Kate's thoughts. Early darkness gave the feel of nightfall to Kate, though by the clock, it was only late afternoon. She opened the door and stepped inside, leaving Mike to close the door for himself.

Inside, she took off her running shoes without untying them and threw her wet umbrella into the holder. Water dripped from her clothes and spotted her mother's wooden entryway. Wet jeans clung to her legs, and her hair, doubled in volume by the rain and wind, stood out from her head like a clown's wig. Shivering, she opened the front closet and hung up her raincoat. "I'm going upstairs," she said. "I plan to soak in the bathtub until I can feel my feet again."

"All right," Mike said, leaning against the wall beside the front door. She felt his eyes watching her as she made space in the coat closet. Brushing water from her cheeks, she looked down at her fingers and noticed the black sludge of runny mascara. *Rain,* she assured herself. *Not tears.*

Without looking at Mike, she went upstairs, let herself into her bedroom, and closed the door quietly behind her. Too tired to be angry, too wrung out to cry, she slumped down on her bed, wondering what she would do with Mike in the house. Before he'd shown up on the front steps, she'd made up her mind. Kate wanted a divorce.

She could not bear the anguish of trying to piece together a relationship with someone she didn't trust. After all, Mike admitted being with another woman. And of course, she'd seen it. She could never again close her eyes without seeing the pictures.

But his being here in the house threw her off. The smell of him, the nearness of him—even the sight of him—conspired against her, weakened her resolve.

She would not give in. No. Kate would close the door on her past and fasten the dead bolt. Never again would she risk the kind of pain she'd experienced over the past weeks.

Today, Kate's emotions had gone around and around with the ferocity of a dough hook. First church and the concern of her church family. Then Kate had been confronted again with her father's age and frail health. She recognized her mother's vulnerability. Too many losses. Too much pain. Things had spun out of Kate's control, and she wished she could bring it all back, dust it off, and line it up. But she could not.

Tears filled her eyes and spilled down her cheeks, making the bedroom swirl out of focus. She brushed the tears away and saw an old family portrait sitting proudly on the end of her dresser. There, in the gilded frame her mother had chosen, stood a beautiful, trusting young woman. Who was she? Some innocent young mother foolish enough to believe that promises were enough? She looked at Mike, holding Keegan in his lap, his face a picture of pride. What had happened to the man she married?

Kate let herself fall back onto the bed, covering her face with her hands. Still cold and overwhelmed with grief, she wished the bed would swallow her. She wanted more than anything to be set free from the anger and confusion she felt about Mike. She wanted, as well, to be free of the deep and intense feelings that overpowered her whenever he came near. If she could only cut herself off from those feelings, perhaps the pain would end.

Grabbing her robe, she went out the door and crossed the hall to the bathroom. She leaned down to start the water, holding her hand under the spout, letting steam build up as the water grew hot. A hot bath would certainly warm her cold feet. But would anything ever warm her frozen soul? Her nose dripped as she leaned over the tub, and she brushed it with the back of her wrist. _Trust me_, she heard the voice again.

"Why?" she asked out loud. "Lord, why on earth should I ever trust you again?"

When Kate came downstairs, she found her parents in the kitchen nook. Rain continued to drum the pavement outside. For a moment Kate watched her mother set the table for the evening meal. Her father occupied his usual place, sipping hot tea from his favorite cup, reading the Sunday paper. "There you are, Katie-Doll," he said. "You look all warmed up. Feel better?"

"My feet feel much better," she acknowledged, taking a chair beside him. Kate noticed that her father's eyes seemed brighter, his voice stronger than after church. His shoulders had grown straighter, too, somehow. The afternoon rest had been good for him. If only she could be so refreshed by a nap.

"Oh, there you are," Mike entered from the kitchen carrying two soup bowls. "Feeling better?"

"Warmer," Kate answered, shrugging.

"Your mom has soup and sandwiches for dinner." He placed one bowl in front of her father, the other at her mother's place.

"I thought it might take the chill off of this miserable weather," her mother said. "So like spring. Beautiful one day. Miserable the next."

"I've always liked your soup, Mom. Not like that canned stuff," Mike smiled at Kate across the table and went back for more soup.

"Well, I always use your father's tomatoes," Rosemarie answered, smiling. "Campbell's could never compete with tomatoes picked and canned in the same afternoon."

"Even Kate can't grow tomatoes like you do here," Mike said from the other side of the kitchen counter.

"Not enough heat out there by the ocean," her father said.

"And our season is too short." Mike brought in two more bowls and turned to reach for a platter of sandwich halves from the counter.

"But you don't have much time for gardening, do you, Mike?" Kate's mother sat down and unfolded a blue linen napkin, spreading it carefully over her skirt.

"I haven't," he agreed. "Not recently. Kate is actually the gardener at our house. But I've been doing a lot of thinking lately. I should cut back on work. Spend more time at home."

"A wise choice," her father said, glancing at Kate. She ignored his look.

When Mike took his seat, her father held out both of his hands and said, "How about a blessing?" Rosemarie took Patrick's hand in her own and offered her other to Mike. He reached for Kate, who glared at him. Protectively, she closed her hand into a tight fist and hid it under her napkin.

"Father," Patrick began, "we thank you for the day you have given us, and for the church family that we enjoy, and for the family here in this room. How good you are to us. How wonderful are the relationships we share together. Thank you, Father." In the tiny pause that followed, Kate glanced up to see her father, eyes closed, smiling gently as he prayed. "And thank you for this food. Bless now our time around this table. Be at the center of our conversation, we ask, in Jesus' name."

Somehow, Kate managed to make it through the meal. Her mother chattered. Michael flattered. Her father contributed an occasional question or comment. No one seemed to notice that Kate said almost nothing. Inside she fumed.

How dare Michael come here like nothing had changed? To see them here, no one would ever know what he'd done. No one would suspect the destruction his choices had caused. How could her father treat him as though nothing at all were out of place? With every passing moment and every polite exchange, Kate's anger grew.

Before long, the muscles of her jaws hurt. Her appetite vanished. She could no longer chew or swallow. The foolishness, the audacity of the situation, seemed to grow until she could hardly contain herself. Eventually, her emotions boiled up and spilled over like spaghetti in a pot.

"Oh yes," her mother said, "I've forgotten to put clean towels out. I'll put some on Kate's bed for you, Mike."

"Thanks, Mom." Mike placed his spoon across his plate and reached for a second sandwich.

"We just changed her sheets yesterday, so the linens are fresh. . . ."

"You don't have to trouble yourself, Mother. He isn't staying."

An echoing silence filled the nook. Her mother's hand, holding a coffee cup, froze midway from the table to her mouth. The arctic moment seemed to last for an eternity.

Kate's father cleared his throat.

"I don't understand," Rosemarie said, glancing back and forth between Patrick and Mike. "I don't understand." She put her cup down and wiped her lips with her napkin.

"You don't understand because I haven't said anything. And I'm sorry for that." Kate put both hands on the table beside her plate. "I know that you have heard that something is wrong. But the truth is that Mike and I have decided to divorce. And I haven't told you because I didn't know how—not with all the worry about Daddy."

Kate's mother seemed completely stupefied. Her wide eyes blinked, not believing her daughter's words. "No!" She covered her mouth with one trembling hand. "Oh, dear God, no!"

"It's true," Kate said. "And I don't know why he's come here. But he isn't staying."

"Did you know about this?" Rosemarie looked desperately at her husband, her eyes filling with tears. "I mean, the divorce?"

He nodded.

"And you didn't tell me?" Her voice trembled, but she continued, "How could you not tell me about this?"

"I thought that Kate should tell you. I knew that she would explain it all when the time was right."

"I guess it's time." Kate sighed, heavy with misery. "And Mike isn't staying. Not overnight. Not here."

Patrick took a deep breath. "Well, Katie-Doll, I'm afraid you're wrong there. Mike is still my son-in-law. And this is my house. We have a guest room, and he can stay there for the night." He pushed his plate away and leaned forward, his elbows on the table. "Whatever problems you two have are your own. I won't interfere with your decisions. But I'm not sending Mike away in the middle of a storm. He can stay for as long as he needs to."

Rosemarie had given in to gentle weeping, making tiny gasping noises, her face cradled in her hands. Mike reached out and gently patted her shoulder. "I'm sorry, Mom," he whispered. "I'm so sorry." His eyes glistened.

"All right," Kate said, her voice a controlled fury. "Whatever you decide, then. I think I'll go upstairs to bed." She pushed her chair away, folded her napkin into precise quarters, and put it down beside her plate. Using her fingers she pressed the folds firmly in place. "I'm really not hungry anyway." Standing, she picked up her plate and walked into the kitchen.

Using all of her self-control, she rinsed her dishes, placed them in the dishwasher, and closed the door firmly. As she passed the table again, she noticed Michael pinching his eyelids between his thumb and index finger. Catching tears. *Well, it's about time.*

"Good night, everyone," she said.

Eighteen

LATE MONDAY MORNING, Norm Walker drove Gwen Saunders along country roads on their way to the rental house. Armed with a search warrant, they planned to enter the home seeking evidence as to the identity of the deceased. All the way from the Federal Building, Norm had played a Wynton Marsalis CD. By the time he picked up Gwen, he'd become completely absorbed in the rhythm and patterns of great jazz.

He really didn't expect to find much at the house. "I don't know why we're even trying," he told her. "After all, the perp is dead. There isn't anyone to convict."

"No. But even criminals have mothers," Gwen argued. "Somebody has to figure out who this guy was and let his relatives know what happened."

"We should let the locals do it." Norm much preferred chasing "really bad guys," as he called them. Petty thievery bored him. "We have too much to do as it is."

"True," she conceded. "On the other hand, maybe someone else is involved. Someone still alive. We might catch a bad guy yet."

"I doubt it."

"Okay. Even if we don't find anything, we might figure out the guy's real identity. Once we do that, we can close this case and move on to real crime."

He mumbled reluctant agreement.

"Should be the next right," she instructed, looking up from the map she held in her hands.

"Got it." Turning the car onto a dead-end street, Norm watched for house numbers. Spotting the rental, he pulled the car into the driveway. Two- and three-bedroom houses situated on half-acre lots lined the street. "Seems like a quiet area. Not your usual high-crime neighborhood."

"Never can tell." Gwen gazed at the dark green house at the end of the driveway. "Well, at least we know the floor plan."

"No kidding," Norm agreed. Like thousands of tract homes, it had the same small front porch, single front door, living room to the left, and three bedrooms down the hall to the right. The dining room would be directly across from the entry, with the kitchen behind the garage, overlooking the backyard. This house, like millions exactly like it, had been recreated in countless communities across the nation. "I hope we haven't wasted a whole day driving out here," he declared.

The linings of torn drapes, grayed from filth, hung over part of the front window. Duct tape, in the pattern of giant spider legs, held together shards of severely broken glass. Great cracks wandered up from the lower right corner. Norm wondered briefly how duct tape could stick to that filthy glass. Weeds overflowed the flower bed below the window, and thick cobwebs hung where the siding met the porch ceiling.

Foundation plantings had grown unchecked around the house until they obscured most of the bedroom windows. In what was left of the lawn, even winter precipitation had not grown grass through the carpet of dandelions covering the yard.

Norm expected filth but wondered if his partner could take the smell. Though she'd searched hundreds of homes, her stomach still reacted violently to bad smells. Criminals rarely cleaned up after themselves.

"Ready?" Norm asked.

"Might as well get it over with." She opened the car door and slid out.

From the front porch they rang the bell. No answer. They had not expected one. Norm knocked on the door. They waited. Again, no answer. Though they would enter with guns drawn, neither feared ambush.

As expected, they had no trouble entering. The front door, faded and warped from exposure, had a weak, inadequate lock.

With a light heave from Norm's shoulder, the lock gave way entirely, and the front door swung open.

"FBI," he called. "We have a warrant." No response.

The smell from the house slammed his nostrils even before he stepped inside. Mildew, animal waste, toilet smells. Norm fought the urge to wretch and turned away to take one last deep breath of fresh air. Inside, he heard an unusual dry crunch, like the sound of someone walking on puffed rice. He looked down.

At the base of the front door, hundreds of dead houseflies lay like confetti. Dry. He glanced back at his partner just in time to see her shake her head in disgust. She'd put her left hand up over her nose in an effort to block the smell. She followed Norm cautiously into the house, gun drawn and held tightly in her right hand.

"FBI," Norm stated again. "We have a warrant." He didn't shout. The condition of the house confirmed that no one remained inside. Who would stay in a mess like that? He nodded to her, and they separated, each going to search opposite ends of the house.

He found the first two bedrooms completely empty. No furniture. Nothing in the closets. In the third he found a sleeping bag. No pillow.

In the only bathroom, stench from an unflushed toilet assaulted his nose. Backing out, he noticed that the tin cupboard over the sink was completely empty. Whoever lived here never meant to stay. "Nothing here," he called backing into the hallway.

"All clear," she called back. "But I think you should come take a look at this."

Holstering his gun, he followed the sound of her voice into the dining room, where she stood beside a card table and one folding chair. A Styrofoam container holding moldy bits of leftover food lay open on the table, lid up. Empty envelopes of soy sauce lay nearby. The house had been empty for a while.

Together they moved into the kitchen. A coffee maker containing several cups of black liquid sat on the counter. Islands of mold floated on its oily surface. Gwen turned away.

Then the sight of dishwashing suds mounded above the sink seemed to catch her attention. Norm watched her move closer. One step, then another. She reached out and almost touched the suds.

"Don't touch that," he said, suddenly realizing what they were.

She had been fooled by nothing more than the puffy fiber of

mold bubbling up from unwashed dishes. She dropped her hand and turned away, clearly disgusted.

"Are you coming? Or are you planning to wash the dishes?" Norm stood in the doorway of the kitchen, completely filling the frame with his bulk.

"I'm coming," Gwen said. "Don't be so impatient." She wiped her hand on the back of her trousers.

Norm turned away, toward what he believed to be the garage or perhaps a laundry room. Just beyond the kitchen they discovered a small addition. On one wall, a high window faced the Taylor property, exposing lilac bushes.

Surrounded by dark imitation wood paneling, a single bulb hung from an uncovered ceiling fixture, providing a dim, depressing gloom. Directly under the bulb stood one long folding table. A blue folding chair faced elaborate computer equipment spread out along the entire length of the six-foot table. At one end stood a cheap card table.

"Well, now we know where all his money went," Gwen offered, putting her gun away. The equipment included a large flat-panel monitor, several hard drives, a modem, and a laser printer. A tangle of cords hanging from the back of the table connected the equipment to an elaborate backup power supply. "But what is this?" Gwen moved to the machine resting on the card table.

"That, my friend, is what he used to produce the credit cards," Norm answered. Moving behind her he pointed to a stack of plastic in one corner. "Those are the blanks."

"Okay, so now what?"

"Well, I guess we try to figure out what's in all this machinery. Then we find his friends."

"So you don't think this is just some greedy kid?" Norm could sense the satisfaction Gwen felt in being right.

"Nope," he admitted with a tinge of regret. "I think this guy had help. Not only that, I think he had a buyer." Norm put both his hands on his hips and turned slowly around the room. "Someone was buying those cards from him. But to figure it all out, we're going to need to get everything we can out of this computer."

"We may have one really big advantage here," Gwen said, smiling.

Norm turned to her, waiting patiently for an explanation.

"It might be that his friends don't even know he's dead."

Norm's mouth twitched while he fought a smile. Outsmarting bad guys gave Norm great pleasure, and nothing made him happier than finding a new angle or surprising break. "If they don't know he's dead," he began, "then we might be able–"

"To become bad guys ourselves," she finished. "Sounds like fun." Flipping her hair behind one ear, she put her hands on her hips. "But can we talk about it outside? I think better when I'm not about to vomit."

———

Though Kate had been the first to bed, she'd been the last to sleep. When she entered the kitchen Monday morning, her eyelids were swollen, her eyes bleary. She walked straight to the coffeepot.

"It's decaffeinated."

She turned to find Mike leaning in the doorway of the sun porch, holding a mug in one hand, his Bible tucked under his other arm. The sight of him holding a Bible nearly made Kate sick. She turned away and began fishing through the kitchen cupboards.

"I found real coffee in those bags that look like tea bags," he offered. "On the second shelf to the left of the sink. You'll have to nuke some water, but at least it's real stuff."

"Thanks." She found the box and took a mug from the rack. "Dad isn't supposed to have caffeine. I guess Mom has put us all on the same regimen." She placed a rose-printed mug in the micro- wave and punched in the numbers. Leaning against the counter, Kate turned to face him.

"You'll be happy to know I'm leaving today," he said. "The air- port transporter should be here soon."

"Oh? Too bad."

He winced. Somehow seeing his pain did not give her as much pleasure as she anticipated. She sighed.

"I thought you'd be relieved," he said. "How long will you stay in Kansas?"

"At least until Dad clears his next checkup. His first rehab course takes six weeks."

"What about your job?"

"Sally has a granddaughter who's a marketing major. She's cov- ering for me."

"So you *will* be coming back to the coast?"

"I can't be certain."

His eyebrows rose, and he shook his head as if her words stunned him. "I guess I should have expected that. What about the kids?"

"They're all grown up. What we do now is private."

"It's never private."

"Yes, that's something you should well understand. What you did with Cara Maria wasn't private, was it?"

He bit his lip and glanced away.

"I've made it clear that I don't want the kids in on this yet."

His face darkened, and Kate wondered for a moment what he might be thinking. She would not ask. "When will you be leaving?"

"In a few minutes. I have my things in the entry hall."

"Well, don't let me stop you. I wouldn't want you to miss the plane." The machine behind her beeped, and she turned to pull her mug from the microwave. She yanked the coffee bag from the wrapper, and holding it by its string, danced it in and out of the water. Steam rose from the cup as the liquid turned dark. The smell of coffee held promise, and she drew in the aroma greedily.

Saying nothing, he stepped up behind her, putting his hand on her arm. She felt his nearness and the depth of his emotion. "Kate, I'm asking you to reconsider." His voice was low, pleading. "We've had so much together. It's been so good. So many years. We could recover from this."

"You have nothing to recover from," she said, keeping her back turned to him, her voice cold. "And I think it's pretty cavalier of you to tell me what I can or can't recover from. I can never recover, Mike. Not ever. You should have thought of that before you took up with Cara Maria." She gasped, a hoarse, throaty cry escaping before she could stop it. "I could never trust you now. You should have thought." A car horn sounded in the driveway.

She felt his body tense behind her and the fingers of his hand on her arm tighten into a gentle squeeze. "I am sorry," he whispered. "And I'll pray. There must be a way through this, Kate. I promise, I'll pray. Don't give up." With a final rub of her arm and another squeeze, he set down his own mug and left the room.

From the kitchen, she heard the front door close quietly behind him. She waited, tense and unmoving, until she heard the van speed off down the street. Then, certain he had gone, Kate collapsed on the counter. More tears. When would they stop?

————

Anyone observing Mike Langston as he sat huddled in a molded black chair at the Kansas City Airport would have recognized that something was wrong. He wore the clouded, deeply chiseled expression of the careworn. He slumped low in the chair, one tennis shoe slung across his other knee, wiggling rhythmically. His right elbow rested on the chair arm, his chin on his thumb. He stared at nothing, running his index finger over his lips one way, then another, completely oblivious of other passengers waiting with him for a San Francisco flight.

Though cheerful families visited around him and the loudspeaker announced arrivals and departures, nothing seemed to puncture the bubble of concern and hurt that consumed him. Even a curly-headed toddler in pink overalls, who stumbled over his long white tennis shoe, did not distract him. She lurched and caught herself, both hands reaching out to touch his knee. Her tiny face looked up expectantly, anticipating a smile and word of encouragement. But the dark-haired man with the big shoe did not see her. Unresponsive, he continued to stare at the floor. Surprised, she toddled away toward her mother.

Truthfully, the man inside the pain bubble was very much alive. In fact, at that very moment, the common torment of all men caught by the stupidity of their own mistakes had begun to burn in Mike's conscience. This morning, on the trip from Lawrence, Mike Langston had begun the process of devouring himself, from the inside out.

In his mind, he heard the same words over and over. *I've lost Kate. She will never forgive me. Who was I to think that she could? That she might?* He slid lower in the chair. When at last the ground crew announced the boarding of his flight, Mike had nearly slithered onto the floor in misery and self-deprecation.

Mike used his frequent flyer miles for a seat upgrade. This morning, Mike's pain demanded space. Lots of space. The new seat assignment gave him the opportunity to board first. He picked up his bags and walked down the Jetway, lost in his own thoughts. Absently, he threw his weekender into an overhead compartment, stuffed his carry-on bag under the seat in front of him, and fell into the window seat. He buckled his safety belt as passengers began to fill the plane behind him.

Mike Langston stared vacantly out the window, only vaguely aware of the people who jostled for storage space in the aisle beside him. At last a voice caught his attention. "I'm sorry, ladies and gentlemen," the male voice said. "We've just heard from the ground crew that we have a small problem with our air circulation unit. We're going to stay here while they replace a defective part. It should take just a few minutes, and then we'll be pushing back from the gate."

"Oh, great," said the twenty-something hulk in the seat next to him. "Just what we need. A delay."

Mike acknowledged his comment with a noncommittal murmur and turned away. Staring out the window, he watched the ground crew. The delay stretched to thirty minutes while air in the plane grew hot and stale. The cabin attendant began to circulate with a tray of ice water in crystal glasses. "Water?" she asked. "Or can I get you something else?"

"I'll take a chilled white wine if you have one," his seat partner said.

"No, thanks." Nothing in an airplane galley could help Mike Langston.

Nineteen

AFTER MIKE LEFT, Kate experienced a grief so heavy she could barely move. Her arms and legs felt weighted, as though she dragged tires along the floor behind her. Exhausted, she took her coffee upstairs and lay back down in her bed. *I got up too early,* she told herself. *I just need to catch a little more sleep.*

For nearly an hour, she lay curled on her side staring at the bedroom wall, the coffee mug resting on the sheets. Nothing had changed in this room. Her mother kept it exactly as Kate had so many years before. Peach and white striped wallpaper, which Kate had chosen herself the summer before she entered high school, still covered the walls around her. Now faded and yellow, the intervening years had somehow changed the paper. Flaws in the plasterboard showed clearly now. The white ceiling had yellowed as well, and tiny cracks had formed near the window frames. Stress forced separation, Kate concluded, in walls as well as in people. Though the room itself had not changed; neither had time left it alone.

Had those years been as cruel to Kate? She fought aging by exercising regularly and watching her weight with the precision of a physicist. She wore sunglasses religiously and swallowed a handful of antioxidants every morning. Though she applied sunscreen with tenacity bordering on obsession, Kate had begun to notice tiny lines in her upper lip. Sagging tissue had begun to replace her previously fit triceps. The skin below her chin had developed a bit of drop to it, and in pictures, Kate thought it resembled a double chin. In spite of her vigorous effort, Kate felt the advancing years every time she started running up a hill. Her hamstrings ached where they attached to her pelvis. Climbing made her feel sluggish and heavy. Though she resisted, the pace of her daily run had slowed.

Had aging been the force behind Mike's betrayal? Had he become disenchanted with her appearance? Kate didn't want to believe that. After all, he looked older too. The folds between his nose and his mouth had grown deeper, his waist thicker, his hair thinner. For that matter, the crown of his head now revealed more skin than hair. He'd taken to wearing a baseball cap whenever he went outdoors, which Kate knew he did to avoid painful sunburn on his bald spot. She pictured him applying aloe vera to his head and smiled. Everyone aged; there was no way around it. She refused to believe that a changing body explained Mike's choices. . . .

"Kate, dear, are you up?"

"Not really, Mom."

"I'm about to make breakfast. Would you like something?"

"No, thanks, nothing for me."

She heard her mother's footsteps move softly away from the door. Though she hadn't slept, couldn't sleep, neither could she get out of bed. Sadness pinned her to the mattress, the same sadness she had come to Kansas to escape.

Nearly two hours later, Kate pulled on jeans and a long-sleeved T-shirt. She ran her fingers through her disheveled hair and went downstairs. Entering the kitchen, she found her mother washing crystal from the dining room buffet. Kate poured herself a fresh cup of coffee.

"So you're finally going to get up?"

Kate chose to ignore her question. "What are you working on?"

"I kept some breakfast for you," her mother said. Lifting a glass from the rinse water, she placed it carefully, stem up, on a kitchen towel. "In the fridge. You can heat it in the microwave."

"Thanks. I'm not hungry."

The squeak of dishrag on crystal sounded harsh to Kate. Her mother continued washing. "I see Mike left this morning."

"I guess so," Kate took her cup to the kitchen table, where she pulled out a chair and sat staring at the backyard. Her father, in an old hooded sweatshirt, stood over a garden bed with a hoe in his hands. Beside him, a pile of weeds wilted on the gravel. Why couldn't he rest for one whole week?

"What did you say to make him leave?"

Kate did a mental double take. "I'm sorry, I don't think I heard you."

"Well, Kate, he came to see you to try to make things right. You must have said something to send him away."

"I don't want to talk about it, Mom. There isn't anything else to say." She glanced at her mother's face just in time to see a pained expression flit across her features.

"Kate, you may not want to say anything. But I think someone has to." She lifted another glass from the water and turned on the faucet. Hot water glistened as it slid over the crystal goblet. She set it gently on the counter and dried her hands. "You've got to listen to someone."

"Please don't start, Mom."

"Kate, we didn't raise you to divorce. This is a good Christian family. We honor the Scriptures."

"Mom, trust me. You have no idea what you're talking about."

"I most certainly do. The Bible says that God hates divorce. Why if your dad and I had bailed out every time we had a little difficulty, you wouldn't even be here."

"I know, Mom. Everyone has trouble. Don't you think I know that? Don't you think I've been there? I'm not a quitter."

"Then why are you quitting now?" Her mother reached for her own coffee mug and brought it around the counter to sit beside Kate.

Kate looked into her mother's dark eyes and saw them fill with tears. She couldn't stay angry with those loving eyes. "Mom, he has a girlfriend. I know, because I saw pictures of them together. Horrible pictures."

"There must be some mistake. Certainly Mike wouldn't do that to you."

"He didn't do it *to* me, Mom. He just did it." Kate pushed hair out of her eyes and took a deep breath. "He—I didn't even have any idea it was going on."

"But why? What did you do to make him do it?"

"Mother, how can you ask that?" Kate put down her cup, jarring the coffee inside, spilling it onto the table. "I didn't make him do anything. This is about choice. His choice. He chose to do this thing—all by himself." In spite of her desire to stop them, her tears began again. "Who knows why anyone does this?"

"But surely you can get him back."

Her mother's old-world thinking did more to kick Kate out of her self-pity than any pep talk might have. "You don't understand, Mom. I don't want him back."

"But you have to do whatever it takes to save your marriage."

"That's where you're wrong. I don't have to. No one can make me. Even God says I don't owe anything to Mike now." Holding both hands around her mug, Kate shook her head firmly. "I don't have to, Mom. And I'm not going to."

———

The cabin attendant smiled at the man beside Mike. "I'll be right back with that," she answered.

Whatever part the ground crew needed apparently had to be shipped by Pony Express. The delay continued as Mike's frustration mounted. He only wanted to get back to California. By now he could have walked. Eventually, the attendant returned with a stemmed glass filled with a pale liquid.

"Ladies and gentlemen, I'm sorry to let you know we're still waiting for clearance on that replacement part. They tell me that we should be another thirty minutes or so." A collective groan rose in the cabin.

"So what do you do?" The man next to him asked, leaning closer. Mike smelled alcohol.

"Software," Mike answered, hoping that short answers would discourage him. He did not feel like talking.

"Good business these days. Who do you work for?"

"DataSoft, San Francisco."

"Oh, good company?"

"Not bad," Mike answered.

"Here on business?" This guy was entirely too friendly.

Mike nodded, desperately trying to avoid conversation altogether. His thoughts were sluggish, his emotions weighing him, but a plan came to mind.

If I were reading, he thought, *the guy would leave me alone.* But Mike had no book and no business material along on this trip. His mind clicked through the items in his carry-on. Wait! A Bible. That would do it. Nothing turned off a conversation faster than a Bible. He leaned forward and pulled his black nylon bag out from under the seat. Opening the zipper, he pulled out the Bible he'd been reading on the sun porch at Kate's parents' home.

His neighbor watched with interest. Then, as he recognized the soft leather cover and gold foil pages, Mike saw him frown. Clearing his throat, he pulled an in-flight magazine from the seat pocket and began an intense search through its pages.

I've got to make this good, Mike thought. He flipped the book open, grateful for the effectiveness of the deception, yet feeling vaguely guilty for his tactic. Truthfully, he didn't feel like reading. Especially not the Bible. He felt certain he had fallen beyond the help of any book, especially the Bible. Too late. He must continue the charade.

Mike felt the stranger beside him glance over as he opened the cover. The man moved his drink to the other armrest. Mike smiled—a tiny, almost imperceptible smile. The presence of the Bible seemed to make his neighbor feel guilty about the wine. Wouldn't he be surprised to know that Mike, who so openly held this Bible, was himself an adulterer? The word stuck in his mind, stabbing his thoughts with the reality of its accusation. *Adulterer.*

Then another thought came to him. *You aren't the first, you know.*

He winced. Some comfort. So there had been other adulterers before him. Big help. But something about the word stuck in his mind. Who? He turned to the back of the book and looked up the word. Yes. In Samuel. King David had been an adulterer, falling into the same horrible sin. Mike looked out his window, lost in thought. Had King David felt as desolate and hopeless as he felt this very morning?

Why don't you look?

But where? Where would Mike find David's feelings? And anyway, what difference would it make if David felt as miserable about it as Mike?

Look anyway.

For a moment, Mike had an almost irresistible urge to laugh. Here he sat, in a stifling airplane, arguing with himself about how David felt after—well, after . . .

The Psalms.

Right. He remembered now. There had been something in a psalm about David and his sin. He turned to the Psalms and began flipping through—certain that the bold subheadings in his Bible would lead him to the passage. Then it jumped out at him.

Psalm 51. A Psalm of David after his sin with Bathsheba.

Mike skimmed the passage once, hungry yet fearful. Mike didn't need more guilt. He'd had plenty of that. He needed something more, but he didn't know what. When he felt certain the passage was safe, he let his eyes wander to the top and read it again, slowly, carefully. Savoring the words, he saw the passage in a new—almost electric—way.

David did know. He had experienced the same horrible pain and regret—unable to let go, unable to forget. David knew. Mike drank in this realization with a deep sigh; he was not alone. Mike read the psalm again, completely identifying with the words and emotions depicted there. He, too, wanted forgiveness, cleansing. He wanted to be truthful. To start over.

I desire a broken spirit.

Mike had a broken spirit all right. Broken beyond repair. Could he ever find a new start? Could he ever face anyone he loved again? Without realizing it, Mike's eyes filled with tears. The words appeared as under water. He blinked, cleared his eyes, and read the entire psalm again. *Create in me a clean heart,* David asked. *And make my spirit new.*

Mike, empty and utterly defeated, realized that he needed a clean heart every bit as much as David ever did. He turned to gaze out the window again. "Me too," he whispered. "Me too."

With a lurch, the plane backed away from the gate, and the passengers began to cheer enthusiastically. "Ladies and gentlemen, we have been cleared for takeoff," the pilot said. "We're number three in line, and we should be on our way momentarily."

"About time," the man beside Mike said.

They began the long slow ride to the end of the runway. Mike, enveloped in his own thoughts, let the words of David's psalm seep into his soul. Each line transformed itself into a prayer. *I want a clean heart, Lord. I want a new spirit. I need your forgiveness, Lord. If Kate never decides to trust me again, I still need your forgiveness. That's all I need,* Mike breathed.

With engines screaming the plane accelerated down the runway. Mike's spirit soared long before the wheels left the ground.

Two days later, Norm was busy in his office, his head tipped severely in order to hold the telephone and use both hands at the same time. The muscles of his face felt tense, and he knew he was talking louder than necessary. While he listened to the voice on the phone, he scrolled though a report on his computer screen, his frustration building. "No, I don't have that," he barked. "How'd you get it?"

While he waited impatiently for a response, Gwen knocked lightly against his cubicle wall and stuck her head over the side. He waved her off, but noticed that she stayed leaning against the frame, a smirk on her face.

"All right," Norm sighed. "Okay. Thanks for letting me in on it. Fax me a copy, would ya?" Without further niceties, he hung up.

"Ooh, charming this morning, aren't we?" Gwen mocked him as she raised one eyebrow.

"Don't mess with me. My coffee shop was closed this morning."

"Well, then, this little piece of information should cheer you up." She held a file folder in one hand and waved it temptingly under his face.

"Not as much as coffee would."

"Let me give it a try, okay?"

In an attempt to humor her, he leaned back in his chair, his hands clasped politely, waiting. "All right, I'm all yours."

She stepped into the cubicle and pulled an oak chair up to his desk. "I have the results of the search of our John Doe house. It seems he had a post office box."

Norm raised his eyebrows in response.

"He used his driver's license for ID, but he gave the rental house as an address. I've already gotten a warrant and emptied the box. I was right. He wasn't acting alone." She smiled, her dimples in full glory. "And get a load of this." Leaning forward, she slipped an envelope directly in front of him. He reached out to pick it up; his eyebrows creased as he read the return address. United Airlines. Inside, he found a ticket packet, including round-trip tickets to JFK. The name on the tickets matched the name on the driver's license.

"Notice the date?" his partner asked.

Norm flipped the first page of the packet open again, reading carefully. "He must have been heading to pick up these tickets, then catch his flight."

"Yep. Dated the day our driver on the Narrows was killed. My guess is that he was delivering to someone in New York."

"Any idea where this came from?" Norm carefully put the packet back in the envelope and tossed it on his desk.

"No clue. It came in a business envelope, directly from the airline, I think. The postmark was Chicago."

"Okay. So our John Doe had a credit card scheme. I'll admit it. You were right."

"Thank you. I'll savor that for a while."

"I hate to interrupt you while you gloat, but what do you suggest now?"

"Actually, I'm glad you asked. I've had a look at this guy's computer. He spends a lot of time on the Net. Lots of e-mail. Lots of programming stuff I'm not familiar with. I'm no expert, but I think that we should call in Dan Namura."

"So you think there's more in that machine than we can see?"

"I'm certain of it."

"Can we justify calling in the big boys? We can't afford to waste their time."

She nodded, her lips pursed tightly. "Norm, I know you hate it when I say this, but I think it's more. Something big. I just have a feeling." She shrugged and leaned her chin on one hand. "I can't explain it."

"Far be it from me to neglect a woman's intuition." He smiled. "All right, you see if we can get Namura. In the meantime, I want you to do your best to try to trace this guy's contacts." Norm poked his index finger at the file she held. "Figure out who everyone on his e-mail list is. Find out who bought the ticket. See what you can discern from all the mail in his P.O. box." He thought for a moment, absently tugging on his earlobe. "We don't have a lot of options here."

"It could be that these guys don't know he's dead. If they don't, we might be able to draw them out."

Norm considered her idea. He knew his partner was good at role playing and trying to think like a bad guy herself. "We don't have enough time. He didn't show up on the ticket. It won't be long before they start to wonder what went wrong." Norm rocked back in his chair. "I think it may be too risky to suddenly show up as the dead guy. No. That's out."

"Okay, then let's see if we can figure out who he was meeting. Maybe we can figure out exactly where he was going with a briefcase full of cards."

"Right." Norm made a note to himself on a yellow pad, tore the page off, and stuck it onto the front of the envelope. "But we'll have to work fast. You get Namura in here ASAP."

"No problem," Gwen agreed. "I'm on it."

Twenty

FIVE DAYS LATER, Norm met with Gwen and Daniel Namura in a windowless conference room in the center of Union Station. The old railroad depot, which had been restored at great expense by the city of Tacoma and a group of private investors, had been leased to offices of the federal government. Norm wondered why they'd done the entire restoration without including windows in the conference rooms. He hated a room without windows.

"And this is Norm Walker," Gwen was saying. "Norm, this is Daniel Namura, FBI Internet Investigations Division." The two men shook hands and took their seats.

Gwen reached for the water pitcher and poured a tall glass of ice water. Offering one to Norm, she continued, "Daniel comes to the FBI from the Federal Computer Incident Response Team."

Norm raised his eyebrows, "Not standard FBI training."

"No, sir," Daniel said, smiling. "Actually, I was recruited. I never thought I'd end up being a 'good guy.' "

"We don't wear white hats anymore, Namura," Norm said, taking a drink of water. He sat back in his chair eyeing the young man. "Well, we might as well get on with it." He pulled his chair up to the table. "Tell us what you've found."

Norm watched Gwen as she pulled out her legal pad and began taking notes. Though Namura would turn in a formal report, Gwen always wanted to write down questions and leads as they occurred to her. Norm never took notes at a meeting; he found it distracting.

And he never understood his partner's preoccupation with pen and paper.

"All right." Namura opened his file. "I've been here two days, and this is what I can tell you about your suspect." He brought out a sheet of typed notes. "John Doe had a pattern of being online every day for hours at a time. He had DSL."

"Direct service? Out there?" Norm interrupted. "Who was the provider?"

"Must have been expensive," Gwen noted.

"It was expensive. I called. More than sixty bucks a month."

In his mind, Norm flashed back to the rental property where they'd discovered and confiscated the suspect's computer. The two facts didn't mesh: expensive DSL and a cheap, filthy place to live. Unless, of course, someone else was paying for the direct service line.

"He had a serious addiction to porn sights," Namura continued. "Visited more than one every single time he went online," Namura continued. "He also spent a lot of time at some unusual commercial sites."

"Commercial sites?"

"Yes, and he did this late at night—or at least late relative to the host computer."

"Okay," Norm said. "So he likes spending time at commercial sites. What was he doing there? Can you tell?"

"I can't be certain yet. But I think they're the source of his credit card numbers. The real question is how was he doing it?"

"And who was helping him?" Gwen added.

Norm glared at her. "Gwen here thinks he's part of a conspiracy."

"We don't know he isn't," she said, glancing at Namura.

Norm smiled. He and Gwen engaged in regular verbal sword fights. They had long ago discovered that bickering augmented the investigative progress. In spite of the added cloud of irritation, the interaction often helped them solve cases. One of them always played the devil's advocate.

"I could fill you in on every little line and connection I have, but you'd be bored to death." Namura turned his page of notes over, pausing to read something he had written before continuing, "I have enough to go visit the system administrators of the various

Internet sites that our suspect spent time with. If we ask the right questions, we may be able to tell exactly what he was doing and how."

"Is this really important?" Norm asked. "After all, we don't know that anyone else was involved. The guy is dead. So is the crime."

"You may be right," Namura answered. One hand tipped his fountain pen end over end. They heard a knock on the door.

"Come in," Norm said.

"Excuse me, Gwen," a woman said through the partly opened door. "You asked me to interrupt if anything came in from the airlines."

"Sure. Come on in."

The door opened, and a small woman in a navy pantsuit entered. "We just had a call from United. They traced the ticket."

"Good. Who bought it?"

"It was purchased on their Web site."

Norm leaned back, shaking his head. The anonymity of the Internet had become a painful thorn in his side. He liked the good old days, when people had names, addresses, and phone numbers.

"They traced the purchase to an IP address in New York City. The name may be fake. But the provider has the phone number of the computer making the purchase. We can come up with the address."

"At last—something you can see." Norm nodded.

"Thanks, Cindy." Gwen dismissed her.

"No problem. I'll work on the location for you." She backed out.

"All right, Norm," Gwen said, "I think that eliminates any question of this young man doing all of this by himself. Right?"

"When you're right, you're right," Norm answered, shrugging.

"There's more." Namura slid pages from one pile to another, looking for something. "Here it is," he said. "Your suspect liked to encrypt his files. Much of his e-mail is encrypted."

"Not your usual family news," Gwen observed.

"Not at all. Most of it consists of only one or two lines of text."

"What did it say?" Finally something piqued Norm's interest.

"I can't be certain." Namura leaned one elbow on the table and clicked the end of his pen on and off, on and off. "I know for sure there were several 'two key' encryption programs on the computer you confiscated. Some of the messages we were able to break down. Others we haven't decrypted yet." Namura handed Norm a slip of paper. "Here's one."

Tipping his head back so he could focus through his bifocals, Norm read, "New York City, March 13."

"That's all?" Gwen asked.

"That's all in that one. Your suspect obviously had some encryption software that he hid somewhere. We'll find it, eventually. But he had hundreds of files, many of them untitled. And he had a bunch of disks—both floppies and zips. I need time."

"At last this thing is starting to get interesting."

Gwen looked up from the message she had snatched from Norm's grip. "Interesting? We have a dead guy, fake cards, sick German shepherds, airline tickets from New York. For crying out loud, Norm, what does it take to get you excited?"

Namura chuckled at Gwen's words. "What I haven't said," he began, "is that there may be more to this than we can already see. I'm going to go to the system administrators. If I can look at their systems, I may be able to prove a great deal more than theft by hacking."

"You think you can?" Gwen asked, a hopeful tone in her voice.

"I know I can," Namura answered.

"Well, then, let's get to work," Norm stood. "Keep in touch, ladies and gentlemen."

———

Mike went back to DataSoft that week, full of hope. None of his circumstances had changed. But Mike had. With forgiveness and a promise of continuing guidance, Mike felt he could finally face and conquer the mess he had made of his life.

On Thursday morning, he had begun the process of answering his messages when the phone on his desk buzzed. He punched the intercom button. "Yes, Brooke."

"I know you said you don't want to be disturbed, sir. But I have Brenda McCoy out here. She says she needs to speak with you."

Mike frowned at the telephone, his mind swimming with responsibilities and deadlines.

Brooke's voice took on a tone of irritation. "She says it's critical." Her voice dropped to an urgent whisper. "She's crying."

Mike sighed. Speaking in an exaggerated tone, he said, "Then by all means send her in."

Why would Doug McCoy's ex-wife come to him crying? What problem would bring her to Mike? *If she only knew,* he thought. *Like coming to a raving maniac for a mental health checkup.* He pushed his chair away from the desk and stood.

A little knock and Brooke led Doug McCoy's ex into the office. Dressed in gray linen trousers and a short-sleeved sweater, she had a jacket draped over her arm. In one hand she carried a purse, in the other a tightly wadded tissue. She walked directly into Mike's arms and gave him a long hug. He felt her shudder.

"Thanks for seeing me, Mike," she said into his shoulder. Her normally soft voice held quivering tears. Mike's response to her tears surprised him. He found himself patting her shoulder, wanting to ease her discomfort. Whatever had driven her to his office had been sufficiently serious to break the pride of this normally strong woman.

"Come sit down," he said, ushering her to his leather couch. "Brooke, could you bring us ice water?" His secretary nodded and left.

She sat, bringing the tissue to her eyes. "I'm so sorry to just show up like this. But I didn't know what else to do."

"Brenda, we've been friends for years. You're welcome to come here any time." Mike took the chair nearest the couch, leaning forward with his elbows on his knees, watching her face. "What is it? What has you so upset? Are the children all right?"

"The children are fine." She seemed to pull herself up by the shoulders, brushing her face with the tissue. Composing herself, she continued, "I'm here about Doug. And money." She sighed. "He isn't paying his child support, Mike. I'm trying to care for the kids without any help from him. I know he has it. Money, I mean." She gathered her silky hair into a ponytail and tossed it back over her shoulder. "I know he drives an expensive car; he lives in a great condo. And Mike, you've got to believe me. I'm barely making it."

"That doesn't sound like Doug. Why isn't he paying?"

"It's more like Doug than you know. He's never forgiven me for getting a divorce. I've always had to grovel for support payments. They've never been regular." She sighed. "But at least they used to come. But it's been seven months."

"Without any help?"

"None at all."

"Is he coming to see the kids?"

She shook her head; her gaze focused on the tabletop as she blinked away tears. The office door opened, and Brooke entered carrying a tray. She set two glasses on the coffee table near Mike and placed a pitcher of ice water beside them. She smiled politely at Brenda and turned to leave.

When the door closed again, Brenda spoke. "I think this is more than getting back at me, Mike," she said. "I'm worried. Something's wrong. You're his best friend. Maybe you can figure out what it is."

"What makes you think something is wrong? If he's been delinquent all this time, what's different about this?"

"I can't explain it." She answered, twirling a strand of fine blond hair around her finger. "I just feel it. Josh has been in the hospital twice this spring. His blood sugar gets harder to control every year. The doctor says it's puberty. But Doug never came to see him. When Josh was in critical condition, Doug never even called." She turned to face Mike, tears threatening to spill over her cheeks. "I think something else has him. Otherwise he would never have missed coming to the hospital." She turned her face away. "No matter what Doug feels for me, he always adored the kids."

Mike remembered visiting Josh in the pediatric ward. Years of battling childhood diabetes had put a constant strain on the McCoy family. "You say something else has him. What, Brenda?" Mike asked. "I can't begin to guess without some clues. Has he been a drinker? Used drugs?" Though he couldn't imagine his friend being involved with these things without his noticing, Mike realized that he might have missed the hints. After all, Mike had been consumed by plenty of his own problems lately. He spread his hands in appeal. "What is it that you suspect?"

She stared at Mike as though she did not see him, blue eyes blank, and Mike wondered if a memory lay behind that expression, just under the surface. "What is it?" he prodded. "You must suspect something."

"I don't know anything for certain. But I wonder." She looked toward the windows and suddenly seeing the water pitcher, leaned forward, asking, "May I?"

"Of course," he said, "let me." He poured water into a tall glass and then reached out to hand her the glass.

"Thanks, Mike." She smiled a weary halfhearted smile that never quite reached her eyes. "I've never told this to anyone before." She paused, and Mike nodded. "I thought it would betray him to tell. But, while we were married, Doug sometimes . . ." she paused so long that Mike's imagination began to wander. It seemed to him as though she could not bear to say the word.

"What, Brenda? What are you trying to say?"

"Sometimes, he gambled," she said. And for a moment she seemed to resemble a balloon from which all the air had been let out. "Not often, really. But it frightened me."

"Did he lose money?"

She nodded and then smiled as the absurdity of the question hit her. "That's what makes it gambling."

Mike laughed. "Sorry." He poured himself some water. "I guess I meant—did it seem to be more than recreational gambling?"

"It was to me," she agreed. "But I wouldn't gamble on the spelling of my own name." She thought for a moment. "But it was cyclical. Sometimes he'd go for months without ever betting on anything—other than an occasional lotto ticket." She set her glass down and brushed her lips with the tissue. "Then there'd be times when he seemed energized by it. He'd go to Las Vegas a couple of times a month and come home happy and proud of how he'd done."

"Are you saying he quit gambling?"

"Oh no, Mike. I'm saying that it was part of what drove us apart. No matter how much money I have, I'll never have enough to risk. He thought I was childish, frightened. He said that the company itself was a gamble—and that only gamblers succeed in business."

"How long have you two been divorced?"

"I left him three years ago."

Mike sat back in his chair and brought one Wilson court shoe up over his knee. Had he noticed a change in Doug over these past years? He couldn't think. Doug had always been mercurial. Mike assumed that was part of Doug's creative nature. And then a memory struck him. It was the moment in the last trade show, when

Doug had failed to show up for the presentation. What was it he had said? Mike struggled to remember. Something about what he'd been up to. Then he remembered.

Doug said he'd been winning.

Perhaps Brenda had guessed correctly. Perhaps Doug had gotten stuck in a serious addiction right under Mike's nose. Had Mike been so involved in his own relationship with Cara that he'd failed to see it? The thought squeezed his insides. Could he have missed something this important?

He sighed and stood. "All right. You may be right. Doug may be caught in a horrible habit. But whether he is or not, he should be taking care of you." He moved to his desk and took out a large leather portfolio. "Our company didn't really do well until after your marriage ended. But I have no doubt that you—and Kate too—may have paid the highest price for our success." He bent forward and wrote briskly with a pen from the set on his desk. He tore a piece of paper from the book and took it to Brenda.

Standing, she reached out to accept it. When she realized what he'd done, she said, "Mike, this isn't what I came for. I didn't mean for you to take care of us."

"It's a small thing," Mike said. "Consider it an advance on Doug's support payment." He grinned, trying to appear more cheerful than he felt. "I can always take it out of his hide."

She held out her hand. Mike shook it. "Thank you so much."

"You deserve it, Brenda—for putting up with that lug as long as you did."

She held the check between trembling hands, as though she could not believe the words written there.

Pay to the order of Brenda McCoy
Ten thousand dollars

Twenty-One

KATE BEGAN TAKING her dad to rehab every morning. The trip gave her time out of the house and away from her mother. By Thursday she'd developed a habit of dropping her father off and driving to a nearby coffee shop. Kate discovered a love for a particularly potent frozen concoction made with coffee, covered with whipped cream, and drizzled with caramel sauce. She never would have indulged herself this way at home. But this was Kansas, not home, and many things had changed since the end of her life in Tiburon. In the quiet of the coffee shop, Kate sipped her drink and read the morning paper. By the time she met her father, she felt refreshed and eager for the day.

At the end of her third week in Lawrence, Kate sat in an overstuffed velvet chair, sipping her drink, completely immersed in the *Wall Street Journal*. The shop bustled with customers, most of whom bought their beverage and went on to work, which suited Kate just fine. That is, until a cell phone tucked in someone's coat pocket began to ring. She glanced at the man sitting at the table across from her and frowned deliberately. He smiled back, pulled out the phone, and switched off the power, never bothering to answer the call.

Startled, Kate turned back to her paper. What kind of man would carry a phone, then turn it off while he had coffee? She found herself curious, and she stole secretive glances across the room. He looked successful—navy blazer, khaki slacks, maroon tie. A normal working guy. She tried to glance at his face but found it hidden behind the sports page. Only soft brown hair peeked out over the headlines.

A few moments later, she glanced at him again, only to find him staring directly at her. This time, she noticed that gray frosted his mustache and eyebrows, though his hair was still a startlingly youthful color. Embarrassed, she looked away. She heard his chair scrape across the tile floor.

"Excuse me," he said, from beside her chair. "I know I'm too old for this line. But I really do think we know one another. I'm sure of it. But I can't remember where."

"I don't think so." Kate tried to ignore him.

"Are you sure? Can I sit down?" He reached toward the table beside Kate and pulled out a wooden chair, but did not sit. "I've lived in Lawrence all my life. And in my business, I meet so many people. Forgive me, but I'm certain that I know you."

The words "forgive me" struck a funny chord in Kate's memory. He said it just like someone else she once knew. She looked up again, scanning the features of his face with care, looking for something familiar. "I grew up here too," she said. "But I've been gone a long time."

"Katie?" His voice filled with a kind of wonder. "Katie Killian? It's me. Greg," he said. "Remember me? Greg Harris."

Something about the gray-blue eyes seemed familiar. But she could not place him—even though he'd offered his name. "I'm sorry," she apologized. "Obviously you remember me, but I . . ."

"We went to South Point Baptist together. Remember? Remember Pastor Chuck? We were at church together every Wednesday night."

The memory came back at last. Greg Harris had grown a good five inches since Kate last saw him. Naturally, over the past thirty-five years he'd filled out. Kate hardly recognized the fun-loving kid in the man who now stood above her chair. Still, she could not deny it. There could be no mistaking those gray-blue eyes.

Delighted, she stood. Throwing her arms around his neck, she hugged him happily. "Greg, it's so good to see you," she said. He tipped slightly off balance, and they both nearly fell over sideways. "Sit down," Kate said. "Do you have time to visit?"

"I do," he answered. "I mean, if you do, I'd love to." He pulled out the chair beside her. "Kate, I can't believe running into you like this. Are you here to see your folks?"

"My dad. He's had a heart attack."

"Oh, I'm sorry. How's he doing?"

"Well, he's at rehab right now. But they say he has a lot of damage."

"Rehab. You mean right this minute?"

"Yes, actually." Kate lifted her wrist to check the time. "I have to pick him up in about fifteen minutes."

"Must be hard on your mom."

"It is. She's doing as well as she can. But she's frightened. Can hardly let him out of the house."

A long silence stretched between them. Kate picked up her drink. As she brought the cup to her face, the straw poked her in the lip. Nervous, she brushed her hand across her mouth, smiled, and sipped. He stared out the storefront, almost unaware of her.

"So, Greg, tell me about your family."

"I have two boys. One is a mechanic at a car dealership. Loves engines. Has since he was old enough to lean over a car. And the other teaches history over in Cottonwood Falls."

"Any grandkids?"

"The teacher isn't married. But the mechanic has two."

"How wonderful for you. I'll bet your wife is thrilled." Kate did not remember whom Greg had married. A hometown girl? A childhood sweetheart? After all, it had been a long time.

"My wife died two winters ago. Breast cancer."

"Oh, I'm so sorry," she said. "That must have been hard."

"It wasn't easy." His face tightened in a bittersweet smile. "But I'm doing much better these days." He took a deep breath. "Tell me about your family."

"Well, I have two grown children. Drew is an engineer in Salem, Oregon, and Keegan attends law school at Pepperdine. Neither is married yet."

"A daughter in law school. That must make you proud."

"I am. I just wish I didn't have to help pay for it." Kate grinned.

"It's so nice to see you again." He looked directly into her eyes. Something about his gentle expression seemed vulnerable. She smiled again and glanced away.

"Well, I guess I should really get going. My dad hates to wait," she said. Standing, she picked up her purse and pulled the strap over her shoulder. As she bent to reach for her trash, he caught her hand with his own.

"Kate," he said. "You haven't said anything about your husband."

"Oh, that." She pulled her hand away, shrugged, and stuffed a napkin into her empty cup. "There isn't anything to say, really. He owns a software company in California. I met him at the first job I had after graduating."

He looked disappointed. "So he's waiting in California?"

"Not exactly," she said. "We're divorced." The lie surprised her. She gestured to the door, backing away from the table. "I need to get going."

"Wait." He stood and followed her. "Can I call you? We could catch up on old times. Old friends."

She hesitated. After all, she had no idea how long she would be in Lawrence. She would enjoy a break from her parents, and it would be fun to hear about all her high school chums. "I'd love that," she said. "My folks are listed in the phone book." She gave a small wave with one hand. "Gotta go." Just before she opened the door, she stuffed her garbage into the tall stainless steel trash can. If only she could dispose of her past so easily.

———

Norm met Gwen in the lobby of their New York City hotel. Together they hailed a cab and headed downtown to the city jail. With any luck, today might move them one step closer to identifying the dead driver. Perhaps they could even prove a conspiracy behind the credit cards.

Norm was oblivious to the sights of the city passing by the car windows. He focused instead on his takeout breakfast—a roll and coffee—which he had purchased in the hotel lobby. Between long swigs of dark black coffee, Norm managed to spill crumbs from the roll onto the lapel of his sport coat.

Gwen watched the city pass through the car windows. "I hate New York," she said. "No one talks to anybody here. I mean, what's wrong with a simple hello? Nobody here opens a door for a stranger. No please or thank you." She turned to look at Norm. "I tell you, we can't get out of here soon enough. It's cold here."

"Should have bought some coffee at the hotel."

She glared at him. "I'm not talking about body temperature."

"Oh yeah. Sorry."

At the jail, the cab driver jerked the car into a circular driveway, throwing Gwen across the backseat against her partner. "I told you," she said, voice low. "No courtesy." She opened the car door and climbed out.

In an indistinguishable accent, the driver mumbled something to Norm. He pulled a twenty-dollar bill from his wallet.

"Receipt?" Norm asked. The man shrugged and handed over a tiny scrap of white paper.

Norm heard himself slip into big-city shorthand. Why use a sentence when a phrase will suffice? Why use a phrase when a single word will do? Maybe Gwen was right. Maybe the city did that to everyone, driving out what few human kindnesses might remain. Language seemed to be the most severely affected of missing civilities.

Gwen led the way into the building. At the security station, she placed her briefcase on the belt into the X-ray machine, turned over her handgun along with her identification badge to the officer in charge, and stepped through the metal detector. As Norm completed the same routine, Gwen waited on the other side of the security desk.

"Where is Johnson?" she asked.

"They told me to check in on seven," he answered, falling into step beside her. "What did you find on the background check?"

"Lots. This guy was born bad. He's been in and out of every jail in New York State."

"Exaggeration doesn't become you," Norm said.

"Okay, not every jail. Just most of them," she conceded. "I talked to New York City Police this morning. The guys in blue are holding him in connection with grand theft—auto."

Norm's eyebrows rose.

"Nothing clearly related to our case. Apparently, when they booked him, he had a wallet full of credit cards. None with his own name. But he won a free night in the city jail for lifting a Lexus."

"Any idea where the cards came from?"

"I couldn't get that much, at least not this morning."

At the elevator, Norm pushed the Up button. "Did you get a fax from Namura this morning?"

"The concierge slid it under my door."

"Anything new?"

"Not really. He just wanted us to know that they can pin Johnson to the tickets in our John Doe's post office box. Hands down. No question."

"Anything else?"

"Well, unofficially, they say this Johnson character we're here to see is connected to New York mob families. Namura says we can use that as a threat. Maybe he'll spill his guts."

"Great. Now we have a computer guy telling us how to interrogate."

"You have lemon filling on your lip there," Gwen pointed with her index finger.

Norm swiped at his upper lip with the side of his wrist. "Thanks." They stepped inside. "What does he think, we're new at this?"

Gwen stepped in beside him and turned to face the elevator door. "Nah, couldn't be that," she said. "Anyone can see you've been at this for years and years."

It took a moment. Then, just as the doors closed, Norm figured out what she meant. This time, it was his turn to glare.

———

"Look, Mom. I'm only going to eat lunch with the guy." Kate slipped one arm into her sweater. "I'm not on a date. We're just friends." She leaned over her mother's chair, squeezing her shoulders. "Be back in a couple of hours."

Kate stepped over to her father, who sat in his recliner, completely absorbed in a novel. "See you later, Dad," she said, kissing his forehead.

"You going somewhere, Katie-Doll?"

Kate smiled. "Dad, do all men miss as much as you do?"

"Of course, dear. It's hormonal." He grinned up at her, holding his finger in his place on the page.

"I'm going to lunch with a friend." Kate picked up her car keys and headed for the front door. "Try to keep Mom busy. She's already started worrying about me."

"That's hormonal too," her mother piped in. "All mothers do it. You should know that."

Kate couldn't argue with her mother on that point. She'd put in enough hours worrying about her own children. But still, when your daughter is approaching fifty, a mother has to let go. Kate pulled her car out of the driveway onto the quiet lane where she'd spent her entire childhood. Things change. At some point, mothers don't make choices for their children anymore.

Kate planned to meet Greg at a small Southwestern style restaurant in Old Lawrence, her favorite part of town. Kate looked forward to seeing the small storefronts lining quiet streets. This part of town still resembled small-town America. Dress stores, hardware stores, a five-and-dime—all still there, just as she remembered from her childhood. She pulled into angled parking in front of the restaurant and turned off the car. Feeling her heart beat fast, she wondered why lunch with Greg should make her feel so nervous.

Why be frightened? It's only lunch. He's an old friend. I deserve to have a nice lunch with a friend, she thought. She pulled the rearview mirror to the side and checked her makeup. Still in one piece. She ran her middle finger along her lower lashes, tidying up a smudge. Pulling her lip gloss from her purse, she moistened her lips, then tugged at her hair with her fingers. *If I don't stop stalling, he'll think I've stood him up.* She got out of the car, tucked her keys into her purse, and headed for the restaurant.

Greg waited at a small round table near the front window. "You've come!" he said, greeting her. "I don't know why, but I wondered if maybe you'd chicken out."

"Of course not," Kate said with far too much cheer. "Why would I do a thing like that?" She slid into the chair he held for her. "I'd never pass up a free lunch."

"But there's no such thing as a free lunch," he quipped, sitting down in the chair opposite her. "Everyone knows that."

"I know nothing of the kind." She picked up her menu. "I'm starved. What's good?"

"Me too," he agreed, smiling.

A dark-haired Hispanic woman came to the table. "Can I get you something to drink while you decide?"

"Just water for me," Kate said.

"The same," he said. When the waitress had gone, Greg smiled into Kate's eyes. "I still can't believe that I ran into you after all these years."

"I know," she set her menu aside. "What a surprise. Tell me, Greg, what are you doing these days?"

"I sell real estate," he said over his menu. "Mostly commercial. The area is growing so much, I can hardly keep up with the demand for square footage."

"Did you work in real estate before . . ." she hesitated, "before your wife got sick?"

"I started right out of college," he said. "I used to have my own business. But after Gena died, I just didn't have the energy to work at it." He gazed out at the sidewalk. "Too worn out, I guess."

"I didn't know Gena. Where did you meet?"

"She was in one of my classes at the University of Kansas."

"When did you marry?"

"A week after I graduated."

Kate smiled. "Oh yes, the summer of changes."

"True for us. I graduated, got married, got my first real job, and moved into a brand-new apartment—all within three months."

"Good thing they don't expect people our age to do that." She laughed. "I'm too tired to get that much done anymore." Even as she said it, it occurred to Kate that she had chosen this same course again. Changing everything, overnight.

"What?"

His question startled her. She thought she'd been clear enough. "I don't understand."

"You had this thing, this, uh, expression—I saw it go across your face just now."

She nodded. "I guess I was thinking about the divorce. How everything can change so suddenly. It's a little like that first summer after college, isn't it?" Kate took a sip of water. "Tell me about your wife."

"Well, she was an artist. Loved to paint. She sold her work in local galleries. She stayed home to raise the boys. And just when they were far enough along that she could concentrate on her own life, she got sick. She planned to go back to school, but she never made it."

"I'm sorry."

"Me too." He sighed. "But we had a wonderful life together. Lots of happy years. I'm thankful for the good times."

"Not angry about the ones taken away from you?"

"Exactly," he agreed.

"But it isn't easy, is it? That's the way I feel about my divorce," Kate said. "Like I need to get on with my life, be grateful for the good times, and let go of the years I didn't get." She ran her fingers through her hair and sighed. "Once in a while, though, I still get stuck in the angry part."

"Not being angry takes time. I heard once that anger is just another form of sadness." He smiled and pushed the menu away. "It was sure true for me."

The waitress approached the table. "Are you ready to order?"

"I'll have the chicken taco salad," Kate said, passing back the menu.

"Make that two," Greg added, grinning. "Two is a good number, don't you think?"

Twenty-Two

AT THE SEVENTH FLOOR reception desk, Norm introduced himself to the officer sitting behind bulletproof glass. Immediately, she announced their arrival. Moments later, a uniformed officer led them through double security doors to a small room at the end of a narrow hallway.

Inside, five heavy wooden chairs surrounded a long rectangular table. A dark glass mirror, an observation window, covered one wall. Gwen pulled out a chair and sat down. Norm wandered over to the mirror, adjusted his tie, and then, sticking his face close to the glass, opened his mouth and began picking at his teeth with the nail on his little finger. After giving a tiny wave, he turned back to face Gwen.

"You love doing that, don't you?" she asked.

He shrugged and gave a little grunt. "Just my way of saying hello."

"And for that they must be grateful."

The door opened, and a policewoman escorted the prisoner into the room. Stepping aside, she gestured to the single chair on the long end of the table. He sat, placing cuffed wrists on the table. "I don't talk without my attorney," he said, shaking long hair out of his eyes.

"We expect him any minute," Norm said.

Gwen began, "We might as well introduce ourselves. My name is Gwen Saunders. This is Norm Walker." She flashed her identification badge. "We're Federal Agents from Seattle, Washington."

"I don't talk to nobody without my attorney in the room."

"We understand. We've spoken with him by telephone. He should be along any minute," Norm repeated, leaning against the back of a chair.

Johnson did not respond. Staring straight ahead, he sat frozen, unmoving. His brown eyes focused on the wall beyond them.

Again the door opened. This time a gargantuan man in a double-breasted suit entered. The dark charcoal suit fabric shone from endless pressing. His overstuffed briefcase, an old portfolio style, bulged. Broken buckles hung uselessly from worn leather straps. Without acknowledging his client, he stepped to the end of the table and dropped into a chair. Norm held his breath as the man went down, hoping the chair could withstand his falling weight. "I'm Stuart Cole," he said, throwing his briefcase onto the table. "I represent Robert Johnson." He nodded at his client. "We can begin any time you'd like."

Norm noticed that beads of sweat formed on the attorney's upper lip. "Thank you for coming downtown, Mr. Cole."

Gwen began the introductions as Norm took the seat beside her. "We need to speak with your client about a case in Washington State. Nothing terribly serious. At least nothing as serious as the charges you have on your hands here in New York."

As Gwen spoke with the attorney, Norm watched Robert, who sat calmly staring forward, as though engrossed in a television program being shown just over his attorney's shoulder. Serious acne marred his forehead and cheeks, and he had grown a beard consisting of no more than a dozen hairs. He might have hoped that facial hair gave him an air of maturity, though the entire effect was that of an overeager adolescent.

Gwen swapped niceties with the breathless attorney and then turned her attention to Robert. "We came to New York hoping you could help us identify the driver of a car, killed in a Washington State accident," she began.

"Must be a pretty important driver to bring in the FBI," Cole commented.

"Seems he might be." Norm glanced at Cole and then back at Robert. At only twenty-two, this kid had managed to get himself in serious trouble. Norm removed an eight-by-ten glossy black-and-white from a stack of documents before him and slid it across the table to Robert. "Do you recognize this photograph?"

With the tips of his fingers, he picked up the photo and awkwardly managed to turn it toward himself. "Should I?"

"Just answer the question, please."

"No. Never seen the guy."

"Are you quite certain?"

"Look, if you're gonna ask me the questions, maybe you better take the answer I give ya."

"You might want to rethink your answer. You see, we found a post office box belonging to this man. The box was loaded," Gwen said.

Norm watched Robert carefully. In spite of handcuffs, his fingers clutched one another tightly. He squirmed in his seat.

"So what do I care about this guy's post office box?"

Gwen answered him. "Inside we found an airline ticket. Made out to the dead driver. The guy was supposed to fly to New York City on the day he died."

"So I guess his seat went empty."

Mr. Cole sat picking at his cuticles, apparently ignoring the entire proceeding.

"We traced the ticket, Robert." Norm pulled out another document and slid it in front of the prisoner. "You bought the ticket, didn't you?"

Suddenly Cole sat up, his eyes sparking. "You don't have to answer that."

He barely glanced at his attorney. "No, I didn't."

Norm nodded to Gwen. "We know you did, Johnson. We traced the purchase from the airline to your Internet address. That address led us to your telephone. You bought the ticket—though you didn't use your own credit card—and mailed it to the driver in our car accident."

Again, the prisoner shrugged, staring off into a corner of the ceiling.

"Now, here's the important information." Gwen leaned forward, using her index finger on the table. "We have enough to connect you with this guy on a RICCO charge. It won't be fun. We know he was stealing credit card numbers from Internet sites and producing cards in big quantities. He was making the cards—but someone else was buying. Maybe you?"

Norm took his cue. "The driver is dead. We can't charge him. But we could still hang you. Wouldn't be too hard. I hear that the car theft case is pretty circumstantial. Maybe this guy here can get you off. Then what?"

"Should be fun, trying to defend yourself in two separate cases," Gwen added. "Two separate states. Do you have the money for that kind of representation, Robert?"

"Now, Gwen, it isn't that terrible," Norm deliberately took the tone of a patronizing parent. "We might be able to bargain for some help in our case," he opened his hands and spread them on the table. "We're really not here to give the kid jail time. We'd just like a little help, that's all."

"What is it you want?" The kid seemed confused. "I don't know the guy. I never met him."

"So why buy him an airline ticket? Who asked you to do it? Were you the contact?"

"Don't answer that." The attorney sat forward, his palms flat on the table, his gaze darting back and forth following the conversation.

Robert glared at him. "What have you done for me?" His voice rose, his composure at last blown. "I've been sitting in this stinking hole for two days, and what have you done?"

"We're prepared to make a deal," Gwen pressed. "If you'll help us, we can reduce charges against you."

"In the car theft?" Robert seemed eager.

"We can't help you there," Gwen admitted. "But in the RICCO, we can forget you were involved, provided you tell us what we need to know. After all, we wouldn't want a conspiracy charge hanging on your record for the rest of your life."

"Who have you been working for, Robert?" Norm spoke calmly, his fingers laced together as though he'd just ordered fries at a local McDonald's.

"I don't really know," Johnson began.

"Stop it. Now. Don't say another word." Cole slammed his palms onto the table.

"I'll say what I want," Robert Johnson shot back. He lifted his hands and ran them through his greasy black hair. "I got instructions from an old boss of mine. Money. Sometimes I bought a ticket for Seattle to New York. Sometimes for San Francisco to New York.

I carried computer disks a couple of times. That's all. Nothing criminal. I didn't know what they were doing."

"Who was your boss, Robert?"

"I got orders from a family on the East Side."

"People you've worked for before?"

"Once or twice."

"Who was in San Francisco?"

"I never knew who it was."

"What part did San Francisco play?"

"That's it. No more questions." The attorney pulled himself up, his chair screeching noisily across the concrete floor. "Guard," he yelled. "We're through."

The door opened, and the officer returned with a slightly puzzled expression on her face.

"We're finished. You may return the prisoner to his cell," Cole commanded.

The guard took Robert by one arm and led him into the hall. Norm and Gwen remained sitting. Stuart Cole picked up his briefcase, his face red, expression tight. "If you ever intend to speak to my client about immunity again, you may begin at my office." He started across the floor and stopped suddenly, turning. "I want every offer in writing, signed by your supervisors."

————

Kate relaxed back into the neck support of the padded salon chair. As the beautician's gentle fingers massaged her face, she willed herself to let go of the tension between her brows, the tension that gave the skin between Kate's eyes a perennial wrinkle—as though she wore a constant frown. She imagined the moisturizer sinking deep into the cells of her skin, bringing with it life and warmth.

"There," the cosmetologist said, spreading the liquid with her thumbs, brushing Kate's cheeks lightly. "Now this moisturizer has an SPF of twenty-five. It will not only protect you from the sun but also from environmental pollutants." As she moved around to work from Kate's other side, Kate forced her eyes to remain closed, determined to spend this hour completely pampered, completely relaxed. "With your fair skin, you need to be especially protective. Unless you wear a sunscreen constantly, you'll find that age spots and freckles will cover that creamy skin of yours."

Very effective. What woman would choose age spots and freckles over creamy skin?

"Now we're ready to add new color." Her voice moved away, and Kate sensed that she had turned to face the counter. "I'd suggest a neutral palette. Something to go with the green in your eyes. Like this." She turned back, and Kate saw her holding a soft brown shadow. "Isn't this luscious?"

Kate nodded, and she continued. "Now I'll use a matte sponge to apply the shadow to the lower portion of your eyelid only. You'll want to purchase a sable brush for yourself—much more gentle. And all you need is a tiny bit of color."

With an effort Kate kept her eyes closed against the rasping tug of the sponge applicator. The woman began to work on her other eye. "I have the perfect liner to go with this," she added, turning back to the counter. "Called 'mink.' I like it because it's less harsh than what most women wear. This is far more natural. It goes beautifully with your warm blond hair." She rested the edge of her hand on Kate's cheek. "Now, look up at the ceiling."

Kate obeyed while the woman ran a crayon along the lower edge of both eyelids.

"And glance down." She touched the pencil to Kate's face again. "I'm only doing the outside edge," she explained. "Because I want to draw the eyes apart." Kate looked up as the woman made her fingers into a "V" shape and did a Batman motion. Kate stifled a smile.

"And now, just the slightest touch of soft brown mascara." She stroked it on. "There, what do you think?" She handed Kate a large hand mirror.

Afraid of what she might see, Kate took a deep breath and looked down at her own reflection. The changes surprised her. Her hair, once long and wavy, had been cut and styled into a dramatic wedge. The back, now shorter than the sides, had been layered severely, while the bangs and sides had been kept long, waving freely around her face. The effect startled Kate. In one hour Kate had gone from a worn-out look to a fashionable professional image. She smiled.

Kate had never worn much makeup—other than for formal occasions. The vast choices of colors and materials daunted Kate.

But this cosmetologist had made a marvelous transformation. She had given Kate glamour and a style perfect for her age and position. Her new look might have illustrated a magazine article titled "Not Older, Just Better."

In spite of herself, Kate grinned into the mirror. "I love it. Really."

"I'm so glad," the woman said. "It's much more fun to do a makeover on a woman who has such natural beauty."

Her words struck Kate. A natural beauty? Healthy, yes. Athletic, yes. On a particularly generous day, Katherine Langston might even give herself credit for handsome. But beautiful? She never thought of herself that way.

The woman began writing down the colors and products she had chosen for Kate's makeover. "Do you have any questions?"

"Yes. Can I buy it all?"

"All of it? Really?" The woman looked at Kate, her mouth slightly open, clearly surprised. "Oh, of course, I'd be glad to ring that up for you." She went around the corner to the cash register, unable to suppress a happy smile.

———

"So do you have a copy of the kid's rap sheet?" Norm asked, slumped against the door of the cab. "Maybe he's worked with someone we know. Maybe that's where we go next."

Gwen, her knees squeezed tightly together, balanced a heavy manila folder on her lap. "Am I hearing you admit that this is indeed a conspiracy?" Gwen asked, shuffling through a pile of print-outs.

"You aren't hearing anything of the kind."

"Of course not. You never admit anything." She handed him a sheet of paper.

"Not until we get a conviction." He accepted the paper, glancing at it briefly. "Oh man, this kid has quite a resume, doesn't he?"

"No more than any other. Car theft. Burglary. Armed robbery. Possession of stolen property." She shrugged. "The usual."

"Okay, what do we know?" He stole a wry look at her and then fixed his gaze at the scene passing by his window. He began tugging at his earlobe.

"We know the kid was a runner. He got information from an

unknown and delivered it to our boy in Tacoma." Gwen put her legal pad on top of the pile. She jotted notes to herself.

"Could be the information was tied to the stolen credit card numbers."

"But we aren't certain," she said. "And we know that he bought airline tickets on a phony Visa card for our boy and for someone in San Francisco."

"We think he's connected to one of the crime families here in the city."

"That's pretty easy to figure out. But it may not help us come up with the big plan." She pointed out the window. "Here we are."

The cab pulled out of traffic into the hotel drive-through. "Right. Only tells us who bought the cards," Norm agreed. Getting out, they continued speaking over the top of the cab.

"So what now?" Gwen asked.

"Now?" He handed the driver exact change and stood up. "Now we go find us some lunch. I'm starved."

Gwen shook her head. "Of course. What did I expect? But after lunch—what then?"

"Then I think we catch a flight home. That defense attorney isn't going to let us talk to Johnson again." He reached the lobby doors in front of her, holding one open. "I'm thinking that Namura might be able to guess what's in San Francisco." As she stepped in front of him, he continued, "But we'll have to hurry if we're going to get a dinner flight out of New York."

Twenty-Three

IN SAN FRANCISCO, Norm walked into the CEO's office behind a blond secretary and blinked with surprise. Though he'd been in plenty of luxurious office suites, he'd seen nothing as opulent as this. The size of the room astounded him, perhaps a full thousand square feet. The carpet, a soft blue-green, sank beneath his steps. A magnificent U-shaped unit, custom designed of some peculiar wood—teak perhaps—served as a working desk.

"Feel free to take a seat. Mr. Langston will be right with you." The blonde gestured toward the couch. Norm did not move. "Would you like something to drink while you wait?" the secretary asked. She stood waiting, posed in the exact center of the room with her hands folded in front of her waist.

"Do you have some iced tea?" Norm asked, smiling.

"I'll have some sent up. Anything else?"

"No, thanks." Norm said. He slid his hands into his pockets and bowed slightly.

When she closed the office door, he walked to the windows, angling his pathway to pass by the screen of the desk computer. From this position, he watched the screen saver. Sailboats of every size and variety undulated across the screen on computer-generated waves. *The guy has a thing for sailboats.* Norm made a mental note to check on this. *A place to hide extra money, perhaps?*

Standing in front of the window, as though he enjoyed the view, he took a quick inventory of the desk itself. Post-it notes hung like drying laundry along the lip of the upper cabinets, each neatly printed note sitting exactly the same distance apart.

Unlike token executives, this man seemed to do real work. Several yellow legal pads covered with notes and diagrams had been laid out carefully along the working surface. Beside his multiple-line telephone, a tall stack of messages written on preprinted forms awaited action. Several matching pens had been lined up exactly parallel with stacks of waiting files. The guy liked padded handles—the kind of pens purchased in twelve-packs at warehouse stores.

Norm wondered whether he should step closer for a better look. As he contemplated this slightly illegal search, the door opened, and a man dressed in tan shorts and Wilson court shoes strode purposefully across the room. Holding out his hand, he said, "Hello, I'm Mike Langston."

"Norm Walker, FBI."

They shook hands. Norm looked Mike directly in the eye, judging him to be about equal in height, with eyes so dark that the pupils seemed hard to find. Olive skin, a perennial tan, Mike appeared to be nearly twenty years younger than Norm. And much thinner. *Probably has a personal trainer,* Norm thought grudgingly.

"You know I haven't changed my mind," Mike said, still smiling.

"Your mind?"

"About the advisory panel."

Obviously, Mike Langston referred to something Norm knew nothing about. Rather than cover his confusion, he asked, "I'm sorry. I don't know what you mean. I'm not here about an advisory panel."

This time, Langston looked confused. He shook his head. "When your man was here a couple months ago, he asked me to sit on an Internet security panel. I told him I don't have time for that kind of stuff." Mike slid his hands in his pockets. "I thought you were here for the same thing. Sorry."

"No," Norm smiled. "Actually, I'm here on a criminal matter. Do you have time to talk?"

"Let's sit," Mike said, pointing to a leather couch.

"Thank you." Norm followed him across the room. In the area around the couch, an Oriental rug had been set into the outer carpet at exactly the same height. An iron coffee table held a slab of natural stone—something golden and polished to a slick shine. At one end of the couch, a linen tube stood in a black wrought iron frame. The lamp, which appeared to be an original, reflected some Chinese or Oriental style. Norm didn't like it. Norm didn't like anything that smelled like money. "I'm sorry to bother you like this, Mr. Langston. I can see you're a busy man."

"True," Mike agreed. "But Brooke told me this is urgent. I can give you a few minutes. What do you need?"

As the two men took their seats, Norm noticed that Mike sat easily, relaxed, one foot crossed over the other knee. His fingers rested without motion on the arm of the overstuffed leather chair. He showed no sign of discomfort. No shifting. No fidgeting.

"I appreciate your time," Norm began. "First I'd like to ask a couple of questions related to an accident investigation I'm involved in."

"Go ahead." Mike nodded.

"Now, am I correct in my information that your company provides the software for businesses functioning on the Internet?"

"Yes, that's partially true."

"Can you explain to me exactly what it is that you do?"

"We design encryption software, what some might call 'shopping cart technology.' Perhaps you've heard of *Amazon.com*? We do designs like that. The idea is that anyone can buy something on the Web using a credit card, and the entire transaction is encrypted—put in code—and sent over the Web to the host company. We do unique designs—different for every company we work with—depending on their individual needs. But our work guarantees the security and privacy of the transaction."

"And companies don't do this themselves?"

"Not usually. It costs too much to keep a design and engineering team on staff. It's far more efficient to sub the work out. Naturally, because we specialize in it, we're fast and effective."

"So companies hire you to design the site?"

"Yes and no. We don't design informational sites. Just sites that require encryption for sales—that kind of thing."

"I see." Norm thought for a moment. "I think I should explain what brings me here. In Tacoma, earlier this spring, a young man was killed in a car accident on the Narrows Bridge. As yet, we don't know who the man was. But we do know that he was in the business of making false credit cards." As Norm spoke, he continued to watch Mike carefully, noting every nuance of expression, movement, and emotion. Mike remained quiet, relaxed.

"Please, go on."

"Of course, by itself, we don't care about the kid making cards. After all, he's dead, right?"

"Mr. Walker," Mike Langston wore a perplexed expression, his index finger pointing into the air in front of his face.

"Norm, please."

"Norm, I'm not following you. What does all this have to do with me?"

"It doesn't. At least not directly." Norm paused in his explanation to gaze around the room. "Beautiful office, Mr. Langston. You use a designer?"

Impatience flitted over Mike's face, but he made no comment.

"Anyway, we've decided that the kid wasn't acting alone. We brought in a computer expert. And we've followed a few leads."

"And?" Mike rolled his hand palm up.

Norm enjoyed dragging explanations out, watching his prey carefully before making the final dive. "And we think that someone in this company may have been helping our suspect."

"This company? You mean DataSoft?"

"Yes."

While Norm observed, Mike's eyebrows moved closer together in an expression of surprise and confusion. "Who? Who is doing it?"

"I was hoping you could tell me."

"You don't know?"

"We have an idea." As Norm watched, Mike lost his calm, relaxed appearance. He sat forward, uncrossing his legs.

"Mr. Walker, it seems to me that you have a lot of nerve coming in here like this. You have no concrete evidence, no solid suspects, no ideas, and yet in spite of that, you want to ruin the reputation of this company on pure speculation."

Mike's tone grew hard, cold, and Norm made a note of it. "Not at all. You misunderstand." Norm chose to remain calm and relaxed, hoping to deflect the executive's indignation. "I'm certain that you value the reputation of your company. I'm also certain that if I'm correct—that someone is actually using your company to steal credit card numbers—then no one wants to put a stop to it more than you." Norm leaned forward, put his elbows on his bent knees. "Isn't that right?"

"Mr. Walker, you've made a very big jump in your thinking. I'm not ready to assume that you are correct. Our systems are airtight. No one can break into them. Not even someone from our own company."

"I didn't say anyone was breaking into anything."

"No. Actually, you've managed to make accusations without any of them being grounded in fact." Mike stood and paced in front of the coffee table. "You have no evidence. No substantive vehicle for the crime itself." Mike whirled to face him, pointing with his index finger. "You have no idea the damage this kind of accusation might do."

"Not accusing. Actually, I was hoping you would help us. If someone here is messing with your product, then no one stands to lose more than you."

"Don't you think I know that? These things don't stay quiet. Our business would be ruined if word got out that we have a security problem—no matter where it comes from."

"So here is my offer. I think things might go better for you and the company if you find out where the problem is."

"You want me to do your dirty work?"

"No. I'm saying that your cooperation might help convince a prosecutor that you aren't involved in anything illegal."

Following a soft knock, Brooke opened the door slightly, and Norm saw that she held a tray of iced tea in glass tumblers. "Iced tea, Mr. Langston," she said.

"No, thank you, Brooke. Mr. Walker was just leaving." Mike kept his anger barely concealed in short terse words.

Her eyebrows rose. "I'm sorry, sir," she said as she backed out of the doorway.

"Mr. Walker, I think I've heard just about enough. If there is something illegal going on at DataSoft, I'd suggest you come back with a search warrant and prove it." Mike walked across the room, opened the door, and held it for Walker.

Norm stood, buttoned his sport coat, and walked slowly across the room. Not about to be hurried, he said, "Well, I'm sorry you feel that way. A judge might have looked at things more favorably if you'd chosen to cooperate." He offered Mike his hand. "But it's been nice visiting with you this morning."

Mike kept one hand on the doorknob, the other deep in his pocket. His face had frozen in a concentrated effort to control his rage.

"By the way, nice office," Norm repeated. "Federal offices aren't nearly so plush." He turned to the door. "Oh yes, I'll be hanging around. If you change your mind, let me know." He took a business card from his breast pocket and held it out to Mike. "You can call me anytime at that number."

Mike took the card. "I won't be calling, Norm," he said, dragging out the agent's first name. As soon as Walker cleared the threshold, the door slammed shut behind him.

Not exactly the kind of interview Norm had hoped for. That guy had a temper.

On Sunday morning, Mike rose bright and early. First, he calculated the time difference between California and Kansas, then dialed Kate at her parents' home. No answer. Out to breakfast before church? Must be. Frustrated, he hung up and went downstairs to the kitchen.

He managed to scramble three eggs and fold cheddar into the mix before plopping it onto a plate. The whole thing slid unchecked from the pan; half of his omelet landed on the stove top. He scooped what he could and left the rest. Oh, well, he shouldn't eat that much cholesterol anyway. He ate while reading the Sunday paper. In the middle of a second cup of coffee, the chiming of the grandfather clock in the hall startled him. With barely enough time to shower and dress for the early service, he dashed upstairs to change.

Just as Mike turned off the engine in the parking lot of Sunset Community Church, Dave Holland approached the Mustang. Mike pulled his keys from the ignition and waved at him through the windshield. "Hey, Dave," he said through the open window. "You don't look too good. You feeling okay?"

"No." He stood on the other side of the curb, his hands on his hips.

Mike got out, and the two men shook hands. Walking toward

the foyer entrance, Mike asked, "What's going on? Your family okay?"

"Yeah, family's fine." Dave shoved his worn Bible under one elbow and tucked both hands in his pockets.

"So what is it? Your face looks like a storm front."

"Thanks a lot."

"What's happened?"

"Remember I told you I was going to get a dentist to come in and cover for me?"

"Right, so you and Valerie could take your dream cruise."

"Well, last night, the whole plan washed out." Dave stopped walking and turned to face his friend.

"How?"

"The dental student I asked to come in called us at home." Dave managed to nod and force the edge of his mouth to turn up in a vain attempt at a smile. Mike followed his gaze and saw a family getting out of a car nearby. Mike waved.

Dave said, "He flunked his boards."

"What?"

"He was supposed to take his licensing exams three weeks ago. Then, when he passed, he was going to come in and work part time until we left on the boat. But he flunked." Dave shook his head. "It never occurred to me that he'd flunk."

"What can you do?"

"I don't know, yet," Dave answered, walking again. "But Mike, please, whatever you do, don't even mention this to Val."

"She's pretty upset?

"I'd say so. When I told her, she locked herself in the bathroom."

"The bathroom?" Try as he might, Mike could not picture Valerie locking herself in the bathroom. He chuckled.

"Yup. Spent about four hours in the bathtub. It's her way of coping with frustration." He stepped from the parking lot onto the sidewalk. "I don't think I've ever seen her this frustrated."

"Yeah, wow, four hours. Long time." Together they went through the double entry doors into the church foyer. "Well, Dave," Mike chuckled, "at least you know she likes the water."

Dave scowled, and Mike suddenly found himself hoping Pastor

Rick had a great service planned. His friend desperately needed one.

————

Norm dialed the phone in his hotel room. After three days in the Bay Area, he'd failed to turn up any helpful information. "We're going to have to do some serious investigating," he told Gwen. "The whole thing makes no sense. How soon can you get down here?" Norm spoke in the low, intense tones he used over the telephone.

"The trial might last another three or four days," Gwen answered. "I could be there as soon as the prosecutor is finished with me."

"All right, then I'll keep snooping. We might have to put someone undercover."

"Have you talked with Langston at DataSoft?"

"Absolutely."

"And?"

"He's edgy. I think he knows something."

"All right. Keep in touch," she said. "Anything I can do from here?"

"Yes. I need the financial reports for DataSoft and IRS returns for all of the corporate officers."

"Okay. How many years?"

"The last five."

"You got it. I'll fax it to you at the San Francisco office."

"Thanks, Gwen."

"Right. And Norm, be careful. You've almost made it to retirement. It'd be a shame to lose you now."

"Wait a minute. This sounds like an 'I care about you' speech."

"No such thing. I just don't want to have to break in a new guy in the middle of a case." She chuckled softly. "Take care," she said, and hung up.

Twenty-Four

MIKE WENT HOME from church by way of the Fifth Street Deli. In the weeks since Kate left, he hadn't made any attempt to buy groceries—other than milk, which he purchased at the same convenience store where he bought gas. With everything falling apart at work, he'd simply eaten when and where he could. Mostly, he'd managed with cold cereal in the morning, skipped lunch, and then grabbed a bite on the way home from work. In the process he'd lost some weight. Not a bad thing, considering he'd put on a few extra pounds over the years.

Today, by the time Mike entered the deli, his stomach played a symphony of growls; he was starving. He waited in line with the other after-church couples, smelling the delicious aromas and feeling his stomach squeeze in anticipation. At the order counter, he chose a tall glass of Mountain Dew, lasagna, a fresh garden salad, and two slices of cheesecake. He paid the man who waited on him, picked up his salad, and turned to scan the room for a seat. As he watched, a couple left a table for two overlooking the bay. He scooted between several chairs and made a run for the empty table.

Putting down his tray, he began moving the glass and utensils onto the table. He placed the plastic covered order number on the edge of the table where a waiter could easily see it and sat down. Just as he did, he remembered how much Kate liked this place and that this was just the type of thing she loved to do. To sit together at a tiny table in an old dilapidated deli, overlooking the ocean. To share a huge restaurant serving of lasagna after church. He looked out over the water. From the street below, the remnants of a burned-out dock jutted into the harbor. Gulls floated and squealed in the afternoon breeze. And the thought that Kate should be here enjoying this with him brought a squeeze of pain even more intense than the hunger he'd felt earlier. This brought tears to his eyes, and he bent his head over the table in anguish.

"God, I know that I deserve this pain. I earned it. But I'm asking again. Forgive my sin, Lord. And help me to forgive myself." He pled quietly over the table. "And Jesus, give me whatever I need to undo the damage. . . ."

"Mike," a female voice called across the room. "What a surprise!"

He looked up and scanned the faces around him.

"Dave, look, there's Mike!"

Mike glanced to the entry, where he found the hulking silhouette of his friend Dave Holland, backlit by sunlight flowing through the deli windows behind him. Valerie, his wife, stood waving from behind his shoulder. Mike stood and smiled.

"Mike, are you here all by yourself?" Val called, dodging chairs and customers and waiters. She had a distinct tone of sorrow in her voice, which seemed to catch the attention of several people around him. Dave followed her path across the room.

"I didn't think there'd be anything to fix at home," he answered quietly. "It looked easier to go out." Mike gestured to the chair opposite him. "Why don't you join me?"

Val glanced up at Dave, who shrugged and stuck his hands in his pockets. "Well, I guess," she said. "You sure we wouldn't be bothering you?"

He shrugged, "I'm all by myself anyway."

"I'll go order," Dave said. "Val, what do you want to drink?"

"Hot tea," she answered. "Herbal, please." She pulled out a chair and sat down opposite Mike. "What did you order?"

"Lasagna."

"Oh, that sounds good. We always share the cannelloni." She wiped the checkered cloth with her palm. "The food here is wonderful."

Moments later, Dave arrived carrying a tray. He pulled a chair from a nearby table and sat beside them. After handing his wife her salad, he placed his own on the table. Leaning over, he slid the tray under his chair. "So. A surprise to find you here."

"Kate and I used to eat here all the time, after the kids went away to school. It almost became our Sunday routine."

"We haven't seen you here lately," Val piped in. "I mean," she lowered her voice, "I mean, before Kate went back to see her dad."

Though Mike knew she didn't mean to, her words brought fresh accusation, and he fought another wave of guilt. "Actually, our routine didn't last long. I guess I should have made those little things more important." He shrugged and cleared his throat. "Maybe I wouldn't be eating here alone."

Valerie reached out to cover his hand with her own. "Mike, don't keep killing yourself over this." She took a deep breath. "Things happen. Like the boat and us. It's no use trying to beat the whole thing up. It just is. That's all."

Mike looked up into Val's pale blue eyes and smiled. She had to be nearly sixty. Her youthful shape had long since abandoned her for middle-age bulge. She kept her white hair colored blonde. Some weeks her hair looked the color of brass bathroom fixtures. Sometimes, it was the soft color of fresh cream. Still, she had a good heart, and Mike understood why Dave loved her. "Thanks, Val."

She smiled and picked up her fork, then changed her mind and set it beside the plate. She reached out and added more dressing to her salad.

"It doesn't have to be the way it is." Dave said, chewing salad noisily. For a moment, Mike did not follow him. But Dave continued, "Just because it is, doesn't mean that we have to leave it like that."

"What do you mean?" Val asked. "We planned this wonderful cruise. But it isn't going to work out. We can't change that."

"Well, maybe we should. Maybe there's a way." He put down his fork and reached for a glass of water. "I told Mike a couple of weeks ago that he needed to think of this thing with Kate as a challenge." He waved his water glass in the air. "Like a business challenge."

Mike nodded. "You did. And I went to Kansas to talk to Kate." He smiled up at Val's surprised expression. "I did. And she threw me out." He shook salt onto his salad.

"That didn't work," Dave continued, "so you try something else. If you were the product and I was the advertiser, I'd try to figure out a reason why Kate needed you. Then, I'd do a Madison

Avenue job of presenting her with her need."

"Gentlemen," Valerie objected, "this is a marriage, not an advertisement. Kate is not a consumer, and Mike is definitely not a product."

"I know that." Dave set his water glass down hard enough to splash some onto the tablecloth. "And I think the marriage itself will draw Kate in. She loves Mike. She's just hurt. She isn't willing to admit that she loves him. Not yet."

"I've tried, Dave. It's a no-go."

"You just didn't have the right ammunition," Dave said, his mouth full of salad.

"Wait. Wait." Val dropped her fork onto the table. Her eyes shone with the brilliance of some unexplored idea. "Ammunition isn't the right word. What you need is bait." Her face lit up with a wide smile, and she held her palms toward Mike. "Oh, I'm masterful. Dazzling, actually."

"Cut it out, Val." Dave said, still chewing. "Just tell us what you're thinking."

Mike chuckled. This banter between Dave and Val had been going on for as long as he'd known them.

"What about this?" she asked, her voice urgent. "What if Kate and Mike delivered the boat to the South Pacific for us? We would have more time to find a replacement dentist. The boat would already be there when we get away from the office."

Dave's eyebrows rose.

She didn't give her husband time to interrupt. "We could have your brother join us in Hawaii or Fiji or someplace. We'd just fly there and meet the boat. Wouldn't that solve the problem with the hurricane season?" Other customers had begun to glance toward them.

"It's an idea," Dave almost whispered, his gaze focused thoughtfully on the harbor beyond the windows. "It would solve our problem completely. We'd have the boat delivered and still have enough time to find someone to take care of my patients." He slapped Mike on the shoulder. "And if anything would convince Kate to stay with you, it would be a romantic cruise to Hawaii or maybe even farther south."

"Dave, you're nuts. I've never taken a boat so far offshore alone. I wouldn't have the foggiest idea how to do it."

"Not so. You've done short cruises with me. You crewed with me in that race. You like the boat; you told me so. I can help you provision. We can plan the trip together. Go over the equipment. The repair. The rigging. It might just solve both of our problems."

Mike ran his hand through his hair, thinking hard. *Would it work? Would Kate make a trip like this with him? She'd thrown him out before. Why did this idea bring such a wildly exhilarating feeling of hope into his chest? Could this be his answer?* "But Kate won't go for it. I know she won't."

"We'll just have to figure out a way to make it worth her while," Dave said, as though it were an easy problem to solve.

"And it won't hurt to pray," Val said, chiding her husband.

"It never hurts to pray," Mike confirmed. In fact, he'd already begun.

————

Kate had never been to the Maison de la Berge. The old house had been renovated long after she moved to the West Coast. The inside of the dining room took her breath away. White enamel woodwork set off wallpaper in soft rose taffeta. Every table, covered in white damask, featured a hurricane lantern surrounded by a wreath of fresh flowers. Waiters wore tuxedoes. Waitresses wore period costumes from the old South. A small orchestra played music from a raised stage along the side of the ballroom. Below them, dancers enjoyed a plank dance floor. Except for the twentieth-century music, Kate felt like she had entered the set of *Gone with the Wind*.

Wonderful French cuisine, a beautiful setting, and Greg's company contributed to an almost perfect evening. Kate had borrowed a silk party dress from her mother and reveled in the luxury of the fabric against her skin. In this setting, with this dress and her new makeover, Kate felt a bit like Cinderella. Certainly, she had not been this relaxed since the day she retrieved the pictures from her mailbox. For dessert, she ordered crème brûlée, her favorite, intending to savor every bite.

She could always go running tomorrow.

As the waitress placed the dessert plate in front of Kate, their conversation took a sudden and unexpected turn.

"Actually, I'm not exactly sure how long I'll stay," Kate answered

Greg. Without looking at him, she toyed with her dessert, using her fork to chip off tiny pieces. "I came because my dad asked for me. When I got here, Mom seemed so crazy, so completely frazzled by his hospital stay, that I just stayed. She needed me." Kate brought one tiny piece to her lips.

"What about your work?"

"You're right. I have to decide about that sometime." She put her fork down and brought her napkin to her mouth, dabbing gently. "But I had vacation time, they had a replacement, and I just decided to take the time away." She rested her chin on her hands, gazing across the room.

As the orchestra began a new number, couples near them began to move onto the dance floor. Kate watched an elderly man at a nearby table help his wife to her feet. The man held her elbow gently as he led her to the edge of the dance floor. Then, with an almost synchronous motion, the tiny woman slid into his arms, and they began moving. It was a motion born of many years and thousands of dances just like this. Tiny and bent, her cupped hand barely reached her husband's shoulder. Moving with striking grace, she kept time with his rhythm. As he turned his wife toward Kate, she glimpsed the elderly woman's left hand. Kate spotted a wedding ring, a simple band so tiny she knew it could not have been removed over her disfigured knuckles. Kate found herself wondering how long the ring had been on that hand. Sixty years? More? The two had been together forever, and the thought of it stabbed Kate's heart.

For a moment, she wondered where Mike was that evening. Was he with Cara? Greg's voice brought her back to the present.

"Kate, I've been thinking," Greg said, holding his coffee cup between two hands. "I'm wondering . . ." He put the cup down. "I know this seems silly. We've only been together a little during these past seven days. But, what if you stayed? What if you got a job here in Lawrence?"

Kate nearly choked. Realizing that he had caught her off guard, Greg began to laugh.

"That's ridiculous," she said. "We're friends. That's all."

"I know, Kate. You're right. But your mom and dad are in Lawrence forever. It will be much easier to help them here than from the West Coast. Our kids are grown. They can fly out to visit."

He reached out and touched the back of her hand. "If you stayed, we might be able to give our friendship a chance to grow."

She pulled her hand from underneath his. "What are you saying?"

"Kate, relax. I'm not asking you to marry me." He smiled and continued, "We're both too old for any whirlwind stuff. But we've been friends all our lives. We have the same faith. The same background." His eyes seemed to plead. "We might be able to make something more of our friendship."

"But my life, my friends, are in San Francisco."

"I know. But perhaps it's time to start over." He pulled his napkin from his lap and laid it beside his dessert plate. "I've been alone for two years now. Long enough to know that I don't want to spend the rest of my life that way. We'll never know what might have happened if you go back to California."

His words so startled her that she had to deliberately close her mouth. "I don't think so." She shook her head. "It's too much change. Too much to decide so soon." Her lips had gone completely dry, and she took a sip from her water glass. "Really. Let's not talk about this again."

"All right, Kate," he said, clearly disappointed. "If we can't talk, at least we can dance." He stood up and came around to hold her chair. She stood slowly, still shaken by his words, and let him take her hand. When they got to the pale wooden floor, he pulled her into his arms and whispered into her ear. She felt his breath warm and moist against her ear. "If you won't talk about tomorrow, then I guess I'll just have to enjoy tonight."

Part Two

Second Chance

Twenty-Five

LATE SUNDAY NIGHT after her date, Kate let herself into the house as quietly as possible. One of her parents had left a light on in the entry hall and another at the end of the couch as well. She slipped into the living room to turn off the table lamp.

"So, Katie-Doll, how was your evening?"

The voice startled her, and she turned suddenly, her hand over her chest. "Dad, what are you doing up?" She glanced at the clock. "It's after one."

He smiled and set aside his book. "Believe me, I'm not up to check on you. I've slept so much over the past three weeks, I don't think my body knows what time of day it is anymore. Your mom went to bed hours ago." He leaned over to touch the lever on his recliner, sliding it into the upright position. "You haven't answered my question."

"I had a nice time." Kate sat down at one end of the couch and leaned back into the cushions. "I've never been to the Maison before. What a gorgeous place."

"When the Duplissey family bought it, everyone in town thought they were nuts."

"Not anymore, right?" She slipped off her shoes and put both feet up on the coffee table.

"Well, I'm not sure. The place is a success, all right. But it cost them so much to restore, who knows if they'll ever make any real money?" He toyed with the corner of his novel. "You look beautiful tonight. Reminds me of the first time I saw your mother in that dress."

"Thanks, Dad." She leaned over to massage the toes of one foot with her thumbs. "The dress is too short, though. And Mom's shoes nearly killed me."

"You get your height from me." He laughed. "I guess that makes for long feet too. Did you dance in them? The shoes, I mean."

"We did." The massage felt good and painful at the same time. She began working on her other foot.

Her father sighed and took off his glasses. "When I'm feeling better, I'd like to take your mom there for dinner."

"Really? You'd have to dress up, you know." For as long as Kate remembered, her father had resisted every occasion demanding formal dress. He'd even resisted wearing a tuxedo for her wedding, but Kate's mother had stood her ground, and he'd reluctantly agreed. On Kate's wedding day, her father had worn the expression of one walking with a knife stuck in his back—stiff and frightened. His miserable expression had slipped into every one of her wedding pictures.

"I know. Scary, huh?" He laughed. "A heart attack has a way of forcing you to rethink your more rigid opinions."

Kate crossed her legs at the ankles and leaned back. Though her father's voice continued, she stopped listening. She fingered the tiny beads embroidered near the hem of her mother's silk Georgette dress. Miniature jet black beads floated on blue smoke silk. Each hung precariously by a single strand of thread. As she turned a single tube on the thread, she realized how much her life resembled these beads. Her marriage had hung by a single thread. The thread of faithfulness. And Mike had managed to sever the thread.

". . . Don't you think?"

"What?" Kate looked up into her father's questioning expression. "I'm sorry, Dad, I missed the question."

"I was saying that now I might be able to dress up and enjoy it. After what I've been through, it's better than the alternative. Right?"

Kate laughed. "I think if you dressed up to take Mom out, she'd be the one to have the next heart attack."

"Which proves two things."

Kate laughed. "What two things?"

"It proves that people can change when substantially provoked. And it proves that even your mother has rigid opinions that could use some adjustment."

"I guess you're right, Dad." With her index finger, Kate traced a tiny invisible circle on the end table beside her. The freshly polished surface gleamed. Looking around the room, she noticed again how neatly her mother kept house. White couches. Fresh lilies in an enameled Chinese vase. A perfectly spotless glass top on an antique gold coffee table. At one time, Kate had resented the rigidity in her mother's housekeeping. She saw the same rigidity in her mother's choice of clothes, her scheduling, her overorganizing of every event. When Kate married Mike, her mother's lists and demands had nearly driven Kate to tears. Even her mother's quilting showed a rigid adherence to pattern and color. Kate wondered if the same rigidity stood behind her mother's determination to make Kate responsible for saving a failed marriage. But her father?

"Dad, aren't we supposed to be rigid? I mean, right and wrong will always be right and wrong."

"Of course. But I'm not talking about right and wrong." He set his glasses on the table beside him. "I've raised you to believe in absolutes. Those things don't ever change." He shifted in the chair. "No. I'm talking about preferences. Responses. Love makes me stretch outside my comfort zone. I do love your mother, Katie-Doll." He smiled.

Kate sighed, remembering this teaching style from her days at home. "Dad, why do I get the feeling that we aren't really talking about dressing up anymore?" She folded her hands in her lap and leaned her head back against the couch. "What are you trying to tell me?"

"I'm not trying to tell you anything. I'm talking about misconceptions. Sometimes we build rigid opinions to protect ourselves from scary things. From taking risks. Like wearing a tuxedo and dancing with my wife in front of strangers."

"I've never thought of you as rigid, Dad."

"Everyone is, Kate, in their own way. Everyone sees life in firm parameters. Growth is about letting God stretch us. Learning to let go of cans and can'ts and trusting God to build something new inside." He scratched at his chin and yawned. "What did you have to eat?"

Kate loved this about her dad. He never overdid a teaching opportunity. Once when Kate was a teenager, all her friends were changing their hair color. Kate had gone to her father asking permission to die her hair brown. He'd answered thoughtfully, *"You can if you want, Katie-Doll. But I was just thinking how pretty your hair is getting to be. Like your mother's. I've always loved the red in your hair."*

Kate had decided against the color change, not because her father forbade it, but because he loved her hair exactly as it was. The memory made her love him all the more.

She smiled. "I ordered a steak, Dad," she said in a mocking tone. "It came smothered in Hollandaise sauce and asparagus, and it was wrapped in a slice of bacon."

"Don't." He held his hands up as if to fend off a brutal beating. "You'll be guilty of provoking jealousy. I don't think I can face one more carrot stick sitting alongside a freshly broiled chicken breast."

Kate laughed. "Mom loves you, Dad. She wants you around for a long time."

"I know. But if I have to eat chicken for the rest of my life, I'm not sure I want to hang around." He slapped his thighs. "Want to go out for french fries?"

Kate laughed, a lighthearted, genuine laugh, and it felt good. How long had it been since she had laughed? "Why not just go for a double scoop at the ice cream parlor?"

"That's an idea. Do you think your mom would figure it out?"

"She'd smell peanut butter and chocolate on your breath." Kate sat up and pushed herself from the couch. "Would you like some tea, Dad?"

"Nothing for me. I'd have to get up in the middle of the night." He stood and picked up his novel. "Well, if you won't help me escape for ice cream, I guess I might as well go to bed." He stepped toward her and wrapped his long arms around her. "You do look beautiful tonight, Katie. So much like your mother when she was younger." He kissed her forehead. "Good night now," he said and turned to go up the stairs. "Don't forget to turn out the lights."

————

On Monday morning, Doug McCoy went to work early. With

one hand he carried his briefcase, in the other the daily paper, scanning the front page as he walked. As the electric doors opened onto the lobby of the Keegan Building, a ringing telephone caught his attention. He glanced in the direction of the sound and noticed a new face at the security desk. Deliberately he focused on the paper, opened it, and folded it in half. He tried to appear entranced by an article.

Standing in the lobby holding this pose, Doug observed the man behind the security console. Much younger than Buzz and wearing a slightly different uniform, he had an alert, intelligent air. As Doug watched, the man stroked the keys of a computer terminal. His fingers flew across the keyboard, and from Doug's viewpoint, he moved rapidly from screen to screen. Putting on a casual air, Doug tucked his paper under one elbow and walked toward the counter. "Good morning," he said, with as much cheer as he could muster. "Where's Buzz today?"

Just as Doug spoke, the screen before the new employee suddenly went dark. "Good morning, sir," the man said. "Can I help you find someone?" Doug noticed that his gray shirt appeared brand-new, the fabric fresh, creases firm.

"I asked where Buzz is."

"And you are?" The security man glanced at Doug's collar.

"Doug McCoy." Doug resisted a rising tide of indignation. He never wore a name tag on company property. Everyone knew him. "I own this company. And I'd still like an answer. Where is our security man?"

"I couldn't tell you, sir. I work for a temp agency."

"A temp agency?"

"Yes, sir." He placed both hands on the counter. "All I know is that I was asked to report here for temporary duty."

Doug laid the paper down on the counter and pulled a pen from his pocket. "Which company do you work for?"

For an instant too long, the man hesitated. A movement of his eyes. "Bayside Temps."

Doug wrote the name on a small piece of paper. "And did they tell you how long you would be working here?"

"A few weeks, sir."

Confused, Doug asked, "Weeks?"

"Yes, sir."

"Thank you." Doug slid the pen back into his pocket. "That's all." He scooped his paper off the counter and tucked it back under his arm. Picking up his briefcase, he headed for the elevator. Something about this new man aroused Doug's suspicion. Why a new security man? Why now? What had happened to Buzz? When Doug found a telephone, he had a few calls to make.

When the elevator doors opened onto the Technical floor that same morning, Mike found the busy sound of production nearly overwhelming. On this floor, nearly thirty computer techies, each in their own cubicle, worked at individual portions of various projects. Mike walked down one row of partitions, heading for Doug's office. Conversations continued back and forth over half walls, phones rang, music played, and Mike wondered how anyone got anything done with this level of ambient noise.

About halfway down the aisle, a young employee in faded cut-offs and green suede Vans came careening around his partition. Mike saw him glance the other way for traffic. With his head turned, he nearly ran into Mike, who managed to sidestep him just in time.

"Oh man. Sorry, Mr. Langston." The employee, still in pimples, blushed.

"No problem. I saw you coming."

The boy stuck out his hand. "Thank you, sir."

Mike shook it, wondering why young men in the company treated him this way. Though Mike founded the company and had been part of turning it into a business success, it seemed the kids on the front lines thought of him as some kind of shipping mag-nate—the Aristotle Onassis of computers. He didn't understand their reverential thinking.

He reached Doug's assistant just as she answered the telephone. Wearing a headset with a tiny microphone in front of her mouth, she pushed a button on the phone and spoke, "Mr. McCoy's office." It looked a little strange to see her smile directly at Mike while speaking to someone else. She pushed the Hold button and quickly buzzed an extension—all in an efficiency born of practice.

"Hi, Liz," Mike said. "I'm here to see Doug. Does he have a minute?"

"I think so, sir." She pointed to a door at the end of an aisle to her left. "He just got back from a meeting."

"Thanks," Mike said. "You don't have to announce me." He walked past her, giving a little wave. As he knocked on Doug's door, he noticed she had rolled her chair back to her keyboard and begun typing vigorously.

"Come in." Doug's preoccupied voice came through the solid wood panel.

Mike opened the door and stepped inside. "Sorry to bother you, Doug," he began. Doug sat with his back to the door, with his head leaning against the back of his chair. Walking around him, Mike found Doug sitting with his eyes closed, tears streaming down his face. "What in the world?"

Doug blinked and brought a tissue to his eyes. "Allergies," he said. "I hate spring." He screwed the cap onto his medication bottle.

Mike smiled, "Eyedrop season, huh?"

"Yeah, I don't even have to check the calendar. I just wake up one morning and feel like I want to scratch my eyeballs out. It's tree season." Doug opened his pencil drawer and threw the white bottle inside. "I never go anywhere without those things." He turned to face Mike. "Have a seat. What do you need this morning?"

"Well, I don't exactly know where to start." Mike chose the padded chair across from Doug's desk.

Placing his round glasses back on his nose, Doug's eyes seemed to disappear behind the lenses. Mike wondered for the thousandth time how bad his friend's vision actually was. "So start at the beginning," Doug said.

Mike crossed his leg, draping one foot over the other knee, letting his foot bounce a rapid pattern in the air. He hadn't really planned this meeting. Doug sometimes found insult where none was intended; how could Mike discuss the current situation without provoking Doug's wrath? Mike needed to let him know about the federal investigation and talk to him about Brenda's visit. And at some time, he needed to talk about Cammie's complaints. But that could wait.

On top of all of that, Mike needed to approach Doug about taking time away to deliver the boat. For a moment, he regretted coming. He should have planned this more carefully.

"Do you have a few minutes?" Mike asked.

Doug wheeled his chair around and punched a series of keystrokes on his computer. "I have a meeting at one. And I'd like to get some food before that. Until then, I'm yours."

"Want to go for lunch?"

"No, this doesn't sound like pleasure. I don't think lunch will make it any easier. Let's get through it."

"All right," Mike agreed. "We have trouble. Lots of it. And I have trouble of my own. We're going to have to work together to solve it all."

Doug leaned forward, put both hands on the desk, and folded them patiently. Suddenly he seemed to have all the time in the world.

In a long and careful monologue, Mike laid out his visit with the special investigator. "It seems they're convinced that someone at DataSoft is in on the credit card deal."

"How did you respond?"

"After I threw him out? Or before?"

Doug smiled. "You threw out the FBI?"

"Yes. Though I wish I'd kept my head. Before that, I told him we're clean, and that I'd stake my life on it."

"So what now?"

"I'd like to do some internal investigation. But I'm not sure how." He uncrossed his legs and slid down in his chair. "I'm sure you can think of something. If we really do have a problem, it seems to me that it would be someone here—in your area." He stood up and walked to the window. "I've been thinking about it. Either the Feds are wrong or someone out there," Mike pointed to the space outside Doug's office door, "has figured out how to visit the sites we're creating and lift credit card numbers." He paced back and forth again. "I don't know enough about what you guys do to solve the case. But I think together we could figure out who might be messing with our software."

Doug let out a long sigh. "I had no idea the federal government had been here. Why would they suspect us?" He reached up to scratch absently over one ear. "I personally investigate every person we hire here. Department security is one of my biggest priorities."

"I know that." Mike stopped and turned to face his friend. "We've both sacrificed our lives for this company. And if we lose security, we're finished. If he's right, it may already be too late." Mike shook his head, still not quite believing the whole situation.

"There is one more thing. The Feds are threatening charges against us as well."

"All right," Doug said, taking notes. "I'll work on that. You said there was something else?"

"Two things, actually. Both are personal." He put his hands on his hips. "I'm afraid one might make you a little angry."

"Okay, so you warned me." Doug's voice sounded hard, and he tipped his chin as if daring his friend to speak.

"Brenda came to visit me."

Doug's eyebrows rose, though his expression remained frozen.

"She told me you weren't paying child support." Mike walked over to the chair and sat again. "I told her I'd talk to you about it."

"Okay. You've done that," Doug said, his tone even, steely.

Mike knew it would be best to let the matter drop, but he couldn't. "Look, Doug, those kids are your responsibility. She can't take care of them without your help."

"This is really good." Doug threw his pencil down on the desk and chuckled. "I saw the pictures, remember? You have a lot of nerve, lecturing me about moral responsibility."

Mike clenched his teeth, determined to keep his temper. "I thought you might go there. Look, I promised I'd talk to you; I wrote Brenda a check."

"You gave my wife money?"

"Not a company check. My money is mine to give to whomever I please. But that doesn't excuse you. Your kids need you." Mike cleared his throat. "But I won't say anything more about it. Then there is one other thing."

"You never run out, do you?"

"Last Sunday, Dave Holland asked me to deliver his sailboat to the South Pacific. Maybe Hawaii. I'm not sure yet." Mike put both his palms on his knees and bounced an up-and-down rhythm with his toes. *Why do I feel so anxious?* "Anyway, I'm thinking about taking some time away. If Kate will go with me, I'm going to do it."

"And why are you telling me this?"

"Because if I do, you'll have to cover for me. The trip could take anywhere from three to five weeks. I think—if Kate will come—that maybe we could save our marriage. It would be worth that for me. I need you to do this for me, Doug.

"I'd miss at least one board meeting. Then, of course, there's the FBI thing. It's horrible timing. I've been struggling all week with the question of whether or not I should take the time off. But if you'll help me, I want to try."

"What makes you think Kate will go along?"

"Actually, I haven't asked her. I'm going to fly to Kansas this weekend."

"What about the FBI?"

"I'm going to do my own investigating. This thing has me really upset. If we can figure it out, I think it'll go better for us. We might save the business."

Doug stared at him, his face motionless. Then, as though he'd been invited to go on a cruise himself, he smiled. And Mike thought his smile seemed to blossom in slow-motion photography. "I'd be glad to help you out, Mike," he said simply.

Twenty-Six

AS SOON AS MIKE left his office, Doug picked up the phone and buzzed his secretary. "Liz," he said, leaning forward with both his elbows on the desk. "Get me someone in HR."

"Do you have a preference, sir?" she asked.

"No." He said, tapping his temple with his index finger. "Wait. Yes. I want Gibbons."

"Yes, sir." As she put him on hold, sultry jazz came through his telephone, and Doug fought with impatience.

At last a voice answered, "Marsha Gibbons. How may I help you?"

"Marsha. This is Doug McCoy."

"Hello, Doug." He heard a smile in her voice. "What can I do for you?"

"I have a quick question," he said, straining to keep an even tone.

"Shoot."

"This morning I noticed a new guy at the security desk. I asked him what happened to Buzz, and he couldn't tell me." With the eraser of his pencil Doug tapped a nervous rhythm against his desktop.

"Hmm," she answered thoughtfully. "I didn't know anything was wrong with Buzz." The sound on the telephone became muffled, then her voice came back. "I found it," she said triumphantly. "I have a memo here saying that Buzz is taking a leave of absence."

"Why?" Doug tried to sound as though he had a personal concern. "I hope he isn't ill."

"Actually, I don't know why he took time off."

"Who made the request?"

"Just a minute." He heard typing in the background. "I think Mike did," Marsha answered. "Funny, huh?"

"Just one more question. Are you happy with Bayside Temps?"

"Bayside?"

"The new guy said he's from Bayside."

"I don't know," she answered. "Actually, I've never used them. Mike told me he'd take care of replacing Buzz himself."

———

Thursday afternoon, Kate's mother disappeared into her sewing room. Hours later Kate found her there, bent over her worktable cutting out pieces of a new quilt. In one hand Rosemarie held an Olfa cutter, while the fingers of her other hand held fabric in place. Kate watched for a few moments from the doorway. "I've never gotten the hang of using one of those," she said, nodding to the circular blade.

"There's a trick to it," her mother said, without looking up. "It used to drive me crazy until I learned how many pieces I could cut at one time." She straightened, removed her reading glasses, and let them drop onto the beaded chain around her neck. "I did throw away a lot of fabric while I learned though." She smiled. "Don't tell your father."

"Your secret is safe with me."

"Good." Rosemarie walked around the table, looking for a new angle to approach her task. The motion reminded Kate of a pool player. Tipping her head, stretching her arm, her mother made several false starts before she settled down, leaned against the table, and began cutting again.

"Mom, I came up to ask if I could cook dinner tomorrow night."

Her mother laughed. "Are you kidding? I'd never turn that down."

Kate smiled. "I thought that might be the case. I'm planning to invite Greg Harris to join us. He's been so good to me while I've been home." Her mother glanced up, her eyebrows raised. Kate ignored the look and wandered over to the project board Rosemarie kept hanging above the sewing machine. Kate removed a suit pattern that her mother had thumbtacked to the cork. "Ooh, I love this jacket. Are you making this?"

"Yes. But I haven't found the right fabric yet." Rosemarie put down her cutter and walked toward Kate. "Why did you invite him? You're a married woman."

"Because I want to return his kindness, Mom. That's all. Don't go imagining things that aren't there. It's the least I can do."

"What will you cook?"

"It's a surprise. But I do have to run to the store. Is there anything you need while I'm out?"

Rosemarie made no effort to hide her disapproval. Sighing, she said, "No, dear."

Kate leaned over and kissed her mother's cheek. "Dad's on the porch reading today's paper. Keep an eye on him for me."

———

On Friday morning, Mike had trouble concentrating on his work. He couldn't keep his mind off the decision he faced. Did he have enough sailing experience to safely deliver a yacht so far away? Could he do it alone? Would Kate go with him?

He envisioned his first trip offshore, remembering his own sense of smallness in the midst of miles and miles of empty ocean. At the end of that trip, Mike had stood on the bow of the boat adjusting the jib when he suddenly recognized the approach of land. After twenty-one days at sea, standing on the deck of a small sailboat, it seemed miraculous to actually find an island rising from the ocean. The first impression he had had of landfall had come from his nose. He had smelled it—the rich, sweet fragrance of earth floating to him on the wind. Then he'd seen mist rising above the ocean. At last Mike had spotted the silhouette of land on the horizon.

Squinting over the vast blueness, an almost overwhelming sense of surprise and relief crashed over Mike like an errant wave. It began deep inside him and bubbled up into an almost hysterical squeal of laughter and delight. "Land ho!" he had cried. "Land ho!" Dave, watching from the wheel, had smiled and nodded. Across the length of the boat, the two men had locked eyes, and a silent "We did it!" passed between them.

Mike made that trip to Hawaii as part of a race crew nearly twenty years before. Dave's self-assurance had been evident from the first moment Mike stepped on board. But now, twenty years later, Mike did not feel so confident. The thought of being responsible for a boat belonging to someone else frightened Mike more than any idea he'd entertained in years. Dave's boat represented more than three hundred thousand dollars in equipment—nearly all of Dave's liquid assets. But more than that, sailing the boat with Kate could mean risking their lives. Could Mike do it? Should he try?

This pummeling back and forth—yes, he should go—no, only fools would try—had driven him to distraction all morning. Mike decided to take the rest of the morning and the afternoon off. He couldn't work anyway; he needed time to think. Mike needed to make a decision based on more than emotion and wishful thinking.

He'd done some research. Thursday night, sitting in his favorite chair, he'd read through Jimmy Cornell's *World Cruising Routes*. According to this resource, Mike did not have time to deliver the boat any farther south than Hawaii. He couldn't leave DataSoft that long. But he could take Dave's boat to Hilo, Hawaii, a trip expected to take no more than four weeks. From there, Dave and Valerie could cruise the Hawaiian Islands or take off in a southerly direction. According to the book, May proved to be the best month for a trip from San Francisco to Hawaii—late enough to avoid winter gales and early enough to avoid summer hurricanes. But if Mike wanted to sail in May, he had to make a decision soon.

It would take time to get the boat ready. Time to provision. Time to take some shake-down cruises with Dave's supervision. Time to convince Kate to come along. Most importantly, Mike needed to settle the question for himself before he pitched it to Kate. He needed to be confident that he could do it. And at this moment, he felt far from confident.

He drove away from the office in his Mustang, planning to take the afternoon off, to take time to pray about this crazy proposition. Mike needed fresh air and a place where work pressure would not affect his thinking—or hearing—should God decide to answer this prayer. Mike hoped to clear his mind with a long walk on his favorite beach.

When Mike arrived at the beach, he found the parking lot deserted. An empty beach suited him just perfectly. He pulled on a light jacket and zipped it closed as he walked down the rocky trail to the beach. Already his mind churned with the decision he faced.

DataSoft employed 113 people. Each employee represented others—nameless families—who depended on DataSoft income. Families, obligations, bills. Could Mike afford to risk the security of his employees by leaving the business now? What if, while he sailed away, the FBI found sufficient evidence to bring charges against someone in the company?

Could Mike trust Doug to safely direct damage control? What would happen if Mike went on this voyage and the whole criminal investigation came to a head? Would Mike sacrifice his own future and the future of the entire company all for some foolish notion that time away with Kate could save his marriage?

This responsibility hung heavily on Mike's shoulders. DataSoft had grown into a successful company. But it would never be successful enough for Mike to betray the trust of the people who depended on him. He turned to face the water. "Lord Jesus," he began, "I came here to listen. Please tell me what to do."

The wind blowing off the water felt cold against his neck. He turned up the collar of his coat and decided to sit for a moment. Sticking his hands in his pockets, he sat down on a small elevated patch of sand watching the waves lap along the shore.

The barking of a large dog just fifty feet down the beach drew his attention, and Mike looked up to discover an older woman approaching. She walked behind an energetic and unleashed Australian shepherd. As Mike watched, the woman stopped walking and began clapping her hands, calling after the dog. "Lucy, come back!" she shouted. The dog did not obey.

Lucy had discovered a gull with a limp, some old injury that kept the bird from leaving the ground as quickly as the others nearby. The dog ran tight circles around the frustrated bird, teasing, but never attacking. The woman tried to call her off. "Lucy, come!" she shouted.

Suddenly, Lucy stopped chasing and sat. Then, looking toward her owner, Lucy began a pitiful whine. *Please,* she seemed to beg. *Let me just wear it out; I promise not to kill it.* The woman clapped her hands again, calling the dog's name. Lucy paid no attention. As the woman approached the dog, Lucy stood up and ran away. Always staying just out of the woman's reach, Lucy continued to torment the gull.

The frightened gull fluttered and jumped, trying desperately to leave the ground.

Mike turned away from the drama, focusing again on his own problems. Silently, desperately, he began to pray. *God, I need your help. I have so many concerns. So many problems. I don't know what to do. Do I take the boat? Do I try to talk to Kate? And what about the company? How can I leave them now?*

As he prayed, the fierce teasing of the injured gull continued. Mike fought to keep his attention on prayer. *Or should I just stay here and do nothing? God, I'm trying to hear you. I don't want to go off on my own again. I need your direction. Tell me what to do.*

He listened, but Mike heard only the sound of the water on the sand and the barking dog.

Then he heard something else. A pitiful cry coming from the bullied bird.

Well, if I can't get an answer from God, at least I can go rescue that stupid bird. Mike stood, brushing sand from his shorts and started down the beach to the dog, calling as he did, "Lucy, come!"

When he got to the seaweed, where the dancing and circling dog had trapped the bird, Mike made a sudden lunge and caught Lucy by the collar. "Lucy. Stop," he said in his most commanding voice. Immediately, she sat. Looking up at him with sad eyes and twisted eyebrows, she whined. *Please let me torment the thing,* she begged.

"No way," Mike said out loud. "You've had your fun. Now it's over. I'm calling you off." Mike held her collar firmly with one hand while he stepped toward the bird, shooing her off with the other. With a long run, the bird scuttled and bounced down the beach. At last the wind caught her wings, and she took off. Rising into the wind, the gull soared above the water. Mike held the dog, both of them watching the gull. Lucy whined, desperate to follow the bird. Suddenly the gray bird turned and dipped, swooping down over them with one last cursing call.

"You're lucky she didn't try to dump on us," Mike said. "By the way, what were you doing, circling and teasing like that?"

The woman came forward, catching the dog's collar with her

free hand. "Thanks for catching her. She can be such a nuisance." The woman looked up at the bird, shading her eyes. "Lucky for her Lucy's a chicken."

The dog whined again, and the woman bent down to attach a leash. "Thanks again," she said, and started away. The dog followed reluctantly, still eyeing the bird.

Mike watched them walk away. A chill had settled on the water, and it threatened to settle on his soul as well. He started his walk in the opposite direction.

As he walked, Mike couldn't get his mind off the bird. This surprised him. After all, what is a seagull anyway but a shoreline garbage collector? Why should he care? Suddenly he stopped walking. Mike cared because he identified with the bird.

Unable to fly, he, too, had been tormented and circled by an enemy. His enemy, unseen but as genuine as Lucy, seemed just as determined to wear him out, to keep him from flight. "God, is that what you're telling me?" he asked out loud. "Are you telling me to go? Will you hold the enemy—just like I held the dog—while I try to put my life back together again?"

Something inside of Mike gave way, and he felt another wave. A wave of peace. He couldn't explain how he knew, but he knew. He'd come to the beach to ask, and he'd gotten his answer. God would hold back the dog. It was Mike's job to take all the time he needed to get off the ground.

Mike turned suddenly, a complete change of direction, and started walking, nearly running for the car. "I need to hurry," he said out loud. "I have lots to do."

He broke into a jog, laughing as his mind hurried ahead of him. *I have airline tickets to buy. A trip to make. A wife to win back.*

————

Doug McCoy could not shake the questions running through his head. How much did Mike know? What steps had he already taken to flush out the company turncoat? The man at the security desk frightened Doug. But how could he ask Mike about it without arousing suspicion?

He decided that he needed to find out more about the company that sent the replacement for Buzz. If he was from a genuine security firm, Doug could at least lay aside his concern over that issue.

What had the guy said? Bayside Temps? Doug picked up the telephone and dialed the number for information.

"For what city, please?"

"For San Francisco and vicinity," Doug said.

"For what listing?"

"A business listing. Bayside Temps."

A long pause. Mike tapped at his desk with his pencil.

The male voice came back on the line. "Could you spell that name?"

"B-A-Y-S-I-D-E." Doug barely covered his irritation. How could anyone not know how to spell the most frequently used business name in the area?

"I'm sorry, sir," he said. "I have no listing for that business."

"What?"

"There is no listing for Bayside Temps." The operator seemed to be losing his patience.

"Did you check the vicinity—Richmond, San Rafael, Oakland?"

"Our listings cover the entire Bay Area. I'm sorry, there isn't anything here. Will there be anything else?"

Doug hung up without responding.

Twenty-Seven

FRIDAY AFTERNOON, Kate managed to stuff Cornish hens with rice and pineapple filling and put them in the oven without requiring stitches herself. Next to the hens, she had placed split sections of butternut squash upside down to bake. On top of the stove, a glaze of soy sauce and honey sat cooling in a pan. In a second oven, Kate baked a pie from her father's blueberries, which she'd found stashed in the garage freezer. Though she'd bathed her face in flour in the process, she felt comfortable with her progress. She had only to run upstairs and clean up.

She showered and put on fresh makeup, carefully applying all of the products she'd purchased at her makeover. Then she wrestled with her new hairstyle. Try as she might, she could not yet recreate the look the hairdresser had produced. Her waves refused to assume the controlled but spontaneous look she'd seen when it was first cut. She did her best, then gave up, frustrated.

In her room, she chose silk pants in a soft pale teal and a matching sweater. After spritzing Anais Anais onto her neck, she stopped to take one last glance in the mirror. "You try too hard," she said with disgust.

Back in the kitchen, she cut up vegetables for a fresh salad and prepared a homemade honey and mustard dressing. Her father came in, sniffing the air. "Mmm. Smells good in here. Must be company coming."

"Good guess." She laughed and gave him a kiss on his cheek.

"So who is it?"

"Greg Harris. I asked him to join us. He's been so nice while I've been home."

"Good. I'd like to meet him." Her father squeezed her shoulder. "Have you seen today's paper?"

"In the living room, I think." Kate opened the oven and drizzled the soy mixture onto her birds. "Dad, you've met Greg before. We went to church together in high school."

"Sorry. I've had so many kids in my classes, I hardly remember you."

Kate laughed. "Well, all right. You can meet him again tonight." Her father leaned over the salad bowl and began picking out cherry tomatoes, eating them one at a time. She reached over and slapped his fingers gently. "Dad, you know better than that."

"But I've had a heart attack." He gave his daughter a pathetically helpless look.

Kate laughed. "Sorry. Not good enough."

"All right, then I suppose I should volunteer to help. Anything I can do?"

"You could set the table." She saw him scowl. "Or you could go out to the garden and bring in some greenery for the flowers I bought."

His face brightened. "Want me to put them together?"

"Would you?" Kate put the pan back on the stove. "I'm hopeless with flowers."

"Not a problem." He picked up his kitchen scissors. "Be right back."

———

By early Friday evening, Mike was already at the Kansas City Airport picking up his rental car. Expecting the trip to Kate's parents' house to take just over an hour, he wondered for a moment if he should call ahead. But as he opened the car door, he glanced at his watch. No need to call; he should arrive just after eight in the evening. Not too late for a visit.

He pulled into traffic and headed for I–70. As he settled into the small import, he decided to enjoy some soothing music. He began shuffling through the stations on his car radio looking for jazz or classics. Nothing.

Frustrated, he switched off the Power button. He'd been

through so much since he'd last been in Kansas; Mike felt like a rubber band stretched beyond its limits. He couldn't take much more. Deliberately he relaxed into the seat, stretching his left leg, shrugging and relaxing his shoulders. He willed tension to seep from his neck out through his fingertips.

He remembered the gull and the barking dog on the beach at home. Praying as he drove, he said, "Call off the dog, Lord. I can't do this by myself. You've got to do it for me. I'm doing my best to save what you've given me."

By the time he arrived in Lawrence, he had no more peace than he had at the airport. Mike Langston operated now on strict obedience and raw determination. He found Kate's parents' home with ease and pulled into the driveway. "I'm here, Lord. Please help me convince her to try."

Turning off the engine, he gazed up at the house. Light fell from the front windows illuminating the box hedge below the sill. In all the years he'd known Kate, this had been her parents' home. Mike appreciated the old house with its simple design and perfect symmetry. He liked the paned windows, the shutters. He loved the brick sidewalk and the half pillars framing the door lights beside the entry. He'd always referred to it as a "Leave it to Beaver" house. Kate insisted it should be called "revived colonial."

Whatever the architectural designation, the house felt like home to Mike. After twenty-seven years of warm welcomes, coming to see Kate's parents always felt like coming home.

Uttering one more quick prayer, Mike took a deep breath and got out of the car. At the front door, he raised his hand to knock. A noise caught his attention, and he thought he heard laughing inside. Hesitating, he glanced around and noticed for the first time a bronze Camry parked against the curb. Did the Killians have company? He rang the bell and waited.

At long last, Kate's mother answered the door. "Mike," she said, her face registering absolute astonishment. "We didn't expect you." She held the door open with one stiff arm, her body frozen in surprise.

"Hi, Mom," he said. "I know this is a surprise. I guess I should have called." Mike shifted his weight and awkwardly stuck his hands in his pockets. Moments passed. His mother-in-law seemed unable to respond. "Can I come in?"

She snapped out of her daze. "Oh, of course, forgive me. Come in, Mike." Stepping back, she swung the door open and stepped out of the way. "We're just about to have dessert. Won't you join us?"

"Sounds good. Is Kate here?"

"Yes, in the dining room."

Mike followed her through the living room to the formal dining room. It surprised him that they would eat dinner in here on a Friday night. Kate's mother reserved the room for special occasions, preferring to serve most meals on the old farmer's table in the kitchen. In the formal dining room, Mike found low candles burning. A soft butter-yellow cloth and fresh flowers accented the china dishes. The room looked soft and inviting.

As Rosemarie entered the room, Patrick looked up and saw Mike. "Mike! You're full of surprises these days." He pushed his chair from the table as though to stand.

"Please. Don't stand." Mike came around the table and offered his hand to his father-in-law. "I'm sorry to surprise you all like this. Looks like I've come at a bad time."

They shook hands warmly. "Take a seat, son. We always love to see you."

"Actually, Patrick, I came to see Kate." Mike stood, embarrassed, behind a side chair.

"She's bringing in dessert. Are you hungry? I think we have leftovers."

Kate's mother cleared a little space in front of Mike and chose another table setting from the buffet at the end of the room.

"No, thanks," Mike held his hands out. "I ate on the plane. I just got in, actually. . . ."

Entering the room from the door to the kitchen, Kate froze when she saw him—a tray of china dessert dishes in her hand. "Mike, what are you doing here?" She moved to the table and set down the tray. She turned to glare at him, putting both hands on her hips. "Why are you here?"

The noise of china bumping as she set down the tray drew Mike's attention. The dishes held large wedges of blueberry pie, each nestled beside a perfectly round scoop of vanilla ice cream. He could see specks of vanilla bean in the mounds. In spite of himself, the dessert made his mouth water. But before he could answer, another voice came from the kitchen.

"I couldn't find the crystal pitcher, so I had to bring out the plastic."

All faces turned to the doorway just as Greg Harris came in carrying a blue Tupperware juice container. Seeing Mike, he smiled, "I'm sorry, I didn't know someone had come in." He put the pitcher down and brushed his damp hand on his slacks before offering it to Mike. "Hello. I'm Greg Harris, and you are?"

"I'm Mike Langston," Mike said, his voice low and controlled, "Kate's husband." The two men actually had their hands extended over the table before Mike's pronouncement hit Greg. The handshake never occurred.

Obvious shock drained the color from Greg's face. It took a moment before Mike realized why Greg seemed so surprised. Glancing at Kate, he saw the unmistakable look of embarrassment cross her features. The skin of her neck began to blotch, and redness crawled up her throat until her cheeks flamed.

"I'm sorry, I don't understand what's going on here." Greg regained his voice and turned to face Kate. "I thought you told me you were divorced."

"I'm going to be, Greg," she said.

"Going to be?" His voice rose in surprise.

"Yes. It just isn't finished yet. I saw the attorney before I left San Francisco."

Before Mike could stop himself, jealousy surfaced in angry words. "That's not quite true, is it, Kate?" Mike put both hands on his hips, trying hard to keep from punching Greg Harris squarely in his prissy mouth. "I'm afraid Kate isn't quite telling you the truth. You obviously didn't know you were hitting on a married woman. So I can overlook this one mistake. But until she actually has a divorce, I'd suggest you keep your hands off my wife!"

Kate seemed to fight to stay in control, her features tightened, her lips narrowed. Taking up the dessert dishes, she began serving, first her father and then her mother. Rosemarie Killian leaned over the table, her forehead resting in her fingers, her face completely ashen. "Please sit down, Greg," Kate said. "Mike isn't staying."

"I'm sorry," Greg said, the unmistakable sound of anger expressing itself in a tremor. "I thought the divorce was final." He shook his head, blushing. "I feel very foolish." He turned and left the room, saying as he did, "I'll be going now."

"Wait, Greg," Kate called. Brushing her hands on her trousers, she gave Mike a hate-filled look and followed Greg into the living room. "Don't leave. Mike shouldn't be here. I didn't expect him."

The dining room fell silent. Miserably, Mike pulled out a chair and sat down. He'd managed to lose his temper and embarrass Kate in the process. It seemed as though he'd just been caught in the end zone by the other team. The tackle was excruciatingly painful. From the dining room, Mike heard the opening and closing of the front hall closet. Then the unmistakable sound of the front door slamming. Mike put both elbows on the table and buried his face in his hands.

———

At home in San Francisco, Doug had taken to letting his voice mail catch all of his phone calls. His sense of impending discovery left him vaguely anxious, unable to start or finish projects—either at work or at home. On this particular Friday evening, Doug had just finished rinsing the last of a sink full of dishes and closed the door to the dishwasher when his phone rang. Hoping for a distraction, he grabbed the phone hanging just above the counter. "Doug McCoy," he said, holding the phone with one hand and wiping the counter with the other.

"Yes, I'm calling about a delivery," a man's voice said. Doug recognized the voice. He could never mistake that low menacing tone.

Doug felt his heart speed up. Throwing the rag in the sink he asked, "Who is this?"

"Don't matter who this is," the voice answered. "You've been paid to deliver a product. And my suppliers inform me that you haven't followed through."

Doug clearly recognized an East Coast accent. He glanced around the kitchen as though someone might be watching, listening, and ran one hand through his hair. "Look, I know what you want. But things have changed." He took a deep breath, trying to calm himself. "The Feds are involved. They're watching the company."

"I'm sorry to hear that," the voice said without a trace of sympathy. "But when a supplier is paid, he's expected to deliver. Your problems ain't my business."

"But I can't do it again; I'll be caught. They'll tie me to your organization."

"Look, I don't care what you have to do. But you understand that we don't pay for services we don't get. If you want to live, you figure out how to deliver. Got it?"

Doug's mouth had gone completely dry, and he swallowed in an effort to speak. Before a word could form in his mind, the line went dead.

————

From the dining room, Mike listened as Kate ran up the stairs. "If you'll excuse me," he said to her parents, "I think I'd better go apologize."

Kate's father nodded, and Mike saw a look of sadness settle on his features. "Good luck," he said.

Mike climbed the stairs slowly and turned the corner to Kate's room. From the hallway, he heard her crying, and he hesitated before knocking on the door.

"Don't even think of coming in," she answered.

"Kate, I'm sorry," he said through the closed door. He ran one hand over the top of his head. "I didn't plan to embarrass you by coming tonight. I didn't realize there was someone else—someone you were seeing."

"Shut up, Mike."

He heard bedsprings creak. "I would never have done this on purpose. I didn't come just to spoil your evening."

The door to her bedroom opened, and Kate stood just inside, her eyes already swelling and her face splotchy from crying. "Come in. Don't stand out here yelling. My parents are listening."

"I wasn't yelling."

She turned her back on him and plopped herself facedown onto the bed. Mike glanced around the room wondering what to do next. He had no place to sit. She clearly didn't want to talk. He sent an arrow prayer toward heaven. *Jesus, you promised you'd help me!*

Mike walked over to her dresser and leaned against it. Slipping his hands in his pockets, he stood watching her. She lay on her front, one hand tracing the hand stitches of the quilt on her bed. "Kate, what was that guy doing here, anyway? I mean, we're still married."

She made no response nor did she look up. He fought an urgent desire to lift her chin and gaze into her eyes.

"I mean it, Kate. Why did you tell him that you're divorced?"

"You have a lot of nerve," she said, still looking down at the quilt, her tone full of menace. "After what you did. How dare you call me a liar."

"Kate, I'm not calling you a liar. I didn't mean it that way. I only meant . . ." Mike stopped speaking. He never intended to start a fight, but seeing her with another man had shocked him, tumbling his confidence. He sighed. "Look, I don't mean to make you angry. Actually, I came to give you what you want."

Her face shot up, her brows questioning. Still she said nothing.

"I've spoken with my attorney, and I'm prepared to give you a divorce. You can have the house, all of our retirement, the cabin, and fifty percent of the value of the DataSoft stock." He watched her face carefully as he spoke.

Her head tipped to one side, and her eyes narrowed. "What's the catch?"

She did not swallow his offer easily. "There is a catch," he admitted. "It's a little four-week investment I want you to make."

"What do you mean?"

"Just this. I've promised Dave and Valerie Holland that I'd deliver their forty-five-foot sailboat to Hawaii."

"What does that have to do with me?"

"I can't deliver the boat alone. I need someone to help me."

"And you're asking me?"

"Yes." He crossed his arms over his chest. "I'm prepared to give you what you want. The divorce is yours. All you have to invest is four weeks. After those twenty-eight days, you get everything—including your freedom. You can even have him," Mike tipped his head toward the door. "If that's what you really want."

"Mike," Kate said, nearly spitting. She rolled over and sat up. "I'm not stupid. I know what this is about. You think you can convince me to stay with you if I spend four weeks cooped up with you on a sailboat."

"That's true. But really, it's a business deal. If you put in the four weeks, you get what you want, and I get my chance. That's all I'm asking for. A second chance."

"I want you out of my life. I can never trust you again," she said, bitterness lacing her words.

Mike winced. "I don't deserve your trust." The silence between them lengthened and stretched like saltwater taffy. "But I want a chance to earn it back. Maybe I'll never convince you to stay. Or to forgive me. Or to believe that Cara was the biggest mistake I've ever made in my life. But I have to try. Sailing away with me—even for twenty-eight days—is the only way I know to get that chance." As he spoke, the room swirled out of focus, and he blinked away tears. They spilled over, and he jabbed at the corners of his eyes with his thumb to wipe them away.

"My last request," he whispered. "I'm not going to pummel you with all the reasons you should go. I'm only going to promise to give you exactly what you want, as soon as we get to Hilo. If you need a contract in order to come along, I can give you that as well. I'll send it to your lawyer."

"I don't need a contract." She began tracing the pattern on the bedspread, slowly, thoughtfully. "A contract never meant anything to you, anyway," she said pointedly.

She certainly knew how to deliver a verbal blow. Silence filled the little peach bedroom, and Mike fought the urge to talk through it. He wanted to try to convince her. To make wild promises. But Kate needed time, and he understood that. "I'll think about it," she said softly. "If you'll go home and promise not to call me for one full week, I promise I'll think about it."

He smiled. It must have been a triumphant smile, because Kate frowned. "But listen, Mike. It won't work. Even if I go, it won't work."

"All right. That's fair."

She pointed at the bedroom door. "Get out of here," she said. "I mean it. Don't call. And don't get your hopes up."

Twenty-Eight

WITH A TREMBLING HAND, Doug put the receiver down, slowly and carefully. Wondering what he should do, he wiped his forehead with the back of his hand. This was not the kind of problem you talked about with your attorney.

He glanced at his hand and noticed moisture. He had begun sweating heavily in spite of the comfortable temperature inside his condo. These people meant business, and for the first time, Doug began to regret the commitment he'd made.

When he had first considered their plan, a few credit card numbers seemed harmless enough. In fact, he had never provided actual numbers. Rather, Doug had only provided the method. For a few dollars, he had simply given them the key to the back door. How criminal could that be? They made the cards. They were the real criminals.

Doug picked up the phone and dialed quickly, his finger punching a rapid staccato. A woman's voice answered. "I just got a phone call," Doug spat. "They want another delivery."

"I know. I've heard from them too."

"Did you tell them that the FBI is watching the company?"

"It wouldn't do any good."

"What do we do now?"

"We," she said, emphasizing the word, "will deliver exactly as promised. It's the last delivery. Only this time, they want you to hand it over."

"Me? Why not you?" He heard panic in his voice and cleared

his throat. "I mean, why change things now?"

"I don't know." She sighed, frustrated. "But that's what he said. No questions. He's going to pick it up this time."

"How will I know when?"

"He said he'd call."

"Great. Just great," Doug said. "I might as well call the Feds for a ride to the office." Doug nearly whined, "Why didn't you convince him to leave the deliveries alone?"

"Because you don't argue with these people, Doug," she answered. "Certainly you recognize that by now."

You don't argue. That part, Doug had definitely figured out.

————

Mike's late-morning flight from Kansas to California passed as uneventfully as his night at an airport hotel had. As soon as he let himself into the house, he went to the kitchen and called Dave Holland.

"Are you calling from Kansas?"

"No, I've already been there and back," Mike answered.

"How did it go?"

"Not as well as we'd hoped."

"Did you talk to Kate?"

"Sort of," Mike admitted. "I promised her a divorce if she'd come along."

"Well, that's one way to do it. Though I hoped you wouldn't have to." Dave's voice held doubt. "Did she seem interested?"

Honesty seemed the best policy. "Not at all," Mike said. Taking a deep breath, he continued, "Kate has a—a friend—in Kansas. Her dad tells me he's someone she's known since she was a kid." Mike paused to let that sink in.

"I'm sorry to hear that, Mike. It makes things harder."

"I've decided to deliver the boat."

"You can't make that commitment yet. Kate hasn't made a decision."

"I know. But I'm committing—no matter what she decides. If she won't come along, I'll hire a crew. I need four weeks away from here, on the ocean. And . . ." Here Mike hesitated, not knowing quite how to explain this to Dave. "I just have this feeling she's going to say yes. If for no other reason than to be done with the marriage. She wants out bad. Real bad. We need to be ready to go."

"All right. When do you plan on leaving?"

"I'd like to shoot for May fifteenth."

"Only four weeks?"

"I think we can do it. I'll focus on it, and with your help, we can get through some sea trials, as well as provisioning and planning."

"I don't know. That isn't much time. The boat needs a lot of attention."

"I know. But it's a weather window. The winter storm season is over by May, and the tropical storms won't have started yet. It's the safest sailing. We should have a smooth passage."

Dave hesitated, and Mike smiled as he heard his friend begin thinking aloud. "We could work all day every weekend. And Valerie could do the galley provisioning."

"We'll need to go over the rigging and electronics piece by piece."

"Right." Dave's voice still held doubt. "It might depend on how shipshape everything is. If we have to do a major repair or haul her out, it would delay everything."

"Dave, I thought you had this thing all planned out."

"I did. But I threw away the schedule when my dentist flunked his test."

"We can get back on schedule." Mike chuckled. "Do you really think I can sail?"

"I have every confidence. If God is in this, nothing can stop us."

"All right, when do we start?"

"Just a minute." While Mike waited, Dave covered the telephone and spoke to someone nearby. "How about tonight? Val says we're having steak."

"I can be there by five o'clock sharp."

———

After a restless night, Kate woke early—even before the birds. She slipped on a pair of sweatpants and a long-sleeved T-shirt and left the house quietly. Perhaps a run, a long exhausting run, would drive the tumbling doubts from her mind.

At the end of the driveway she paused to stretch. Sitting on the ground, she reached gently for her toes. Then, putting one leg behind her, she leaned forward slowly. A blue Ford Escort drove down the street on the wrong side. She paused to watch as the car slowed at the house next door and a leggy teenager jumped out of the car and ran up the driveway. Hurling the paper onto the porch, the boy pivoted and started back to the car before Kate heard the thud of newspaper hitting wooden steps.

A normal Saturday morning. Daily papers. A sleeping neighborhood. Only Kate seemed to be churning with the weight of a life-changing decision. The car pulled up to her father's driveway, and the boy jumped again from the passenger side. He repeated his routine without ever seeing Kate. The driver, a man in his midthirties, drank coffee from an oversized mug.

Kate stretched her hamstrings and inner thighs and then started down the street at an easy lope. Questions whirled through her mind. Should she accept Mike's challenge? Why not? With anyone else, under any other conditions, a four-week trip to Hawaii would be a great stress reliever. And no one needed a stress reliever more than Kate. She imagined the sun setting on tropical beaches. The color of the water, the sky, the gentle rocking of the boat. She missed sailing with the family. Those had been pleasant memories. Did she still know how? Could she still guide a boat through the water using only the wind?

Questions without answers. Kate rounded the corner and started toward Massachusetts Street. In the back of her mind, it occurred to her to run all the way to the river and back via Watson Park. A good long run might drive these fluky thoughts from her mind. Perhaps she would come home with an answer.

Fluke: A sailor's term for an unsettled wind, a wind refusing to blow steadily from the same direction. Where had that word entered her mind from? Like an unsteady wind, Kate's thoughts would not settle down. She shook her head and picked up her pace. Soon she settled into the heavy, even breathing of a seasoned runner. "God, help me," she said out loud. "I have no desire to sail with Mike."

Kate's run had not helped her decide what to do. She returned exhausted and confused and found her father in the kitchen, reading the gardening section of the morning paper. Water for tea heated on the stove.

"Dad, you're up early."

"Couldn't sleep."

"I'm sorry. Aren't you feeling well?" She opened the fridge and pulled out the water pitcher. Empty.

"No, I'm fine," he answered, folding the paper into quarters.

Kate opened the lid and looked inside. The dial on the filter indicated that it needed changing. "Where do you keep the filters, Dad?"

"Above the refrigerator."

She dragged her mother's step stool over to the cupboard and climbed up. "So why can't you sleep? Should we call the doctor?"

"No," Patrick laughed. "He couldn't help me here. I can't sleep because I'm worried about my girl."

Kate, balanced on one foot, her arm stretched up into the cabinet, froze. *Here we go again.* She didn't want to discuss everything all over again. Patiently, she opened a box and removed a fresh filter. "Daddy, you don't have to worry about me. Your only job is to get better."

"Kate, *it is* my job to worry about you. I'm a father. That's what fathers do. Tell me why Mike came to see you and then left all in the same evening."

Kate climbed down off the step stool and came around the counter to the table. Kate pulled out a chair and sat beside her father. Leaning her elbows on the table, Kate told him everything. "I've been running, hoping that the whole thing would fall into place. Hoping I'd know what to do. I didn't mean to make you worry, Dad. I just want you to work on getting well."

He smiled and pushed the paper aside. "Kate, my heart is blown. No amount of rehab is going to make my heart new again."

Her eyes filled with tears, "Please, Daddy, don't talk like this."

"It's true. I don't know how long I have. But it isn't long." His voice seemed to Kate to come from some other faraway place. "We can pretend, but it doesn't change the facts."

"Daddy, please." Boiling water made the teakettle begin to whistle. Kate ignored it.

"Kate, I have to say this," her father began. "You can't— mustn't—stop me." He looked into her eyes, and for a moment Kate felt as though he were staring into her very soul. "I know that I'm dying. Or at least I'm close. But I have no regrets." He put one hand over hers, grasping it firmly. She felt his hand close, giving her three tight squeezes. She returned the secret code. From the time she was little, this had been the "I love you" code between father and daughter. Three tight squeezes. One for each word. "I love you."

He smiled and continued, "No regrets, Katie-Doll. I've loved your mother with all my heart. I've served the Lord with everything I have. I'm ready to go home. I've done the best I could."

"I know you have, Daddy," she whispered. "But I don't want you to go."

"Unfortunately, we don't get to choose the time. But I take comfort in knowing that I've done everything I could to live out my faith. Of course, I've made mistakes."

"Everyone does."

"True." He stood up and moved around the counter to the stove. Lifting the whistling kettle, he continued. "Everyone does. And I'm no exception."

"Daddy, why are you telling me this?"

"Because your mother won't talk about it with me." He poured hot water over his tea bag and put the kettle down. "And I need to talk. And I think you need to listen."

Kate wiped tears from her cheeks and watched him come back to the table. "What are you really saying, Daddy? I know you mean something else."

He smiled. "I'm saying that I know you're wrestling with this crazy idea of Mike's. And I think I'm wrestling too. I want you to be happy—more than you could ever know. I hate that Mike has hurt you. I don't want you to be hurt again. All parents want their kids to be happy. We want our kids to live without pain. If we could have our way, they would never experience sickness or sadness. They would never fail."

Kate nodded. She knew the feeling. She'd put in lots of anxious hours praying through the problems of her own kids.

"But I want something more for you. Something bigger."

Kate knew what he was thinking, and she didn't want to hear it.

"When you get to this same place in your own life, I want you to be able to say—in spite of all your mistakes—that you did everything you could to follow God. Everything."

"But I have, Daddy."

"Everything?"

"I think so."

"What about going sailing?"

"But, Daddy, when is enough, enough? After all he's done, are you saying that I should go with Mike?"

"No. I would never tell you what to do. You must make your own decision."

He fingered the edge of his cup, his eyes down. Kate watched his white mustache tremble slightly, and she knew he fought with his own emotions. "But when you are in my place, Kate, and you face the end of your life, I want you to feel the complete freedom of having done everything you could. No regrets. No sorrows."

"But you've never been hurt like this."

"You don't know what hurts I've had. Not everything." He looked into her eyes. "I've had to make choices too. Oh, not the exact same choices—but the same issues. Tough choices. Faith is one long succession of tough choices."

"I can't go through anything this painful again." Tears clogged Kate's voice. "And if I sail with him, I might . . ."

"I know. Every relationship involves risk. No one can protect you from that. But the reward is worth the risk. If you don't try, you'll never know what might have happened."

"You're saying I should go with him."

"I'm asking you to think. How will it feel, at the end of your life, if you don't give it a try?"

Kate stood up, brushing away tears, and leaned over her father. Wrapping his shoulders in both her arms, she leaned down to kiss his head. "I love you so much."

Twenty-Nine

MIKE CAME AWAY from the Holland home, his appetite satisfied, his heart warmed, and with twenty sheets of yellow legal paper tucked under his elbow in a file labeled "Marriage Delivery." Though they had not accomplished a single thing on the boat itself, the sheets detailed step after step of preparations to be made for the voyage. Beside each task, a name had been written and, beside that, a date indicating the goal for the chore to be finished. Even Valerie's name appeared throughout the list.

Mike's enthusiasm felt slightly dampened by the daunting list of assignments for the passage. Dave, a detail man by nature, had tripled Mike's preliminary list.

They arranged to transport the sails to a tennis court near Dave's house and go over the stitching, looking for signs of wear and chafing. They planned a day to go up the mast to check all the fittings and rigging, with the goal of buying replacement pieces for anything questionably worn. They set aside a day to go over electronic equipment. Mike still had to learn to operate the Global Positioning System, the autopilot, and maritime Sail Mail—all of which had been invented after Mike and Kate sold their last boat. The new electronic equipment made Mike feel a little like a sailing Neanderthal. He hoped he could learn it all before the time came to cast off and head south.

These preparations filled his head, dancing and catching all through the night. He slept anxiously, fitfully, though not by grief or guilt. In a way, it felt wonderful. At long last, Mike could do something, take action. Now he had direction, a plan. How wonderful to move toward a goal! While he tossed, Mike decided to keep a lined tablet by his bed. Then at least he would be able to write down his nighttime thoughts and perhaps sleep more soundly.

———

Doug McCoy went to work before five on Monday morning. Parking as close to the building as he could, he decided to use the north entrance. He did not want the temporary security man to notice his arrival. Not this morning.

He placed his key in the lock and slid his card through the security pad beside the door. Punching the numbers with his right hand, he held the door handle with his left, waiting for the beeping alarm to signal his entry. Doug waited. No beep.

He pulled at the door. Locked. He slid his card and punched the numbers again, this time with greater force. No beep.

Suddenly, a message came up on the LED screen above the security pad. "Access denied." Doug let go of the door. He must have made a mistake. Too much anxiety. He'd simply made an error. He looked at the card again to make sure he hadn't slid his library card through the slot by mistake. Right card. He checked the magnetic strip. Everything seemed fine.

Glancing toward the empty parking lot, he began the entire sequence again, forcing himself to act with slow deliberation. Again the same message: "Access denied." Doug swore softly to himself. What could possibly cause the system to refuse access?

He shuffled through the possibilities. For a moment, he wondered about the FBI. Then he remembered Mike's words in his office. What had he said? *"I'm going to do some internal investigation."* But hadn't Mike wanted Doug to flush out the source of the illegal credit card code?

Wait. Had Mike actually said that the code was faulty? Doug went back through the conversation in his mind. He could not remember. Had Mike said or only implied that the code was faulty? Doug swore again. Fear had begun to run his mind in circles, and he could no longer separate imagination from reality.

He stepped back from the door and walked to the sidewalk surrounding the parking lot. Doug would have to enter through the lobby, pass in front of the security man, and use the main elevators. Well, it couldn't be helped.

He hurried around the building toward the front entrance, when suddenly he realized that he did not have his usual coffee and paper. Perhaps with his face hidden behind a paper, the security man would not notice his early arrival. Doug jogged back across the lot to his car, opened the door, and riffled through the backseat. There, he found an old business section from the *Chronicle* and an empty Styrofoam coffee cup. Putting a lid on the cup, he balanced it in his hand as though it were full.

The whooshing of compressed air and moving lobby doors announced his arrival. Doug glanced briefly toward the security desk and back at his newspaper. The man from Bayside Temps stood behind the counter, watching a monitor that sat just out of Doug's line of sight. That guy sure took long shifts for a man from a temp agency. As Doug passed by, he did not look up.

Doug walked briskly past the desk and headed toward the bank of elevators. He punched the Up button and watched the light above the doors, waiting impatiently for the elevator to arrive.

"Excuse me," said a man's voice. Doug jumped. "I need you to sign in."

"Sign in?" Doug turned to face him.

"Yes, sir." The temp man had been transformed. His voice held no trace of recognition. The friendly tone he'd had when they last spoke had vanished. "New company policy. No one gets in or out of the building without checking in."

"That's ridiculous. I'm a partner here. I don't check in with anyone." Doug turned back to the elevator, willing it to arrive. "Besides, where did this policy come from? I haven't been consulted about this!"

"I couldn't tell you, sir. But I'm under orders. Just doing my job." He held a clipboard toward Doug. Taped to the back of the board, a string held a ball-point pen. "If you'll just sign in, sir."

As he accepted the board, Doug blew air through tightly pursed lips. "All right." He signed his name.

"And your badge number, sir."

"Badge number?"

"Right there, sir." The temp pointed toward the slot beside Doug's name.

With short angry strokes, Doug wrote down his six-digit employee number. Just as he shoved the clipboard back toward the uniformed security man, a bell rang, and the elevator doors opened. Doug stepped in and turned around.

Through closing doors, Doug saw the security man check his watch and write the time of Doug's arrival beside his name.

————

By Monday morning's commute to work, Mike's head was still filled with arrangements and lists. He stopped by a convenience store for coffee, choosing speed over taste. Mike had no time for a latte. He had work to do.

On one side of his office desk, he managed his DataSoft responsibilities. On the other, he managed his sailing venture. Always, in the back of his mind, he prepared the boat.

So when Brooke called to announce an unexpected visit from Doug, he was caught off guard. "Send him in," he said.

The door opened and Doug stormed in. Dressed in wrinkled cargo pants, Teva sandals, and a stained T-shirt, it looked to Mike like Doug hadn't slept in months. He moved directly to the oak chair in front of Mike's desk and flung his green canvas shoulder bag onto the carpet. He dropped into the chair, his knees spread, his hands gripping the arms. Though Doug and Mike had been friends for years, Mike had never before seen his friend in this condition.

"What is going on around here?" Doug demanded.

"I'm not sure what you mean."

"You know exactly what I mean."

Doug had always been the casual type, but today he looked like Richard Dreyfuss in the first *Jaws* movie. Curly disheveled hair, thick round glasses—the resemblance was so striking that Mike bit his lip to keep from chuckling. Considering the dark cloud hanging over Doug's countenance, Mike knew better. "I'm sorry, Doug. I can see that something has you all lathered up. But until you tell me what it is, I can't help you. What're you so upset about?"

Doug leaned forward and spoke through tight lips. "I mean that I came in at four-thirty this morning. I went to the north entrance, and I couldn't get my security card to work."

Mike nodded, at last understanding the source of Doug's frustration.

"Security is your department," Doug continued. "And I want to know why I've been cut out."

Mike smiled turning his hands up. "You haven't been cut out, Doug."

"Then why can't I get into the building?"

"It isn't just you. Don't take it personally. I had security beefed up for the night hours. The main entrance is the only one anyone in the company can use before seven in the morning."

"And what good is that going to do?"

"For one thing, it guarantees that all personnel going in and out of our building have to pass in front of the security team. It just might reduce the chance of illicit nighttime activities." Mike watched Doug's face closely. He seemed unconvinced. "Listen, I didn't know this would inconvenience you. I only wanted to be certain that anyone coming and going in our building belongs here. That everyone knows we're watching things carefully."

"We always watch carefully."

"Right, but if something illicit is going on here, don't you think that it's most likely to happen when no one else is around to watch?"

"There isn't anything illicit going on." Doug nearly spat the words.

"I agree. But for some reason the FBI thinks we're involved in a crime. I don't know why; but I'm as anxious to prove them wrong as you are. I've started several extra security precautions with that in mind."

"What precautions?"

"You just said security is my department. I have it under control. But really, I am sorry about this morning."

Doug sat for only a moment longer. Mike hoped to see signs of relief, relaxation. Instead, he watched what seemed to be a thousand emotions flicker over Doug's face and eyes. Doug lived in his own world. At last, he seemed to put on a mask. A controlled closed expression covered his features. "I'd appreciate it," he said in cold even tones, "if you'd at least let me know the next time you decide to change things around here. I don't like being stuck in the parking lot—unable to get into my own building."

"I'm sorry, Doug. Things have been really hairy around here lately. I'll try to tip you off next time."

Without another word, Doug left the room.

The meeting left Mike feeling uneasy. For some inexplicable reason, Doug seemed overly offended about the security issue. Perhaps Mike didn't understand the kind of pressure Doug faced. After all, Mike didn't know much about the delivery schedule downstairs. Perhaps he would respond the same way if Doug had made unilateral changes.

Still, in general, responsibility for company security had been placed squarely in Mike's portfolio. He had only chosen to do his job. He could not be responsible for his partner's hurt feelings.

When Brooke buzzed him on the phone, he nearly barked at her. "Yes."

"A call on line three."

"I'm busy, can't you take a message?"

"I thought you'd want to take this one, sir," she said quietly. "It's Mrs. Langston."

Mike felt foolish, "Thanks, Brooke." He punched the flashing line number. "Kate," he said breathlessly. He leaned back in his chair and closed his eyes, rubbing his forehead with one hand.

"Hi, Mike. Sorry to bother you at work."

"Never a problem."

"I've been thinking about your idea." Her voice gave no clue as to her decision.

"And?"

"Did you really mean what you said about the divorce?"

"I did."

"That you won't fight me?"

His breath caught in his throat. "I won't fight."

"And you'll give me the house and spousal support?"

Mike took a long slow breath. "Yes, I promised all of those things." He'd hoped this conversation would progress differently.

"Then," he heard her sigh, "then I will sail with you."

His heart seemed to miss a beat. Victory and fear surged through his bloodstream, both at the same time. Kate had taken the bait.

"Mike?"

"I'm here."

"Did you hear me?"

"Yes, I guess I'm just surprised, that's all."

"When do we cast off?"

"I hope to sail May 15."

"I'll come home in a couple of weeks. But I don't want you at the house."

"I'll live on board."

"All right, then," she said.

"Great." He could think of nothing else to say.

"Mike," she said, her voice weary, "I meant what I said."

"What?"

"Don't get your hopes up."

Mike resisted the urge to forget work and run to the marina. He wanted to be doing something. Fixing, cleaning, repairing—anything other than sit at his desk. But he had work to do, and racing to work on Dave's boat would not keep DataSoft running.

He picked up his latest production schedule and began to check efficiency numbers. The phone startled him.

"Mr. Langston, Mr. Walker and Mrs. Saunders from the FBI are here."

"They don't have an appointment."

"I know, but they say it's important."

"Show them in." Mike could hardly savor one success before being hit with another problem. He cleared his desk and waited for the door.

This time, Walker followed a woman into the room. With hair the color of cloves and a beautiful figure, he would never have guessed this woman worked with the special investigator. He stood as she crossed the room.

Walker lost no time introducing the woman, who seemed to be nearly twenty years younger than he. "This is my partner, Gwen Saunders. We've both been working this credit card case for some time."

The woman offered her hand, which Mike shook. "Please have a seat." This time, he offered only the chairs before his desk. The entire situation had begun to wear on Mike, and he hoped the desk would serve to support his appearance as a respectable business-man.

Saunders began, "Agent Walker has briefed me on your last conversation. I'm very familiar with this case, Mr. Langston. And, according to what I can find about your company, I believe you when you tell me you are innocent."

Her words surprised Mike. When Walker left his office, Mike felt certain that the agent wanted to throw him into federal prison forever. He let the discrepancy pass.

She continued, "I've come to ask your help. I'd like to place a Federal Agent in your company."

Mike's eyebrows rose.

"I can place a person in your business without a warrant—with or without your permission. However, I am limited as to what information we can use in court."

"What do you propose?" Mike asked her.

"A sniffer," she answered without flinching. "I have a man who could monitor a sniffer from anywhere in the company. He would watch the information traveling over your systems for signs of intrusion. Though the information he gleans would not be admissible in court per se, it would allow us to pursue our investigation more accurately. Our man could tell us what he finds, but we could not bring the information itself to court as evidence."

Mike spoke firmly. "No way."

"We can obtain a court order," Walker added.

"I don't think you can. You don't have enough evidence."

"Whether we do or not is of little significance here," Saunders said. "I'm offering you a way to help us without compromising your own security. If you are truly innocent, then a sniffer would help to find the guilty party and let you get on with your business."

Mike rolled his chair around to face the window, thinking fast. Technologically, a sniffer could watch all the information in the company—everything from every computer on the network. The person monitoring would know everything. Contacts. Projects. Codes. Schedules. Finances. It seemed like a lot of information for anyone to sort through. Too much access for an outsider—even a Federal Agent outsider. Everything in him said no. But his mouth said something altogether different.

"I'd like some time to think about it."

"That's all we can ask," Saunders said, smiling.

"Will that be all?" Without giving them time to answer, Mike stood and led them to the door.

"You have my number," Walker said, and Mike nodded.

———

After a long morning, Mike headed for his car. He planned to take the rest of the afternoon to accomplish several tasks. These included dropping a quarterly financial report off to an investor in the financial district. After that, he would cross the Bay Bridge and visit the rigging shop at Svendson's on Alameda Island.

The roller furler on Dave's boat needed a new motor, and Mike wanted the rigging experts to recommend a replacement. The motor would likely have to be ordered. Mike didn't have a lot of time to wait. Before he made it home, he would drive a complete circle of the Bay Area.

Mike could hardly see his feet over the plastic file box he held with both arms. On top of the box, he balanced his briefcase. Over his shoulder, the strap of his laptop computer dug into his neck. For the first time, he felt grateful for electronic lobby doors.

Outside, warm sunshine greeted him, and Mike headed straight for the Mustang. He set his bundles on the pavement and unlocked the trunk. Sliding things around, he stuffed things inside and slammed the door.

He threw his warm-up jacket on the back seat and slid behind the wheel. Hot. Too hot. He decided to drop the convertible top on the car. As he reached up to unlock the right side of the top, the release lever broke off in his hands. *Shoot.*

The lever had been rattling for weeks. *What did I expect of a thirty-two-year-old car?* He tossed the handle onto the floor in front of the passenger seat.

Suddenly he remembered a wrecking yard in Oakland—not far from the airport. He could drop into Oakland and stop by the wrecking yard for a new handle. It wouldn't be far out of his way, and he could put on the new handle himself.

Hours later, with his errands finished, Mike headed south on the 880 freeway. He hadn't thought about lunch until a giant hunger pang nearly doubled him over in his seat. Normally Mike wouldn't choose to eat lunch in Oakland. But certainly he could grab a bite at some place near the airport. He pulled off the freeway at the next exit.

Two blocks later, he found a small pub advertising a lunch special. The full parking lot seemed as good an advertisement for food as any billboard. Mike walked up to the hostess station where he found a long waiting list for tables. "I'll sit at the bar," he said, smiling.

"That's no problem. We can seat you right away," the hostess said.

Mike followed her into a dimly lit room filled with smoke. Dark paneling lined the walls where small booths held a lunch crowd composed largely of truckers and construction crews. Hard hats dotted the floor and tables around the room.

As Mike took a chair at the bar, a waitress handed him a menu and reported the daily special. "Halibut and chips," she said. "And that comes with your choice of chowder or salad."

"Sounds good. I'm starved." Mike gave the menu back. "I'll have the soup."

"I'll get it right out."

Mike ordered a tall Coke from the bartender and sat patiently waiting for his lunch. The sugar in his drink managed to stave off the hunger that had driven him into this restaurant. He took another long sip. Then, just as he put the drink down, a movement in the mirror over the bar caught his attention. Without turning around, he scanned the booths behind him.

There, in a booth in the corner, Mike spotted his partner, Doug McCoy.

Thirty

MIKE SLIPPED OFF his barstool and walked over to Doug's booth smiling. "Hey, Doug. I can't believe I've run into you here."

Doug glanced up and then did a double take. For a moment, he seemed shocked, but he recovered quickly. "Mike, man, you're a long way from home." He slid over on the vinyl bench, tucking a briefcase out of the way. For a moment, it looked as though Doug would invite Mike to join him. Instead, an awkward silence followed.

"True. I had some errands to run," Mike said. "And the handle on the Mustang's convertible broke this morning. I thought I'd run out to Stein's Wrecking to pick one up." Mike gestured toward the highway with his thumb. "I got stuck on the Bay Bridge and hadn't had lunch." He slipped his hands into his pockets, waiting to be introduced to the man sitting with Doug.

Taking the cue, Doug began, "This is, uh, Larry. Larry Williams."

"Good to meet you," Mike said, offering his hand. Larry only nodded.

"We were just having lunch," Doug said. He picked up his coffee mug and took a drink, eyeing Mike over the rim of the cup. Larry turned away, saying nothing.

Feeling strangely excluded, Mike made an excuse. "Well, I guess I'll leave you two to visit. My lunch should be coming." He went back to his seat. When the waitress brought his food, Mike explained that he had changed his mind. "Could you put it in a doggy bag or something?" he asked.

She smiled, "In a hurry, huh?"

Mike paid his tab and left the restaurant. He couldn't shake the eerie sense he'd gotten from running into Doug so far from the office. Over and over, he replayed the scene, wondering what might be bugging him about the meeting. Nothing came to mind. Just two men having lunch.

And then he remembered the briefcase. Something about the briefcase seemed out of place. What was it? Mike accelerated, merging into heavy freeway traffic. It was new—a formal style—made of leather. Then it dawned on him. For years Doug had carried an old green canvas shoulder bag. Mike tried to remember the last time he'd seen it. Just days ago, Doug had carried it into his office. Had Doug suddenly gone urban? That had to be the explanation. Doug had finally decided to dress the part of a successful businessman. *About time,* Mike conceded.

Without signaling, a two-trailer semi pulled into Mike's lane. Glancing over his shoulder, Mike wheeled around him, narrowly avoiding an accident. *If I go on daydreaming like this, I won't live to take the boat trip,* he thought. And he headed for the wrecking yard.

———

For the next two weeks, Mike Langston and Dave Holland worked feverishly. In spite of a full patient load, Dave spent every evening with Mike. Though the effort exhausted both men, they pressed on. First they tuned the diesel engine and went over every inch of it with a marine mechanic. They purchased spare parts— pumps, motors, electrical equipment, and repair kits—storing everything carefully on board. A service center inspected and re-packed an inflatable life raft, which they stowed on deck. Together, they made a list of supplies for an abandon-ship kit.

The cost of provisioning the kit surprised both men; but undeterred, they bought it all—flares, an Emergency Position Radio Beacon, a freshwater-maker, fishing supplies, a GPS, and a handheld VHF radio with spare batteries. Neither of these men spent money recklessly, and the bill nearly killed them.

They packed all the new supplies in a waterproof floatable container and placed the kit in a storage compartment under the rear cockpit bench. In case they had to abandon ship, they could throw the kit into the ocean before inflating the life raft.

When weather cooperated, they took the boat out, practicing sail changes and reefing techniques. Mike had never reduced sail in heavy seas, but he expected to have lots of opportunity on this passage. Dave insisted he repeat the procedure until he could bring down the main and tie it in place single-handedly.

Dave chose and purchased an emergency medical kit—unlike anything Mike had ever seen. The kit, enclosed in an enormous red nylon bag, featured color-coded medical supplies. Each tool or supply was sealed in a clear plastic pouch with a broad colored band on the outside edge. The kit's instruction book had color-coded pages. Each procedure had an assigned color. Lacerations were green. Broken bones were blue. Heart attacks were orange.

When an accident occurred on board, all Mike had to do was identify the injury, open the book, and remove the corresponding color-coded packages. Then, by following the directions, Mike could treat any onboard injury. The kit made him an instant emergency room. They stowed the bag in the forward storage area, and as they closed the compartment, Mike silently prayed that he would never have to use it.

Together the two men went through the toolbox, cleaning and replacing worn or rusty tools. Dave added rubber exam gloves from the dental office, dental mirrors, and tools. They stowed waterproof epoxy, deck sealants, seacocks, and sail repair supplies. They purchased a collision mat, which in case of a collision could be draped around the hull and held in place by the pressure of the ocean itself. The mat would allow them to remain on board waiting for rescue even after serious hull damage.

The work felt endless, overwhelming. But both men knew how dangerous a voyage of this distance could be, even under the best conditions. Saving the boat and their lives depended on covering the details.

———————

Two weeks later, Mike packed a few suitcases and moved to the boat. He'd promised Kate that he would be out of the house when she returned. But more than that, he felt he needed time to bond with the boat, even if he only lived there at night. No matter how silly it sounded, Mike wanted to be so familiar with Dave's boat, so certain of the normal sounds and feelings on board, that he could sense any change before it proved dangerous. He wanted to listen to her creaks and feel her shudders. Mike wanted to learn to sleep on board and instantly recognize—even in his sleep—abnormal conditions. No matter what Kate requested, Mike wanted to live on board.

During the daytime hours, Mike continued at the office. He worked relentlessly, through his lunch hour and late into the afternoon. Some days he left early and, with the help of his cell phone, worked from the boat. With time, Mike learned the tricks of communication via onboard laptop computer. He perfected his ability to retrieve and read weather faxes via the Inmarsat-C system. He still had trouble interpreting the data occasionally, but he felt confident that he could run the equipment.

Eventually, Mike found himself counting the days until Kate's return.

———

On her last night in Kansas, Kate enjoyed a quiet dinner with her parents. After the fateful night of Mike's unexpected arrival, she had not heard from Greg Harris. Though his silence hurt, Greg had been right. She did need to close one door before opening another. Kate frequently reminded herself that this trip was simply her way of closing the door.

She said good-night early, kissing both parents before going upstairs to finish packing. She laid out her clothes for the next day and changed into her nightgown. In the bathroom, she gathered her things and put them in her travel case. Looking into the mirror, she told herself firmly, "It's only a trip. After all, what is there to worry about? When the trip is over, so is the marriage. It's exactly what you want."

Somehow Kate didn't quite believe the woman in the mirror.

Kate had an unmistakable feeling of anxiety. Why had she allowed Mike to convince her to go? She sat down on the edge of the bed and pulled her Bible from the nightstand. Kate needed comfort.

Am I doing the right thing, Lord? She wondered.

Trust me. She heard the words again—the same words she'd

heard several times over the past several weeks. But the words did not pacify her fear.

She sought her favorite verse but found it cold and empty. She looked through the Gospels, but received no solace. Restless, she stood and looked out the bedroom window, down onto the street where she had played as a child. "I'm afraid, Lord," she said aloud, brushing tears from her cheeks. "I'm just plain scared."

———

Norm was just reaching for another donut hole when Gwen Saunders suddenly stuffed her hand in the bag of goodies he was holding. "You could ask, ya know," he said. "Besides, you don't eat junk food."

"Sorry. I guess I'm just tired of listening to you eat." She popped a piece of sweetness into her mouth as they continued their vigil.

Their unmarked Grand Marquis sat on a hill overlooking the marina where Dave Holland kept his boat. Norm was licking sugar off his fingers as his partner raised her binoculars and looked out over the water to the F dock, where the *Second Chance* floated on a mirrorlike calm.

"Can you see him?"

"Not now, he's gone below."

"What about the other guy?"

"The big one? He's got his head in a locker near the wheel."

As Gwen watched the boat, Norm kept his eye on the traffic going in and out of the lot. After a bit, he stretched and asked, "So what do you think?"

"I think we're wasting our time."

"We know he's leaving."

"We know they're provisioning. We know the dentist isn't leaving his practice. I guess we *think* Langston is leaving." Gwen shrugged, never taking her eyes off the boat.

"Maybe he's making a contact."

"Doesn't make sense."

"Why not?"

"Because all of the other contacts went to New York City or Seattle. Why would they change things now?"

"They know we're watching."

She shrugged again. "Hey, I don't mind the overtime. But Langston isn't our man."

"Well, then, I think it's about time we figured out who is."

"We could call about the sniffer."

"Seems like the easiest way," he agreed.

———

Kate allowed her parents to drive her to the airport, though she insisted they drop her off rather than walk her to the gate. She didn't want her father walking through a busy airport just to say good-bye. They pulled up to the curb nearest the United Airlines check-in counter, and Kate unloaded her bags. When she closed the trunk, both her parents stood on the curb waiting.

She hugged her mother first, feeling her tiny frame, soft and squishy. "Bye, Mom. Thanks for calling me. Thanks for letting me stay so long." She kissed her mother's cheek.

"Your daddy needed you, honey. I'm so glad you could come."

"Me too." Kate hugged her again, and stood back. Glancing at her father, she noticed that he blinked back tears. "Daddy," she said, stepping into his arms. "Oh, Daddy. Please take care of yourself. Do everything they tell you, all right?" They hugged, squeezing each other.

"I'll do my best, Katie-Doll," he answered. He left one hand resting on her shoulder as though he couldn't let go. She felt him squeeze her upper arm with the three-squeeze code. "I'm still praying for that miracle."

She hugged him again. "I don't think you should waste God's time, Daddy," she said, wiping a tear from her face.

"God never wastes time, Kate. Not His. Not ours."

Kate shook her head, a smile spreading across her face. "You are incorrigible, Daddy. And I love you, so much." Tears stung her eyes, and she rejected the question that frightened her most. *Will I ever hug my daddy again?*

She didn't want to let go, but she had to. She had to catch her plane. She had to take this trip and put her life with Michael behind her. When she looked up at her father, she saw that he, too, had tears streaming down his cheeks. "I'll call as soon as we get to Hawaii," she assured him.

He nodded, too overcome for words.

Kate stacked her overnight bag on the top of her rolling suitcase and pulled up the handle. When she had balanced the whole contraption, she smiled again, "Well, then, I'd better go. I love you guys."

"We'll pray for your trip," her mother said.

"We'll pray for everything," her father added.

As she walked away, Kate glanced back at her parents and waved. She took one last mental picture of them, standing together on the sidewalk—crying and holding hands.

———

Doug McCoy found himself sitting at his desk, unable to work, unable to concentrate. His fingers endlessly drummed the Formica surface. He tried to calm himself but could not. He had too much to lose. Too much at stake. And at this moment, it looked to him like his whole world might come crashing down on top of him.

He pulled a yellow legal tablet from the top drawer of his desk. Carefully, he wrote down the growing list of suspicions that threatened his plans. First he printed in tight capital letters the words *Security Man.* He knew Mike had brought in the officer at the front desk. He wrote *Why?* next to the words. He had no idea. At the same time, he knew the man had lied about being from Bayside Temps. No such business existed.

He might be a "plant." Perhaps he had been brought in to watch the corporate computer system. What if Mike had hired someone to install a sniffer? Had all of Doug's work been traced? He printed the word *Who?*

Doug felt his pulse thump in his temples. The tension in his jaws began to grow into a headache. He had to figure this out. He had to stay one step ahead of the game. He stood and walked to a nearby cabinet where he had hidden a bottle of scotch behind his software manuals. He pulled out the books, grabbed the bottle, and drank. Doug didn't need a glass, he needed comfort—immediately.

As he felt warm liquid burn its way down his throat, he took a deep breath, determined to out-think his opponents. Leaving the bottle on the counter, he went back to the desk. After all, he designed software. They could never match his wits.

He picked up his pen, read over the list, and then listed *Access Denied.* Next to these words he printed *Others?* Mike had changed some of the most primary security procedures at the building. Perhaps being denied access at the north entrance meant more than he realized at the time. Perhaps other security measures existed that he had not observed. He would think this through later. For now, Doug wondered if he had been caught in a net he did not yet see.

Below this he printed *Feds* in slightly larger letters. The presence of Federal Agents in Mike's office—not once but three separate times—alarmed Doug. Tiny beads of perspiration formed on his forehead. These he brushed away with his hand. Though he had no details on their first visit, the second two he knew about from Mike himself.

Doug still had one ace up his sleeve: Mike's trust. Doug had complete confidence that he would be the last person Mike would suspect, yet so many things had gone wrong.

He drew an extra large question mark beside the word *Feds*. How much did they know? How much had they told Mike? He wished he knew, but he had no way of finding out.

Clearly, Mike had not put things together yet. But still one event troubled Doug. More than all the others, this one thing kept Doug at his bottle of scotch. Kept him from sleeping. From working. He printed the word *Delivery*. Though he did not recognize it, Mike had actually caught Doug in the process of a transfer.

This one error he could not erase. And it ate away at Doug more than any other event. If someone, anyone, asked the right questions, Mike could put Doug away. He'd seen a face. Knew of a place. Saw the two men together.

All of this led Doug back again and again to one important question, a single question that threatened to drive Doug to the brink of despair. How much did Mike know?

Doug picked up the phone and dialed. A woman's voice answered. "I think we have serious trouble," he said without introduction.

"I've told you never to call me here."

"I had to. I'm worried. I don't know how much Mike knows."

"That much is obvious," she said. "Perhaps the time has come to eliminate the question."

"What do you mean? I can't do anything like that," he hissed.

"I'm afraid you've already done something like that. You're in over your head, Doug. Too many people know about you. Someone," she emphasized the word, "might go to the police about your involvement."

"No one can connect me with anything."

"I can." She let that sink in. "Only one person can put the whole thing together. It's time to get rid of him."

Doug heard only the soft click of the telephone as she hung up.

———

Mike arrived ninety minutes early for Kate's flight. He wore neatly pressed khakis, a dark polo shirt, and dark socks under his Top-Siders. All week, he'd worried that traffic might make him late. So he came early and set up his laptop and cell phone, determined to work while he waited. His stomach fluttered with anxiety, which surprised him. His body seemed to be reacting as if this were his first date.

Long-stemmed roses from a shop near the office waited on the seat beside him. Mike had had them boxed in gold foil. Every few minutes, he stopped working to check his watch. Frequently, he rose and walked toward the bank of monitors to check the arrival schedule.

Eventually, Mike gave up. He closed his laptop, stuffed it into his briefcase, and moved to a window where he could gaze out on the Tarmac. Soon Kate would be back. Could he do it? Could he convince her to try again? Doubt threatened to bubble up and swallow Mike whole.

Oh God, I'm dying here. Please help me.

Her plane arrived precisely on time. With building anxiety, Mike watched as the ground crew extended the Jetway. He waited, holding his breath, while they opened the door to the waiting area. Strangers streamed past, and Mike's emotions bounced like a brisk chop on the bay, as families greeted passengers coming off the plane.

Then she came. He noticed her hair color first, the soft strawberry-blond he so loved. He noticed her face and hair above most other passengers, for Kate was taller than most women. He'd already noticed some of the changes she'd made in her appearance when he saw her a couple of weeks ago in Kansas. Her wavy hair was shorter and softer somehow, framing her face with light wisps. She wore makeup, and he could not think of the last time he had seen her in makeup. Kate had always had a natural, soft beauty. He could not remember that she'd ever dressed it up with cosmetics before. He wondered about it now. Why had she made these changes?

She came through the doorway slowly, almost timidly, her eyes scanning the room. Mike noticed the moment she saw him and regretted the stiff look of recognition that came over her face. He walked toward her, one hand out, the other holding her roses. She stopped before him, still awkwardly holding her bag and purse. "Mike," she said, nodding. "Thanks for coming to meet me." She might have been greeting a business associate.

"I'm so glad to see you," he said, reaching for her hand. Taking her purse, he pulled her gently toward him; he gave her cheek the softest kiss he could manage. She resisted, her body stiff and unyielding. How desperately he wanted to pull her into his arms and hold her. Instead, he offered her the flowers. She dropped his hand and accepted them with a nod.

He refused to babble on about how much it meant that she'd decided to come. *Let her come around in her own time,* he told himself sternly. "Let's pick up your luggage," he said, smiling.

I refuse to worry about tomorrow, Lord, he prayed silently. *For now, she is here.*

Thirty-One

AT THE BAGGAGE CLAIM AREA, they picked up Kate's luggage and went out to the parking area. Mike carried the larger piece down the stairs. Trying to sound casual, he said, "Kate, you've changed your hair."

She stopped walking to stare at him. "No, actually, it's still mine."

"No, I mean it's shorter. I like it, really." Why did women always do things like that, change their hair and then resent it when men didn't compliment them correctly?

At the car, Mike wondered for a moment if he should put up the convertible top. Maybe she would want to protect her new hairstyle. He dropped her luggage into the trunk and slammed it shut. Kate had already climbed into the front seat. Apparently, she didn't care about the wind.

He got in and pulled out of the lot. "Where would you like to go first?"

"I'd like to go home," she answered, sounding very weary.

Mike noticed that she slid down against the seat, resting her head against the back, her eyes closed. "All right," he agreed. "Your wish is my command."

"Please don't do that," she said without opening her eyes. "You aren't going to win me back, Mike. And I refuse to let you treat me with this stupid deference. It isn't real. It doesn't suit you. If we're going to be together, then just treat me like you always have."

The words stung. "I'm sorry," he said. "I was only trying to lighten things up." They rode in silence for a moment before he began again. "Actually, I wondered if you'd like to see the boat, or if you needed groceries, or if you wanted to stop somewhere for something." He glanced at her just in time to see her lips tighten in an expression of disgust.

"I'll see the boat soon enough. Right now, I just want to go home."

Looking at her again, Mike noticed that though the wind blew her hair wildly around her face, a tiny tear had escaped, making its way unchecked down her left cheek. He wanted desperately to reach over and wipe the tear away, but instead he forced himself to keep both hands on the wheel. His own betrayal had caused those tears and many others just like them. Wiping them away would not heal her wounds.

Kate allowed Mike to carry her bags into the house, to show her where he'd kept her mail, and give her a list of phone messages he'd taken for her. She listened halfheartedly while he gave her a tour of the refrigerator and the pantry. She leaned against the kitchen counter, her arms folded across her chest, while he told her about the boat and the trip he had planned.

"Valerie told me that she's going to help you provision. She should be calling real soon."

Kate nodded.

"I guess she thinks it will be easier for you if you do it together. They'll be taking the boat on after we deliver it. She wants most of her galley supplies on board when we leave San Francisco."

"I don't know anything about a long-term voyage," Kate said. "The only experience I've had is the little trips we've made around the Bay. Even then you did all the sailing."

"I know. Dave and I have been working hard to prepare the boat. It's seaworthy, Kate. You shouldn't have to do much."

"What exactly do you mean by 'much'?"

"Well, until we get out of the shipping lanes, we'll have to have someone on watch full-time. I can't do that myself."

"How far is that?"

"About two hundred miles off the California coast."

She nodded, pressing her lips together. The idea of taking a boat to Hawaii with Mike grew more ludicrous with every sentence.

Why had she agreed? She couldn't take a watch. She had no idea how to handle a boat as large as Dave's. Everything inside her wanted to back out. With a divorce she could move on with her life. It might almost be worth it to let him have everything—if she could get out of making this stupid trip.

She watched him sitting on the kitchen island, ankles crossed, feet swinging, and wondered how many times she'd seen him there, just like that. Her mind wandered back over the years. This position, this little-boy position, was the way he had told her about new products DataSoft brought online. Nearly every night, when things were good, Mike had jumped onto the island counter and chatted while she made dinner. Five years ago, they'd planned Drew's graduation party just like this. When things were good.

"Have you thought about the clothes you'll need?"

His voice startled her, and she realized that she had not been listening. "I haven't thought about anything," she answered truthfully. "I just want to get this stupid trip over with."

Kate watched his face fall and the light go out of his eyes. She'd wounded him, and she felt a twinge of regret. The regret surprised her. *He didn't regret wounding me,* she told herself sternly. *I don't owe him anything.*

"Well, then, I guess I'll go down to the boat. You can reach me on my cell phone."

Lifting himself by his arms, he dropped off the counter and moved to the back door. Without looking back, he went out, quietly closing the door behind him.

————

At their first meeting, Kate and Valerie Holland managed to develop a series of menus to cover both the California to Hawaii trip and the Hollands' sail through the South Pacific. From those meal plans, they came up with a grocery list several pages long. Two days later, Valerie met Kate at a warehouse-style grocery store.

"You're on time!" Val called, coming across the parking lot toward Kate's car. She scooped Kate into a warm hug.

"Nice to see you too," Kate answered. With the beep of her automatic lock, Kate turned toward the store. "Well, shall we get on with it?"

Purchasing supplies took most of two days. For canned goods, they went to the warehouse store. For freeze-dried foods, the sporting goods store. For medicinal supplies, a warehouse drugstore.

The list of purchases and preparations seemed overwhelming to Kate, who considered herself an organized person. Valerie carried all of her lists in a leather portfolio—separate pages covering each supply category. Beside each item, she listed the size required and the number of units to purchase. As she put items into the cart, she wrote the purchase price on her list. With this methodical approach, Val might have provisioned the entire Pacific naval fleet. Next to Valerie, Kate felt like a scatterbrain.

The women spent two full days repackaging the supplies. For this, a simple sealing appliance became their right hand. They made "night watch" packages, filled with high-calorie, high-energy foods, and sealed them into watertight packages. They made storm packages—foods that required only boiled water for preparation—and sealed them into single meal containers. Any food that might be susceptible to water damage—like pasta, beans, and rice—was double-sealed. They made separate containers of vitamins, Band-Aids, and alcohol wipes. They double-sealed packages of matches. Though Kate assured Val that she never became seasick, they even prepared tiny seasickness packages of herbs, medicines, and suppositories.

"You've never been out in a really big storm," Val assured her. "Fifteen-foot waves can make anyone seasick. Better be prepared."

As they worked, they anticipated where to stash each item. On a diagram of the boat, Valerie kept a record of the storage areas. Eventually, when everything had been safely stowed on board, Valerie would take the labeled sheet and have it laminated. This copy would hang in the galley as a permanent record.

In Valerie's garage, they labeled all of the canned goods with permanent marker before shellacking them against the ravages of saltwater. The work was hard, smelly, and very messy. Shellac ended up everywhere—on their clothes, in their hair, and all over the garage floor. In spite of this, through long hours together, the two friends gradually shared more than hard work. They shared their lives.

Though they never actually spoke of Cara Maria or the pictures, Kate knew that Val understood. She knew her friend had experienced a similar pain in her past—though Val never revealed all the details. During their time together, Val exposed her own wounds and told Kate about her road to healing. Valerie Holland never instructed or lectured; she simply shared her own experience.

"At one point, I remember deciding that I would never forgive Dave," she finally admitted. "But looking back, I see that by forgiving him, I became whole again." She shook her head. "That doesn't make sense, I know. After all, it was his wrong choice. But I admit it. It's true. Somehow, my letting go of him helped me."

Kate didn't want to hear about forgiveness. She didn't want to know about healing. But she valued her friend. Val's vulnerability touched Kate. She didn't want to seem disrespectful—even though she knew she would never follow her friend's example.

Mike's betrayal had wounded Kate beyond any ability to forgive.

"Keegan thinks our trip is a sign that all is well between us." Kate said, as she filled small bags with cashews.

"You've told them?"

"We called them a few days ago, Drew first, and then Keegan. Just like old times. Mike was on the extension, and we told them all about our plans."

"What did they say?"

"Well, Drew didn't really know anything was wrong. You know how boys are. But I know Keegan thinks we're back to normal. I could hear the relief in her voice. She was thrilled about it."

"But you aren't thrilled."

"Val, I'm making the trip so that I can get a divorce. I couldn't tell Keegan that. Not now. And part of me feels horrible about letting her believe a lie."

"It isn't a lie yet," Val said. And then, changing the subject, "Could you hand me those chocolate bars? I think we should put some chocolate in with the cashews before we seal them."

In spite of her determination to remain detached from the entire voyage, Kate found herself enjoying the work. Then, to her horror, late Thursday afternoon she realized that she'd even begun to look forward to the trip.

Eventually, they finished gathering supplies and stacked everything in carefully organized piles. Opening the garage door, they took pictures of one another smiling over the evidence of their hard work. Then they began loading it into Valerie's minivan.

With so much to transport, they decided to make more than one trip to the boat. Refrigerated and frozen items could go on board only at the last minute. Other things could be stowed immediately. So, early Saturday morning, Kate met Valerie at the house to take the first load to the marina.

"I should have known better than to do this on a Saturday morning," Val muttered as she drove through the crowded parking lot. "But it isn't like we have a lot of flex time in our schedule." She turned the corner and started through the lot again. Cars occupied every spot and overflowed in bizarre patterns onto the street and alley. "Okay," she said, swinging into the loading area near the locked gate. "Here's the plan. I drop you off here and go across the street to park. You ambush the first family that comes out of that gate with an empty dock cart and bring it over to me at the car. Got it?"

"You mean one of those wheelbarrows?" Kate pointed down the dock with her finger.

"That's it. Don't come back without one."

"Aye, aye, Captain." Kate saluted and got out of the car. Smiling to herself, she walked to the security gate. Val pulled out and drove across the street.

Nearly ten minutes passed before Kate pushed a cart to the car. Trying to avoid a second trip, they loaded the cart high. Kate pushed, and Valerie walked beside the cart, trying to keep the whole heap from falling over onto the sidewalk. The women managed to lower it slowly down the dock ramp. Eventually they arrived beside the boat. Kate carefully lowered the cart handle while Val climbed the plywood stairs to unlock the safety lines. Dropping them to the side, she stepped on board. "Why don't you come up and check the place out first? Then we'll start lugging all the stuff on board."

Kate stood rooted to the dock, her eyes roaming over the length of the *Second Chance.*

"Your mouth is hanging open," Val said, laughing.

"I—I didn't expect it to be this big."

"Forty-five feet," Val said, nodding. "Seems big—until you're stuck on it in the middle of an endless ocean. Then somehow it shrinks."

"It's beautiful." Kate walked up the stairs and stepped on deck. As she paused to admire the height of the main mast, her neck objected to the angle. Massaging her muscles, she looked down and noticed teak slats lining the decks. She knelt to feel their smooth silver surface.

"They don't get as slippery as fiberglass when they're wet." Val stepped into the cockpit and squeezed around the wheel. Moving to the hatch, she unlocked the padlock that secured the sliding door to the salon below.

Kate followed, stepping onto the cockpit bench and ducking under the awning. "We have foam pads for the benches down below," Val said. "I like them, but Dave thinks they aren't safe. Says they slide when you step on 'em." She set the padlock down on one of the seats and slid the hatch cover out of the way. "Still, the pads are easier on your backside than teak." Folding the door out of the way, Val locked it in place. "Well, here she is, your home away from home." With a sweep of her arms, she disappeared down the steps. Kate took a deep breath and followed.

The wooden stairs down to the main living area were steep, but rails on each side helped Kate descend without difficulty. Inside, her eyes took a moment to adjust to the darkened cabin. What she saw surprised her.

Kate couldn't remember ever being on a boat this large. An oval table, large enough to seat six, sat on the right side of a broad living area. Around the table an L-shaped bench covered in light green tapestry made for comfortable seating. Constructed of wood, the blond table featured a lip designed to keep dishes from sliding onto the floor. Opposite the table, on the port side of the cabin, a matching bench rested just beyond a desk full of navigational equipment—most of which Kate did not recognize.

Directly to her right, behind the stairs, Kate found a circular galley. A little gasp slipped out when she saw the two-basin sink and three-burner stove over a medium-sized oven. Louvered cupboards, six in all, completely covered the wall above the counters. She stepped down into the tiny area and ran her fingers over laminate countertops. "It's so beautiful. And so much storage." Kate reached up to unlatch a cupboard.

"Functional too," Val agreed. "When we brought the boat back from Texas, we had lots of stormy weather. The galley is tight enough that you can wedge yourself in there and not be thrown around too much. You'll appreciate that."

Still awed by the cooking area, Kate noticed a tiny porthole above the back wall behind the stairs. Standing up on her tiptoes, she found that she could see the bottom of the cockpit steering wheel. For a moment, Kate pictured Mike's shoes there on the deck while he steered the boat. She imagined cooking a dinner while he steered. From this position she would be able to feel the swell of the ocean beneath the boat and watch him from this very window.

"I'll have to teach you how to light all the cooking surfaces," Val said. "I hope I know where I stored the galley towels." Val walked into the main salon. "What I liked most about the *Second Chance* were all her clear hatches. Not many boats have this much natural light below deck."

Kate had to agree. She counted four hatches in the salon—all letting sunlight into the cabin. She shook herself from her day-dreaming and turned her attention to Val. "What about the beds?"

"The most important part of any ship." Valerie walked to the nav desk and made a sharp turn toward the back of the boat. "The center cockpit leaves space for a nice big aft cabin. I think you'll like it. It's my favorite spot."

They stepped through a hall near the navigation desk into the rear cabin. A spacious captain's bed rested high on the rear wall of the boat. Four drawers had been built below the bed itself, and Kate noticed that the wall on her right held another bank of drawers. Sunshine filled the space, spilling in from another large hatch above the bed.

"New boats don't have nearly this much storage," Val said, watching Kate run her fingers over the drawers. "That's partly why we chose an older boat. This one was built in Taiwan—back when craftsmanship was still available." She took a few steps into the room. "Here's your bathroom." She opened a door, and Kate peered into a marine bathroom with white fiberglass walls and a teak bench. "It's also the shower," Val said.

"So roomy."

"You do like it!" Val said. "I could live here, I think—that is, if Dave ever really decided to retire."

"What about the forward cabin?" Kate tried to sound casually curious. She had no intention of sharing a room with Mike on this trip.

"Oh yes. I forgot. Not as nice, but handy. I nap there when I'm all salty. Keeps the sheets clean." She stepped back into the hall and walked through the salon. "Look at that door," Val said, pausing before the most beautiful wooden door Kate had ever seen. "Amazing, isn't it?"

An arched doorway led to the forward cabin. The door itself had been carved from a single piece of lightly grained wood. The finish gleamed as perfectly as the finish on a carameled apple. Opening the door, Val folded it into a single five-inch slab, which she secured out of the way with two latches. Kate paused to rub a hand over the gleaming surface. The texture reminded her of an elegant grand piano.

Stepping into the forward cabin, Val pointed out the bed on the right and a desk on the left. "I generally keep my own work here," she said. "That way the ship's log and charts and so on are undisturbed in the nav center."

Kate nodded.

"And here is the second head." At the very end of the forward bunk, Val opened a full-sized door to reveal a second marine toilet.

I'll have to get used to all this marine talk if I'm going to sail again, Kate told herself.

"Beyond there, in that cupboard you'll find the sail compartment. You can stuff unused sails from the deck directly into the boat. Then you can access them from inside if you need to make repairs or swap sails." She closed the cupboard, firmly snapping the lock in place.

They went back to the salon. "Here are the under-floor storage areas," she said, bending over and turning a brass ring set down inside a teak panel. The floorboard lifted, and Kate looked down into an irregularly shaped white compartment. "All of these spaces drain back into the bilge area. No water will accumulate here—unless you're sinking." She laughed. "By the time you two cast off, we'll have every one of these spaces stuffed with supplies."

"No wonder you're keeping a diagram."

"You'd never find anything without a storage chart." Val shrugged, smiling. "Believe me, I've done it the hard way." She dropped her hands and shrugged. "Well, should we go up and haul that stuff down here?"

"After you."

The two women started up the stairs when a thought occurred

to Kate. "Hey, Val, I can haul this stuff on board by myself. Why don't you go back to the house for the next load?"

"But dragging it down the companionway stairs is the worst part. I hate to leave you with the really hard work."

"By the time you get back, I'd be done with the cart. I could meet you at the car, and we'd unload right at the gate."

"You're right. It would be easier than waiting to get another one. Are you sure that's okay with you?"

"No problem," Kate said. "I'll see you in about forty minutes."

Kate watched, her hands resting on her hips, as Val stepped off the deck and jumped with a thud to the dock. With a little wave of her hand, her friend trotted back toward the parking lot.

"Well, I might as well get started," Kate said out loud. Sighing, she started down the steps to lift the first box off the cart.

Kate, kneeling on the salon floor, had one hand deep in a cupboard below the port bench when she heard footsteps on the deck above her. The sound startled her, and she wondered for a moment if she had lost track of time. "Shoot. I forgot to go up to the gate." She straightened up, bumping her head on the bench above her.

Narrowly avoiding an oath, Kate rested her face on her forearm for a moment and rubbed the sore spot on the back of her head. "Sorry, Val, I didn't watch the time," she said into the floor. No answer. Hearing movement on the companionway, Kate looked up to find a pair of navy blue trousers above women's shoes coming down the companionway steps. Who could this be?

"I'm sorry to bother you," the female said as she emerged below. "Are you Kate Langston?"

"Yes." Kate stayed on her knees, too surprised to stand up. "And you are?"

"Gwen Saunders, FBI." The woman pulled a badge from her jacket pocket and showed Kate. She did not flash the badge the way Kate remembered from movie scenes. Instead, she moved slowly, deliberately.

Kate stood up and offered her hand. "What can I do for you?" she asked.

"I came to talk to you about your husband," the dark-haired woman replied.

Thirty-Two

"WHAT ABOUT MY HUSBAND?" Kate fought a rising tide of irritation. Tension filled her neck and shoulders. Deliberately, she willed herself to relax, rolling and stretching her neck. Whatever this woman had to say, it had nothing to do with her.

"It's a long story. Do you have time to talk?"

Kate looked directly into the woman's dark eyes as she searched them. *Can I trust her? Will she tell the truth?* "Sure, I guess." Kate shrugged. "How about if we go up on deck? It's lighter there, more comfortable."

"Great." The woman smiled.

Kate reached into the closet behind the engine room and brought out the green foam pads for the cockpit benches.

"After you," the woman said, waiting for Kate to climb the stairs.

Saunders stepped into the afternoon sunshine and waited while Kate put the cushions in place. "Thanks," she said.

Kate nodded and took a seat, unwilling to volunteer a single unnecessary word. "Mrs. Langston, I'm going to be completely honest with you," Saunders said. "We've been involved in a very extensive criminal investigation that has landed directly on your husband's doorstep."

Kate tried not to let surprise register on her face. "What kind of investigation?"

"Well, I can't tell you everything. But I can tell you this. We know that someone at DataSoft is involved with organized crime—

what we used to call the Syndicate. Someone has written malicious code into DataSoft software."

"Malicious code?" Kate had never heard the term before. In all of her meetings with Mike, he hadn't mentioned anything about trouble at the company. "I don't understand."

"It isn't something you hear about every day. We know that the Syndicate has been harvesting credit card numbers off the Internet. A very profitable activity, I assure you. We caught them in the process of producing false cards."

"But what does that have to do with DataSoft?" Confusion swirled through her head. Who was this woman? What did any of this have to do with Kate?

"We've traced the numbers to sites built by DataSoft. We talked to the system administrators. They didn't even know they'd been hit." Gwen Saunders paused and took a deep breath, blowing it out slowly. "We know it wasn't a break-in, Mrs. Langston. Someone probably got paid a huge amount of money to design what programmers call a 'back door' in the software. Then that same someone gave the keys to the Syndicate, who harvested the numbers and made duplicate credit cards. It's all very layered. Covered up. But we know for certain that it started at DataSoft."

"Why are you telling me this?" Kate leaned forward, resting her hands over her knees. "I don't know anything."

"Mrs. Langston, we know that you don't have anything at all to do with the company. We're quite certain that you aren't involved." Uncrossing her legs, the woman leaned forward. Her eyes narrowed. "At the same time, we know that you have plans to leave with your husband. I'm here to warn you."

"Warn me of what?" Kate fought to keep panic from her voice.

"If your husband has had anything to do with this—anything at all—he could be in grave danger. These people don't play games." She stood, walking to the rear of the cockpit and gazed out over the other boats. "And if your husband is in danger," she said, turning back to Kate, "I don't need to explain that you may be in danger as well."

"Mike would never be involved with anything like this."

"Mrs. Langston, according to my information, your husband has been involved in several activities lately that have surprised you." She folded her arms across her chest. "I should think you, of all people, would know better than to make broad assumptions about his innocence." The agent reached into her jacket pocket and pulled out a business card. Handing it to Kate, she said, "If you know anything, anything at all, I'd suggest you help us. After all, your marriage is over anyway. Why not shut this guy down? Turn him in."

Kate took the card. "We've been married for twenty-six years, Miss . . ." she glanced down at the card, "Saunders." Her words breathed ice. "If anyone knows my husband, I do. Whatever he may be, he is not a criminal."

"For your sake, I hope so. You wouldn't be the first woman to be surprised by her husband's activities."

"I think it's time for you to go." Kate stood, gesturing toward the dock.

Gwen Saunders moved toward the rear door of the cockpit, then turned to offer her hand. "If you change your mind, or if you think of anything or hear anything that would help us, please call that number. You can leave a message any time of the day or night." She stepped onto the bench. With one foot on the deck, she turned back, "Please, Mrs. Langston. Be careful. These people play for keeps."

Kate stood silently, her arms folded across her chest. Sighing, Saunders turned and left the boat. Kate watched as she walked down the dock to the ramp and started up toward the parking lot. Kate followed Saunders until she had disappeared in the crowd onshore.

When Val came back to the parking lot, she found Kate, her shoulders raised, her features tight, pacing in front of the locked gate. Valerie pulled into the loading area and unlocked the rear door. "Am I late?" she asked, coming around the rear of the car.

"No." Kate pulled the cart into place and lifted the hatch. Silently, she began dumping packages into the cart.

"What on earth happened?" Val asked. "I've never seen you this uptight." She lifted a tin of sugar from the back of the car. "You look like someone put you in a corset and tightened it with a winch."

"I had a visitor," Kate admitted.

"Who?"

"The FBI."

Val stopped suddenly, dropping a can of powdered eggs onto the pavement. "What? What were they doing here?"

"Relax, Val," Kate said. Glancing around, she bent to retrieve the container. "We can talk about it later. I'm not under arrest or anything."

Later in the boat, Kate gave an account of her visit from Gwen Saunders, Val slapped her thighs with the palms of her hands. "It can't be Mike. He wouldn't do that."

"Oh, wouldn't he? Seems to me Mike has done lots of things we didn't expect him to do."

"But not this," she objected. Val stood and paced through the cabin. "He wouldn't do it. Why would he? He doesn't need the money."

"So . . . you're saying he needed an affair?"

"Cut it out, Kate. I didn't say that at all." She sat heavily on the bench. "What are you going to do? Ask him about it?"

"I don't know what to do." Kate shrugged. "It was like she just wanted to see me react. She was watching me, eyeing me. Like she was trying to bait me into telling her something by making me really afraid."

"What will you do?"

"I don't know what to do." Kate opened a cupboard and began loading cans. "One thing for sure, she accomplished the task." Kate stopped and looked up. "I am afraid."

———

Cruise preparations continued for most of the next week, throwing the two couples into nearly constant contact. Frequently, the men squeezed themselves into the engine room together while Kate and Val worked in other parts of the boat. Kate had no real understanding of their activities. Occasionally they appeared in the salon covered in grease, dripping sweat, triumphantly displaying some old part they had successfully replaced.

Whenever they were together, Kate watched Mike carefully, trying to decide how much of what Saunders had told her might be true. Could he be involved in something illegal? Did this explain his relationship with Cara Maria? Kate wanted to tell Mike about the FBI. But every time they spoke, the air seemed to fill with electricity—though not the pleasant voltage of attraction. It seemed as though they spoke through static—the kind of static you hear on a car radio as you drive under high voltage wires. No matter how hard Kate tried to stay focused, they both found innuendos in every sentence.

On successive tangents, their conversations moved further and further from the mark, each of them defending their original meaning to the other. The whole process of speaking with Mike exhausted Kate. So rather than talk, she settled for stiff but polite exchanges, knowing more confidently than ever that there would never be healing between them.

The two women planned onboard housekeeping techniques. Val taught Kate how to wash clothes and take baths on board and still conserve fresh water. The secret is in the rinse, Kate learned. You can wash anything successfully in warm saltwater—even your hair—provided you rinse with the tiniest amount of fresh.

Kate and Val made lists continually. Once during the week, on a particularly beautiful but cold spring afternoon, the two couples took the boat for a short sail. A brisk wind and mild midweek traffic made for an enjoyable sail. Everyone took a turn at the wheel, and Dave captained his crew through sail changes and reefing techniques. Kate tried to look confident and enthusiastic. In truth, she held a deeply hidden terror about the boat and the trip—a terror only partly born in the difficulty of the ocean passage.

———

At last the weekend before their departure arrived. Val planned a small going-away party at the Hollands' home. In some ways, it would be her going-away party as well. Val and Dave planned to leave San Francisco for the Pacific soon after the *Second Chance* arrived safely in Hilo. The new dentist had begun work in the office, and they were in the process of shutting down their stateside obligations.

Most of the people from Kate's office came to the party, including Sally and Don Crandall, her old secretary, and most of the office and design staff. Though Kate was happy to see Sally again, she resented her determination to see Kate's marriage healed. Sally put too much pressure on Kate. She was way too eager to give Kate more time off from work when she'd explained why she needed it.

And tonight, Sally spent the evening beaming approval over the trip, certain it would prove to be the answer to all their troubles. If only Sally knew the whole truth.

The closest of Mike's friends attended as well. The staff from Dave's dental office arrived, having packaged a surprise to be opened when Dave and Val crossed the equator. Brooke brought a package for Kate and Mike to open halfway to Hilo. For a moment, while everyone laughed about the package, Kate hoped that the dark waterproof plastic held nothing more surprising than beef jerky and a can of aged cheddar. She'd had about as many surprises as anyone could handle in one year.

Amid much laughter and many hearty well-wishes, their friends toasted their voyage with sparkling apple cider.

After Val finally closed the door behind the last of their guests, the two couples began cleaning up. Mike carried a garbage bag through the house, disposing of paper plates and napkins. Dave wiped down the living room tables. Together, the women put away leftover food and filled the dishwasher.

"There's coffee left," Val offered as she rinsed the kitchen sink.

"Decaf?" Kate asked. Her friend nodded.

"Sounds good," Dave said. "Let's sit for a minute." He pulled four mugs off the rack and grabbed the coffeepot. "By the way, where was Doug tonight? I thought he would come to send you off."

Mike pulled out a chair. "He called me on his cell phone. Told me he wasn't feeling well."

"Maybe we should be glad. I don't think we could have fit any more people in this house," Val said.

Dave laughed. "I've never seen that much Poppycock disappear in one night."

"Don't worry, honey," Val offered. "I bought it at Costco. And I saved an extra can in the pantry just for you."

Kate picked up her mug. For a moment she hesitated, thinking to herself, *If ever there were a safe time to bring up the FBI, this might be it.* Dave and Val could help to keep them on track. She could ask questions and get real answers without the tension she and Mike struggled with when they were alone. She needed to know. Needed to reassure herself. She needed to slay the monster of fear that threatened to engulf her.

"I had a visitor the other day, at the dock," she began, putting the mug down.

Val glanced at the two men. Neither reacted.

"I thought maybe we should talk about it—before we leave." Kate ran her finger around the lip of the mug. Though the men appeared attentive, no one responded. "It was a woman. Her name was Gwen Saunders. She told me she was with the FBI."

Mike let out an audible sigh and squirmed in his seat. "I wondered if they might do that," he said. "Why didn't you tell me?"

"I've tried. You have to admit, we don't do really well with communication."

Val spoke up, "Tell them what she said."

Kate saw Mike wince. He obviously wasn't happy about Val hearing this news before he did.

"She said the FBI is investigating DataSoft for writing some kind of false code into the software they sell," Kate said, feeling her fear rise again. "Somehow, the false code is connected to the Mafia—or whatever they call it these days." Kate searched her friends' eyes, begging for help. "Agent Saunders suggested that Mike might be involved."

Mike slammed his hand on the table. "How dare she do that? How dare she imply something like that without proof?" His features tightened, and Kate saw a flash of fire in his dark eyes. "I've spoken to my attorney. I've cooperated with them as much as I can." He looked directly at Dave, as though seeking support, "I've even done some investigating of my own."

"So you're saying you don't know anything about it?" Dave asked.

"Nothing." Mike pushed his mug away. "Well, almost nothing." He leaned forward on his arms. "At least not enough to do anything."

Val looked at Kate. "You should tell them everything."

"Everything?" Mike asked. "There's more?"

"She said that the boat trip could be risky. If you are involved—and she didn't really say you were—the people paying you are dangerous people. She said, and I quote, that they 'play for keeps.' "

Mike buried his face in his hands. "Oh great," he said. "I'm doing my best to do the right thing. To help a friend and save my marriage. And look at this."

"Maybe you should start at the beginning," Dave said, his voice low and calm.

For the next hour, Mike described the strange things happening at DataSoft. "The problem is," he concluded, "that I have a bunch of pieces I can't put together."

"What did your attorney say?" Dave asked.

"He advised me not to talk to the agents. He told me to document everything. And to try to figure out what is going on by myself."

"And have you learned anything?" Val sat across from Mike, completely absorbed in the story.

"Not enough."

Kate had to ask. She had to know. Taking a deep breath, she voiced the threatening fear she'd wrestled with through the past week. "Mike, I don't believe you'd be involved with this yourself. But I have to ask." She glanced at the other faces and back to Mike. "Do you think we're in danger?"

"I don't see how. I don't know anything. I haven't done anything." He took a swig of cold coffee. "I've thought about it over and over. It's kept me awake at night. Whoever did this has to be someone from DataSoft. They are the ones who should be afraid of the investigation. Not me. Since we aren't involved, why should we be in danger?"

"Is it safe to leave town with this going on?" Dave asked the practical question. "Doesn't DataSoft need you now?"

"I don't really know the answer to that question," Mike said. "There's never a great time to go away. But on the other hand, there isn't any more I can do here." He reached over and put his hand over Kate's. Though she didn't pull away, her hand stiffened with his touch. "The investigation continues, whether I'm here or not. I didn't do it. So I shouldn't have anything to fear." His hand squeezed hers. "The fact is, I've spent way too much time worrying about that company as it is. The only thing I care about now is sitting right here beside me." She heard the slightest break in his voice. "The only thing I care about is saving our relationship."

He looked directly into her eyes and stared, unblinking. "If I can't save my marriage, I don't care about the company."

Thirty-Three

ON MONDAY MORNING, two days later, Kate met Mike at the Alameda Marina just after sunrise. He stepped off the boat carrying an oversized mug full of fresh coffee. "Thought you might need this," he said, smiling as he gave it to her.

She took the mug, careful to avoid touching his hand. "Thank you, Captain," she said stiffly. "The six A.M. traffic around here is miserable. I thought I'd never get to the marina." Handing him her small makeup case, she started up the stairs to the boat. She and Val had stowed her clothes the week before. Only these small items remained. She stepped into the cockpit and stood out of the way for Mike, who led the way down the stairs to the salon. "When is high tide?" Kate asked. Balancing her cup in one hand and holding the rail with the other, she followed him down.

From below she heard Mike say, "It was about four-thirty this morning. We'll cast off in an hour and a half. That way, we'll ride the outgoing tide out of the bay." She heard banging around in the galley. "With the extra speed, we should be moving pretty fast by the time we hit the Gate."

Kate knew he referred to the Golden Gate Bridge. Unbidden, visions of tidal pools and seawater rushing past bridge supports came to mind. "How fast?" She stepped off the companionway and turned to watch.

A small ringing sound came from his chest pocket. He pulled out his cell phone. Flipping it open, he held up an index finger, frowned, and said, "Mike Langston."

She waited, poking through the nav station while he spoke on the phone. "No hurry," he said at last. "Just get it done. And let me know what happens." He put the phone away and turned toward her. "Now, what were you saying?"

For a moment, she couldn't remember. "Oh yes. How fast is the current at the Gate?"

"It should give us three or four knots. But the wind will be coming right at us there. So we'll lose some speed to the wind." He sat down at the salon table with a fresh cup of coffee. "Here. Look at this." He smoothed out a navigational chart. "This tells us everything we need to know."

She sat beside him, careful to keep some physical distance between them, and stared down at the chart. After a moment, the squiggly lines and tiny letters transformed themselves into recognizable landmarks. She saw the San Francisco Peninsula and the Golden Gate. She recognized Treasure Island, Alcatraz, and Richardson Bay. Running her finger along the chart, she located the Alameda Marina, where *Second Chance* had been moored for the installation of rigging for a second jib. Mike's phone rang again.

He pulled it out. "Mike Langston," he said impatiently.

She gazed at the chart while Mike spoke in low tones into the phone. She thought about the old trips, to Point Rincon and Horseshoe Bay and south to Alviso and Redwood City. She heard Mike's voice rise into the phone. "You'll have to figure it out. I'm on vacation." He snapped the cover closed and slammed the phone onto the table. Kate blinked. "Sorry," he said, his voice still dripping with irritation. "I should think those guys could get along without me for a day or two. Where were we?"

"How long to get out of the harbor?"

He pushed the phone aside. "If we sailed out, around six hours. I don't know about the wind yet. It's so early in the morning, we'll probably use the motor most of the way."

She glanced from the chart to his face, watching him scrutinize the diagram. His eyes sparkled with excitement over their adventure. He gazed at the waterway on the diagram and ran his finger over their course. "We'll go out here." He pointed, leaning forward. "At this hour, on a Monday morning, we shouldn't see much traffic. But here," he tapped the table, "and here, we'll both have to be watching for commercial vessels."

"Don't sailboats have right-of-way?" She took a sip of coffee, trying to swallow her own fear and frustration. If only she had more experience with a boat this size.

"Only on paper." He smiled at her, and she recognized the disarming boyish smile of his youth. "And only if the sailboat is under sail. We may not be. In the bay, commercial vessels tend to watch out for us. But in reality, they get paid to deliver cargo." He turned his attention to the chart. "On the ocean, right-of-way belongs to the biggest and the fastest. That's why we keep a continual watch— all the way to Hawaii. That and containers."

She nodded. Theoretically, containers rarely ever drop off cargo ships, even in the worst of storms. But years ago, Mike and Kate had sailing friends who had run into a container on a trip to Mexico. Fortunately, damage to their boat had been minimal. But the collision had frightened them so much that they refused to sail offshore again. Kate couldn't imagine the horror of slamming into something solid in the middle of the night. Or the fear of water pouring into the boat. She shuddered. Mike didn't seem to notice.

"Ahoy, Captain. Permission to come aboard." Kate recognized Dave's voice.

Mike looked at Kate and smiled. "They're here," he said, tipping his head toward the dock. "Wouldn't let us cast off without them."

Val came down the companionway first, carrying a small paper bag. "Brought some treats for takeoff."

"You shouldn't have," Kate said, standing to accept the gift.

"Actually, they were Dave's idea."

"Don't talk about me," Dave said, backing down the stairs. "I don't like to have you talk about me when I can't defend myself. Where's the coffee?"

Mike stood and poured two more cups. "I knew you'd come down to see us off," he said.

"And you braved Bay Area traffic to do it," Kate added. "I wouldn't do that. Not after this morning's trip."

"We're going to do better than just wave good-bye," Val said, smiling. "We came to pray you off." She opened the bag and spread donuts out on napkins. "After coffee, of course."

Moments later, the two couples sat around the galley table,

heads bowed, hands clasped, commissioning the voyage to the Captain of Captains.

Kate watched from the cockpit as the *Second Chance* passed under the Bay Bridge and floated past Treasure Island. Behind Alcatraz Mike brought the boat into the wind and put the engine in Neutral. "Time to put the sails up," he said over his shoulder.

Together they removed the cover on the main and raised it to the top of the mast. It fluttered uselessly, clanking against the rigging, while they prepared the rest of the rigging.

"This one lifts the boom," Mike said, pulling hard on a rope near the mast. Tying it off, he chose another line and said, "This one pulls the sail tight. Watch the creases." He pointed up. Kate focused on the massive triangle above her head. "There, see how the cloth hasn't any wrinkles now?" Kate did not see, but she nodded anyway.

Will the whole trip be like this? Filled with endless little lectures about sailing? Did Mike bring me on board simply to make me feel stupid and useless? Yes, that was it. Mike's midlife crisis—for that was what the Cara Maria thing seemed to be—had now expanded to include making Kate feel both betrayed and stupid. She sat unmoving on the cockpit bench. Arms folded, she fumed.

"We're ready now." He smiled and jumped down into the cockpit. Turning the wheel, he adjusted the mainsail against the wind. "Could you pull the jib in as tight as you can?"

Kate looked up, trying to hide her anger. He seemed determined to make her feel inadequate. "How do you propose I do that?"

"That sheet, on that side," he said pointing.

"Sheet?"

"The rope. Right next to your hand."

She rolled her eyes. Mike had never used these terms on their little cutter. After all, it wasn't her fault she didn't understand the unfamiliar rigging on this enormous boat. She needn't feel embarrassed. And why did sailors always choose to call things by some name other than the obvious? Why couldn't a rope just be a rope—not a "sheet"? She leaned forward, pulling hard. When it refused to give further, she glanced around, looking for someplace to secure the rope. Then she spotted a cleat shaped like a clamshell. She pulled the rope through and tugged hard, until she felt certain the rope—no, sheet—would not slip. She might not know exactly what she was doing, but she would not give Mike anything but her best.

Mike nodded. "Good job." He turned the wheel and moved the boat out into the bay. Mike watched as the sails filled and the boat moved forward. "There." His voice held satisfaction. Leaning over the controls, he pushed in the fuel valve and turned off the motor. A wonderful whispering quiet enveloped them.

Until his phone rang again. He frowned and pulled it from his shirt pocket. He started to open it and then seemed to change his mind. Slamming it shut, he winked at Kate and threw the ringing phone high into the air. Arching above his shoulder, it flew out over the water. Together, they watched as the phone sailed, still ringing, through the air and splashed into the bay.

"We aren't able to come to the phone right now," he said, his voice teasing. "Leave us a message, and we'll get back to you—in about twenty-eight days." He laughed as the boat rolled in the wind. For a silent moment Kate watched the San Francisco skyline slide by. Soon, Coit Tower fell behind them.

Kate refused to look north, determined not to see Richardson Bay disappear from view. She refused to watch her home fade behind her. She hated to leave. Hated to be alone on the ocean with Mike. No. Instead, she would concentrate on the Marina district. Rather than watching her life disappear, she would watch for tourists.

Five hours after casting off, the *Second Chance* cleared the Golden Gate. Though still not actually out to sea, Kate noticed the jade green of the bay fade to the darker hue of the Pacific Ocean. With certain dread Kate watched the pale golden sand of Baker Beach slip past the *Second Chance*. She said a secret good-bye to the row houses perched above the shore. On the north side of the waterway, she watched the harsh, barren hills around Point Bonita. For a moment Kate wondered if she would ever see them again, and she fought a horrible sense of dread. She did not want to be in that huge empty ocean with a man she didn't trust.

But here she was, floating along, watching land and security fade into the distance behind her. Sitting in the cockpit, she watched from the stern as the bridge and the land around it blended into the horizon.

The gentle rocking of the bay gave way to a more serious ocean chop. She heard the lapping sound of the water turn to a rhythmic banging that echoed in the cabin below. Suddenly the wind, which had been hatching at them from first one direction and then another, seemed to come at them directly from the bow of the boat, forcing Mike to point the boat into the wind. With the sails tucked in as tightly as strength could manage, Kate felt the boat roll over on its side in response. She moved to the "uphill bench."

"She rides well into the wind," Mike said, his voice floating back to Kate. She watched him at the wheel, dressed in his Oakland baseball hat, aviator sunglasses, and DataSoft sweatshirt over a denim shirt and worn jeans. His face radiated pure joy. "See how close we can point without stalling?"

"Stalling?" Would this terminology never end?

"No boat can go straight into the wind, or else the sails won't catch any air. There has to be some pressure blowing against the sails." He smiled at her. "You'll remember. It'll all come back to you—as soon as you take the wheel."

I can't wait, she thought. Nodding, she glanced back toward San Francisco. With a shiver she zipped her sweatshirt, pulled up the hood, and tightened the string under her chin. Then, aware of the light reflecting off the water, she reached down to the bench and put her orange sun hat on over the hood.

"We'll have to beat into the wind for a while," Mike said over his shoulder. "Then, as we get farther from the coast, we'll catch a northerly off the starboard beam." He pointed off the right side of the boat—as though she should be able to see the wind coming. In spite of herself, Kate glanced north. *Beam?*

Beam. Kate thought hard for a moment. Mike had to be referring to points of sail. Vaguely, she remembered a diagram of the outline of a boat sketched around the face of a clock. Confused and frustrated, she tried to remember the importance of the sketch. Though she'd asked Val to help her refresh her sailing skills, it had been too long since her days on the bay with Mike and the kids. Beam. Oh yes. The middle of the boat. "Wind off the beam" referred to wind aimed directly at the middle of the boat. How would they trim the sails in that position? Kate had no idea.

She glanced up at the main mast. A tiny arrow floated high above the deck, attached by a pin to the mast, always pointing into the wind. Kate remembered that she had watched the same arrow on their own boat during her time at the helm. But she couldn't remember why. Nor could she remember how to bring the boat into the correct position. She dug deep into her memory and came up with nothing—only that the tail of the arrow had to stay out of the markers or the boat would lose power. This had to be what Mike meant by stalling. She shook her head. *I'll never remember enough to keep up with Mike.*

Kate scrunched herself down on the bench, trying to stay out of the wind. The air had grown cold. Leaning against the corner of the cockpit, she hugged her knees and glanced around at the water. Though ocean traffic was relatively light, all kinds of vessels floated around them. Sailboats, powerboats, commercial vessels. She watched anxiously as a freighter seemed to come at them from the left. Had Mike seen it?

"Mike," she called, pointing to the ship.

He glanced at Kate and then to the end of her finger and nodded. "Freighter off the port side. Thanks, Kate." He made no obvious change of course.

Port side. What is he trying to do? Make me feel like an idiot? How she resented his sailing lingo! If Mike would only speak English, perhaps she could catch up more quickly.

She looked forward again and noticed that the morning fog had begun to lift. *Second Chance* headed into the afternoon sun, and she turned her face to avoid the glaring brightness that hung in the sky just off the left side of the bow. As the wind picked up, the sun broke out over the water, and the light burst into thousands of perfect reflections glistening on the top of the ocean. The beauty of the scene and the fresh air lifted Kate's spirit. She took a deep breath and enjoyed the warm sunshine on her face. *Thank you, Lord. I see your hand in this beauty.* She could not keep a smile from sneaking onto her lips.

But rising wind had other effects as well. Hours later the chop turned into moderate waves, and still Mike held the boat into the wind. As Kate watched the bow of the boat rise and fall with every wave, she began to feel as though she were perched on the end of an enormous seesaw. As the bow rose, the cockpit seat fell. Then, as she went up higher and higher, she watched the bow silhouetted against the blue of the sea. Normally, Kate did not experience seasickness, but this endless motion began to make her feel queasy. *How on earth can I get seasick now?* Recognizing the feeling, she sent an arrow prayer heavenward. *Lord, help. I have almost four weeks to go on this carnival ride.*

As the wave action continued to increase, so did the misery she experienced. She glanced at Mike and saw that he had not yet stopped smiling. He had not noticed Kate turning green. Still watching vessel traffic, he had changed tack and was now beating into the wind from the opposite direction.

Suddenly, Kate stood and climbed out of the cockpit onto the rear deck. As the wind hit her face, she threw her hat back into the cockpit and dove for the side of the boat. Holding the lifelines, she heaved over the rail. Waves of nausea and vomiting overcame her while icy wind bit into her face and salt spray froze her fingers to the stanchions. Finally, when her stomach seemed entirely empty, she felt better. Crawling back to her seat, she resumed her position on the bench, this time trying desperately to keep her stomach from rolling. She rested her forehead on her knees.

Still Mike had not noticed her dilemma. Her miserable nausea continued, and Kate could no longer sit up. She slid down the bench and curled up into a ball.

Something about her movement caught Mike's attention. He glanced back once and then again, frowning. "What happened? You look awful."

"Sick," Kate managed. She closed her eyes and dreamed of a lounge chair sitting completely still in her garden.

"You should sit up," he said. She glanced up and saw his eyebrows furrow, concern in his expression. She let her eyes drift closed. "Look at the horizon," he called. "Don't close your eyes."

Under other conditions, his advice would have made her angry. But too sick to care, Kate ignored him and pulled into the shell of seasickness. Focusing on her nausea, she concentrated only on keeping her stomach contents inside.

In this position, she drifted off, vaguely grateful for the cloak of sleep protecting her. But her relief was only momentary. She woke suddenly, needing to reach the rail again. This time, from behind the wheel, Mike watched as she dove for the side of the boat. As Kate hit dry heaves, Mike set the self-steering clutch and disappeared down the steps. He returned with a polar fleece blanket, lined on one side with a heavy nylon fabric. He stood next to the bench, waiting for her to settle down, and then tucked the blanket around her. "Stay here," he said, and dropped back down the stairs. At his touch, she opened her eyes again. He stood before her with a pillow in one hand, a steaming mug of tea in the other.

"I can't," she objected.

"It's ginger," he said. "From the health food store. Guaranteed to stop queasiness. Try it."

She sat up and accepted the cup. Holding the hot cup felt vaguely comforting, though now an accompanying dizziness seemed to make the nausea worse. She felt herself sway, completely separate from the motion of the boat, and thought for a moment that she might black out. She closed her eyes against the swirling horizon.

In that moment, Mike took the cup and slid into the seat beside her, holding her steady with one arm around her. "Steady, girl," he coaxed. "Try a sip, and then you can lie down again."

She opened her eyes fleetingly and tried to sip. The hot liquid burned her tongue and throat as she gulped more than she anticipated. "Oh." Her eyes watered against the pain. She leaned into his side, resting her head on his shoulder.

"We have medicine for this," he said.

"No medicine," she said weakly. "I'll beat it." She wished she didn't have to lean against him. Wished she didn't have to smell him so close. But she could not sit up, could not resist.

"It works better if you use it right away."

"Then it's already too late," she said, her stomach rising again. She shivered and pulled the blanket up around her neck. He rubbed her shoulder with the palm of his hand. "I just want to die," she whispered.

"Not today, Kate," he said. Without leaving his seat, he used one foot to disengage the clutch. "It won't last long. I promise." Guiding the wheel with his foot, he held Kate with both hands as she drifted back to sleep. "When the wind changes, things will be more comfortable," he said softly, kissing her hood.

Thirty-Four

BUT THINGS DID NOT IMPROVE. The predicted change of winds did not arrive on schedule. In fact, a series of small squalls, each carrying moderate wind and pelting rain, drove themselves one after another over the *Second Chance*. Troubled seas manifested themselves in a rolling motion that exacerbated her symptoms. Kate would not eat. Could not eat.

Mike moved her to the forward bunk, where she could be closer to a marine toilet. For nearly thirty-six hours, Kate slept full-time in the bunk, rising only to empty her stomach contents into the forward head.

Mike worried. He had not planned this kind of trip. By now, Mike had hoped to explain what had happened with Cara and how much he regretted it. He'd planned to be at the "happily ever after" stage of the voyage. Instead, he drove the boat west and south while Kate slept and vomited.

Mike had no opportunity to sleep, other than brief catnaps on the cockpit bench, and fatigue started to wear him down. Driving into the wind forced him to make continual changes in the sail positions. The close proximity of vessel traffic required that he frequently radio his speed and course to ships nearby. He kept a close eye on the weather fax, trying to avoid the roughest of oncoming systems—aware of the effect of the boat's motion on Kate. Mike e-mailed Dave regularly to report their position and progress.

Dave, Kate continues severe seasickness, yet refuses medication. Piloting alone, I haven't slept. The weather continues to be unpredictable. I have to get Kate to the helm soon.

Finally, desperate for her help, Mike dug through the medicine bag Valerie had packed. Then he went forward to wake Kate. In her sleep, her face looked thinner, ashen. She had not combed her hair or brushed her teeth since they left the dock. She slept as one drugged, and he regretted having to wake her.

"Kate," he said, shaking her shoulder gently.

She moaned and rolled away.

He tugged again. "Kate, I have something here. I'd hoped we wouldn't have to use it, but I understand it works."

"No drugs, Mike," she mumbled.

"Kate, you have to eat. You need your fluids. I need your help. I can't sail this boat all the way to Hawaii by myself. Please."

Her eyes flitted open, and grimacing, she swallowed. She rubbed her face with both hands and tried to sit up.

Mike wrapped his arm around her shoulders and helped her up. She pulled away.

"What kind of medicine?"

"A suppository. Prescription. That way the medicine really gets into your system, without upsetting your stomach."

"Oh, good," she said, sarcasm dripping from her voice. "I wouldn't want to get an upset stomach."

"Kate, I promise you'll feel better. If I'd known you would be this sick, I'd never have asked you to come along."

She rolled her eyes and swung her feet over the side of the bunk. "I'll try it," she said. Pushing up with her arms, she tried to stand.

Kate swayed dangerously, and Mike reached out to grab her just as she pulled herself up by the desk across from the bunk. She flashed him a warning look. "Sorry," he said. "I thought you were going to fall."

She made no comment, but staggered forward to the head. As the door closed behind her, Mike realized that she reminded him of a drunk he'd once seen staggering along the street near a pub.

The medicine seemed to work. Over the next few hours, Mike left the wheel frequently to go below and check on her. Though she slept like a dead woman for hours after the first dose, Mike noticed that color had begun to return to her cheeks. She stopped moaning in her sleep, and he never once saw her dash for the bathroom. *Now, if she can only keep liquids down.*

Five hours later, she surprised him by crawling up on deck, wrapped in an orange and brown afghan. "Hello, Captain," she said, a small smile playing at her face.

"My, my. I think we have a stowaway on board," he returned, chuckling.

"I wish." Using one hand, she felt her way to the rear bench and landed there. She pulled the blanket up tight around her neck. "If I were a stowaway, you'd be obligated to put me off as soon as possible. There's nothing I'd like better."

"I'm sorry you've been so sick. You look better."

"Actually, I'm a little hungry."

"Good. I think you should get something in your stomach. What do you feel like having?"

"I just drank some water. Soup sounds good."

"Great. Why don't you take the wheel, and I'll go down and fix something hot."

"Me?" She looked out over the ocean, the wind blowing her hair behind her. She shivered. "I have no idea what to do."

"No time like the present to learn." He gestured her to his side and moved out of the way. "Come here, and I'll give you a lesson."

"Boy, you sure don't let anyone take advantage of sick leave around here, do you?"

"You want soup or not?"

Kate looked out at the ocean and back again. Shrugging, she nodded, "Okay, what do I do?"

Still hugging the afghan, she moved to the giant silver wheel. "Here you go." Mike stepped aside, leaving only one hand on the wheel. "Make very gentle turns," he coaxed. "The boat responds slowly." He pointed at the compass. "See the compass heading?" She leaned forward to see better and nodded. "Try to keep that arrow pointed on the same number. And keep an eye on the wind. That's all there is to it." He grinned.

"Wait. What do you mean?" He saw confusion in her wide eyes.

He pointed up to the mast. "The arrow at the top of the mast points to the wind. If you keep the heel of the arrow just outside that left mark, that's perfect. If the arrow moves, either you've changed course or the wind is changing. Just turn the wheel gently until you get it back where it belongs." He turned the wheel while Kate watched the arrow. "See? I've turned away from the wind. Why don't you turn us back?" Keeping her eye on the arrow at the end of the mast, Kate moved the wheel.

"Don't turn too much. You'll overcorrect." He started to step around her.

"No. Don't go." She held the wheel firmly, and he saw the muscles in her hands and forearms tighten in fear. "Stay for a minute until I get the feel of it."

He moved back to the rear bench. "I'll sit for a minute. The weather is clear, and the wind is steady. You tell me when I can go down." He sat down and stretched his legs out in front of him, allowing the muscles of his back to stretch and relax. He'd been at the wheel for an eternity, and his joints felt frozen. From the bench Mike watched Kate.

With her thumbs sticking through the stitches of the afghan, she held the blanket loosely around her shoulders. Her hair, golden in the late afternoon light, had curled into a crown of fluffy curls. The wind brought pink to her cheeks. She swayed gracefully with the motion of the boat, and he thought he saw pleasure in her expression. He enjoyed the break from his hours at the wheel and leaned his head back over the deck. Soon the motion of the boat and his extreme fatigue conspired to force his eyelids closed.

"Mike, wake up," Kate shook him roughly a few hours later. "The wind, Mike. It's gone."

He groaned and rubbed his face with his hands. "What?"

"I don't know what happened," she answered. "But it got weaker and weaker, and now it's completely gone."

She stepped aside as Mike stood and looked up at the sails. Both the mainsail and the jib hung limp above the boat deck. He stretched and yawned. "Not unusual," he said, putting his hands on his hips. "Near the coast, the wind sometimes dies at night."

"Why?" Kate gazed out over a flat, dark ocean.

"In California, when the sun heats up the Central Valley, the air above it warms and rises. Air from the ocean rushes in to fill in the space. At night the temperatures between the valley and the coast are more similar, so the wind dies." He shrugged.

"What do we do now?" Kate glanced at the wheel of the boat

and noticed that it moved listlessly in rhythm with tiny waves.

"We wait," he said. Stepping over to the wheel, he locked the autopilot in place. "We could motor through the night—but I hate to waste the fuel. We only have 165 gallons, and we don't know when we'll need it." Mike disappeared down into the cabin. When he came back up, he carried two sleeping bags, and smiled broadly. "In the meantime, we could crawl into our sleeping bags and catch some sleep outside."

"Like a slumber party?" Kate glanced up at the black, star-studded sky. "Sounds okay to me."

"I'm going to bring you something easy to eat," he said. "How about a roll and some hot soup?"

"Thanks, that'd be nice."

While Mike scrounged for food, Kate sat in the silent cockpit enjoying the still air. Stars glimmered over the sky, like something from a Disney movie. She pulled the afghan up around her shoulders.

When Mike came back, he carried a plate with buttered rolls and two mugs of hot tomato soup. While Kate sipped soup, Mike unzipped the canvas cover of the dodger, rolled it up, and tied it out of the way. Bending over one of the benches, he stretched out a sleeping bag. "There you are, madam," he said. "The most beautiful view on the planet."

Kate finished a roll and sat down on top of the sleeping bag. Tucking her legs inside the flannel lining, she slid all the way down and pulled the bag up around her neck. Realizing that cold air still seeped in from around her, she reached down to pull up the zipper. The still cold air stung her face, but inside the bag, she felt delightfully warm. "Mmm, nice," she said. "But I need to do something about the pillow." She reached behind her and rolled the top of the bag into a cushion behind her neck. "There, that's better."

"Isn't that something?" Mike said, pulling his bag around his shoulders. "Don't see views like this in the city."

"Not ever," she agreed. "Reminds me of our first little rented house in town. We'd go up on the roof and gaze at the stars."

"I'd forgotten that," he said. "That was BK—Before Kids. We did more on that roof than just watch the stars." He chuckled to himself. "Seems like a long time ago. . . ."

"Look," Kate said, pointing. "What's that? It's moving."

"A satellite."

"Wow, I don't think I've ever seen one before," Kate sighed. "I guess I've never stopped long enough to really look up."

"Probably the only moving light over San Francisco is an airplane. See that over there?" Mike asked, pointing. "That's a planet."

"Which one?" She turned her head to follow his arm.

"Venus, I think," he said. "But I'd have to look at a chart to be certain."

"You sure could fool me," Kate laughed. "I don't recognize anything other than the Big Dipper."

"Me either, really," Mike said, his head resting on his arms. "I've always been amazed by the old mariners who used to navigate with nothing more than the stars." A long comfortable silence floated between them as they lay there—together, yet separate. Each watching the heavens. The *Second Chance* floated quietly on the calm sea.

"He leads them out by name," Kate said, quietly.

"What?"

"The stars," Kate said. "Somewhere in the Bible it says that God leads the stars out across the sky and that He knows every one of them by name." She shivered. "I'll have to look it up."

"Means more when you're looking at a sky like this to think that each one of those tiny sparkles has a name, a place, and an orbit." Mike laughed, "You know, I'm suddenly remembering more about that first house."

"The one on Park?"

"Yeah," he agreed. "The one where the walls roared when the toilet flushed. And the landlady." He shook his head at the memory. "She was something else."

"She used to call me every night as soon as I unlocked the front door. It was enough to make me wish that you got home before I did. Used to make me crazy. I tried not to answer the phone. But she just kept calling till I did."

"She was a lonely old lady."

"All alone." Kate closed her eyes, thinking. "No kids. No husband. No friends. If I hadn't been so young and impatient, I would have been kinder to her."

"I know," Mike said. "I used to pay the rent after she went to bed—just so she wouldn't invite me in for coffee. I slipped the check into her mail slot like a criminal."

"Not quite like a criminal. They don't put checks *in* the mail slots. They take them out." Kate laughed. "I didn't know you did that."

"I miss those days," he said. She heard the sound of longing in his voice. "Things were so simple. We were so close." He rolled over onto his side and rested his head on one hand. She felt his eyes staring at her, even in the dark. "We were working together, saving for a house. We spent all our time together. Nothing got between us."

Kate felt herself stiffen with the words. Without her bidding, the pictures came burning back into her imagination. *If only I hadn't seen them,* she thought. *I could handle this if I hadn't seen those stupid pictures.*

"It's my fault, Kate," Mike went on. "The whole thing is my fault. The pain, the mess we're facing. It's all my fault." She thought she heard tears in his voice. "I've hurt you and the kids."

"Please don't, Mike. It's over. Let's not go there."

"I wish that were possible. But it isn't. There isn't a day that I don't wish I could undo the whole thing."

"You can't." She heard a bitter tone in her own voice. Though she wished it were not true, Kate felt both angry and bitter. "We've had good days. These are the bad days. Now it's over. You can't undo it."

"I know. But I've thought about it so long. Tried to figure out how I got into it."

"And what have you discovered?" Even as she asked, she regretted the cynicism that crept into her voice. If Mike had figured this thing out, she certainly didn't want to miss his explanation—not that it would be entirely accurate.

"I can't really say. I think I was lonely. The kids left home. You seemed so happy. So content. You had a job and friends. And you seemed so satisfied." He rolled onto his back, tucking his hands behind his head. "But somehow, I wasn't."

"Satisfied? With me?"

"No, that's not it at all. Satisfied isn't quite the right word. It's more like—I don't know—restless, maybe. All the challenges were over. The business was doing great. We'd expanded and grown.

We'd moved into the new building. But I still felt restless. I don't know, almost worried that life was over. Like nothing would ever happen to challenge me again."

"So you decided to have an affair."

"No, Kate. I don't think I ever decided. No matter what any pastor says. For me, it came slowly; I was into the whole thing before I ever thought about what I'd done. It was just like you hear people say—like heating water under a frog. I really believed the thing with Cara was innocent. And then, suddenly, it was like a trap springing closed. Even after I realized it was wrong, I spent a long time trying to justify it to myself."

She felt tears stinging her eyes in the dark. *I might as well let them roll,* she told herself. *There's no one here to see them.* "It was wrong, all right."

"I tried to break it off." A mocking sound escaped from Kate. "I know. That sounds so lame now. But I did—even before the pictures. I tried . . ." She heard the rough sound of his hands rubbing his face. "But I didn't do it. I didn't break it off. That's what counts. I didn't until the pictures."

She turned her head away and focused on the tiniest star she could see—in the farthest portion of the black heavens above her. Focusing on the star made it disappear. But when she glanced away, the star returned, as if by some supernatural trick. It would be nice to have the pictures disappear like the stars. But not trying to see them didn't help. They were there, floating in her mind whenever she closed her eyes.

"Please, Mike," she said, tears rolling out of the corners of her eyes and down her face into her ears, cold and damp. "Please don't talk about it. Not anymore. Not now."

"I won't," he said. His voice sounded tired, worn. He sat up and got out of his sleeping bag.

"What are you doing?"

"Just checking. We need to watch for vessel traffic, even when we aren't moving." He sat down on the rear bench near her head and put his hand on her hair, running his fingers softly along her forehead. "Can I pray, Kate?" In spite of herself, she stiffened at his touch.

"Can I pray?" Right. What am I supposed to say to that? "Whatever, Mike." She rolled away from him. "You can do whatever you like."

He left his fingers on her forehead, and she felt the warmth of his hand resting there. "Lord, if you can keep track of all those stars, you know where we are. Right here. Right now. In the middle of this huge ocean, you are leading us. I'm asking for you to touch Kate. We need you to heal the pain I've caused. I did it, Lord. As surely as if I'd used a knife. I'm not asking you to make her forgive me. I'm not even asking for her to take me back. I'm just asking you to ease her pain. To feel you here beside her, Lord. Help Kate to trust you, even when she can't trust me. No one can do this kind of healing but you, Lord. Please."

She felt tears burn her eyes, and she huddled down in the sleeping bag, holding herself perfectly still until she heard him stand and go down the companionway. How dare he ask God to heal her? Her pain wasn't God's problem. After all, Mike himself inflicted the injury. He came back up the stairs carrying a comfortable pillow and another blanket. Bending over Kate, he whispered, "Get some sleep. If you get cold, you can go below. I think I'll sleep out here, where I can keep watch." Kate made no motion. Without another sound, she cried herself to sleep.

Thirty-Five

WHEN KATE WOKE, her bones ached with cold. For a moment she forgot where she was and, rolling over, nearly fell off the narrow bench. The sky seemed lighter near the stern of the boat, but the sun had not yet risen.

"Morning," Mike said, stepping into the cockpit from the bow. "I've just put up the spinnaker. We have a little wind. Enough to get moving again. Would you like to take another turn at the wheel?"

"What do I do?"

"Try to keep us moving," he laughed. "Come over here." He gestured with his hands to the wheel. "See? This is the direction we want to go." He pointed again at the compass. "Same routine as before. The spinnaker is a very light sail. Lots of surface area. If we get any wind at all, it should fill and move us forward."

She nodded. "Captain, do you mind if I go to the bathroom before I take my shift?"

He laughed. "Sorry. Go ahead and go on down. I guess I'm a little overanxious."

"I'll say. Overtired, too." After she used the bathroom, she splashed a bit of fresh water on her face and started water for tea. She fished around in the cupboard with the nightshift snacks and brought up two. "Okay. Ready, Captain," she said, handing him a sealed package. "Have you checked the weather?"

He accepted the bag and tore into it greedily, immediately choosing a smaller bag of cashews. "The fax says we should have a system coming toward us sometime today. We can dodge it, but frankly, I think we should go after the wind. If it gets too strong, we can swing out of it." He sat down on the bench behind her. She glanced at him and noticed that the sun had started to make a glossy pink stripe across the horizon behind him. Beautiful. She turned back to the wheel, glancing once at the wind indicator. Satisfied, she turned back, intending to point out the sunrise to Mike. But she did not. Mike had curled up on her sleeping bag and fallen sound asleep, his snack bag still clutched in his hand. She stepped away from the wheel long enough to throw the extra blanket over his shoulders.

Kate enjoyed the predawn silence. She set the autopilot and went down to the salon looking for something to keep her mind busy while Mike slept. Digging through the bookshelf behind the kitchen table, Kate found a secondhand novel belonging to Val. Before long, she sat on the starboard bench with a book in one hand, holding a mug of hot tea with the other and steering with her feet.

Twice, rising wind sent her below for warmer clothes. She enjoyed the solitude, the view, the beauty of the brightly striped spinnaker as it filled with wind moving the boat over gentle swells. The sound of the rigging in a gentle breeze felt friendly. Kate managed to keep the boat on course without trouble. And once, around eight A.M., she thought she spotted a porpoise in the distance. She leaned forward, trying to catch a glimpse of the beautiful animal, but it disappeared as quickly as it had arrived, leaving Kate and the *Second Chance* behind.

About nine o'clock, it started to rain. Though it was not a hard rain, it felt cold. Before long, water dripping on Mike's face woke him, and he sat up. Creases from the teak benches striped his cheeks. "How long have I been asleep?"

"About four hours," she answered. "Hungry?" He still had the snack bag on his lap. "You didn't eat before you went to sleep."

"Starved," he said, standing up. "I think I'll cook. What do you feel like having for breakfast?"

"Something hot," she answered. "Surprise me."

He disappeared down the companionway stairs. She wondered for a moment why she couldn't hear him working in the kitchen. And then she realized that the wind had picked up. The rigging and the sails made their own noise, and she could no longer hear below deck. *What if we get so much wind that I don't know what to do?* She kept one eye on the wind speed indicator. Though the direction remained steady, the velocity had risen. She wondered how long the spinnaker should stay up. Could the light sail take the rising wind? She shook off a tiny shudder of fear.

"Mike," she called below. "Mike, the wind is rising."

He didn't seem to hear her, and she turned the wheel to move directly into the wind. For a moment, it seemed to ease the pressure on the spinnaker. Mike popped his head up the companionway, and she saw him glance around. "How fast?" he asked.

"Around ten. I think it's rising," she answered.

He jumped out onto the deck. "Need to drop the spinnaker," he said, moving forward.

She reached out and grabbed his sweatshirt. "What about a lifeline?" she asked, trying to keep her voice calm. They had rigged a line from the bow to the stern just after passing under the Golden Gate. Up until now, her seasickness and the relatively light winds had caused Kate to forget that they might really need to be harnessed to the boat. But as the wind rose, the motion on the bow increased. Occasionally, a wave broke on deck. At this moment, Kate felt like a circus rider standing on a bucking bronco. How could Mike stay securely on a deck that flailed up and down above rising waves?

He looked at her and smiled. "Right. I'll get my harness." He ducked below and came up with a sea jacket and a tether. Mike had chosen an expensive foul-weather jacket and harness combination to replace his worn jacket from their sailing days. This jacket featured an integrated harness, and the jacket itself would inflate should the wearer be thrown overboard. Though the jacket was expensive, at this moment Kate was more than happy with his choice. She watched as he clipped his tether to the lifeline and started forward. Moments later, he dropped the spinnaker onto the deck, opened the sail compartment, and shoved it below.

"We still need to reef the main," he said, moving toward her. "Bring her into the wind, and I'll drop it."

For a moment she panicked. Reef the main. That meant bringing the sail down and tying it off. But she hadn't done it on this boat. "How?" she shouted. But Mike, holding onto the mast, had turned to look off the bow, and the wind carried her voice behind her. She glanced up to the wind direction indicator and took a deep calming breath. "Help me, Jesus." The wind came off the right side of the boat. She turned the wheel to the right. The boat responded, and soon the main flapped uselessly above her.

"Now drop the halyard," he shouted. "I'll flake it as it comes down."

She glanced over the cleats in the cockpit and found one labeled "main halyard." She loosened it and let go, running the line through her hands. The sail dropped.

"Good job," he said. "Hold it there until I get all the reef ties." He worked quickly and efficiently, tying the strips around the beam so the sail would be firmly held in its new smaller shape. He moved back to the cockpit, brushing saltwater off his face. "Good. Now tie it down tight. We could put up a little bit of jib. But I think I'll hold off." He looked up at the sky. "I'm not sure how serious this little system is going to be. Better to have too little sail than too much." He stepped to the wheel and held his arm out to the boom. "Can you hold this?"

She reached up to grab the huge piece of metal on which the bottom edge of the triangular sail was attached. As he had indicated, she pushed it into the wind.

"Hold it," he said, letting the wheel respond gently. Before long they were underway again, skimming across choppy seas that seemed to grow angrier by the minute.

Feeling useless on deck, she asked, "Should I finish breakfast?"

He turned toward her, brown eyes smiling. "Would you? I'm a better sailor than cook."

"And I'm a better cook than sailor. Be right back."

"Bring a hat, would you?" he called after her.

Below, she found that Mike had started cooking a batch of hot oatmeal. He had fruit out; apples rolled in the sink with the motion of the boat. Raisins sat on the counter waiting to be added to the cereal. It looked inviting, and Kate noticed how good it felt to feel hunger pains again. She began peeling apples.

While she stood working in the galley, a large wave suddenly slammed into the bow of the boat. The motion startled her, and she dropped both her paring knife and the apple, slamming her hip into the cupboard beside the sink. "Ow!"

She looked around the galley and noticed the safety harness that had been bolted to the wall behind the companionway. Val had warned her to use it in heavy seas. First, though, she had to get the knife. Bending over, she reached out just as another wave threw the boat into a trough. Her fingers closed around the handle of the knife, and the motion of the boat smashed her forehead into the corner of the companionway stairs. She narrowly avoided letting an unladylike term express her discomfort. The apple, banging into the wooden step, caught her attention. Holding on to the counter, she snatched the apple as it began to roll down the floor away from the galley. This kind of cooking held far more challenges than her kitchen at home in Tiburon.

The weather had clearly deteriorated. She slipped into the harness and clipped the ends together. *Well, I'm going to eat, no matter what.* She reached the sink to rinse the apple that had fallen on the floor, and began peeling again.

She managed to chunk the apple into the oatmeal and open the package of raisins. Just as she held the raisins over the open pot, the boat lurched into another wave. This time, a loud crash sounded in the salon over the galley table. She looked forward just in time to see the galley window fall onto the table, followed by what seemed like an entire ocean of seawater.

"Oh no! Mike, help!" Kate started forward into the salon as water poured into the cabin, crashing through the open space that had been the window. But her harness held her in the galley. With shaking fingers she unfastened the clip and stepped out of the galley. Cold seawater rushed over the salon table and splashed onto the floor. Kate waded through it as it flowed back toward the engine room. She screamed Mike's name again. Kneeling on the bench, she reached up to the window with her arms—as though she intended to hold out the Pacific Ocean with her bare hands.

"Kate," Mike yelled, coming down the stairs. "Get away from there." He jumped the last two steps onto the floor of the salon, sloshing toward her. "I'll cover the hole." He grabbed her shoulders, pulling her away from the bench. "Don't panic," he said urgently. "Just go up and drop the main. Then steer us into the wind. Keep the boat going down the waves at an angle." Using his hands, he indicated the pathway the *Second Chance* should take down a wave. "Just like this," he said. "You can do it."

She nodded, suddenly terrified and bitterly cold all at once. Her teeth began to chatter. Shivering, she hugged herself. Could she do as he asked? Even as she wondered, she knew she had no choice. Mike grabbed the cushions around the salon table and heaved them, full of water, through the open door into the forward compartment. "I'm going for a piece of wood and my drill. Please, Kate, steer so the waves don't break over the bow."

Their survival depended on keeping water out of the boat. For what seemed like an eternity, fear kept her immobile. Then another wave poured in, and Mike bolted for the engine room.

Suddenly, Kate heard the motor of the automatic bilge pump whirl into action. Water building in the bottom of the boat had thrown the pump switch. Another wave crashed through the window, and the cold water shook her from her daze. Frightened and cold, she started for the companionway.

Stepping onto the deck, a new scene surprised Kate. The wind, which had been building steadily, now came in gusts and spurts. A heavy blowing rain splattered the deck, and Kate wished she'd taken the time to put on foul-weather gear. Too late now, she realized; she had to steer. She could warm up later.

Grabbing the wheel, she glanced up, trying to determine where to turn the boat. The wind, accompanied by huge waves, came hard on the starboard side, the same side where water had blown out the window in the salon. She turned the wheel to the right, directly into the wind, and the boat responded, though more slowly than before.

A huge wave crested over the bow, and ice-cold water crashed all the way to the cockpit, soaking Kate to the skin. A strong wind blowing hard on her wet clothes chilled her even further. Her shivering increased, though she believed it was more from terror than cold.

Keep your senses, Kate, she told herself. *You can do it.* Another wave crashed over the front. She needed to steer past the wind, so the waves and wind would hit the boat on the other side—away from Mike and the broken salon window. She fought the wheel further, turning away from the wind, then past it, until the indicator above the mast told her that the wind was coming from the port side.

In her mind she visualized Mike's hands as he described the way to steer into the waves. She had not yet managed that angle, and the crashing wave had been her punishment. When the bow came to the top of the next wave, Kate turned the wheel, trying desperately to make the boat skim down the other side at a slight angle. The stern rode to the crest and started down. But an oncoming wave rolled the boat over dangerously, and Kate's feet slid on the wet deck. Frightened, she pulled herself up on the wheel until she stood upright. She had overcorrected, and the next wave crashed directly into the empty window.

Second Chance righted herself, and Kate glanced up again at the wind vane. She needed to hit the next wave at a better angle. The flapping sail caught her attention.

She'd forgotten to drop the main! Setting the self-steering gear, she loosened the halyard and climbed out of the cockpit. Wait! Her harness. She clipped on and moved forward. The wind caught the sail and tried to rip it from her hands and throw it into the sea. Kate fought back—valiantly scrunching and pulling—unable to flake the sail correctly, until at last she grabbed the end of a nearby rope and tied the sail to the boom. Using sloppy, unprofessional knots, she managed to wrap the boom in several places with the same rope. Not the way a sailor would do it, but the rope would hold it in place until Mike had a chance to fix it.

Back in the cockpit, she found the boat easier to steer. The bilge pump ran continuously, and she wished she could see the progress below deck. How were repairs coming along? Did Mike need her help? Time passed slowly, and it seemed to Kate that it had been hours since water had blown through the salon window. Still soaked and cold, she wasn't sure how long she could persevere in this weather.

Rough seas continued, though it appeared to Kate that the wind speed began to decrease slightly. Her shivering increased as she steered through wave after wave. Eventually, she mastered the technique. Just as Mike taught her, she guided the boat smoothly down the backside of each crest. No longer did she slam the bow into the bottom of the hole between waves. Instead, the *Second Chance* skimmed down like a professional surfer.

"Kate, I've got it," Mike said, stepping onto the deck. "I put up a piece of plywood and screwed it into the frame around the window."

"Will it keep water out?" Chattering cold made her lips feel like logs, her words nearly indistinguishable.

"I drilled holes with a hand drill. Then I put a waterproof sealant between the wood and the frame. With the wood screwed in place and the sealant, it should be as good as new. But we won't be able to see much." He smiled a triumphant smile, and Kate wondered how he could so easily let go of such a frightening experience. "I'll take the wheel," he said, moving toward her.

She stepped aside and nearly fell onto the seat beside him. She looked down at her aching hands, frozen in the same stiff, clutching position they'd been in for the past hour—as though they still held the wheel. Mike looked hard at her, and his gaze seemed to take in her wet clothes and the exhaustion in her face. "You need to get below and dry off. Put on some dry clothes, wool socks, and boots," he said. "Then put foul-weather gear on over everything before you come back on deck."

She didn't move for a moment. Aware of all she had been through, she tried to relax, willing her body to let go of the fear. She took a deep breath and blew it out between tight lips. "Thanks for fixing the window, Mike."

He looked directly at her, surprise in his expression. A moment passed, and a slow smile spread over his face. "Thanks for driving."

He frowned suddenly, "One more thing. From now on, every time we come on deck, we're going to snap on. No more being on deck without a lifeline. I should have made that a rule as soon as we left the bay. I guess I took it easy because of the weather." He reached down and tugged her shoulders, coaxing her off the seat. "No more. Now go down and get warmed up." She started down the stairs.

"Hey, Kate."

She turned to look at him.

"Do you think we could have that breakfast after you dry off?"

Thirty-Six

MIKE DIDN'T THINK oatmeal had ever tasted so good, and after breakfast he volunteered to take the dishes down and clean up the galley. Actually, he needed time to sort out what had happened, evaluate the window seal, and contact Dave Holland. Dave would want to know about the blowout immediately, and he might have other suggestions for keeping water out of the salon. Through a relatively new technology called Sail Mail, Mike and Dave spoke regularly, even across the Pacific Ocean. When Dave introduced Mike to the system, he had no idea they would be using it for disasters like this.

Mike typed,

> *Dave, we had a major problem with the forward salon window on the starboard side. Today in rough seas, a rogue wave blew out the window. I have made a temporary repair, using plywood and waterproof sealant. You will need to order a replacement window and have it waiting in Hilo. Of course everything below is wet, but drying out should be no problem. What bothers me is this: What made the window give way? I have looked the window over carefully and can see no sign of fatigue on any of the support brackets. It appears as though the screws holding the frame actually fractured. I cannot imagine a wave strong enough to cause this kind of damage. Fortunately for us, the remaining fiberglass around the window is in good condition. The experience frightened Kate, though we are both fine. Her seasickness has abated at last. I had hoped for our trip to be less eventful.*

Mike pushed the Send button and closed the laptop. Silently, he thanked the Lord that whoever designed the *Second Chance* had tucked the nav station on the windowless side of the salon. Only a small piece of wood designed as a room divider had kept the seawater from completely saturating their navigation equipment. Though manufacturers boast about water resistance, no one makes guarantees. That one wave might have left them out in the ocean with no way of contacting anyone. The thought made him shudder.

In the meantime, Mike's relationship with Kate continued to haunt him. Emotionally, she had not yet given an inch; her behavior demonstrated her resistance in a hundred tiny ways. Yesterday, when he offered her a fork, she had gone to great lengths to avoid touching his fingers. She never looked him in the eyes. For the most part, she spoke only when spoken to. And now, only a week into the trip, she'd been through horrible seasickness and a near disaster. *I was stupid, Lord, thinking I could win her back under these conditions.* He opened the log and made a short entry.

Day seven, May 28. 1130: Rogue wave takes out forward salon window at 0950, starboard side. Repairs made. Seems watertight. Holding well. Kate badly frightened.

His log would never tell the whole story.

When Mike came back on deck, Kate excused herself to work on water damage to the cabin. She mopped and dried and wiped until the skin on her fingers wrinkled. Eventually, she put things away enough to maneuver around the cabin. She dragged the cushions to the sink and squeezed seawater from them. Then she filled the front compartment with drying covers and cushions, towels, and books. No more room to sleep there. Kate and Mike would have to share the aft cabin, at least until things dried out. But since they never slept at the same time, this prospect did not bother Kate.

For the next few days, calmer weather prevailed. Mike and Kate managed to get themselves into a routine of sorts, splitting the night watch into two major portions. Kate took the early shift, staying at the wheel from nine P.M. until two or three A.M., while Mike slept. When he woke, he made a hot snack and brought it to her in the cockpit. They ate together and visited for a while before Mike took the wheel and Kate went to bed.

When Kate woke, they had breakfast together. During the day, they split their watches into three-hour shifts. Both took catnaps whenever the need arose. Theirs turned out to be a relaxing, restful approach to the passage, and Kate found herself thinking less and less about the circumstances under which she made the trip.

The work of voyaging demanded all of her energy. Everything aboard the boat—cooking, cleaning, even straightening up—took much longer than on land. Below deck, every chore demanded the additional strain of balancing against the motion of the boat. Most of the time, Kate felt tired. But she relished the genuine weariness of hard work. And she liked it far better than the stress of life in the city.

In spite of the circumstances, she enjoyed being with Mike. She always had. Their long-standing friendship surfaced again on board *Second Chance.* As she watched him work, she enjoyed his ability to manage the boat. He had always been a handy kind of guy, clever with tools, able to fix anything. She enjoyed his sense of humor, his pleasure in sailing. She even enjoyed his reluctant acceptance of the slow pace of life aboard the boat.

At first, Mike wanted to be busy every moment of every day. He was always fixing or adjusting something. Once she'd even caught him in the cockpit moving things from under one bench to the other—though she saw no real reason to move things. Mike seemed unable to simply sit and watch the water flow by.

His restlessness seemed normal to Kate. Mike had pushed himself through sixty-hour workweeks for nearly ten years. Now, in the middle of the ocean, he had trouble allowing himself to relax.

She mentioned it once—that he should calm down and enjoy the trip. He smiled a peculiar, sad smile and went back to cleaning and lubricating some part of the boat. After another week, though, her words seemed to soak in. Once, she'd even caught him reading a novel, lying on his back on the foredeck.

"Mike," she called up to him. "Better put that down!"

He rolled over and looked back at her, surprised. "What?"

"It's a novel. That means fiction. Lies. Untruth. Fiction is written for no other reason but pleasure. You don't like pleasure." She smiled broadly.

He made a face at her and rolled over. "No. You've got it all wrong," he said in a phony English accent. "Pleasure is my life!" He moved the book close to his face to block the sun. Laughing,

Kate turned the wheel in a vain effort to throw him off balance. "Won't work, sweetie," he called. "Can't throw a person off a sailboat."

———

By their fifteenth day at sea, the weather had warmed. Though they continued to hit occasional squalls, for the most part, the wind came at them off their starboard beam, just as Mike had predicted. No storm lasted more than an hour. Rain came less and less frequently.

Kate felt proficient working in the tiny galley, and Mike had begun to catch fish to add to their menu. Often, during the afternoon hours, they talked, sitting lazily in the cockpit, both in shorts, protected from the hot sun by the canvas dodger. At first their conversations covered vast subjects, rarely personal. But after two weeks, they returned to their past, to the years they'd shared, to the children and the memories of their life together. For Kate, these memories held both pleasure and pain. Pleasure in the happy years past. Pain in the empty years ahead. In spite of the peaceful passage, Kate continually reminded herself that her future with Mike would end as soon as the *Second Chance* docked in Hilo.

This voyage is only an interlude, she told herself. *A time between injury and freedom.* Though the voyage seemed to ease her pain, it did not have the power to heal her wounds. She refused to be healed.

Mike continued to be thoughtful and attentive. He never pushed. Never tried to touch her or make advances. In fact, there were times when Kate thought that he looked at her with an almost visible agony, as though seeing her brought him physical pain.

One night, as Kate guided the *Second Chance* through a moonless night, she heard the sound of the automatic bilge pump. *Funny,* she thought. The pump had not run for a long time. She concentrated on the boat, listening and feeling, but could not sense any significant change.

When Mike came up, he brought crackers and cheese and hot chocolate, which she accepted happily. "Right on course," he said, moving forward to make an inspection of the rigging.

"Naturally," she said, chewing. "I can manage to keep the boat moving in the right direction." She sat on the rear bench, holding the mug on the deck between her tennis shoes. Mike came back and took off the self-steering. Standing at the wheel, he turned the boat ever so slightly and frowned.

"How long has the boat felt like this?"

"Like what?" Kate bent forward and picked up her drink.

"Heavy, sluggish." In the light spilling from the cabin, she saw deep creases in his forehead as he concentrated on the feel of the boat.

"I did hear the bilge pump tonight," she offered. "But it hasn't been running constantly. Everything seemed okay."

Mike stood aside. "Would you take the wheel while I go below for a minute?"

"What are you going to do?"

"Check the engine room." He went down the hatch before Kate could stand up and take the wheel. She kept the wheel fixed in the right direction, watching the horizon, glancing at the wind indicator. *What did he feel that I missed?* She made a deliberate move of the wheel, trying to sense a change. She did feel it. The boat seemed heavier, slower. She shuddered. *What now?*

More than ten minutes later, Mike came up the stairs.

"What is it?" she asked.

"Bad news," he said. "There's water in the bilge. I think it's coming from the rudder, but I can't see for certain."

Her face must have registered fear because, laughing, he added, "Relax, Kate. The pump is managing the water. The rudder box looks a little loose. I've tightened the screws. When the sun comes up, I'll do a better inspection." He took the wheel. "You look really tired. Why don't you catch some sleep?"

Kate crawled into the berth in the aft cabin. The aching fatigue in her muscles reminded her of the flu. In spite of exhaustion, she could not sleep. The whirring sound of the bilge motor in the engine room riveted her attention. The sea had decided to join them—inside the boat.

Early the next morning Kate hurried on deck, anxious for Mike to evaluate the source of the leak. He spent a long time in the engine room before coming up to explain his discovery.

"Well, we do have a problem," he said, sitting on the bench. "The rudder box is loose. I tightened it up, and it's better. But the motion has damaged the fiberglass where the controls go through the hull. That's where our water leak is."

"What can you do?"

"I'm going to try to patch it. We have the material. But it will take time. The worst part is that Dave will need to have the boat hauled out in Hawaii. Could mean a big repair for him."

"Well, Mr. Fix-It, what do you want me to do?"

"Could you make something for me to eat? Then I'll get to work on the hull."

Unable to use the self-steering for a while, Mike drove while Kate cooked. Then Kate piloted while Mike worked in the engine room. With only one porthole and very little air circulation in the engine room, he interrupted his work frequently for water and fresh air. Several hours later, he declared the patch complete.

"I can't figure out how it happened," he said, sitting in the sunshine, drinking a large glass of instant lemonade. "We went over the rudder system twice. It was perfect." He shook his head. "I guess the forces at sea are hard on all equipment."

He took a turn at the wheel while Kate worked on cleanup. She straightened the galley and baked a small coffee cake in the oven. When she brought it upstairs, Mike grinned from ear to ear. "I don't know why, but I'm always hungry out here. That looks wonderful."

She smiled but made no comment. The heeling of the sailboat had caused the cake to bake in the shape of a large wedge, the surface slanting severely from one side of the pan to the other.

They ate quietly. Mike brushed off his shorts when he was finished and said, "I think I'll go below and check things out."

She took the wheel, feeling sleepy and lethargic from her restless night in bed. Light wispy clouds floated across a blue sky above her. *Feathers,* she thought. *Like the end of a quill pen.* A brisk wind kept the sails full, and *Second Chance* skimmed quietly over the sea. Kate sat down and steered with her feet, opening her novel. They hadn't seen another boat in days. It felt good to think about something other than the problems in the engine room. Immersed in her story, she turned only two or three pages before she became completely oblivious to trouble on the *Second Chance.*

Mike immediately wrote to Dave.

We've had another problem. The rudder box came loose, and the extra motion damaged the hull where the controls exit. I've patched the fiberglass, and it seems to be holding. We won't use the self-steering gear until I know the repair is safe. In the meantime, I'm anxious. It seems to me that I still have water entering the hull from some other source. I don't want to sound hysterical, but I can't help but feel something is wrong. You and I worked on the rudder together. Everything was completely solid in San Francisco. Why would this happen? Where is the additional water coming from? I find myself wondering about the woman who spoke to Kate. Have I inadvertently allowed myself to get mixed up with the Syndicate? Isn't it bad enough that I have completely destroyed our marriage? Could I have endangered Kate's life as well? Please pray. And send me an inspection plan. I have no idea where to begin looking.

Mike sent the message and took a moment to pray.

Mike's presence on deck caught Kate's attention, and she turned her book over on the bench beside her. "Kate," he said, staring off to the horizon. "Something is definitely wrong."

She saw that the furrows on his forehead had returned.

"The automatic bilge is working harder than it should. It's hot, and I have no idea how much longer it may last."

"But you said you fixed the rudder leak."

"I did," he said, shaking his head. He crossed his arms over his chest. With one hand, his fingers rubbed his upper lip.

"What is it, Mike?"

"We're getting water inside. Not just from the rudder, but from something else too." He stood motionless, staring off the bow of the boat. "I've got to find out where it's coming from and stop it," he said.

Whispering into the wind, he said, "Or we're going to be in real trouble soon."

Thirty-Seven

IN AN EFFORT to save the motor on the automatic pump, Mike disconnected it from the power line. From somewhere below, he pulled out a portable hand pump, with a long tube that reminded Kate of the built-in vacuum hose at their house in Tiburon. Using duct tape, he attached one end of the hose to the galley sink and took the pump into the engine room and emptied the water from the bilge.

When he came up again, he wore the clear expression of triumph. "It's dry for the moment," he said. "The hand pump worked perfectly. Do you mind if I take a nap?"

"Can I use the self-steering gear yet?"

"No problem. The patch is dry, and it's holding well."

"Then get some sleep." She smiled, and he ducked below. From her seat in the cockpit, she saw Mike sit heavily on the port bench of the salon. He stretched out, landing on his back with his knees folded over the end of the bench. Without taking off his shoes, he fell soundly asleep. Before long, Kate heard him snoring loudly—a noise she recognized from years of sleeping in the same bed. She smiled, glad to have him resting so completely. The rudder repair had taken a lot out of him.

As Kate sat in the cockpit, she felt her own body complain as well. The muscles of her neck ached, and her shoulders felt tight and sore. Through all of the repair process and the morning pumping, she'd been at the wheel. She'd had no time for a catnap. The time on deck was getting to her. Her eyelids grew heavy, and she developed a bad headache. She stood and moved around the small confines of the cockpit, wiggling and stretching in an effort to stay awake.

Though she continued to try reading, exhaustion forced her to read every sentence twice. Eventually she quit, for the words began to swirl out of focus on the page. In frustration, she dropped her paperback into the space below a bench. Maybe something to drink. Tea?

Both Kate and Mike had been avoiding coffee during the passage. They needed to be able to fall asleep without caffeine interference. But Kate wanted something now—something that would help her to fight her own drive for rest. She set the self-steering and went below, careful not to wake Mike. Above the stove, she found a commuter mug that she filled with water from the hot pot. Quietly, she located a bag of blackberry tea, dumped it in the mug, and set it in the sink to steep.

As she turned to start back up, she noticed her face in the mirror above the salon table. Freckles spread across the pale skin of her nose, over her cheeks, and onto her chin. Walking closer, she let her fingers pass gently over her face. How long had it been since she looked at herself carefully? She frowned at the image and decided to put on sunscreen. She hadn't been as careful about sun exposure as she meant to be. The mirror confirmed that her skin paid the price of her negligence.

Creeping past Mike, who hadn't moved in more than an hour, she walked past the engine compartment to the aft cabin. In the bathroom cabinet she found a tube of sunscreen and paused to rub it liberally over her face. She went back to the aft bedroom and dug through her drawers for her wide-brimmed hat. Not there. Where could she have put it?

"I must have left it somewhere," she muttered, and started back toward the salon, looking for her missing hat as she walked. As she passed the door to the engine room, an unusual sound caught her attention. A different sound, something unlike the normal banging of the rigging or of the equipment inside. The engine wasn't running. It wasn't the bilge motor. Something more subtle. A slapping sound. Kate stuck her head in through the opening and looked around. To her amazement, she found water again rising against the white fiberglass floor. Startled, she caught her breath and bit her lip. She needed to tell Mike about this latest surge of seawater.

Though he had been sound asleep, Mike woke quickly and headed for the engine room. "Kate," he called, "please go up and disconnect the self-steering. Keep the same course. I'm going to pump."

She went up the companionway, leaving her tea in the sink.

Mike worked for several hours before he came up on deck. "I think we have a failure in a through-hull," he said, landing on the bench opposite her. "Every boat has places where water can pass out of the hull. Places like the sink or the toilet have valves that control the flow of water through the hull of the boat. But when the valves fail, and sometimes they do, then water can seep in." He sat down, crossing one foot over his knee. "I've traced it to the forward head. Even though I closed the gasket, water is still coming in."

"What does that mean?"

"It means we have to stop the boat and plug the hole. Otherwise, the leak will continue—and maybe grow. It's already letting in more water than we can handle."

More than we can handle. Kate tried not to think about what that phrase might mean. "How do you plug a hole?"

"You'll see," he said. "In fact, by the end of the afternoon, you should be able to do it by yourself." He stood and smiled, though to Kate it looked forced. "First, though, we need to get the sails down and out of the way. Then I'll go over the side and drive a plug into the hull."

"Mike, we're in the middle of the Pacific. You can't just go over the side."

"I have to, Kate, or we'll be in the middle of the ocean without a boat. We don't have a choice. Trust me, we'll be fine." He pointed at the wheel. "Point her into the wind. Then set the gear and help me wrestle down the sails."

Kate was beginning to hate those words—"Trust me." The two of them downed both sails quickly, for by now they had developed a routine. Kate worked from the mast toward the stern, and Mike came forward to meet her in the middle. Mike's height enabled him to reach the boom from the floor of the cockpit—which Kate could only reach by standing on a bench and leaning out over the deck. It felt good to Kate, knowing what to do and how to do it: like being part of the team, no longer an observer. It had taken a long time to get there, and for a brief moment, she cherished the feeling. Her mind skipped back to the summer that they had built a small playhouse for Keegan. Another happy time, long ago, when she and Mike had worked together to accomplish something good. For an instant, Kate forgot her fear.

With the sails down, Mike stripped to his shorts. He pulled a spare harness out from under a cockpit bench and removed the clip from the tether. Digging around until he found a longer rope, he attached it to the clip. He tied one end firmly around the mast; the other end he clipped to the harness. Laying the line carefully along the deck of the boat, he stood up.

"Still need my tools," he told Kate, starting down the companionway. When he returned, he carried his tool bucket in one hand, a mask and fins in the other. Handing her the bucket, he said, "All right, you don't have to do anything, really." He put on the harness. "The rope is long enough for me to climb off the stern and swim around to the front of the boat. If you'll keep the line from fouling on the deck hardware, I'll go around to the bow and try to find the hole."

"What then?"

"Then I'll come up, and you can hand me the plug and the mallet."

"All right." Kate fought with her emotions. She wanted to stop him. To keep him on board with her. The idea of letting him swim away from the boat caused a horrible knot of fear to grow in the bottom of her stomach. She nearly doubled over with the terror.

"Try to keep the rope as short as possible. It should only take a moment to drive the wood into the through-hull." He smiled, reaching out to pat her shoulder. She flinched and stepped back. Pain flashed across his features. "Relax, Kate. When we fix this, the only problem we'll have is that we can't use the forward head." He walked back to the stern of the boat and sat down with his feet over the edge. Balancing there, he slipped on his fins and adjusted the mask over his face. "Okay, here we go." He dropped over the edge feet first and made a small splash at the back of the boat. Kate fed out the line while her heart beat fiercely against her chest. Leaning against the lifelines, she watched for him to come to the surface. "Do you want anything?" she called.

"Nope," he gave her the okay signal with his hands. "Unless you want to turn up the temperature in the pool. It's a little chilly." He stuck the snorkel in his mouth and blew air through it.

She frowned. "No jokes. This scares me to death."

"Okay, here we go. Keep the line free, all right? That's all you have to do."

"That and pray like a saint," she said under her breath. *Oh, Jesus, please keep him safe. Help him do whatever it is he has to do out there.* She walked the line up the side of the boat as Mike swam long, powerful strokes around the side. At the bow, he stopped and adjusted his mask. Pulling out the snorkel, he said, "You can pull in some of the line. But not all of it—I'll have to go under a few feet."

She tried to do as he instructed, forming a neat circle of Dacron at her feet. Mike took a deep breath and ducked down into the water. She watched his bottom go under, followed by a small kick with his fins. Unconsciously, Kate held her breath along with him, feeling her heart pound in her ears. She glanced out over the water; swells rolled the boat from side to side. For once the weather had cooperated. Mild wind, no real waves. "Please help him, Jesus. Keep him." She waited. No Mike. Running out of air, she let her own breath out. Gasping, she wondered, *How can he stay down so long?*

For a moment, she suspected that Mike had gotten caught below the water. In an instant, the peaceful warmth of sunshine and rolling water changed into a vast desert of panic. Again, she glanced out at the horizon. Mike had to make it. He had to fix the problem. Alone, Kate would never find Hawaii. Never sail the boat. Never solve the endless problems that seemed to be determined to sink them.

Stay calm, she told herself. *Focus.* She knelt down and peered over the edge of the boat, straining to see his body under the water. Suddenly she heard air blow through the snorkel, just as his face cleared the surface. "Got it," he called.

"Thank you," she whispered. "Okay, what do you need first?"

"It looks pretty simple. Bring the seacocks over where I can see them."

She stepped away from the edge and returned with his tool bucket. Picking up a small cone-shaped piece of wood, she asked, "This one?"

"Too small."

She held up another slightly larger piece.

"That's it. I'll take that one."

She reached out over the water, holding the cone. He bounced up and took it, saying, "I'll need the mallet too."

She turned back to the bucket and selected the hammer with a soft vinyl end. "This?"

He nodded. With the tools in hand, he took another gasping breath and went below the water. Instantly, he surfaced again, breathing hard. "Dropped the wood," he said, looking around. "It floats. Find it."

She looked over the rail, fighting panic. No wood. She ran around the other side of the bow. "Here!" she shouted, pointing. "I see it."

Mike swam quickly around the boat. He scanned the water, looking for the plug.

"There," she pointed again. "Beyond your left hand."

He turned away from the boat, swam a single stroke, and caught the plug in his fist. He gave her a slight wave and swam for the other side.

Again, she moved around the edge of the deck, still holding his line and watching as he went under, head first. Moments passed. She waited, this time breathing deep regular breaths—as though she provided Mike's air herself. Still, he stayed under. *God, why is this happening? Why is he taking so long? Why don't you help him?*

She glanced up, as though to plead Mike's case, just as he surfaced. "That's it," he said. "Got it." Again, he made the okay sign. He swam close to the boat and handed the mallet up to her. "Now, if you'll help me in." As he swam toward the back of the boat, Kate followed, alert and watching, holding his line high above the deck.

At the stern, Mike paused and dropped his mask to his neck. "Could you give me a boost with the line? I'll just kind of climb up the back."

Kate wondered why the *Second Chance* had no swim platform. Of course, she had a small inflatable dinghy attached to her stern. But a platform would have given Mike a place to pull himself out of the water. She braced her feet against a deck box and pulled as he climbed up the stern of the boat like a rock-climber.

And then, when he stood safely beside her on deck, Kate did a most amazing thing. She threw both arms around his neck and kissed his cheek. "Oh man, am I glad you're back."

The look of surprise on Mike's face made her laugh. Before he recovered, she pulled away and handed him a towel. "You're all wet," she said.

Mike went below, overwhelmed by the simple hug she'd given him. It had been so long. And Kate's arms around him felt so completely wonderful that he nearly cried as he stepped down the stairs to the salon. He dried quickly and put on an old pair of sweat pants. Though the air was quite warm, forty minutes in the ocean had chilled him to the point of shivering.

He poured himself some water from the hot pot and drank it quickly, disappointed to find it tepid. Still, warm liquid felt good in his stomach. *Now to check the engine room,* he thought. He went back and slid the door aside. Water sloshed against the wall of the bulkhead. This he had expected. After all, stopping the water from entering would not remove the water already there. He reached for the hand pump and taped the tube in place.

Mike pumped for nearly twenty minutes, counting his strokes as he did. The water level below the floorboards dropped slowly as he pumped. Satisfied at last, he took a black marker and marked the new water level with a spot on the wall and the exact time. With the wall marked, he could measure the water, watch the time, and record how much change occurred to the water level in the bilge.

Knowing he had done all he could, he went back to the galley and made sandwiches for both of them. His stomach growled, and he felt as though his hunger ached all the way to his knees. He poured a can of peaches into a bowl and pulled out the leftover coffee cake. He put water on to boil.

As he moved about the galley, uneasiness continued to gnaw at his consciousness. Before they left San Francisco, he and Dave had replaced every through-hull in the entire boat. Every single one was brand new. Why had this one failed? Why had so much water poured through the opening? Why hadn't the valve stopped the flow as it was designed to do?

Once again, the thought of sabotage flitted across his mind. With effort, he dismissed it. Sabotage only happens in novels. What did he know about malicious code anyway? After all, he was just a businessman on a trip with his wife. He frowned and placed the food on a platter.

Before he went on deck, he took a moment to retrieve a weather fax. Carrying the entire load upstairs to Kate, he set the food on the bench beside her. "You've been on duty all day," he said. "You haven't eaten lunch, and you need a break." She smiled at him as though he'd just purchased a Mercedes Benz and given it to her as a birthday gift.

"I wondered if you'd think of food. I'm starved," she said, reaching for a sandwich. She let go of the wheel and took an enormous bite.

He sat and helped himself to cake. As he brought it to his mouth, he noticed the weather fax flapping in the breeze, held in place by the platter. He grabbed it with the other hand and scanned the weather sheet.

Kate's face fell when she looked up at him. "Oh no. Mike, what is it now?"

"It's the four-day forecast," he answered. "A bad storm coming down on us from the southeast."

She sat down hard. "Just what we need." Suddenly, her hunger disappeared.

The weather fax had arrived late in the afternoon of their twenty-first day at sea. Mike reassured Kate, saying that in all likelihood the storm would not reach them before they made port in Hilo. Then he'd insisted she eat, hungry or not, and go down to sleep. He'd checked on her twice and found her nearly comatose on the aft bunk. Glad that she slept soundly, Mike began preparing the boat for the possibility of a severe storm.

In the meantime, the wind shifted, now coming from behind the *Second Chance*. This demanded a change in sail configuration, and Mike determined to make the change without waking Kate for help. Clipping himself onto the lifeline, he moved forward to the jib. He rigged a whisker pole on to the forward sail. This pole enabled the sail to stay out as far as possible from the boat, catching the wind from behind. Then he moved to the main. Using a preventer cable, he pulled the boom out as far as possible on the opposite side of *Second Chance*. He clipped the preventer onto the end of the boom and connected the other end to the mast. In less than an hour, Mike had the boat in the "wing and wing" position.

With both sails hanging out on opposite sides of the boat, the wind would push them from behind. Because of the pole and the presenter, both sails remained frozen in position. As the wind picked up, Mike felt *Second Chance* surf down the waves of a following sea. In this position, at this speed, it seemed likely they would reach Hilo before the storm caught up with them. Mike sat down in the cockpit and prayed for a strong wind and swift passage.

The new configuration made for comfortable sailing, with little rolling and almost no heeling. He sat at the wheel, enjoying warm wind at his back, eager for Kate to wake. *She would like this,* he thought. *Provided we make it to port before the storm.*

Thirty-Eight

SEVENTEEN HOURS LATER, Mike and Kate had the dubious pleasure of having made it through another night at sea. Kate had lost the baggy-eyed, sad-faced appearance that betrayed her exhaustion, due in part to Mike's refusal to wake her at the usual time for her watches. Instead, he'd taken longer turns at the wheel, opting to give her the extra sleep she seemed to need.

When she woke on day twenty-two, she appeared cheerful and refreshed. She made breakfast and took it to Mike in the cockpit. So close to their destination, the weather had at last turned warm. Kate wore a tank top and shorts along with her bright orange widebrimmed hat. In the fresh morning air, they ate a quiet breakfast on the cockpit bench, both enjoying the warm sun, partly cloudy skies, and brisk wind driving *Second Chance* toward the islands. When they'd finished, Mike took the dishes down, and Kate took her turn at the wheel.

In the salon, Mike washed up. His usual morning routine included time at the nav station, where he filled out the log, retrieved messages, and recorded their position and progress on the sea charts. On this morning, he retrieved his e-mail, which included his daily contact with Dave Holland. From California, Dave continued to act as advisor coaching them through the various problems they'd experienced aboard *Second Chance*. No one had been more baffled than Dave when the salon window blew out. He'd been equally surprised by the through-hull failure in the forward head. But he reassured Mike that he wouldn't have handled these crises any differently than Mike had. In this morning's message Dave wrote:

> *I can tell from your last e-mail that you are still losing sleep over the trouble you have had with the boat. I don't think you can assume that sabotage is behind your current list of troubles. Sailing is fraught with trouble. If it's not one thing, it's another. You're handling the boat well and making good time. I cannot explain the rudder problem. We went over it with a fine-toothed comb. It should not have happened. The pins in the rudder box are nearly new. Though I must say I'm glad you were able to patch the fiberglass. This is the reason that all sailors must be able to fix every part of the boat. Be glad that the sails are new, my friend, or you'd be patching those as well. (Aren't you glad that you rebuilt your own Mustang?) Val and I will fix the forward through-hull when we arrive. As to the storm behind you, I say this, you wouldn't be racing the storm if you'd gotten to the trades more quickly. But with all you've been through, you've done better than most. Try to make all the distance you can, even at night, and you should be in port in plenty of time. I'm watching the weather from here. I'll send anything I hear to you ASAP. Keep an eye on the bilge. If the water level changes, let me know immediately.*

Mike carefully plotted his position from the GPS and calculated the distance left to port. In less than three days, if the wind held steady, they would be back in the middle of civilization. Paradise, yes. But civilization, none the less. A moment of panic hit him as he realized that he had not yet won Kate. In spite of his determination, he had not convinced Kate to change her decision. Sitting in the nav station, he considered her behavior over the past few weeks. She'd come on board cold and angry, determined to avoid any contact with Mike. Since then, she'd grown more relaxed, even smiled some. But as far as he knew, she had not changed her mind. In fact, every time he tried to bring up the subject of their relationship, he found himself tongue-tied. *Like an adolescent,* he scolded himself. *Almost like asking for your first date.*

He had to admit, as he sat thinking about it, that fear kept him from approaching the subject. If he brought it up and she still wanted to divorce, Mike knew he would be overwhelmed with pain. Truthfully, part of him hoped he could avoid the subject forever. Perhaps they could sail past Hawaii and keep right on going.

Only three more days. What if he couldn't do it? What if she would not reconsider? How could Mike go back to California without her? How could he face life alone?

He felt a horrible fear clamp down on his stomach. "Oh, Jesus, help me," he prayed. "I can't do this. It was a dumb idea. I haven't managed to get Kate to stay. I've even put us both in serious danger. The work has been a constant distraction, and all of these problems with the boat have only drained our energy. This isn't what I planned. Help me, Lord."

Mike tried to shake the downward turn of his thoughts. Turning his attention to the logbook, he scratched an entry noting their position, the weather, time, and sea conditions. He made no mention of the condition of his soul or of his desperate need to save his marriage. None of his most urgent concerns belonged in the log.

Just as he signed off, he remembered that he had not yet checked and recorded the water level in the engine room. He put down his pen and tucked the chair under the desk. Moving down the hall to the engine room, he stepped inside and flipped on the overhead light. To his amazement, water soaked his tennis shoes. Glancing to the line on the wall, he noted that water had risen more than two inches since he'd last marked the wall.

Water? Why now? Had his plug come out? He reached into his tool bucket and brought out a flashlight. What could possibly have gone wrong now? Methodically, he began searching through sections of the engine room. He would find the source of this water once and for all. He got down on his hands and knees and crawled around the diesel engine. Hand over hand, he went around the walls of the engine compartment, feeling the pipes and drains for dripping water. He checked the rudder box and found the screws holding tight. He examined the fiberglass patch he'd made when they first came aboard. Dry and holding.

Perplexed, he turned the light upward and caught sight of the hose draining from the cockpit scupper above him. He moved the flashlight sideways, slowly bringing it along the hose toward the outside section of the cockpit floor. There, a reflection.

He stood up and moved the light back, reaching up to touch the hose. Wet. The hose was wet. At the point where the hose clamped onto the through-hull, water fell steadily onto the floor of the engine room. He moved closer. Standing directly under the hose, he examined the clamp that held the hose to the plastic through-hull. What? A small incision just below the clamp let water drip directly onto the engine room floor.

He reached down for a screwdriver and unclamped the hose. Peering inside, he pulled out the tiniest section of nylon netting, folded across the hose end and held in place by the hose clamp. Why had nylon been inserted into the drain hose? Behind the netting, debris packed tightly against the walls of the hose, forcing water out through the incision near the clamp. All of the debris from the cockpit floor had drained into the scupper and down into this hose, where it had been held back by this tiny piece of nylon— effectively plugging the hose.

He stuck the end of his screwdriver up the hose, dislodging large clumps of smelly debris. As soon as the stuff dropped onto the engine room floor, Mike regretted his action. He should have dropped it into a bucket or a pan. Now he would have to clean the floor by hand—after he pumped out the additional water. He dropped onto one knee, reaching into the water to scoop up some of the mess. His flashlight balanced in his other hand as he felt along the floor. *Wait. What was that?* Something strange floated half submerged in the water near his foot. He stretched his fingers and the thing floated away. He moved the flashlight, trying to look more closely, but couldn't see. Blindly, he put his hand into the water again, feeling along the bottom of the boat for the thing that eluded him. Ah. His fingers closed on the object. He brought it up out of the water and examined it with his flashlight.

In his hand, he held the white lid of a small plastic bottle. He'd seen this kind of lid before. Where? He forced himself to think, to imagine the lid and the bottle it covered. Then suddenly he saw it clearly. This lid was the same kind he had seen on the eyedrops Doug used. Why would Doug's eyedrops . . . ? Suddenly the implication of finding a matching lid on board the *Second Chance* sent a shiver of apprehension down Mike's back.

Mike could fix this latest leak easily. Removing the nylon netting, he cleaned the plug and repaired the hole that he believed had been cut with a knife. He moved the flashlight to the other scupper hose. Once again he found water dripping from an incision in the hose. While he dragged the debris from the second hose, his anger toward his partner boiled. Why had Doug done this? If he'd gotten himself into trouble, that was his own problem, but why try to sink the *Second Chance?* Mike could not understand how his friend could be so cold as to try something this stupid. *Why? Why would Doug consider me a threat?*

Mike cleaned up the mess and pumped the engine room dry. Once again, he got the water below his previous mark. This time, Mike would not tell Kate what he had found. No matter what he believed about Doug, he refused to frighten Kate any further. She had been through enough. He would handle this himself.

As he closed the sliding door to the engine room, another terrifying thought hit him. If Doug were really the one who sabotaged the scuppers on the *Second Chance*, was he also responsible for the window failure, and the rudder box, and perhaps even the through-hull failure? And if Doug were behind everything that had happened thus far, what other misfortune did he have planned? What disaster did they have yet to face?

The thought sent a shiver through Mike. He decided to complete another inspection of the boat. If he went over every inch of the boat—from the top of the mast to the keel—perhaps he might avert the next disaster before the Pacific Ocean swallowed the *Second Chance* whole.

On deck, Kate noticed that the wind had picked up. The moving air chilled her, and she slipped on her sweatshirt. For one strange moment, she actually felt grateful for her experience with the salon window. Because of it, with the wind behind her, Kate knew she could guide the *Second Chance* down the back side of waves accurately and safely. She tried not to look behind her. From her position in the cockpit, it appeared as though wall after wall of water tried to crush *Second Chance*, to topple over on top of her like a leaning tower of bricks. The sight of it made Kate feel sick. Instead, she concentrated on the waves in front of the bow. If she could keep her mind on the sea in front of her, she would be safe.

Mike came up the companionway, and she took her eyes off the water for a moment to glance at him. Something in his expression made her look again. "What is it?" she teased. "You look like you've seen a ghost."

"Oh, just a little adjustment in the engine room."

"Serious?" She focused on the wave in front of the bow, turning the wheel gently, skimming down the back side.

He smiled, "Nothing, really. I fixed it."

"Do you need a nap? You were at the wheel for a long time this morning."

"I am a little tired," he nodded, looking up at the rigging. "But I think I'll just do a little checking around before I sleep."

Something about his face and the tone of his voice made Kate uneasy. She continued to steer as he clamped his tether to the lifeline and moved onto the forward deck. She watched as he went around the deck from one side to the other checking rigging, sheets, and stays. Some he shook, glancing upward. Others he touched and fiddled with, feeling every fray in the wire. He seemed tense, almost nervous, and she wondered if he was telling her everything. When he dropped into the seat beside her, she confronted him straight out, "Something's up. You know something."

"No, nothing like that. I just want to be certain we're ready in case this storm catches us." Putting his feet up on the bench, he lay down on his back, resting his head on his arms.

"Mike, we've been married for too many years to fool me. What was that out there?" She pointed forward to the rigging. "What is happening?" Her voice rose in spite of her effort to maintain control.

He sat up and sighed, looking out over the ocean. "I'm concerned about the boat," he said evenly. "I think maybe someone may have tampered with things before we left."

"But when? We've been on board constantly, for weeks."

"We all went to the bon voyage party."

"But the dock has security."

"It isn't hard to get through a security gate—if you want to." He looked directly into her eyes. "Maybe I'm wrong. But I've looked at the rigging, Kate. And someone has tampered with it. The wires holding the mast have been compromised. I can't fix any of it in this weather. Someone was hoping we'd run into some serious wind."

"But why?"

"I think whoever did it hoped that we would be dismasted."

"Break the mast?"

"I think so. And, when the mast goes over, it would do serious hull damage. In that case, the *Second Chance* would fill with water and go down like a rock. We wouldn't have time to get into a life raft."

She stared hard at him, searching his eyes. "I can't believe that."

"It makes sense. The through-hull failure. The window blowout. Someone wanted water inside the hull so that she would be difficult to steer. Then, a good storm would put extra pressure on the rigging—with a sluggish boat . . . It wouldn't be a pretty picture." Mike gestured with his hands—a palm-up, no-hope shrug that sent shivers through Kate. "We'd have gone down without a trace." He looked into her face. "We've been lucky, though. The water didn't all come in at once. We've been able to deal with things one problem at a time."

"I don't understand, Mike. Who would do this?"

"I don't know for certain. All I know is that I never meant to put you in danger, Kate. Really I didn't. All I wanted was for you to have time alone to remember who I am. Why you used to love me." He looked down at his hands. "I never meant for this to happen."

She ignored his apology. "What now?"

"Now we need to get to Hilo as fast as possible. If we can beat the storm, we'll make it. If it catches us, I think we're in real trouble."

Kate didn't answer. Instead, staring into the sea ahead, she guided the *Second Chance* down building wave after building wave. "So we keep doing what we've been doing," she said. "You need some sleep, Mike. I can't do this alone."

"I am a little tired," he said, closing his eyes. "I think I'll just nap here for a moment." And before she could send him down to a bed, he fell asleep.

As Kate steered and Mike slept, the wind picked up. Before long, a wave coming from behind crashed into the open cockpit, soaking both of them with cold ocean water. "Oh, shoot," Kate said, sputtering, brushing wet hair from her eyes.

Mike sat up and brushed the water from his face. "I think we should bring down the sails a bit," he said. "I hate to slow us down, but she'll be easier to manage if she isn't moving so quickly."

"Can we close up the dodger?" Kate asked. "I'll freeze to death if I'm wet."

"Good idea," Mike agreed. "Why don't you clip on and go forward? You can get ready to drop the main. We'll reef it in and see if things calm down." Mike stood on the cockpit bench and began untying the knots holding the plastic window in place.

Kate had been clipped to the safety line since she'd come up with breakfast. But she didn't bother to correct Mike. She felt safer hooked to the boat; in fact, she had felt almost relieved to have him insist that they tie on whenever they were on deck. She glanced at Mike to make certain he obeyed his own advice. Mike had on his heavy-weather jacket with his harness securely tied to the lifeline.

Standing on the port bench, she stepped carefully up to the deck. Moving forward, she clutched the cabin rail with her right hand. With the main sail winging out over the starboard side, she had chosen the port side to move forward. This way, she could go behind the mast without having to climb under the boom. When Mike had the dodger in place, she would be ready to help him reef the main. She looked forward to a slower pace. If only they could calm the weather. Standing on the forward deck, she clung to the mast, waiting.

Has the wind picked up? Or do things just feel more violent up front? The boat seemed to ride up and down the waves with a hard, frenzied motion. She hugged the mast, swaying with the motion, and glanced back at Mike, who struggled with the zipper of the dodger. The wind blew his clothes forward, and he seemed so focused on the zipper that he didn't notice her clinging to the mast. *Hurry, Mike.*

The sound of a sudden loud snap caught her attention, and she glanced around for the source. The clip of the wire preventer flew into the air, severed into two distinct pieces that fell heavily onto the deck. Movement. She turned just in time to see the boom swing wildly toward Mike. The terror in her chest exploded into one long horrifying scream.

Mike must have heard the sound of the preventer clip snapping. His head came up just as the boom caught him above his right shoulder. It slammed into his head and tossed him over the side. For the tiniest moment, Kate thought she recognized a look of surprise on his face—just before he dropped over the rail into the ocean. Kate screamed again, and the noise of her scream floated uselessly on the wind.

At first, she didn't move. She heard the unmistakable sound of Mike's life jacket as seawater triggered the flow of compressed air.

The boom continued to flap wildly as the bow of the boat turned with the wind. "Mike," she cried, still not moving. "Mike!"

Too terrified to let go, Kate clung to the mast. The *Second Chance* drove forward, and she saw no sign of Mike. She had to do something. More time passed. Reluctantly, she let go and began to feel her way around the opposite side of the boat toward the cockpit. The wind, now caught in the main, slammed the boom back and forth on the port side of the boat. For a moment, she stood frozen on the deck, watching the boom, unsure of what to do. She held her hands overhead, as though she could keep the thing from hurting her should it decide to fly in the other direction.

Stabilize the stupid thing, Kate. She reached for the traveler and pulled hard, fastening the boom to the center of the boat. With all her strength, she pulled the sheet. Then, ducking under the boom, she ran to the edge of the boat and looked over, hoping to see Mike swimming along beside the boat.

She could bring him on board; she had done it before. With her eyes, she followed the rope attached to his harness. Where was he? Why couldn't she see him? Then she recognized his plight. Mike's body was being towed behind the boat, facedown, about fifteen feet from the deck edge. His arm had been caught in the line, forcing his face down. His unconscious body plowed through the water, forcing the sea to curl up over his head.

"Mike," she called, pulling on the line. "Mike." He didn't respond. She pulled harder. "Mike!" she screamed his name, and the sound tore at the flesh of her throat. She pulled until she managed to bring him in slightly, and in the effort, her feet slid on the deck, the rope slid through her hands, and the motion nearly pulled her into the ocean after him.

The force of the wind drove the *Second Chance* forward. Mike rode facedown behind her like a useless dinghy.

"Oh, God, he's drowning," Kate cried. "What do I do?" Tears came to her eyes, but Kate refused to give in to the utter hopelessness that threatened to engulf her. "Help me, Jesus. Help me!" she cried aloud.

Air. Mike needs air. If I cut the line to his jacket, his arm will be free. The life jacket will roll him face up. He needs to be face up. She fought panic. *But I can't cut him loose. How will I find him again? How can I get him back in the boat?*

She hesitated for a brief moment, and then threw herself down the companionway. Her own tether caught on the wooden frame, and she nearly tore the clip open to go below. She tripped over the last stair and fell onto the salon deck. Scrambling up, she grabbed a knife from the sink where Mike had left it. Holding the handle with her teeth, she used both arms to climb the ladder. She clambered out of the cockpit onto the deck and began wildly sawing at his tether with the kitchen knife. Just as she sawed through, the weight of his body tore the last fibers apart. Turning to the rail, she watched his body float away. "Turn over," she whispered. He did not. The moving boat increased the distance between them.

Suddenly she realized that she would need to mark his position or she would never find him again. No one could find anything in this vast ocean. She grabbed a cockpit cushion and threw it into the sea. Green. The stupid thing hardly showed. Something bright. She tore off her sun hat and threw it toward him. She could barely see it against the sun and the waves.

Kate jumped back down into the cockpit and dropped the halyard to the main. Running forward, she pulled the sail down with all the strength she could manage. She didn't know how to sail after Mike with a following wind. But she did know how to start the engine. She ran forward and disconnected the whisker pole from the jib. Without thinking, she dropped it onto the deck, where it rolled wildly with the motion of the boat.

She jumped back into the cockpit and pulled the lever, giving fuel to the engine. "Oh, Jesus, please. Start this stupid engine," she prayed, turning the key. Nothing. No sound, no cranking. She glanced at the battery gauge. Full charge. Again, she turned the key. Nothing.

"Jesus. Please. Help me. I've got to get Mike. Don't let him die, Lord. Please." Tears ran freely down her cheeks. "Oh, God," she said, turning the key again. The engine turned over. "Oh, thank you," she breathed. She reached down and let the jib loose, so that it flopped wildly. She glanced at the compass and put the engine in gear.

Turning the wheel, she brought the *Second Chance* around to face the direction from which they'd come, the wind blowing hard at the bow. Kate looked out over the ocean, unsure of which side of the boat to search. She had at least two things on her side. The wind had been directly behind them just before the boom had swept Mike over the side. So now, if she headed directly into the wind, she would be going in the right direction. She'd also taken a compass heading. Reversing the heading should put her back over the place where he fell into the ocean. Now if she could only spot him in the water.

She moved the boat forward slowly, scanning the water for the cockpit cushion or the orange hat. But she could not see Mike. Instead, she saw only the sun reflecting off of miles and miles of boiling, empty sea.

Thirty-Nine

A VIOLENT TREMBLING took over Kate's body. Panic. She recognized the symptoms. *Think*. Her mind seemed to scream the word at her. What should she do? How should she search for Mike? How could anyone search for someone in the middle of the Pacific Ocean all alone?

"Oh, God, help me," she sobbed. "I don't know what to do. Help me."

Her fear found a voice. *You'll never find him*, she heard it say. *Not out here. What do you know about searching for someone, anyway? You can't even sail a boat.* "Shut up," she screamed into the wind. "Just shut up. I need to think."

Tears filled her eyes and spilled down her cheeks. She dragged at her face with the back of her hand. She couldn't see through her tears. *Mike needs me*, she told herself. *I can't fall apart now.* She glanced out over the rough seas and felt very alone. "I'm not alone," she shouted again. "I'm not alone."

Trust me. The other voice. A voice entirely different from her fear. The same words she'd first heard in the airplane. "Okay," she agreed, still crying. "I'll trust you. Just help me do this one thing. Please, Lord."

She drove the boat forward, searching the seas for Mike. The *Second Chance* fought its way through the same wind and waves that moments ago had driven it toward safety. She set her course back toward the accident, wondering how far she should go in this direction. She glanced at her watch. Three twenty-three in the afternoon. How long had it taken her to start the boat and turn around? She had no idea.

Guess, a voice told her. *Stay calm. I will help you. Trust me.*

Kate blinked hard and tried to think her way through the question. It had taken perhaps five minutes to drop the sails, and the engine had started fairly quickly after that. But, she remembered, during all that time, the wind had been at her back, pushing her west with every minute that passed. All right. Then she must travel in an easterly direction longer than the time it took her to turn around. She must account for the push of the wind. After she went too far east, she could begin a search pattern. Perhaps a box. *But how far is too far?*

For a moment she considered using the radio to call for help. Instantly she dismissed the idea. Every moment Mike spent in the ocean, at the mercy of wind and current, diminished his chance of being found. She was the only person who could help him now. Not Dave. Not the Coast Guard. "Help me, God. We're all he has."

In spite of the wind, in spite of her self-talk, the tears continued. She brushed the moisture from her face and strained to focus on the surface of the water in front of her. Moderate swells rose and fell in front of the *Second Chance.* She called over the engine. "Mike, can you hear me?"

Nothing. She scanned the horizon, hoping to catch a glimpse of Mike or the cushion or the orange hat. She called again, screaming his name into the wind. What was she thinking? No one could hear anything over the sound of this stupid engine. She decided to travel forward, stop the engine, and listen. But even this plan frightened her. What if the engine would not start again?

Trust me.

She turned off the key and called again. Only the sound of wind and swells slapping against the hull answered her. "God, help me," she cried. "Please help me."

Again she looked across the water, hoping to see his self-inflating harness. The bright red nylon should be easily visible against the dark blue of the water. "Mike," she screamed. "Mike, where are you? Mike, can you hear me?"

No answer. She reached forward and turned the key. The engine turned over, and Kate slipped it into gear. The boat began to creep forward. Keeping a close watch on the compass, she stood high on the bench. Should she go below for binoculars? Might she miss him if she went below? She decided to stand on the bench and steer with her feet. Still moving east, she began a systematic scanning of the sea.

Again she stopped and called. No answer. She looked at her watch. Three thirty-seven. Five more minutes and she would turn west again. She called out. No response. Starting the engine, she drove further east, still moving into the wind. If only she could see her hat.

Nothing.

At precisely 3:42, Kate began a slow turn to the right. Using the compass near the wheel, she made a ninety-degree turn and continued her northerly course for about four minutes. Still no sign of Mike or of the items she had thrown over with him. With another careful turn she returned to a westerly course and stopped the engine. She called again. Nothing. This time she found it harder to keep raw panic and terror from swallowing the volume of her voice. Part of her wanted to curl up on the cockpit bench screaming in grief and terror. But another part, a stronger, trusting part, refused to give in. She grew angry with herself for her continuing tears. She couldn't even see the deck through her watery eyes.

"Stop it," she told herself as she started the engine again. "You couldn't see a freighter through all these tears. Just stop it. Now." She paused long enough to blow her nose on her sleeve. Coaxing the *Second Chance* west, she watched her clock as the boat progressed. Facing the brilliant orange of the sun in its downward path, she could barely see the water.

She marked her position and put the engine in Neutral. Setting the self-steering gear, she watched for a moment to determine which direction the boat seemed to drift. She had to be absolutely certain that she could resume her search in the same direction. The boat slid south as its nose pointed west. She ran down the companionway and threw herself into the gear bag under the nav station desk. There, she found an old hat belonging to Mike.

She turned back to the salon and dug through the shelf above the table. Throwing novels and magazines onto the bench, she searched the shelf. Sometime during the trip, Kate remembered seeing sunglasses here. *Where are they?* She found a small nylon bag, and, holding the end of the bag, she shook the contents onto the bench. Sunglasses flew across the salon, landing on the floor below the port bench. She crawled under the bench, grabbed the glasses, and ran up the steps.

Throwing herself onto deck, she was glad she'd stopped for the glasses. She no longer needed to squint against the brilliance of the sun. She made a full turn, calling his name over the sound of the engine. "Mike!" she called. "Mike, answer me!" Still, no sign. She threw the boat into Forward and gave it fuel. Watching her wristwatch, she stopped again to call. No answer.

Then it hit her. When she had stopped for sunglasses, the boat drifted south. Surely the current had done the same with Mike. She needed to account for drift in her search pattern. Kate turned south at the end of the next westerly pattern. She kept an eye on the face of her watch, counting the minutes, scanning the horizon.

At the last minute, she slowed the engine and began a careful spin of the wheel when a reflection off the water caught her attention. She stared hard and realized that she had spotted the glint of sunlight reflecting from Mike's harness. "Mike!" she screamed. "Mike!"

This time, she didn't stop the engine to listen. With her heart full to bursting, Kate brought the boat closer to the body floating in the ocean. Part of her wanted to rev the engine and approach Mike as quickly as possible. But years of water-skiing with the kids and common sense told her otherwise. She needed to approach him slowly and to put the engine in Neutral before she brought the boat too close. As she brought the boat nearer, she watched for motion. *Does he see me? Is he okay?*

"Mike!" she screamed. No response. His jacket *had* inflated, thank the Lord, and rolled him face up on the sea. But he did not move or signal.

Her heart beat furiously. She decided to circle him, determined to approach him from upwind. This approach, she reasoned, might not bring her close enough. Yet from this direction she could be certain the wind would not blow the boat into Mike. She came around his body and turned into the wind. Deliberately, she cut the engine, trying to gauge the distance the boat traveled on its own momentum. It floated a great deal farther than she had expected.

Keeping one eye on Mike, she swung the boat in a large circle. As she did, Kate decided that Mike had to be unconscious, unable to help himself. She would have to rescue him single-handedly. She felt a sudden drop in her stomach. How could she get him on board by herself?

She dropped the engine out of gear, thinking furiously. Never letting her eyes leave his life vest, she tried to think of ways to bring him on deck. One by one, she dismissed her ideas as too difficult or too risky. Then suddenly, she remembered the tether she had cut when he fell overboard. That line, perhaps only fifteen feet long, was still attached to his vest. If she could reach that line and pull it on board . . .

She turned the boat again, moving into a tighter circle around Mike. This time, she cut close to him and put the engine in Neutral as she approached. She scanned the water near his vest and spotted the line trailing off his body away from the boat. She could not reach it from this position. She would have to circle again.

Again she brought the boat around, this time feeling more confident about the distance the *Second Chance* would drift. She needed something to help her grab his line. *What can I use?* Suddenly she remembered the whisker pole that had been tied to the jib. Kate cut the engine and ran to the foredeck. Grabbing the pole, she dropped it into the cockpit and turned the wheel. This time, with her plan firmly set, she circled Mike, put the engine in Neutral, and drifted as close as possible to him. With the pole in both hands she reached out over the water, trying desperately to catch the line attached to his vest. The wind blowing into the bow slowed her down considerably. She could not reach the line. She put the boat in gear and circled him again.

I have to catch it, she told herself. She brought the boat in close and put it in Neutral. Again, she leaned out over the side, the pole poised in her hands. Closer. Closer. The wind pushed the drifting boat toward Mike.

She scooped the pole under the water and caught the line. Inch by miserable inch the soaking wet line slipped over the pole. With a lunge, she tried to wrap the end and stop the line from slipping away. It dropped silently back into the sea. "Oh, God," she said. Desperate, she lunged for his vest, and the pole caught in a ring of the harness. Miraculously, his body lurched as it spun and moved slowly toward the *Second Chance.* Kate dared not let go. She had no option but to hang out over the ocean and pull his body by the tip of the pole. As she brought him nearer, she saw that Mike's eyes were closed, his face swollen, and blood trailed from a wound over the left side of his head.

Her arms ached and her back screamed with pain from leaning so far out over the water. But she couldn't quit now. She might never catch him again. She pulled hard. Walking her hands up the pole, he drifted closer. At last, he was beside the boat, rising and falling with each wave. Kate held on to the pole and leaned out over the deck; she could never reach the line. Instead, she had only one choice. She would have to let go and use the pole to bring the line up to the boat. If she were quick enough, she might grab the line before Mike drifted too far away.

Only one opportunity. "Oh, God, help me."

With one mighty pull, she brought Mike up to the side of the boat. Then, letting go, she dipped the tip of the pole into the ocean, lunging toward the line that dangled uselessly from his side. Caught it.

But the line slid over the pole and away from her as Mike drifted away from the boat. "No! No!" she cried. "Help me, Lord!" She wrapped the pole twice more around the line, and miraculously, the wet line caught on the pole and became taut. She moved her hands quickly up the pole, bringing the line in to the boat. At last, she held the rope in her own two hands. She dropped the pole on deck and fished the line hand over hand until she grasped the end with her fingers.

She had him. Kate knew she did not have the strength to drag him on board herself. *What now?* Quickly, she wrapped the line around a cleat, securing it firmly. Mike floated beside the *Second Chance* like a piece of garbage. Wave after wave crashed over his unresponsive face.

She ran forward to the mast. Picking up the mainsail, she fished through the yards of stiff fabric looking for the hook to the main halyard. If she could somehow fasten the halyard to Mike's line, she could use the winch to lift his body on board. Unhooking the sail, she pulled the line until she brought the clip to the rope holding Mike.

Without unfastening the rope, Kate connected the loose end of Mike's line to the halyard, using more knots than any sailor could ever imagine.

Cautiously, she let the line off the cleat. Watching carefully, she saw that her jumble of knots held. She ran forward again, this time wrapping the winch with the halyard. Stuffing the winch handle into the winch, she began hoisting the line. Slowly, slowly she felt the tension increase. It worked.

She turned the handle deliberately, always with her eyes on the knots holding Mike's lifeline to the halyard. The knots tightened and strained, but continued to hold as slack came out of the line. Before long she felt the weight of Mike's body hanging from the halyard.

Kate was sweating now, both from hard work and complete terror. The tension in the winch told her she had cleared the water's surface. Now she had only to get him high enough to clear the deck lines. Then, thank the Lord, she could swing him onto the deck.

She turned the handle, pushing and pulling with all of her strength, always watching the knots and the line. Though it strained and the knots tightened, the line did not give way. She panted with the effort of turning the winch. And then she saw him. Coming up to the level of the deck, still dripping seawater, his entire body hung arched backward, suspended by the metal ring coming from the center of his chest. His arms and legs dangled limply from his body, his back bent as though he had become some circus contortionist. For one horrible minute, Kate saw the angle of his neck and wondered if he had broken it. After ten minutes of further effort, she brought him up to the safety lines. Cleating the halyard so it wouldn't move, she ran to his limp body.

"Mike," she said, tears again clouding into her vision. "Oh, Mike." She reached out over the lines and pulled him onto his side, effectively dragging him clear. He hung suspended over the deck, and for a moment, she pulled down, trying to lower him. Then she remembered the cleat and went over to let the rope down slowly, lowering him onto the deck.

Again she cleated the line and ran back to his body. Bending over him, she put her ear to his mouth and heard him breathe. "Oh, Jesus, thank you," she whispered. She gave his body a quick inspection, deciding that the boom had injured only his head. She could see no other bruises or cuts.

She stood and unzipped the dodger. She needed to get Mike inside, out of the wind and water. Certainly this much time in the ocean had robbed his body of the heat he needed to survive. She squatted on the deck above his head and tucked her arms under his shoulders. With great effort she inched his head and shoulders nearer the cockpit. Then, repeating the effort, she dragged his legs sideways. When she had him at the edge of the cockpit, she squatted on the bench and dragged him down into the cockpit. He moaned as she let go of his head. "I'm sorry, Mike," she said, aware of the pain he must feel. She stood quickly and lugged his legs over the edge onto the bench. At last, she had him safely on board.

But Mike was in too much trouble for her to rest. She lowered her ear to his face, listening carefully. Air, quiet and warm, flowed softly from his nose. "Thank you, Jesus," she said again, blinking back more tears. She sniffed, and rubbed her nose with the back of her hand. Then she rearranged his body, trying to make him comfortable on the narrow bench. Keeping her eyes on Mike, she reached down to the key and switched off the engine. If she had to drive the boat all the way to Hilo, she needed all the fuel she could spare.

She ran down the companionway, quickly grabbing blankets, towels, and dry clothes. These things she dragged up the narrow passage, throwing them onto the deck while she knelt beside his unconscious body. She threw towels over him, drying his exposed skin. Then she began to undress him carefully. But she could not remove his clothes without rolling him off the bench.

Again, she ran down to the cockpit. Searching through the galley drawers, she grabbed kitchen shears and returned to cut the life vest and clothes from his body. Carefully, she slid the fabric out from under him. With his clothes off, she tenderly dried his skin. He had begun to shiver, and Kate felt desperate to get him into warm clothes and blankets.

Though she did not know how or why, Kate felt confident that his only real injury was to his head. Still, she tried not to move him unnecessarily.

It looked as though Mike had sustained a serious injury to his skull. The skin, broken at the point of contact, was stretched over a lump just above his ear. In the time he had been out of the water, his hair had matted with blood and a bruise had begun to develop behind his ear. Kate applied pressure to the wound on his scalp and moved closer to look at the rest of his face. A tiny trickle of clear fluid drained from his nose. Though she brushed the fluid away with the towel, it reappeared immediately.

Mike was in grave danger, and Kate needed help.

Forty

KATE TORE OPEN a sleeping bag and covered Mike, tucking the corners carefully under his chin and enfolding his arms and legs. His violent shivering continued, though he had not yet opened his eyes or responded to her voice. Under the opposite cockpit bench, she found a length of rope that she tied to a cleat outside the cockpit, tucked under the cover, and ran through the latch below Mike. Her own fear made her tremble, and with shaking hands she took the line back outside to a separate cleat. Tying it as tightly as she could, she formed a rough version of a seabed, hoping to prevent Mike from falling off the bench with the motion of the boat. Satisfied that he would stay put, she stood up to zip the dodger covers closed. The wind inside the cockpit immediately quieted. At least Mike would be warmer.

Though she hated to leave him, her only hope was in the nav station radio. The salon seemed miles away from Mike, and Kate hated to leave him alone. Gently she touched his face, brushing wet hair from his forehead. "I'm going for help, Mike. Hang on," she said. "Please, Father, help him hang on."

Below, she pulled out the seat at the navigation desk and began scanning the dials and screens in front of her. This technology sent a moment of panic through her. What did she remember? Who would hear her if she called for help? She turned the On switch beside the radio microphone and hoped that it would select the same frequency Mike had monitored throughout their trip.

Squeezing the Talk button with her thumb, she brought the microphone to her mouth and spoke. "Mayday, Mayday," she said. She let go of the Talk button and listened to loud static. No answer.

"Mayday, Mayday," she said again. "This is the *Second Chance.*"

Still no answer. Loud squealing static came from the speaker on the radio face. She turned down the Squelch button. "Mayday," she said, "this is the *Second Chance.*" Still holding the microphone, she leaned her arms on the desk and put her head down, crying.

"*Second Chance*, this is U.S. Coast Guard, Com Station, Honolulu, go ahead."

Kate's head came up, and she laughed, brushing away tears. She turned up the volume. Now that she had someone, she didn't know what to say or how to say it. "Oh, God, I'm so glad."

"*Second Chance*, please state the nature of your emergency. Over."

Kate fought to stay calm. "My husband. He was thrown off the boat. I've got him back on board, but he's hurt."

"*Second Chance*, can you tell me how serious the injuries are?"

"No. I don't know."

"Is your husband conscious?"

"No."

"*Second Chance*, what kind of vessel are you broadcasting from?"

"A Liberty Cutter. Forty-five feet."

"What is the condition of the boat?"

"The boat?" Why did this guy want to know about the boat when Mike was injured? Kate stifled an urge to yell at this guy.

"Is the boat in any immediate danger of sinking?"

"No." She felt shame at her anger. "We're fine."

"Are you under sail?"

"No. The sails are down. Please, my husband is injured."

"All right, *Second Chance*, I copy that. You have an injured man on board. *Second Chance*, where are you expected to make landfall? Over."

"Hilo. We were sailing to Hilo, Hawaii." Kate began to cry again.

"All right. *Second Chance*, I'm going to get a flight surgeon on the radio. He's going to ask you some questions. It will take a minute to patch him through. Can you stand by the radio?"

"Yes. I'm here." Kate let go of the button on the microphone and realized that her hands hurt from clutching the microphone so tightly. Slowly, deliberately, she stretched the fingers of her right hand, willing herself to breathe deeply. She tried to relax her shoulders. She rolled her head and rubbed her neck.

"*Second Chance*, this is Com Station, Honolulu. I have a flight surgeon on the line. He'd like to ask you a couple of questions. Go ahead, sir."

"*Second Chance*, this is Dr. Chuck Burns, Honolulu. Can you hear me?"

"Yes, I hear you." Kate hesitated, unsure of radio protocol. "Over," she added.

"*Second Chance*, I'm going to ask some questions. They are very important. Try to take the time to answer as carefully as you can. Over."

"All right."

"First, who am I talking to?"

"Kate, Kate Langston."

"And your husband is injured? What is his name?"

Again, irritation threatened to take over Kate's emotions. Certainly this guy wouldn't ask for her insurance policy numbers. "Mike. His name is Mike."

"Good. Where is Mike right now?"

"He's on the cockpit bench."

"Is he awake?"

"No, I told you. I told the operator. He isn't awake." Kate's voice rose in anger and frustration. "He's out. Cold. If he weren't unconscious, I wouldn't be on this stupid radio."

"Calm down, Kate. I'm not there. I can't see your husband. I have to make sure I understand your situation in order to help you. I'm going to ask you to go to him and check a couple of things for me. You are going to have to be my eyes. All right?"

"Okay. What do I do?"

"I need you to go to your husband and check his breathing. Is he breathing easily, normally? Then I need to know how his heart is doing. You can lay your head on his chest or check his pulse. Try to count the number of beats you hear in one minute. Then I want you to try to speak to him. See if he rouses to your voice at all. Pinch his hand or his arm. Then pinch his legs. Watch to see what happens. Do that, Kate, and then come right back to the radio. I'll be right here waiting. Do you understand? Over."

Kate dropped the microphone onto the desk and ran up the stairs. When she stepped into the cockpit area, she noticed that Mike's violent shivering continued. She turned her head and brought her ear down above his mouth to listen to his breathing. It seemed easy, regular.

She pushed aside the blankets and put her ear over his chest. Bringing her hand up to her face, she glanced at her watch and began counting. Seventy-nine beats in sixty seconds. *Now, what else? Oh yes.*

"Mike. Wake up, Mike. You've been asleep long enough. Time to get up." She tugged at his shoulder. Nothing. She reached down into the blanket and pinched his forearm. Hard. He pulled his hand away.

"Thank you, God."

She reached down to his legs and pinched his thigh as hard as she could. He squirmed. All right. He could feel his arm and leg. So far, so good.

"I'm going back down, Mike. Don't move." Even as she said it, she wondered why. He couldn't hear her voice. Mike was lost in his own black world. She nearly fell down the stairs to the cabin.

"Dr. Burns. This is *Second Chance.*" Kate let go of the button and waited. Static filled the speaker for what seemed like an eternity.

"*Second Chance.* Go ahead, Kate."

"He's shivering, Doctor. About to shiver himself onto the floor. His breathing seems fine. His heartbeat is seventy-nine. He pulled away when I pinched him, but he doesn't answer me."

"Kate, can you tell me exactly what happened?"

"Yes. He was hit in the head by the boom and thrown into the water."

"How long was he in the water?"

"I'm not certain. About forty minutes, I think."

"All right, Kate. I need one more piece of information. I want you to run back to your husband and lift each eyelid. Look into his pupils. Those are the black centers of his eyes. I want to know how they look. Are they the same? Does he respond to the light coming into his eyes?"

"Okay. I'll be back. Wait." She ran up the steps and bent over Mike. Lifting his lids did not seem to bother him. He didn't flinch or pull away. The pupils of his eyes looked the same to her. For a fleeting moment, she thought of how much she loved those beautiful dark eyes. "Wake up," she whispered, wishing again that he would hear her. He did not.

She ran back to the radio and reported her findings. The doctor sounded disappointed—at least it seemed that way from what she could hear in his tone of voice above the static. "I'm going to scramble an Air Force rescue helicopter. I need you to talk to the Com Station operator, Kate. He's going to have you tell us where you are. Then I'll come back on and help you take care of your husband."

Tears came unchecked. She sobbed her relief. Only two words came to her mind. "Thank you," she wept. "Oh, thank you."

"*Second Chance*, this is Coast Guard Com Station, Honolulu. Over."

"I'm here."

"Kate, I've been listening in. I know your husband is in very serious condition. I need you to tell me where you are."

"How can I tell you that if I don't know?"

"Does your boat have any kind of navigational equipment on board?"

"Yes."

"Have you used it before?"

"No." Kate began to cry. This conversation yanked her emotions up and down like a sewing machine needle. Would Mike die because she was navigationally impaired?

"Stay calm, Kate. We can talk you through it."

She gasped a breath of air and held it, forcing herself to concentrate. "Okay, tell me what to do." She wiped the tears from her face.

"Do you have a GPS?"

"A GPS?"

"Global Positioning System. Some boats have a Loran-C. Others have GPS."

"I think we have a handheld unit in the cockpit."

"Good. Have you used it?"

"No. Never."

"Okay, Kate. We're going to talk our way through using the GPS. It isn't hard, but it takes time. So be patient. Can you do that?"

"I can."

"The handheld won't work inside the boat. You'll have to go up to the cockpit, get it, and then stand somewhere out from underneath the cockpit cover. Be sure to tie on to your own lifeline. Then put up the antenna and turn it on. You should get a menu page. Figure out how to move through the menu to an 'acquire position' page. There might be a cursor, or it might just highlight the text. Do you understand so far?"

How could she possibly understand? All she had ever done was hand the instrument to Mike. Though she'd watched him operate it, she'd never even turned it on by herself. "I'll try."

"Good. Once you get to the acquire position page, the unit will do the work for you. But it takes time. I'm going to stand by while you go work on that. It's the most important thing you can do to help us. If we know exactly where you are, we can come right to you. We'll get your husband to the hospital more quickly."

Without responding, Kate dropped the microphone and ran up the stairs. As she bolted into the cockpit, she heard the radio cord banging against the nav desk. She looked for the little instrument. The GPS was not on the dash, as she remembered. She scrambled through the bench opposite Mike. Not there. She couldn't move Mike. Maybe it was downstairs. She ran down and rummaged through Mike's equipment bag.

There! The size of a small cellular phone, it had hidden itself under the zippered pouch at the bottom of the bag. Clutching it tightly in the fingers of one hand, she ran back up to the cockpit, clipped on, and stepped out onto the rear deck.

The wind blew Kate's hair into her face. She spit it out of her mouth. Panting, Kate twisted the antenna into the upright position. She found a tiny button labeled with the drawing of a light bulb. The On button? She pushed it and waited while the welcome screen filled in. Her heart pounded as she tried in vain to be patient. She glanced at Mike. His left arm had fallen off the bench and now swung freely with the motion of the boat. Other than that, he looked no different than he had the first moment she'd lugged him into the cockpit.

When she glanced back at the screen, it had gone blank. She hit the On switch again, saw the welcome screen and watched it go blank. Batteries. Maybe it needed new batteries. She ran back down the stairs and grabbed Mike's gear bag. Shaking it upside down over the nearest bench, she watched as tools and gadgets fell onto the bunk, rolling with the waves. A cellophane-wrapped package of AA batteries fell onto the bench, and she reached for it greedily. As she ran up the stairs, she ripped open the package with her teeth.

Back on the rear deck of the boat, she fiddled with the case, at last finding the battery cover. She dropped the spent batteries onto the teak, letting them roll into the ocean. She stuffed four new batteries into the case and closed the cover. She hit the On switch again. Nothing. Had she installed the batteries correctly? She repeated the steps, this time turning the batteries in the opposite direction.

She hit the switch and waited. The welcome screen returned. This time, a globe rotated in the corner of the screen. *Stupid globe,* she thought. *No wonder the batteries were dead.* The screen switched automatically to a picture of concentric circles, with numbers placed in various positions on the screen. This had to be the satellite page. *Help me, God. Help me work this thing.*

Acquiring. The word flashed. That was it! Hurry, hurry. She tried to keep her breathing steady. Tried to keep her hands from shaking. A bar formed above one of the numbers on the side of the screen. She waited. Eventually, another bar formed. Black filled in the bar-shaped rectangles. *Acquiring signal strength,* the words on the screen read. This is what the operator had described. Finally, the screen switched again to a dial, indicating her present direction and speed. And there, at the bottom of the tiny screen, were the exact details she needed.

She ran back down to the radio.

"Coast Guard Com Station, Honolulu, this is *Second Chance.* I have our position."

"Go ahead, *Second Chance.*"

She read the numbers as they appeared in the center of the screen.

"Okay, *Second Chance,* I'm going to patch Dr. Burns in to you and scramble an Air Force rescue helicopter. You're out of range for our birds. When I have information as to our estimated arrival, I'll let you know. Stand by, *Second Chance.*"

"Thank you, God," Kate whispered. "Thank you."

"*Second Chance,* this is Dr. Burns, the flight surgeon. How is our patient doing? Over."

"The same."

"All right, then I'm going to help you help the patient. Are you with me?"

"Yes, I think so."

"Okay, first, let's get some heat into him. Have you removed his wet clothes and dried him?"

"Yes."

"And wrapped him in blankets?"

"Yes."

"All right, Kate. Do you have a microwave on board?"

"Yes, a tiny one."

"Then I want you to take a towel, soak it in water, and heat it in the microwave. Got that?"

"Heat a towel. Yes."

"Then I want you to put it in a garbage bag and put it inside your husband's blankets, close to his skin. When you're done with that, I want you to look carefully at his head and give me a report."

"Right. It'll be a few minutes." Kate put the microphone down and went to work. She needed to help warm Mike. If there were more people on board, she could get into the blankets with him. That was the best treatment for hypothermia. But she couldn't do that and manage the rescue operation too. She heated a bath towel, put it in a garbage bag, and ran back up the stairs.

"Mike," she said, "Mike, I'm putting a heating pad in your sleeping bag." Though she spoke to him, she did not expect him to respond. She lifted the edge of the sleeping bag and slid the bag down over his stomach. She checked the heat, making certain it wouldn't burn him. Then, tucking him in, she turned her attention to his head.

Mike had a large cut above his left ear. Underneath the cut, she felt a bump—though not the kind of goose egg she remembered from when her children were young. His was a tight, firm knot just above his ear. Brushing his hair away, she took a second towel and dabbed at the cut. The bleeding had essentially stopped. For this she was grateful, but as she cleaned the area around the cut, something else caught her attention. She dabbed at the skin of his ear-lobe and brought the towel into the light. The towel revealed a stain of fresh blood. She turned the cloth, looking for a clean section and pressed it carefully on the wound. Lifting the towel, she inspected it. No blood.

She returned the cloth to Mike's ear and repeated the procedure. This time, fresh blood stained the white terry cloth. Mike had blood coming from his ear. Brushing his hair away for a closer inspection, Kate found the bruise. Below and behind his ear, an angry black spot had started to grow. Frightened, she ran back to the radio.

"*Second Chance*, it's clear your husband has taken a severe blow to the head. He may also have damaged his cervical spine. I want you to try to stabilize his neck."

"How?" Kate had moved from hysteria to an almost dreamlike obedience to the unknown doctor on the radio. "How can I keep him from moving?"

"Try this. Find some tape or rope and a bath or hand towel. Fold the towel into a five-inch strip and slip the towel under the space between his head and the bench. Then roll it around his neck and tape it in place as tightly as you can. Will you do that? I'll stand by."

Kate went back up the stairs with duct tape in one hand and a towel in the other. Folding the towel, she slid it behind Mike's neck. She spoke reassuringly in soft low tones as she touched him and then tore the duct tape with her teeth. Satisfied that he couldn't move his neck, she started down the stairs.

She heard a noise behind her. Moaning. "Mike." She dropped to her knees beside him. He opened his eyes, and a look of fear and surprise came over his face. He moaned again, this time in pain.

"Mike, you've hurt your head. You mustn't move." She bent over him, staring into his frightened, confused eyes. But instead of calming, Mike seemed to grow more agitated. He tried to move, reaching to grab the sleeping bag and throw it off. A stab of pain twisted his features and his eyes closed hard, his brows tight.

"Don't move," Kate pled. "Please, Mike, don't try to move."

His eyes opened again, and she saw confusion. "I can't hear you," he shouted at her. "I can't hear."

Torn, Kate wondered what to do. She needed to stay nearby in order to keep him from moving. But she needed to get to the radio as well. Should she dig out some pain medication? Impulsively, she pushed his shoulders onto the bench with both hands. Then, lowering her face to his, she kissed him tenderly. She bent over his right ear and spoke in clear, gentle tones. "Don't move, sweetie. Please don't move."

She waited beside him until the muscles in his face relaxed. His eyes closed, and he seemed to rest. She went below, anxious for the latest news.

"*Second Chance*, this is Com Station, Honolulu," the primary operator said. "I have a private vessel in your area that is going to divert from their course and come to your aid. They can help you with your vessel. I suggest you heave to and wait for them to arrive. We're scrambling the rescue team. We have a storm bearing down on you from the southeast. However, we should be able to get to you before the weather hits. Should be there inside of two hours. Do you copy?"

"This is *Second Chance*. I copy."

Another voice came over the speaker. "*Second Chance*, this is Dr. Burns. How is our patient?"

"He woke up. But he says he can't hear. He's wild, Doctor. Confused."

"Not a surprise after a bad blow to the head. Go on up and keep him quiet. We'll get help to you as quickly as possible. Don't let him move. If you need help, I'll be monitoring this channel. Call me."

"Doctor, he seems to be in horrible pain. Can I give him something?"

"No. I repeat. No pain meds. We don't want him to have anything that might alter our ability to diagnose his injuries. Do you copy? This is very important."

"All right, Doctor. This is *Second Chance*, out." Kate turned up the radio volume. She wanted to be able to hear the radio from the cockpit. Then she went up the stairs to wait with Mike.

Kneeling beside him, she moved as close as she dared and wrapped one arm over his chest. Lowering her face, she began to pray. In this position, Kate waited through the longest two hours of her life.

Forty-One

"I'M SO DIZZY," Mike moaned, catching Kate's attention. His eyes flickered open, and Kate watched his brown eyes try to focus. For a moment it seemed like he was watching a bird flying across his field of vision, over and over, from the same direction. "I'm going to be sick," he said.

"It's your ear, Mike," Kate said, raising her voice and leaning close. "Something is wrong with your ear. It's bleeding. I think that's why you're so dizzy."

"I can't hear you," he shouted, rolling toward her.

"Stop! Mike, the doctor said you shouldn't move." She threw one arm across his chest and pushed his forehead down with her other palm. Kate watched the muscles of his face slacken as his lids closed. Clearly, Mike hadn't lost his hearing completely. He heard her, responded to her. But he had been injured. Badly injured. And Mike was afraid.

"It's better with my eyes closed."

"Good. Try to relax." She spoke in low soothing tones, like a mother to a frightened child. "Help is on the way, Mike. Just cooperate until then. Please." Though her words seemed to comfort Mike, they did not calm Kate's frantically beating heart. Then she heard the words again. *Trust me.* For a moment, she nearly laughed out loud. Where else could she turn? "I do trust you, Lord," she said.

The wind seemed stronger now, and the boat rocked wildly on rising waves. Kate turned on her knees to catch a glimpse of the wind speed indicator. Without any pride in her nautical ability, Kate realized that she was correct. The wind had picked up, blowing steadily at fifteen knots; some gusts topped eighteen.

Keeping one hand on Mike, she reached through the cockpit cover and tightened the rope holding him in place. "Everything will be fine, Mike. I'm just going to turn the boat into the wind and lash the wheel." With the rope taut, she leaned over his good ear. "Promise me you won't try to move."

He gave an almost imperceptible nod of his chin, and she kissed his cheek in response. "Good. I'll be right here." She stood, moving to the wheel. Without sails, *Second Chance* had no momentum to accomplish a turn. She started the engine and swung the bow away from Mike, taking several waves on the starboard in the process. Eventually, side to side rocking gave way to a smoother bucking motion, not unlike riding a playground teeter-totter.

She turned off the motor and set the steering gear. After another glance at the wind indicator, Kate returned to Mike's side. Where was the Coast Guard, she wondered? She checked her watch. Only forty minutes had passed from their last radio transmission.

"Thirsty," Mike whispered. "So thirsty."

Kate wondered if she should give him water. He had been in the ocean a long time; perhaps he had swallowed a great deal of seawater. "I don't know if I should let you drink anything," she said.

"Please. Water."

"Stay still," she instructed him. "I'll get some." How could she give him water without moving his head or neck? Should she even allow it? Should she radio for permission? She decided against the radio and started down the companionway stairs, remembering a roll of plastic tubing Dave had included in their tools. When Mike fixed the through-hull she'd seen it in his tool bucket. Where was the bucket now?

She found it against the engine room wall. Taking the tubing to the galley, she used a steak knife to cut a six-inch length. Then she fished in the cupboards until she found a tiny plastic juice glass. Four ounces. Certainly that much water couldn't hurt Mike. She filled the glass and took it upstairs.

With the tube between her thumb and index finger, she held the glass to his mouth. Even pinching his lips around the makeshift straw seemed to cause Mike pain. Grimacing, he drank greedily.

"Better," he said. It seemed to be all he could manage, for his expression relaxed again and he closed his eyes.

"*Second Chance*, this is Com Station, Honolulu."

Kate heard the voice coming from the nav station radio. Had something gone wrong? Couldn't they get to her? She glanced at the wind speed. The wind had increased another two knots. "Mike, I have to go down to the radio," she said, holding her palm gently against his cheek.

"This is *Second Chance*."

"I have a vessel on channel 29. The skipper of the *Wind Runner* reports that he is in your area. If you switch to channel 29, you can speak with him directly."

"Thank you, Coast Guard," Kate answered. "I'm switching to 29." She reached for the radio dial and moved off the emergency channel. "This is *Second Chance*."

After a lengthy pause, she repeated the call again.

"*Second Chance*, this is *Wind Runner*," a cheerful voice greeted her. "We are about one and a half hours north and east of you. We have changed direction and are heading your way. We'll be there as soon as possible to render assistance. Can you describe your vessel?"

"Yes, *Second Chance* has a white hull, aluminum mast. She's a forty-five-foot cutter, center cockpit. Sails down. Green trim. Do you have our position?"

"That's affirmative, *Second Chance*. We've been monitoring your emergency transmissions. We understand you need assistance to bring your vessel to port."

"Yes. My husband will be airlifted to the hospital. I can't abandon the boat."

"We copy that. One of our crew will captain your vessel into Hilo. We'll accompany you to port. Do you copy?"

"Oh, thank you," Kate blinked back tears. Then, remembering her protocol, she repeated, "I copy. Thank you."

"We'll stand by on this channel until we make contact visually. Do you have VHF?"

"Yes, *Wind Runner*," Kate acknowledged. "I have VHF."

"When we get closer, I'll hail you on VHF channel eight. At that point, we'll make plans to come alongside. Do you copy?"

"I copy that, *Wind Runner*, VHF channel eight." Kate let go of the Talk button. Then remembering protocol, she brought the microphone back to her mouth. "Over," she said.

"This is _Wind Runner_, over and out."

"_Second Chance. Out._" _Well, if nothing else, I'll know how to use a radio_, she thought. She turned her VHF on and tuned it to channel eight.

Anxious to check on Mike, she returned to his side in the cockpit. He had pulled the sleeping bag up over his chest, his brow furrowed in pain. "What is it?" she asked. "What hurts?"

"A headache."

"Are you still cold?" She reached under the sleeping bag to feel the towel. It had cooled since she placed it there, and she pulled it out. "I'm going to heat this again." Downstairs, she stuffed the towel into the microwave and dialed the timer. She thought about the flesh wound over Mike's left ear and decided to spend her time doing what she could to stabilize the wound. She could clean it; perhaps she could even butterfly the edges together. She dragged the emergency medical pack out into the salon. Unzipping the two halves, she found the instruction book and the laceration package. Grabbing the warm towel and the medical supplies, she took the stairs two at a time.

Upstairs, Mike continued to moan. "Hurts."

"I know, honey," she said, kneeling on the floorboards of the cockpit. "I'm going to put more warmth on your belly." She reached inside his sleeping bag and tucked the towel in place. "Now, Mike, I'm going to work on this wound."

"What?" he shouted.

"Please relax, Mike." She brushed his hair away from his face. "I'm going to work on your head." She spoke louder, her face only inches from his. "I just hope your skull is as hard as I've always thought it was," she muttered to herself.

His head is hard. But his heart is soft.

"I know, Lord."

How is your heart, Kate?

Refusing to answer, yet aware of the painful truth, Kate brushed away tears. She opened the zipper on the laceration package and slipped on a pair of sterile gloves. Easily two sizes too big for her hands, she struggled with the extra latex on the ends of her fingers. Using the scissors, she began cutting away the hair around Mike's wound. Though she tried to be careful, the pitching motion of the boat drove the tip of her scissors against the tender wound. "Ouch," Mike cried, trying to move away.

"Be still, Mike," she urged. "I have to get your hair out of the way so the bandage will stick."

"No." He tried to slide his whole body down the bench away from Kate and the scissors. "Mike, I'm trying to help," she said. "Stay still. I won't hurt you." She held his jaw firmly between the fingers of her left hand. "It will be better if you cooperate."

Kate, will you cooperate?

Caught off guard, Kate sat stock-still on the floor of the rocking boat. For one unmistakable moment, she saw her own hardhearted resistance to Mike. She saw her own unwillingness to trust God's work in his heart. She saw herself squirming away from the painful, but healing, work of the Lord in her life.

"Forgive me," she said, simply. "I was running, Lord. I didn't believe you could heal me." Tears began again. This time, though, they were of sweet relief.

After cleaning Mike's wound as well as she could, Kate went back down to the nav station. She listened again for any sign of communication from the Coast Guard. Nothing yet. A peculiar buzz caught her attention, and for a moment, she thought the microwave was on. But the sound grew louder, and Kate wondered if she heard an airplane. She ran up the stairs.

As she stepped outside, a large plane swept low over the boat. She crawled out of the dodger, clipped her harness to the lifeline, and hurried to the bow. Waving both arms high over her head, she watched as the plane turned to trace a low circle around the *Second Chance*. Dipping one wing and then another, it seemed to Kate that the plane waved back. She rushed down to the radio.

"*Second Chance*, this is Coast Guard pilot Captain Hanson. Do you copy?"

"I do," Kate answered, hearing relief in her own voice. "I mean, I copy," she corrected herself. "Where is the helicopter?"

"Right behind me," a kind but professional voice answered. "I'm flying cover for the rescue team. You *were* close enough for the Coast Guard to come. Good work on the coordinates. Accounting for wind speed and direction, you're right where you told us."

"Good." Kate heaved a sigh of relief. "What do I do now?"

"Hang tight, *Second Chance*," he answered. "When the helo gets here, we'll talk you through every part of the rescue."

The steady *whumpa-whumpa* of rotor blades began before Kate put the microphone down on the nav station desk. At last, they'd arrived. She ran up the steps again, feeling an ache beginning in the muscles of her upper legs. She hadn't done this much stair climbing in years. "They're here, Mike. Do you hear them?"

Again she stepped out of the dodger and waved. The helicopter, a huge white bird with the red Coast Guard stripe and insignia near the tail, hung low behind the stern. The sound of the helicopter was deafening. The rotors blew the sea in wide concentric circles beneath the body of the craft. Kate watched as a man appeared in the side door, waving to her. She waved back. Embarrassed, she realized that they wanted to speak via the radio. Feeling stupid, she ran down to the nav station where the helo hailed her. "*Second Chance*, this is Coast Guard vessel 1435. Do you copy?"

"I copy," Kate answered.

"Good," the helicopter pilot answered. "The seas are rough, and the wind is picking up. We need to get your husband on board as soon as possible. I can't hold my position for long. We need your help."

"What do I do?"

"We're going to try to lower a rescue swimmer to the afterdeck of your sailboat. He'll help you load your husband onto the litter, and our crew mechanic will hoist him into the chopper. Then we'll lift our crewman back on board. We need you to keep the boat as steady as possible into the wind," he finished. "It won't be easy to hit the deck of a sailboat in this weather. We can handle up and down, but can you keep her from moving side to side?"

"I think so."

"All right. Because of the height of your mast, we'll have to drop from pretty high up. And we need to do this in less than thirty minutes. That's all the time we have. Do you copy?"

"I copy."

"So now, if you'll put the boat into the wind, we'll get started."

Kate went upstairs and started the motor of the *Second Chance*. Putting the engine into its lowest gear, she pointed the bow directly into the wind. The boat labored against the waves, but made no progress against the sea. Exactly as she had been instructed.

Glancing over her shoulder, she watched the helicopter move to a position just off the afterdeck of the boat. Slowly, the chopper rose until it seemed to hover over the mast itself. She longed to watch, but could not see through the roof of the dodger. Mike seemed to be aware of the helicopter, though his face had screwed itself into a tight expression of pain. She would have spoken to him, but she knew he wouldn't hear her over the helicopter's roar. Determined to resist watching the deck behind her, she concentrated instead on the gruesome seas before her. Fighting the bucking motion and the cresting waves, she stole glances behind the boat.

After several excruciatingly long minutes, Kate caught a glimpse of black-flippered feet attached to the legs of a red survival suit touching down on the boat deck. The deck rose suddenly on a large wave and the legs of the rescue swimmer buckled as he tried to stand. Tossed onto his seat, he pulled the line toward him as if to give himself slack. But before he could detach himself, the deck fell away again, and he was jerked roughly into the air. This time, his hands were quicker than the sea, and he managed to disconnect the clip of his harness from the line attached to the helicopter dropping onto the deck. The chopper hovered near the bow of the boat now, the wind forcing the chopper to move forward. The seaman and his line had been blown back over the stern where he could safely avoid both mast and stays. As soon as he stood safely on the stern, he sat and removed his flippers. Kate set the self-steering and turned off the motor.

"Petty Officer Rowan," he said, stepping down to the cockpit. He had dropped his diving mask to his neck, and his dark eyes sparkled with kindness.

"Thank the Lord you've come," Kate said, holding both hands over her mouth. Tears of relief and gratitude spilled down her cheeks. "I was so afraid." Suddenly her knees buckled, and she landed on the bench opposite Mike.

Rowan dropped his flippers onto the rear bench and moved to Mike. Crouching on the deck beside him, he introduced himself. Mike did not respond. "What is your husband's name?"

"Mike," Kate answered. "Mike Langston. He seems to have a hard time hearing."

Rowan spoke to Mike again. "Can you open your eyes for me, sir?" he asked loudly.

Mike's lids flitted open. The pupils struggled to focus. Rowan examined his skull, checked his pulse, and unfastened the towel Kate had wrapped around Mike's neck. Running his fingers along Mike's spine, he smiled. "Nothing seems out of place. But I've brought a collar just in case." Next he made a careful visual exam of Mike's trunk and limbs. "What hurts, Mike?" he asked.

"My head," Mike whispered. "I have a headache over my ear. And I'm so dizzy."

From the side of his harness, Rowan removed a flesh-colored splint fastened by black Velcro. Gently, he slid the back half under Mike's neck. Then he put the top half under Mike's chin and strapped it in place. From his harness, he touched the Talk button of a built-in radio, speaking to the chopper hovering behind the boat. "I think we can lift him out of here now."

"How will you get him out?" Kate had moved to the rear bench, her left hand resting on Mike's ankle.

"The chopper will drop a Stokes litter. I'll need you to keep the boat steady, just like you did when I came on board. Can you manage?"

"Yes, I think so."

"Start the engines, then."

He moved back to the stern of the *Second Chance,* and the entire procedure was repeated again. This time, though, Kate had the added security of having a rescuer on board. Certainly he would save Mike. The basket, a wire contraption resembling nothing more than a bread tray, seemed for a moment to catch in something above the deck. Though she didn't feel it hit the rigging, Kate heard the chopper roar up and forward and then move to the starboard side of the boat. She prayed, "Lord, help them get that thing on deck."

Once again, the helicopter settled over the boat, and she heard the litter land heavily on the stern. Before she finished setting the self-steering gear, Rowan dragged the litter toward the cockpit, sliding it beside the bench where Mike lay grimacing.

Tucking it against the outside rail, he began unzipping the sides of the dodger, rolling them out of the way. Kate helped by fastening the walls in place with snaps. Before long, sea spray blown up by the helicopter peppered the air in the cockpit.

"Normally, I could put him in the litter myself," Rowan said, squatting and stepping inside. "But I don't know how stable his spine is. Could you help me?"

Kate nodded and instinctively squatted on the bench at Mike's feet. Fear made her feel strong enough to throw him over her shoulders and climb the mast. It would be no problem to hoist him out of the cockpit and onto the deck. She put her hands on his ankles.

"Okay, we'll lift on three. Ready, one, two, and . . ." With a huff, they lifted Mike, Rowan keeping his spine as straight as possible under the cramped conditions. Once in the litter, Rowan buckled the belt near his waist and fastened the Velcro straps that held him safely inside. "All right. In the litter, he's easier to move. Let's drag him to the aft deck."

"Do you need me to steer into the wind?"

"Not this time. We can drop a line without too much trouble."

Together, they managed to drag the wire basket back to the rear of the boat where Rowan signaled for the helicopter to drop the line. This time, Kate watched as the line came down from the chopper. As she reached out to grab the clip, Rowan pushed her aside. "Let it drop to the deck!" he shouted over the engine noise.

Surprised, she jumped back.

"Electricity. Static generated by the rotors. We have to let it hit the deck to ground it." Rowan smiled. "Don't want to electrocute you." The clip hit the deck hard and line continued to drop, giving them slack. "All right, now let's hoist him out of here." Kate watched as Rowan clipped the line to the basket holding Mike.

He stood, glancing up at the chopper. With his arms, he signaled the chopper to pull the basket. The line began to move upward. Ever so slowly, the slack came out until the harness on the basket itself tightened. With the basket only inches from the deck of the bucking ship, the chopper changed direction, pulling the basket away from the mast and rigging. Holding her breath, Kate watched as the litter swung out behind the chopper. About fifty feet off the stern of *Second Chance*, the chopper hovered, and the basket rose slowly up to the front hatch door. At last, Mike disappeared inside, and Kate could breathe again. With a painful twist in her heart, she realized she hadn't said good-bye.

By radio, Rowan confirmed that the patient was safely on board.

"Where are you taking him?" Kate asked.

"To Barbour's Point. Then he'll travel by ambulance to Hono-lulu. Unless the flight surgeon changes our orders."

"How will I know?"

"You can contact us by radio or telephone. I understand there is a vessel assist on the way." She nodded, blinking back tears. He smiled. "You should be safely in Hilo by dawn the day after tomor-row. From there, you can fly to Oahu and drive to the hospital."

By this time, the helicopter had returned to hover just above the mast, dropping a line to the deck. Rowan had retrieved his flippers and placed his mask on his face. Kate watched as he clipped his harness onto the line and signaled the crewman above him to begin the lift. Again, the bird moved away as soon as he cleared the deck.

In the midst of heavy seas, blowing water, and blustering wind, Kate stood alone on the deck of the *Second Chance* watching Seaman Rowan ascend up to the hovering helicopter. As he was pulled in-side, the mechanic operating the winch managed a wave. Kate waved back, and the side door closed.

Kate watched as the white bird pulled up into the sky and started away. The plane, which had maintained a steady circle around the boat through the entire ordeal, tipped its wings and followed behind. Kate stood there watching until the last bit of plane disappeared from view. In that moment, the most intense loneliness Kate had ever felt buckled her knees and sent her to the deck. At last, Kate gave in to her tears.

She allowed this small indulgence to last only a few moments. Looking at her watch, she realized that the *Wind Runner* would be coming quickly. She wiped her face with her sleeves and stood up on the bucking deck, glancing around the horizon. If the *Second Chance* were to make it to Hilo by tomorrow morning, she needed to get her shipshape and ready to sail.

Forty-Two

WITH ONE HAND, Kate placed her paperback novel down on her knee, keeping the page with her thumb. Then, balancing the book carefully, she slid the same hand up the crease to the corner, where she turned the page. She'd been reading this way all day for three full days. Kate Langston's right hand was busy. With it, she held Mike's. It wasn't easy holding hands through the bars of a Honolulu hospital bed and reading at the same time.

Mike stirred and opened his eyes.

She set the book on the bedside stand. "How you feelin', baby?" she asked, leaning close.

"I've got a whale of a headache," he moaned. "Water?"

"You've been drinking water like a fish. Here," she said. Leaning over the bed rail, she held a glass with one hand and the drinking straw steady with the other. This way, Mike could grasp it with his lips. As he turned his head to the glass he groaned again, saying, "Oh, please. Make the room hold still."

"It's a motion sickness all its own," Kate teased. "You don't even need a boat to get it. Just a lump on your skull."

"Is that what happened?"

Kate laughed. Every day since they'd arrived in the hospital, she and Mike went through this same question-and-answer routine. At first it frightened her that Mike had no memory of the accident or of the explanation she gave him. But his doctor reassured her. Many patients with concussions—especially serious ones—have difficulty with recent memory.

"Yes, dear, the boom hit you in the head and knocked you off the boat."

"How'd I get back on?"

The whole event seemed like a terrible nightmare to Kate, and if she had her way, she would never go over it again. But Mike needed to hear it. And in a way, she found it reassuring to say it again and again. To know that each time the outcome was the same. Mike was safe.

She explained about the storm and the preventer and the uncontrolled boom swinging into the side of his head. She went through the rescue slowly, deliberately, leaving out as many of the horrifying details as she could. "The doctor says you fractured your temporal bone. That tore your eardrum and damaged your hearing. You've had surgery, and they think everything will be back to normal eventually. And that's why you're here using up a perfectly good hospital bed," she finished.

Every time she repeated the story it seemed that Mike had never heard it before. This time, he gave the slightest nod. "It seems familiar."

"Should be. I've told you often enough." She leaned close and brushed his lips with a kiss.

"I remember that," he said.

"I hope so. We've been doing that for a number of years." She smiled. "Oh, Mike, think how close I came to losing you!"

A gentle knock caught their attention, and they both looked up to see Special Agent Norm Walker push open the door with his back. In his arms he carried a vase of flowers and a box of donuts. Kate took the flowers from him, setting them on the nightstand beside the bed. She smiled. "This is certainly above and beyond the call of duty."

"How is our patient doing?"

"Better than when you saw him yesterday," Kate answered. "But his memory is pretty well gone."

"That might be a good thing." He pulled a chair close to the bedside opposite Kate and sat down. "When do they say you can take him home?"

"They expect to discharge him tomorrow morning," Kate answered. "He's been given medication for the swelling and the pain. His hearing will improve in time, and everything seems to be stable.

We should be able to fly home in a week or two."

"Good. That's very good news."

Kate reached through the bars of the bed and took Mike's hand. "I'd like to know how this happened," she said. "That is, if you can tell us anything." Mike made a supreme effort to roll toward the agent, groaning slightly. His eyes made unavoidable rolling motions, and he closed his eyelids.

"Moving makes him dizzy," Kate explained.

"I think I can tell you some parts of it," Agent Walker began. "But I'd be speculating—because we don't know everything yet." He leaned forward, resting his forearms on the bed rail. Starting with the accident in Tacoma, he told her all that he knew. "We traced the cards in the Tacoma car to a kid in New York, who had known Syndicate ties. We suspected DataSoft because you designed all the sites that had been hit. All we had to do was figure out who was the 'bad guy' at your company. I thought you had to be in on it. But my partner didn't believe it. She kept after me. . . ."

"Your partner is a woman?" Kate seemed surprised.

"Actually, you've already met her. Gwen Saunders," he said, nodding. "Anyway, she wanted me to look further. That's when we came up with Doug McCoy."

"Doug?" Kate couldn't believe it. Kate knew only the quiet, intelligent, technical side of Doug. "Why would he get involved in this?"

"I couldn't understand that either." Walker smiled. "But Saunders kept showing me his tax forms. He made plenty of money but had nothing to show for it. That made her suspicious. She uncovered a gambling addiction."

"Gambling?" Kate had no idea Doug had a gambling problem.

"A bad habit. Owed everyone money most of the time. Big money. Saunders confirmed it with his ex-wife."

Mike murmured.

"You knew about that?" Kate asked him.

He nodded the tiniest of nods. "I think she came to talk to me about it."

"Anyway, seems that he and the Calloruso woman decided to make a little extra on the side. She had Syndicate contacts. She set it up, but Doug delivered the goods. Doug built Internet sites with flaws that could be used to steal credit card numbers. He never stole the numbers. But he helped the bad guys do it."

Kate felt a moment of intense hatred run through her. The woman who had been with Mike also had Syndicate ties. "Sounds like something Cara Maria would be involved in."

"You're right. She's a bad one." He glanced at Mike. "Turns out that Cara Maria Calloruso was worried that Mike had figured the whole thing out. She threatened Doug with exposure if he didn't get rid of Mike. So Doug rigged the boat. We didn't know about it until after you sailed. That was when Doug turned state's evidence."

"What?" Kate sounded incredulous.

"He's going to testify against Cara in court. He should be able to supply plenty of details. We would've had a hard time convicting him anyway. And by the way, he told us he sabotaged the boat."

"I knew it was him," Mike said without opening his eyes.

Kate's voice rose. "How do you remember? You didn't say it was Doug."

"As soon as Agent Walker said it, I remembered," Mike said. "It happened before the accident. I found a lid from Doug's eyedrops rolling around in the bilge."

"You did?" Kate couldn't believe this. She had fought horrible fears on the boat. Terrible suspicions. But she never suspected that Doug might be trying to kill Mike. The news made her hands tremble, and her breath come in short tight gasps. She leaned back in the chair trying to relax. The whole thing was over. They were safe. Still she noticed that her hands shook as they rested in her lap.

"But he never meant to have you die," Walker continued. "He said he did what she asked, but he planned it so that it wouldn't happen all at once. He knew that Mike was a fixer—a handyman. He said he hoped that he could get Cara Maria off his back *and* give Mike enough time to save himself. Then he let us know what he had done so that we could rescue you. I guess he figured that Cara Maria would run his life forever unless he faced his own problems. He decided to put an end to her power over him."

Walker looked directly at Mike. "Not only did he figure out how to let the water in the boat, he'd also tampered with all of the rigging. If that storm had caught up with you, the *Second Chance* would have been dismasted."

"We knew that."

"Then this should come as a real surprise. If you hadn't been thrown overboard, the Coast Guard wouldn't have been able to help you. It was the faulty clip on your boom that actually saved your life."

This last bit of information made Kate shudder and close her eyes. Sending Mike over the side didn't seem like much of a lifesaving technique.

"The reason we were able to get to you as quickly as we did is because he warned us."

"What?" This latest news was too much for Kate.

"Doug came into the office with his attorney and told us everything."

"Why?"

"He was afraid that you both might be killed. But most of all, he was afraid that Cara would manage to pin the whole thing on him. He didn't want to face murder charges."

The news kicked Kate hard in the chest. "What exactly did he say?"

"He told us about Cara's . . . uh . . . relationship with Mike. He said she'd initiated the whole thing in order to keep close tabs on Mike—to find out how much he knew about their criminal activities. And of course they wanted to know how much Mike had told the FBI."

"But it started—I mean, I got involved with Cara even before you came to the office," Mike said.

"True. Seems that you had a visit from a Federal Agent before we got involved. And someone told McCoy."

Mike searched his memory and came up blank. "What visit?"

"That's the ironic part," Agent Walker chuckled slightly. "Turns out it was that visit you had from one of the folks from our Computer Security Panel. Remember how you thought that was also the reason I came to see you the first time?"

Mike thought back. Yes. He remembered. He'd been asked to join a panel designed to provide Internet security advice for a government supervisory agency. He turned them down.

"Anyway, that was when she and McCoy decided to keep a—well, a real personal eye on you."

"She set me up?"

Walker nodded. "That's what Doug says. He admits that he sent the pictures. He was afraid that she had really fallen for you, and he didn't want her to turn him in."

"I don't understand." Kate felt dizzy and confused. She had never suspected that the trouble with the boat could be related to Cara and Doug.

"Doug believed that sending the pictures would force Mike to end the relationship. That way, Cara wouldn't be able to betray him." Walker opened the box of donuts and offered one to Kate. She shook her head, and he took one for himself.

"So the relationship was a setup." Mike still couldn't believe it.

"Doug's confession won't save him completely. But the prosecutor will go easier, because with his help, we can nail the families trafficking in credit card fraud. As soon as we heard that the boat had been sabotaged, we decided to keep an eye out for you. Through the whole trip, you were never very far out of sight. We monitored your transmissions, watched you on satellite—we knew every time your marine toilet flushed."

Mike made a weak smile at this.

Kate breathed a quiet grateful prayer. She had nearly lost her husband to murder. The FBI had sent the men in the other boat. Without them, she couldn't have gotten the *Second Chance* to Hilo. She shuddered as reality struck her.

"That's why," Walker continued, "we were able to get to you so quickly. When we realized that you'd made it so far, we knew that something must be scheduled to happen soon. We were waiting."

Kate leaned over the rail and sought her husband's hand. She could not see his face, but she felt the dampness in his hand. They both realized how close they'd come.

"Well, I just wanted to see how you were doing and say goodbye." Walker stood. "I need to get going. I'm flying back tomorrow. I have a meeting with the Federal Prosecutor." He started to the door. "Oh, by the way, you'll need to hire a new technical supervisor. Your partner may not be available for a couple of years. Enjoy the donuts. I'll be in touch."

Kate watched until the door closed behind him. Mike began a slow arduous turn in the bed, trying to roll onto his back. She watched his brows twist and draw together as pain tightened the muscles of his face. How she wished she could ease his discomfort.

She held the pillow, trying to prevent his head from dropping helplessly onto the sheets. "Better?" she asked.

Without opening his eyes, he blew a long, slow breath through tight lips. When his face finally relaxed he opened his eyes, slowly, carefully.

"Room moving again?"

"Tie it down, would you?"

She leaned down and kissed his cheek. "It'll be better soon."

"Kate," he said, looking into her eyes. "There are some things I still remember. Some things I can never forget." He held his head very still, though his eyes focused on hers. "I wish I could. I wish that there were some way to knock those memories from my mind." He blinked, and tears trickled down the sides of his face, following the creases beside his eyes and dripping into the bandage beside his left ear.

She bent and wiped his tears with her fingertips. Holding her face close to his, she said, "I have the only thing I've ever wanted, Mike. I have you." She touched his nose with her index finger. Then, taking on the tone of a mother with a child, she said, "Sometimes, losing your memory is the result of getting clobbered in the head. Other times, you have to be clobbered in the heart before you can make the choice to lose your memory." She laughed a light, gentle laugh. "Trust me," she whispered. "I've made my choice."

Kate leaned down and gave Mike a long, gentle kiss.

He moaned, and she searched his face. "I'm sorry. It's that dizzy thing again, isn't it?"

"Yup," he smiled. "But, it's not the head injury."

"Well," she said, brushing his lips with hers, "you'd just better get used to it. I plan to keep you dizzy for the rest of your life."

Mike smiled. "That's a plan I can live with."

Acknowledgments

Without the help of experts, *Pacific Hope* would not exist. I am indebted to the many, many people who made this story a reality. Mike Rice, of Puget Sound Sailing, taught me to tie my first knot. Under his skilled instruction, I learned to sail. John Neal's Offshore Cruising Symposium proved invaluable in understanding the ocean passage experience. Jan Paton and her husband, Ken, provided much advice in the plotting of disasters on board the *Second Chance*. Alliance Yachts in Seattle, Washington, allowed me to take reference pictures of *Distant Drummer* (the model for *Second Chance*). I am also grateful to the experts at Island Marine (Lopez Island, Washington) and Svendson's Boat Works (Alameda, California) for helping me "sink" my boat. Together, both crews managed to teach me everything I needed in order to sabotage a sailboat; we laughed a lot in the process. Thanks, guys.

I am also indebted to Tim Duplissey and Larry Dill, both of World Vision, and to my brother, Steve Roberts. Their computer-related advice contributed to the plotting of *Pacific Hope*. And to the agents of the FBI and the United States Coast Guard, who willingly shared their experiences and advice, I give my thanks. To the real men who jump into raging seas to save us, I offer my most sincere respect and admiration!

Special thanks to Susan, who reads everything I write, and to Jeannie St. John Taylor, who provides valuable insight and support for my work. I couldn't do it without you two! May the Lord richly bless you both.

And to my many friends at Bethany House, I give my sincere appreciation for your talent and devotion. Because of you, *Pacific Hope* is the best I can do.